CUNARD

Library

Out of respect for your fellow guests, please return all books as soon as possible. We would also request that books are not taken off the ship as they can easily be damaged by the sun, sea and sand.

Please ensure that books are returned the day before you disembark, failure to do so will incur a charge to your on board account, the same will happen to any damaged books.

The Queen's Assassin

Also by James Barclay from Gollancz:

CHRONICLES OF THE RAVEN

Dawnthief
Noonshade
Nightchild

LEGENDS OF THE RAVEN

Elfsorrow
Shadowheart
Demonstorm
Ravensoul

THE ASCENDANTS OF ESTOREA

Cry of the Newborn
Shout for the Dead

ELVES

Elves: Once Walked with Gods
Elves: Rise of the TaiGethen
Elves: Beyond the Mists of Katura

Heart of Granite

The Queen's Assassin

No _____

One of 500 numbered copies
of the first edition of

THE QUEEN'S ASSASSIN

James Barclay

Signed by the author

Published by Gollancz
in association with Goldsboro Books
June 2022

First published in Great Britain in 2022 by Gollancz
an imprint of The Orion Publishing Group Ltd
Carmelite House, 50 Victoria Embankment
London EC4Y 0DZ

An Hachette UK Company

3 5 7 9 10 8 6 4

A CIP catalogue record for this book is
available from the British Library.

ISBN (Hardback) 978 1 473 20246 7
ISBN (eBook) 978 1 473 20248 1
ISBN (audio) 978 1 473 23243 3

Typeset at The Spartan Press Ltd,
Lymington, Hants

Printed and bound in Great Britain by Clays Ltd,
Elcograf S.p.A.

MIX
Paper from
responsible sources
FSC® C104740

www.jamesbarclay.com
www.gollancz.co.uk

This book is dedicated to the memory of Dick Whichelow, who would have loved this one. A great friend and wonderful human being who is keenly missed by all of us who loved him.

Chapter 1

She lost her grip when the soldier convulsed. Blood surged from the torn artery, running down to mix with the churned mud in which she knelt.

'Hold her, dammit, hold her!'

Hands moved to put pressure on the soldier's legs and shoulders. Naida pressed down again, above the tear, fingers deep in the shredded flesh of the soldier's thigh. She had to stem this in the next minute. Had to. The soldier jerked and spasmed in pain from the breaks in her arms and the lacerations to her chest and stomach.

Naida moved one bloody hand from the wound and placed it on the soldier's forehead.

'What's her name?' she hissed at the pale-faced, shivering swordsman nearest her.

'Caryne.'

'Caryne, it's Naida. Relax now. I'm going to save you.'

An ephemeral smile passed across Caryne's mud-and-blood face and her every muscle relaxed. That was always the reaction when Naida used their name and told them they weren't going to die. She returned to her work, letting her fingertips, out of sight of her team, smooth the rupture in Caryne's femoral artery. The bleeding ceased, saving her life.

'Ready with pressure pads and bandages,' said Naida. 'Pinch the wound closed as best you can when I withdraw. Pressure pads to keep the rupture closed, not cut off supply to the leg.'

Horns sounded across the battle line.

'Flay-shot! Flay-shot!'

The eerie whispering and whistling from a hundred catapult baskets cut across the rolling clamour from the front lines. Soldiers dropped to a crouch, snapped shields over their heads and pressed together to lock their defences. Cavalry drove on, hoping to get under the arc, and the front line continued to push. After all, the catapults were what today was all about. And tomorrow.

Naida kept working as the soldiers around her tiled shields over and about her. Others placed their bodies between her and the flying shot of chain-linked, spiked iron fists and bladed carriage-bearings.

'Brace! Brace!'

The horns fell silent, even the conflict line appeared to pause, while the whispering grew in volume and the whistling became a rattling terror from the sky. Naida focused on Caryne's artery, drawing the rupture closed, sealing it with her body's energy. It was a temporary measure, solely designed to get Caryne from the field and onto an operating table, but it would hold.

The flay-shot struck, striking earth, shield and flesh. A severed limb thumped into a shield above Naida and dropped to the ground by her head. She stood.

'Get Caryne stretchered, secured and back to the medical tents.' Naida wiped her bloody hands on her filthy trousers and said, quietly, 'Where next?'

She cocked her head. A human screaming in pain can cut through even the din of full-throated battle. Evolution had designed it that way; its frequency reaching the ears and the heart simultaneously, demanding aid, demanding relief.

Naida ran. She yelled instructions to those running with her. Barely audible over the roar of infantry; the ground-shaking thrum of myriad hooves; the shrieking of metal on metal; and the eerie sounds of flay-shot flung from catapults, followed by the rattle of their fall on metal; their dull thuds against sodden earth; and the sick ripping of flesh.

The battlefield was crowded. Across two hundred yards of mud, blood, and bodies, the opposing front lines ebbed and flowed across a shallow, rock-strewn stream. Cavalry circled the flanks, hemming in the lines and acting as a deterrent to the enemy Haronic horsemen. Archer and reserve infantry cluttered the space behind the lines where stretcher and medic teams darted in and out, dragging the wounded to triage points and the dead from beneath the feet of the living.

Forays to attack the catapults were frequent, heroic, and doomed. Supporting cavalry were easy prey for archers and heavy bows. Even so, the day was with them: once there had been a hundred and twenty catapults in four ranks. Now there were less than a hundred. But the attrition rate was awful, and Naida's medics were overstretched and increasingly vulnerable.

Naida was aware of her impact, her influence... her aura. Where she ran, hope came in her shadow. Where she was seen, courage surged within those who faced the enemy across a barrier of sharpened steel. They had the knowledge, the unquenchable certainty, that should they fall, Naida would save them.

Of course, she couldn't save them all and, of course, they knew that. Everyone who hurled themselves at an enemy knew a fatal blow remained a fatal blow. But the *chance*, where there had not been one before, that a severe injury might not mean the end, was seized like the most precious of jewels.

Naida was the reason many of them fought at all. They'd long ago forgotten the cause that had taken them from their families, the reason the Queen demanded they fight an enemy whose

3

crimes against Suurken had never been adequately explained. People they had been told to hate for reasons that were forever opaque.

It painted a target on Naida's back. Wherever she ran, the fighting intensified, the arrows fell with greater density, and the catapults were loaded and discharged more quickly. When she appeared on the flanks, enemy cavalry charged. It all left her conflicted, wondering if she should run the battlefield at all when her presence might cause more death, more injury.

But run the lines she did, because to see her heedless of personal risk was a tonic to her people, who often said her mere presence was a mortal threat to the enemy.

Her people.

It was how she thought of them and how they saw themselves. The pressure of it should have crushed her. Military command should have hated her for wielding so much more influence than they ever could. But even the blind could see her value as a talisman. Not just here, but on every front. Knowing she ran the lines every day, rarely suffering so much as a scratch as she saved the lives of their friends and comrades, energised the army.

Naida thrived on it. Belief is a virtuous circle and there is no level it cannot attain. And their enemy's attempts to kill her – from battlefield surges to assassins sent to her tent with poison, knives, even venomous reptiles and arachnids – all failed. And every failure was trumpeted as a victory, as proof of her invulnerability.

Naida slid to the ground right behind the reserve lines, no more than twenty yards from enemy blades. The expected surge was met and repulsed. The wounded spearman was being moved backwards across the mud and through the legs of his comrades. She stared through the thicket of mud-encrusted limbs and hissed through her teeth. The soldier was screaming but no longer in pain.

'Stop! Keep him still! Make me a path.' She crawled through the ebb and flow. Down here in the mud the roar of battle was that bit more muted but the stench of sweat-soaked leather, metal, sodden earth and blood was intense. 'Don't move him.'

Naida reached the soldier's head. His helmet was gone and matted greying hair sprouted in desultory tufts from a balding head. He'd stopped screaming, and she knew why.

'Shattered throne, Hazza, my friend, you don't get any breaks, do you?'

'That is spectacularly bad phrasing.'

'I do my best,' said Naida. 'Any feeling?'

Around her, the infantry heaved themselves forwards, trying to give her space. The howl of voices strengthened, metal clashed, and shields cast a shadow over the ground where they lay. The Haronic catapults would be winding back with a new area to target, and her people would be ready.

'It's all a bit light below the waist.'

'Thought so. Well, I can confirm you *have* a below-the-waist still. Feet and everything.'

Hazza smiled. Distracted by her words and her face right above his, he couldn't sense her hands on his lower abdomen and back, where the flechette had entered his body and sliced into his spine. Allowing herself to move her consciousness into her hands for a flicker, she could feel the cleanness of the break, see the microbes of infection that would threaten a recovery, and the tendrils of his spinal nerve seeking reconnection. She could help with that. But not here; and he must not suffer further trauma.

'How messed up are they?'

'No more than normal. The wound is clean, Hazza. I can save you.'

Hazza relaxed, the desperation behind his bravery replaced by hope. Naida took a breath.

5

'Right,' she said, glancing around to assess his escape route. 'Stretcher! I need this man immobilised and moved with tremendous care.'

The enemy pushed back, her soldiers giving a yard. Medics formed a shield around Naida, keeping careless feet from knocking Hazza's paralysed body. Naida kept her hands on Hazza's shoulders, providing comfort as his nervousness grew. The soldier was mired in mud. He'd be difficult to lift onto the stretcher.

'I need a long shield,' she said. 'And sure hands. And some precious time.'

The roar of battle surrounded her and her team. Flay-shot whined. New screams split the air, overlaying the clashing, thudding, growling tumult of battle. But her message got through like it always did. From somewhere, she cared not where, a long wooden shield appeared. It was cracked, nicked and blood-stained, painted with the open maw of a beast from nightmares.

Naida signalled for calm in the chaos. Arrows landed around them, whispering into earth and flesh, knocking into wood and bouncing from steel. She bound Hazza's legs together with a belt and motioned one of her team to support his head. She stayed at his waist, where the risk lay.

'Kella, position the shield. On my word, we rock him up, slide the shield under, lay him back down. One movement, gentle, fluid.'

The quiet that descended for Naida when she deployed her Talent was surreal. A bubble in which she had complete concentration and could see everything moving as if slowed in time. She knew why but couldn't tell anyone. The consequences for her would be dire.

She could sense the movement of a careless infantry boot that was sliding backwards towards Hazza's legs and diverted it from its dangerous course. She heard the flay-shot and flattened herself over the stricken soldier's body to protect him. She

6

directed the delicate manoeuvre with such precision no one could recall afterwards quite how she did it. And yet there Hazza was, atop the shield then loaded on to the stretcher, awaiting the word to head to the medical tent.

Job done, Naida let reality flood back. Fresh blood, fresh screams, fresh calls of her name. Ignoring them all, she spoke to the stretcher-bearers.

'You cannot run, you cannot slip. One sharp jolt and Hazza will never walk again. Gird yourselves. Dawdling to the camp while the flay-shot whines around you will scare you witless. But you'll make it. I have faith in you and your courage.' She smiled. 'And, Kella, in your outrageous good fortune. Go.'

Naida turned back to the battle. Cavalry from their left flank had made a significant break and infantry was pouring into the gap, rushing towards the enemy catapults. Many of them would not be coming back. Arrows thickened the air, catapult arms cranked. She blew out her cheeks.

'One more,' she said. 'I'm not sure our tables can take more than that.'

Chapter 2

Grim work.

Blood slicked the loose-laid wood floor. The surgery stank of urine and excrement and mud. And wood and alcohol and sweat. Sweat. It dripped from every one of Naida's pores, soaked into her headband and ran down her arms. Every canvas window and door was open to the sultry summer's afternoon. Still it was stifling. So much suffering humanity, so many medics, so much boiling water.

Fighting echoed from the battlefield, reminding everyone in the surgery of six tables and a dozen prep-beds that they were patching up soldiers just for them to come straight back with another hole or gash or shattered limb. On five tables, surgeons cleaned and sewed the simpler cases, calling on Naida only if they had to. Her table, in the centre of the circle, was surrounded by observers, off-duty surgeons trying to glean some teaching from her deft movements, to absorb her unique understanding of human physiology.

And Naida was exceptional, she allowed herself that. She had dedicated her life to understanding how the human body worked, with the express purpose of saving lives others thought unsavable. So here she was, hands deep in Hazza's back, her mind open, using her Talent to examine his wound, knowing that none of those crowded around her could ever hope to see the tendrils of the lumbar nerves that she would soon rejoin to allow him to walk again.

So, whenever she narrated her surgery, her direction was necessarily threaded with lies. Lies to save her life, while she used the Talent within her to save the lives of others. There were rumours, naturally. Naida even encouraged them, played up to them, in the knowledge it was the surest way to puncture them.

Hazza's breathing was regular, his pulse strong, unconscious under the ministrations of dwale, a draft of mandragora, resentha petals and opium. Naida plucked tiny threads of cloth from the wound with delicate tweezers, signalling for hot sponges to clean the deep slash that ran from his right hip and across his lumbar spine. Sometimes lying to the victim was the best short-term strategy. This was a ragged wound, despite what she'd told him, and had she not been there it would have been mortal.

'Now the wound is clean, I can redress the area surrounding the discs, clearing a path to allow the severed nerve to reconnect. He must be still for the healing to take place.'

The lie was an easy one. Scalpel in one hand, Naida eased a string of flesh aside and laid her free hand atop the soldier's spine, tendrils of warmth running from her thumb and forefinger to the trailing ends of the nerve. And while she made a play of easing Hazza's insides back into some form of order within the wound, she gently brought thumb and forefinger together. His body was deeply enough anaesthetised that his lower body didn't react, but the energy flow was complete, or complete enough, once again.

'It's the best that can be done. And so, we move into the hope phase.' Naida smiled and signalled for needle and thread. 'This will be quite a scar.'

'Dammit!' The exclamation from Sennoch, one of her surgeons at another table, held fear. 'Naida! Quickly, the bleeding...'

Naida pointed at Hazza. 'Sew him up, Kella. Make him beautiful.'

She moved quickly to the next table where she could see blood surging from the stomach cavity of a soldier who'd come in with an arrow deep in her gut.

'Pressure on the rupture,' she said. 'How?'

'Removing the head,' said Sennoch. 'Must have nicked something on the way out.'

'Or the head had pierced deeper than you thought.' She looked into the wound and tried not to react, choosing another gentle lie instead. 'It's not as bad as you think, Sennoch. Plenty of blood in all this intestinal nonsense just waiting an opportunity to get out.'

Naida felt the surgeon relax. She picked up a steel-faced wooden clamp, leaned in to fit it while placing her palm over the cut intestine and feeding her essence into the damage, allowing the clamp to snick shut just as her true work was done and the blood-flow lessened almost to nought.

'Clean the wound, then clean it again. Infection is death, we all know that.' Naida laid a hand on the surgeon's forearm. 'This is no fault on you, Sennoch. Next time let the blood-flow show you where you need to apply the fix. You have more time than you think.'

'Thank you.'

'Thank you. This soldier's life was saved because you called, and it is the saving that matters, not the manner of it.'

'Ever and so,' said Sennoch.

Naida looked around the tables. More would come to fill them. The fighting would go on until dusk and maybe beyond if either side felt they could press for victory. She toured the triage beds, assessing the work to come. Nothing here right now demanded her attention. Conventional means would suffice.

'I'll be in my tent if you need me,' she said. 'Recharging for the next wave.'

A few muted laughs saw her out into the fresh air and Naida's first lungful felt like a cascade of cleansing cold water through her body, flushing away the sharp taint of blood and the stenches of effluence and pain. She pushed a bloody hand through her hair, reminded herself she had to bathe sometime and walked slowly to her pavilion, which was pitched very close to the surgery. Too close when she craved a long, idle walk.

Oh, for one of those. Naida smiled to herself and gazed across the sprawling camp beneath the clear sky, its flags and banners snapping in the occasional gust of wind. The generals' pavilions were a little further up the rise, sheltered from the breeze that carried the powerful smells of livestock and horses. She always thought it a shame that so many soldiers chose to burn dung rather than seek wood. It rather tainted the food.

At the entrance to her pavilion – the lordly style of tent made more humble by being pitched among the people she was trying to save – Naida stopped at the sound of a roar rolling down from the battlefield. Every head turned towards the noise.

'I hope that's us,' she said to the sky before pushing the flap aside and walking into her tiny square of calm, knowing she might be called out again before she'd slept a wink.

Inside, it was a sparse affair. A cot and mattress boasting a tangled sheet and rough blanket; a desk covered in papers; a rack for hanging her very few clothes; a battered trunk of possessions and three chairs arranged around an unmade fire pit. Some old rugs covered about half the dirt floor, and a single decorative tapestry hung behind her bed.

Home.

Naida thought to head over to the cook fires for some hot water for tea, but instead sat at the desk, poured a mug of water from the jug, and stared at her papers. Requests for more staff, mostly refused; requests for equipment, mostly refused; standing orders, meetings and agendas. It was all so many random ink squiggles right now.

Naida blew a thin stream of air through her lips. It had been a day and a night since she'd last lain on her tangle of a bed. Not a good state for a surgeon. She drained her water, stood and shook out her bedclothes, pulled off her boots and lay down.

'You are Naida,' she whispered. 'Never forget that.'

Every night, she had to remind herself or fear speaking in her sleep and betraying herself. Because she wasn't Naida. She was the most hunted woman in Suurken. The only daughter of genocidal monsters. An Esselrode. Too terrified to use her Talent for years because they were looking for a Gifted girl her age, and later, a Gifted woman her age.

And now, after years hiding in the army, she couldn't admit her gift to anyone. The psychological barrier was unscalable, the risk that a careless word would bring her enemies to her door was too great. Every morning she awoke afraid, only able to quash her fears when she knew she was Naida for another day.

★

She dredged herself from the chains of sleep, eyes opening to her lantern-lit desk. Fruit and bread sat on a plate next to the light, along with a covered bowl of what she guessed would be soup, almost certainly long-cold. The camp was quiet but for the flap of tent canvas in the breeze, the chatter of guards on patrol and the occasional cry or moan from the infirmary. The distant crackle of a fire.

Shattered throne, she'd slept through the army's return.

Naida raised herself on arms heavy with the memory of rest. Her pavilion had been tidied, her spare blanket folded at the end of her cot and her clothes rehung or laid out for her. She smiled knowing who had visited. She swung her legs over the edge of the cot and stood carefully, trying to work out how long she'd slept.

The answer was on a note left on her desk beneath her rearing-horse paperweight. She recognised the delicate handwriting:

The day was neither won nor lost. We thought to wake you but Sennoch organised battlefield teams and triage. All who survived into surgery still live. Today was a good day. Fresh clothes for tomorrow are laid out for you, as is the dress outfit for your evening being bored to death by our esteemed commander and whichever crusty old soldier is coming to pin another medal on you. Do you have space on your chest for one more?

I'll wake you at dawn. Go back to bed, I know you're reading this in the middle of the night.

As ever yours, my love,

Drevien.

Naida chuckled. Just for a moment, she considered undressing and going back to bed, but there were rounds to be made. She stepped outside, where Drevien was waiting.

'It's almost like I know you,' said Drevien. Three red stripes on her sand-coloured overalls indicated her rank: an infirmary shift sergeant, known as a 'wardlord'. The overalls were covered in stains, not limited to the blood and vomit of her patients.

'It's almost like you're making a blatantly obvious point with your filthy rags.'

'You need rest,' said Drevien.

'I need to keep my patients alive.'

'I'm going to carve that on the plinth of your statue, right after I've polished the heroic glint in your eyes to a blinding dazzle.'

Naida kissed her. 'Thank you for caring.'

'Someone's got to.' Drevien wrinkled her nose at her. 'Come on, let's go see all the sleeping people. Then you can return to bed satisfied you've discharged your stupid-hour-of-the-night duties that are already covered by the night-shift organisation you signed off three days ago.'

'You know, I'm in charge here and that is definitely insubordination,' said Naida. Drevien looked around her while turning full circle. 'What are you doing?'

'Looking for someone who cares.'

Naida burst out laughing, turning the heads of guards and groups of reserves congregated round the nearby dung fires. She waved an apology.

On the hot night, the infirmary tent doors were tied aside and the tent skirt was brailed up. Lighting was low and soft, and the stoves keeping the water hot had been moved outside. Naida toured every bed, noting and reducing fevers with a gentle touch to the brow; checking dressings and requesting changes where she could sense infection gathering. She spoke softly to any who could not sleep, or who had been woken for medication.

Drevien followed her. 'They believe you'll make them better while they sleep.'

'Belief is infectious, we could do with an epidemic of it.'

Naida paused by Hazza and fetched a pin from the dressings kit on her belt. She moved the light sheet from his feet and pushed the pin gently into his left big toe pad. One eye opened and he regarded her, his mouth turned up in a wry smile.

'I am awake, you know.'

'What on earth for?' asked Naida.

'When you think you'll never be able to feel your feet or stand on your own two legs again, and some miracle-worker turns your darkness into light, sleep seems such a waste.'

'All I did was create the conditions. Your body did all the heavy lifting.'

There were tears in Hazza's eyes. The weathered, scarred face that had seen more campaigns than Naida had seen patients, was flushed in embarrassment.

'Sorry,' he said, clearing his throat, voice gruff.

She patted his foot. 'What for? You thought you were done. Turns out you're not. If it was me, I'd be drowning in a lake of my own tears.'

'Thank you,' he said, swallowing and smiling while the tears rolled down his cheeks. 'It is a pretty good feeling.'

Naida clasped his proffered hand. 'Well, don't get ideas about strapping your leather back on just yet. You've a journey ahead before you can fight again.'

'Aye, but I'll be able to walk into the arms of my family. It's all that matters.'

Naida's heart missed a beat. She knew she was beaming. Her mind clutched the joy she felt, holding it tight to her. But it would slip from her grasp when new blood was spilled, like it always did.

'Please don't fight again.'

'You know I can't do that,' said Hazza.

Naida shrugged. 'Never hurts to ask. Right, I can go back to bed now.'

Drevien was beside her again. 'I'll confess this was probably worth your while.'

'How gracious of you.'

'Come on, I'll tuck you in.'

'You could stay.'

'I'm on shift and you would be terrible company.'

They kissed and Naida held Drevien's embrace allowing the weariness to settle on her, though her mind was ablaze with

Hazza's words, and where they would sit in the pantheon of justifications for everything she did and why ... *how* ... she did it.

By the time she reached her cot, sleep all but owned her and she needed Drevien's help to strip off her boots, shirt and trousers. Her tent was hot despite every opening being pinned back, and the air was still, carrying each sound as sharp as the moment it was made. She summoned up the energy to drag Drevien into a final tender kiss.

'Thank you,' she said.

'It's what I'm here for, my love,' said Drevien. 'Now, please, will you rest.'

Naida just about had the awareness to consider these were terrible conditions for sleep before her eyes slammed shut.

Chapter 3

Naida broke her fast with Drevien, a meal of rye bread, fruit and nettle tea eaten quickly to the sounds of an army on the move and the thundering of hooves. Skirmishes had already started, with clashes from before dawn, but the battle orders left on Naida's desk in the early hours noted a change of tactics, to break what was in danger of becoming a messy stalemate.

There was to be no pause, the change was immediate. The medics were going to be busy. While Drevien trotted off to check the triage wagons and brief the stretcher teams and battlefield medics on their new plans, Naida sought out her veterinary peer. She found him at the forward quartermaster's stores, arguing for more gear.

'...are expected to run around behind the infantry lines, right in front of enemy archers, moving injured – and therefore slow – horses, and you think we don't need either helm on our head, nor shield strapped to our back?'

'You bloody fetlock-massagers are all alike. You know full well, Elmridge, that my stocks of armour are near zero and that everyone who joins this army provides their own armour and weapons.' Master Gorvan, a veteran of every sob-story ever conceived, regarded Elmridge with a painful absence of sympathy. 'All I do is replace damaged stuff, which I can send to my smithy for repair and return to my stores.'

Elmridge, a tall strong man with the deftest of touch with animals, stared straight back. 'So I should take the armour from the dead, to trade with you?'

'Or to wear, if it fits,' said Gorvan. 'Either is better than turning up here expecting something for nothing. My advice is to stand in the lee of your crippled nags while you lead them from the field.'

'When I need advice on battlefield safety from a man who hasn't set foot on one for twenty years, I'll come right to your cook fire.'

'You're getting nothing from me. I don't have the stock.'

'If I die today, do me the decency of feeling you played a part in my demise.'

'I shall sing a lament over your rotting corpse, Elmridge.'

Naida had listened as long as she could. Horns had sounded. The enemy had begun their full approach. Suurkene soldiers and riders ran or rode to muster points. Orders fought to be heard.

'Luckily your singing is enough to return the dead to life, Gorvan,' she said.

'Lady Naida, is there anything I can give you? I need nothing in return.' Gorvan's wink was as theatrical as his grin was wide.

'I have everything I need,' said Naida, turning to Elmridge. 'We need to talk.'

'Yes, save me from this cruellest of men who would see my body a pincushion merely to hear the groan of his shelves beneath the weight of his stocks.'

'Ale tonight?' asked Gorvan.

'Wouldn't miss it,' said Elmridge. He gestured towards the battlefield. 'Shall we talk as we walk?'

Naida led the way out of the stores and back towards the infirmary where her team were assembled and wagons, with oxen in their traces, vibrated to the trembling of the ground beneath them.

'Will it work?' asked Naida, waving the note from her desk in front of him. Elmridge was a keen student of battlefield tactics, particularly the actions of cavalry, and was often invited to tactical debates as an expert contributor.

'It stands a chance,' said Elmridge. 'But casualties will be high in the early thrusts. We'll know quickly if we can press any advantage, and from there a rout of the enemy is likely. We have to be aware of the risks to ourselves, particularly in the first contacts.'

'Agreed,' said Naida. 'Things I need you to do: don't try moving horses you know you can't save. They can shield my people. I'm bringing the wagons into the thick of it, and we've armoured the oxen as best we can. They can protect your people too. Walking injured can stay safe by the horses you are taking. Use anything you need, we have plenty.'

'Good for you.' He was a little short.

'Being me has its advantages.'

Elmridge smiled. 'Good for you.'

'What do you think?'

'I think when we work together more lives are saved.'

'Are you at this dinner tonight?' asked Naida.

'Survival-permitting.'

'Such optimism.'

'There's a strong case for not surviving, as a valid tactic for avoiding the dinner,' said Elmridge.

'You will stop me falling asleep in my soup, won't you?'

'Not a chance.'

★

The battlefield energy was intense. The usual raids from either side had come to nought and bodies were being displayed, disfigured and dismembered. But today, the air smelled different. Decisive. Naida could feel it in the thrill running through the infantry that passed her, and in the cavalry she was to shadow on the left flank.

The risks were high, the rewards of victory higher in the lives that would be saved and the strategic ground that would be gained, the diminution of enemy machines and the major step towards the ultimate goal: peace through war.

Just as the Queen desired. She who wanted, above all things, long-lasting security for the people of Suurken. The warrior queen who fought to hang up her armour and announce peace for all time. But to achieve it there must be war and there must be bloodshed.

So went the speeches from the sergeants-at-arms, the cavalry captains and the archer commanders. So spoke the words in Naida's head. Words that might as well have been tattooed on every chest.

Moving on the left flank, past the archer lines, she looked towards the rear of the gathering infantry where the preamble of a day's fighting – taunting, threats, shield thumping and chanting – was well underway. But today it had a different purpose: normality as distraction. The calculations had been made and the dice were about to be thrown. Late attacks on the Haronic cavalry yesterday had proved profitable. Intelligence had backed up one of their theories with hard facts: their foe didn't have the horses, or riders, in great enough numbers.

That news had provoked the bold, risky change in tactics, knowing that its failure would leave them woefully exposed and facing a hurried retreat to the border, four days' fast march to the north. That contingency had not been ignored. Civilians in the camp were making critical preparations for such a retreat, hoping they would be a waste of time.

The move was never going to be perfect. There had been no training or rehearsal for this, just a terse briefing at muster and sketches scratched in the dirt. But when the horns sounded, the army was together enough to take the enemy completely by surprise.

Infantry lines rushed in to engage Haronic swords. The cavalry swept by on both flanks, driving headlong towards the still-assembling ranks of enemy archers, some with half-strung bows. Every reserve rider moved to protect the infantry. Archers raced across the divide to the back of the infantry lines, splitting left and right and ready to loose at enemy cavalry.

Before the Suurkene cavalry reached the Haronic archers, some of the enemy dropped their bows to grab swords. Too few kept their heads and aimed at the wide target area that horseflesh presented. But even they could only nock and loose twice before the first Suurkene cavalry breached their fracturing lines, hurdling their fallen on the way.

Haronic cavalry, uncertain who to attack, split up. Some rode at the Suurkene defensive reserve, only to find themselves under archer attack. The majority turned their attentions to the Suurkene cavalry, exactly as expected. Haronic infantry peeled off from the back of their lines to defend them. Suurkene infantry pressed hard, seeking a critical break. Everywhere, the pressure intensified.

Naida trotted along beside a wooden-roofed carriage pulled by a pair of oxen whose harnesses were hung with thick leather armour. Her team ran with her, and alongside them were animal physicians. Eight carts in all moved over the pitted ground and into the deliberate confusion in which only one side had a plan.

Haronic archers had run and regrouped but clean targets were scarce. The bulk of the Suurkene cavalry had driven straight through the archer lines. Hundreds of bodies lay among broken bows and downed horses and riders. Reserve Haronic forces were trying to stop the cavalry reaching the catapults, which still launched flay-shot into Suurkene territory.

Sucked into the excitement and energy of the attack, Naida ran ahead of the oxen. She felt the breeze of an arrow flashing in front of her nose and heard the wind through its fletching as she gasped and ducked down. More arrows thudded into the wagon and the oxen's leather flank armour.

Kella moved to her shoulder. 'Only you could be that lucky.'

'Stupid,' said Naida, 'stupid.'

Naida fought against the shock that threatened to settle on her. So many times, arrows, swords, catapult rounds ... whatever the weapon ... had missed her by a hair or been blocked by a defender. But every previous time she had been on the ground, trying to save a life.

Her head filled with visions of lying in the mud, blood dribbling from an arrow shaft jutting from her temple. Unable to help those she had pledged to save, instead sprawled face down, helpless just like them, tortured by screams and pain that she could not soothe.

A detachment of reserve cavalry galloped across the front of the cart and ploughed into a group of Haronic infantry heading in to attack the medical teams. Naida shook herself back to focus and ordered the cart to stop. Three others stopped in her wake.

'Get in under shield cover and bring casualties behind fallen horses when you can. Triage on site, stretcher to the lee of the wagons, and help the horse docs if you can.'

Sacks retrieved from the back of the wagon, Naida and Kella headed for the aftermath of the brief and brutal collision between cavalry and enemy archers. Shield bearers ran in front of them, though the threat from arrows had diminished almost to nothing.

Cavalry had broken through to the enemy infantry, spearmen and archers defending the catapults, and had run into significant resistance. They needed infantry support themselves, but the lines were still engaged with no real sign of the enemy fracturing. There was one thing that could swing it, though, and she hoped the battlefield commanders could see it.

Naida slid to the ground by a dead horse. Its rider had been thrown a short distance. Bone was visible through his trousers and blood slicked his face and hands. He was staring at the wound, his body trembling, the adrenaline flooding him which, combined with the shock, allowed him to try to push the bone back into his mangled leg.

'What's your name?' Naida asked, motioning Kella to get the dwale shaken up. The cavalryman was staring at her, through her. 'Name? Give me your name.'

'If I can just push the bone back in, I can mount up again.'

'Maybe you should leave that to me,' said Naida, sharing an anxious glance with Kella. 'Tell me your name.'

Naida needed him to focus. He was lost in his shock, his body numbing his pain, his mind churning out solutions to keep his consciousness from recognising reality. But none of it would last if the thrashing agony came. It would render him untreatable until the horror rendered him unconscious.

'I was fine a moment ago. I'm not sure how this happened.'

'Name,' said Naida, gently. 'You remember that, don't you?'

A great roar erupted behind her. Suurkene infantry bullied through a break in the line that turned quickly to a tear, then a full-blown rout. Enemy infantry scattered, and what remained of their cavalry tried to make room for their foot soldiers to get behind the catapults, only to run into Suurkene riders mopping up every mote of resistance in front of the artillery.

Unable to move their machines, many crews abandoned their posts, leaving those with greater courage to try to protect what was left of their forces. It was a desperate move. Attempting to force a pause in the Suurkene advance, they shortened their arcs and flay-shot whined into the melee, cutting down friend and foe indiscriminately.

Suurkene cavalry gathered and charged at the catapult line. It would all be over soon.

'Per Daniel,' the soldier said slowly.

'Per, I need you to lie back.' Per's eyes began to focus on Naida, reality was about to make an unwelcome intrusion into his life. Naida gestured Kella to bring the dwale. 'But drink this first. It's good stuff.'

Per's eyes spilled over with tears and Naida saw the pain begin to take him. He grasped Kella's hands and drained the cup in a single swallow.

'Please make it stop,' he said, voice a whimper, face dragging down to a scream.

Naida moved closer. 'I will fix you. Sleep now.'

Per sank towards unconsciousness and the scream faded on his lips. Kella was there to lie him back as Naida looked at his leg. It would need straightening before he could be moved.

'Can you really fix that?' asked Kella.

'Guess we'll find out. I can save his life. His leg … is not so clear.'

Across the field, physicians and medics bent to their tasks. Stretchers moved in the shadow of injured horses. Oxen and their wagons moved among the dead and wounded. Medic teams buzzed around them, workers to their queens.

The Haronics were broken, routed. Artillery had been captured in great numbers. The same could not be said for those who threw down their arms in surrender, though they must have known what was coming to them. It was, and ever had

24

been, the Suurkene way, to leave a message on every battlefield. Naida hated the slaughter, and at the same time she understood it. And when she was being practical, just as there were limits to the number of people she could treat, there were limits to the number of prisoners Suurken could manage.

★

Naida stayed away from the celebrations for as long as she could. The formal dinner to fete some crusty old general – probably that terminally dull old letch, Grastin – had turned into a party she wasn't sure anyone had really anticipated. The scale of the victory, the swiftness with which their change in tactics had won the day, had the camp floating on a cloud of disbelieving euphoria from which it showed no signs of descending. It was a strange, almost hallucinatory experience, and it made Naida uncomfortable.

The price of celebration was a massacre of people very few of whom, if given the choice, would have been there in the first place.

So Naida stayed in the infirmary, tending her patients long after her skills were needed and far beyond the point where her rudeness could be excused. Whatever.

Eventually, Drevien cleared her throat often enough to irritate her into changing into her dress uniform. It was a stupid, scratchy, uncomfortable affair that had about as much to do with being a surgeon as did a hat with feathers. And it had a hat with feathers.

The trousers ended at mid-calf, leaving bare skin down to her ankles, which were covered by boots. This was to 'remind the surgeon that they too are flesh'. The shirt, with its ridiculous starched collar that dug into her neck, had sleeves that ended just below the elbow 'to remind the surgeon that their hands are their greatest, most delicate tool'. She had always refused to wear the costume gloves. They were beyond embarrassing.

Around her neck hung a chain adorned with a ceremonial scalpel pendant, the only actual indicator of her role in the whole farcical ensemble. The jacket was a cutaway, cavalry-style affair, deep green with shoulder braids and all; reasonably stylish and with no attendant explanation for its design.

'I look like a stork on the verge of rigor mortis,' said Naida. 'How long before I suffocate, do you think?'

'How long before you starve might be more pertinent,' said Drevien, barely trying to suppress her smirk.

Naida held her head high to try to mitigate the irritation caused by her collar. Drevien was right. How she would eat, when she wasn't sure she could look down at her plate, was a fascination for later.

'Can't I just wear the old one?'

Drevien raised her eyebrows. 'Remember the day you were treating that surprisingly large anal boil?'

'Oh.'

'Be on your way.'

'I could do with you next to me,' said Naida, cupping Drevien's face with her hands.

'Uh-uh.'

'You're enjoying this, aren't you?'

Drevien kissed her forehead. 'Yep. And the duty sergeant-at-arms is waiting outside. Still.'

'Shame. Thought he'd have collapsed with boredom by now and I could escape the crippling embarrassment of being introduced.'

'An order is an order, Naida!' called the sergeant-at-arms. It was Willan, and Naida smiled. 'Anyway, it's a lovely night.'

Naida scratched at her head. Drevien approached her with the feathered hat.

'You're taking the stork thing too far now,' said Naida, then raised her voice. 'Hey, Willan, do I have to wear the hat?'

'It's not strict etiquette but it is a military expectation for senior ranks to behat.'

'I don't do ... "behat"? Did you make that up, Will?'

'No idea.'

Naida wafted a hand at Drevien. 'I don't do etiquette expectations, or behatting for that matter.'

With a florid bow to Drevien that ended in a wince as her collar jabbed into her neck just behind her lower jaw, she cast her tent door aside in as grand a manner as possible and strode into the humid, alcohol-scented evening.

'Take me to my doom, fair Willan,' she said.

Playing his part, Willan offered her his arm and the two walked through the camp to whistles and applause. Plenty of drinks were offered, all refused. It had been a long time since Naida had tasted wine, spirits or ale. Patients didn't appreciate hungover surgeons attempting delicate surgery.

'They love you,' said Willan. 'We all do.'

Naida glanced across at her friend of a decade and more. He had taken her under his wing when she had first walked into a battlefield camp and had been her protector and occasional unarmed combat trainer ever since. Naida would have been lost without him.

The bald veteran was so proud to be escorting her across the camp to the hill. His habitually round-shouldered, reluctant-looking shamble had been replaced by a straight-backed, chin-jutting style. No wonder he hadn't wandered away while she was procrastinating.

'They love the fact I keep them alive when they should die. It's cupboard love, if you ask me.'

'You misunderstand them, then. The devotion is real. Yes, you keep them alive ... shattered throne, I can point to scars of my own that mean I still breathe the air, rather than being bones in the earth. But you give them the courage to fight, the belief in life after battle. You're a saviour who looks after them all.'

Naida squirmed a little, though she'd heard it before. 'You know, quite a lot of them still die.'

'Yes . . . but it's those who walk from the ward who write the story.'

'It's all a myth.'

Willan smiled. 'It isn't, though, is it? You're special. Enjoy it.'

Naida laughed. 'All right, all right! Now stop talking about it.'

The stroll through the camp was a journey through the heady mixture of relief, joy and that most precious of things: the knowledge that a new dawn would rise without an awaiting enemy. The singing was mostly awful but occasionally quite beautiful. The inevitable drunk wrestling contests were as chaotic as they were likely to lengthen her list of patients in the morning. And the cooking smells from stew and spit were many and alluring. Naida was starving.

Sudden cruel laughter and harsh words at odds with the mood of the camp grabbed Naida's attention. She glanced to her left and was marching towards the source before Willan could offer a warning. Having passed two cook fires where celebrations were at their raucous best, and where she smiled away invitations to stay awhile, she knew with sick certainty where the laughter was directed.

A small cluster of tents surrounded a single fire a little apart from the rest of the camp. Walking into the firelight she saw the drunk soldiers, one urinating on the door of a tent, one slapping the canvas, another daubing crude symbols on it.

'Come on out! Join the party. Show us tricks, oh Touched mistress.'

'Yeah . . . we cut you, you heal yourself . . . good old-fashioned magic show for a party night!'

Naida strode into their midst, seeing their faces flushed with drink and the scent of the hunt.

'Put it away, soldier,' she snapped, a single disdainful glance at the soldier's cock enough to shame him into pushing the dribbling member into his trousers.

'Sorry, Lady Naida... I'm sorry.'

The three of them backed off as Willan came to her side, the firelight adding a hard edge to his anger. Naida glanced at the tent, saw the tree root and branch drawings on it – old religious symbols, designed to scare those within. She stared back at the soldiers and they withered in front of her.

'Forris, isn't it?' she said, pointing at the one with the dark stain on his trousers and a long scar from ear to collar bone.

'Yes, Lady Naida.'

'Flay-shot. Glancing blow or you'd have had no head. I remember.'

'Thank you for saving me,' he said.

Naida shrugged. He wouldn't meet her eye.

'I just stitched you up. The infection was brutal though. Your screams... remember those? Myra... she has a name... Gifted Myra in this tent stopped the infection. You owe her your life.'

Forris stared at his feet, embarrassed and angry. His friends, relieved the fire was not beneath their feet, looked anywhere else but at him.

'Nothing to say, boy?' Willan moved up a pace. 'You will look at your superior officer when addressed.'

Forris looked. 'It's not right, sir, what they do.'

'Which bit? Saving your life or not coming out to get soaked in your piss?'

'I—'

Willan put a finger on his sternum. 'Best you say nothing more. Any of you. Get back to your tents and do not move. I will deal with you later. And should I hear of any more abuse of the Gifted, I'll have the skin from your back. Understand me?'

'Yes, sir.'

Naida watched them go, seeing the hate in the set of their bodies, feeling it rising from them.

'Thank you, Will.'

'It's a little worse every day,' he said. 'What was once muttered quietly is now out in the open.'

'I don't understand it. You army lot don't help much, though. Old traditions die hard on the battlefield.' She feathered the tent canvas. 'You all right, Myra?'

'Fine.'

'I can—'

'I'm fine, Naida. Just … let me be alone.'

'Of course,' said Naida, wanting nothing more than to go inside and stay until Myra's fear subsided, knowing that every time anti-Gifted sentiment reared its head, the seeds had been planted by the genocidal crime for which her parents had been executed a decade and a half ago. A crime that it was said they had used their Talent to perpetrate.

It was the same reason she would be hiding the fact she was of the Gifted for the rest of her life since her parents' accusers further claimed it must be in her blood too. And if she didn't hide her Talent forever, if it came out that she was Gifted after all, *someone* would recognise her. *Someone* would say.

'Come on, let's get you to your dinner,' said Will.

They began walking again. Naida smiled, perhaps it would be a welcome distraction after all.

'What's on the dinner table for the likes of me, then?'

'Fruit, small birds and fish, I heard. In delicate and exciting combinations.'

Naida wrinkled her nose. 'Can we stop off for some soup and bread somewhere?'

Willan pulled her back on course with a pinch of her arm.

'No. Any later and the knives might be out for you.'

'I can take it,' said Naida.

'Stop it,' said Willan, his admonishment apologetic. 'We've been spotted, anyway.'

He tipped his head at the grand command pavilion around which the senior military's capacious pavilions were pitched. Torches lined a hastily brushed and weeded avenue, and guards in dress uniform flanked the canvas portico – at the edge of which stood Elmridge, who hurried down the shallow slope of the hill when he saw them.

'Where have you been?' His face was a battleground between irritable and envious expressions. 'I'm the only person in the room that doesn't look like some sort of preening bird doing a mating display.'

'Naida claims she looks like a stork,' said Willan.

Naida gestured at her collar. Elmridge wrinkled his nose.

'Amateur stuff. You should see what's being preened inside.'

'I did have a feathery hat.'

'You still aren't going to compete,' said Elmridge.

'You and me against the birds,' said Naida. 'Willan, shall we?'

'This is where I take my leave,' said Willan. 'Don't forget it's self-defence training tomorrow.'

'Don't I get a day off since we won today?'

'There's always another enemy lying in wait,' said Willan.

Naida kissed his cheek. 'I'll be there.'

Willan blushed, saluted and withdrew. Naida and Elmridge walked up the torchlit avenue, acknowledged the guards and went into the grand command pavilion. She was announced by the Master of Ceremonies, and every head turned to see her.

Naida's gaze caught that of the guest of honour, Lord Marshal Yavin Ludeney, and by the merest raising of his eyebrows in recognition, she was completely undone.

Chapter 4

How she managed to walk further into the pavilion was a mystery because she couldn't feel her legs at all. She gripped Elmridge's arm and the vet smiled at the perceived honour bestowed on him.

Naida felt clammy and cold. She was sweating far more than the heat within the pavilion should prompt, and she had to blink rapidly to stop her vision fogging. Only long years of unconscious control stopped her from trembling but she could do nothing about the clamour in her head, the shrill volume of every sound, or the knowing, repulsed expressions she imagined she could see on every face turned her way. Her mind crammed with the knowledge that every preparation she had made for a day like this was worthless; she was a rabbit in a noose.

An orderly walked by with a tray of drinks and she clutched a goblet of water with her free hand, needing something, anything, to distract herself from the magnitude of the catastrophe that would at any moment engulf her. Here, in an atmosphere of entitlement and celebration, among senior military leaders, captains of cavalry and infantry and the Lord Marshal's entourage, she was about to be unmasked. Exposed for who, and what, she really was.

Naida responded to questions, apologised to the Commander-in-Chief for her late arrival, acknowledged those who thanked her for her service and courage, waved away trays of delicacies – the very scent of which was driving a tidal wave of nausea – and even smiled in most of the right places.

Elmridge noticed, though, and his aura of reflected glory became a brittle smile masking his concern. While the army players strummed and blew reasonable approximations of stirring classics, Elmridge moved Naida away from the centre of the room and the well-meaning but ceaseless attention being shown to her.

Near the tables where they would be called to sit in a carefully curated plan, he found a feeble breeze struggling through the sewn panels of pavilion canvas. To Naida, it was like a winter gale blowing across the hot sands of Cantabria.

Why had she not yet been denounced? The Lord Marshal might have been enjoying her suffering or awaiting a more apposite moment. They were, after all, to be seated together at dinner. Never would a circumstance be closer to perfect.

'What's up?' asked Elmridge.

'Heat and fatigue,' said Naida, far too quickly.

'Must I remind you how long we've been friends?' Naida felt the fog thin for the briefest of moments. Elmridge cocked his head like one of his soppier dogs. 'I mean, you look like you're about to vomit up your lungs or collapse into an invertebrate heap. I just can't make up my mind which.'

'You and I might be friends. The Lord Marshal and I are not.' Naida's heart felt constricted. 'I hadn't thought to see him again.'

Exactly like the first time, his merest glance had rendered her all but helpless; lost in panic. The first time, she had been a child of fourteen and his face, his blank-like-it-was-dead face, had scared her so deeply she had never completely recovered.

Their eyes had locked, just like today, and he had recognised her. He had pointed at her, his words obscured by distance and a pane of glass, and his soldiers had begun to run.

They hadn't caught her that time. She had escaped with the scent of burning strong in the air, and the screams of the dying crushing her innocence like stone dropped on spring blossom.

And now the sacrifice of so many good people was wasted because evil fate had delivered her straight to him and all that she had done to hide her true identity had been for nothing.

It was easy enough to choke back the desire to shed a tear, and her terror faded to be replaced by sadness, knowing that for all the good she had done, all the lives she had saved, the stain of the past would damn her just the same.

Elmridge was staring at her and must have seen her expression change with every thought crossing her desolate mind. In the grand pavilion where seventy would sit for dinner, where the banter ebbed and flowed, and where the orderlies swam through the shifting knots of the officers with trays of food and drink, Elmridge stood sentry against the many who would speak to Naida.

She loved him for it and pitied him for the moment when he discovered what she was — and what he had befriended and empowered over many years. He had been a true friend. The betrayal he would feel made her want to weep.

'He must have done something pretty awful to inspire this sort of reaction. Care to elucidate?'

Naida shook her head. 'It was a family squabble and the people with the power can do harm to those with less.'

'I'm sorry. Perhaps you should withdraw? I can cover for you, tell them you're unwell.'

Naida squeezed his hand. 'I won't ask you to lie for me. And honestly, though your offer is tempting and so warm-hearted,

I fear it won't make any difference. Better to face him, get it done.'

'You think he'll resurrect an old argument?'

'I think it's inevitable,' said Naida.

'If he's an arse, let me know. I've got some really effective horse laxatives.'

Naida snorted and momentarily felt a lightness of mood but then the gong sounded for dinner. Naida clung to her self-control and took her seat in the centre of the horseshoe of tables. Entertainment and speeches would be performed in the round once dinner was complete.

The Lord Marshal moved to his seat last, nodding to the assembled company. Naida breathed in expensive scent, freshly laundered woollens and delicately oiled leather. He was an impressive man, always had been. Tall, as upright as if steel ran through his spine. His hair, swept back from a high and noble brow and gathered in a wide tail that reached the middle of his back, was arranged with enormous care. Not a wisp dared stray.

His face was lined and considered, suiting his gravitas. A thin nose, vanishingly thin lips and a chin chiselled to a point. A theatrical villain's mask made flesh.

His arrival managed to relax the assembled company while terrifying Naida. But then, she knew what his capture of her parents had led to and that he would have visited the same horror on her fourteen-year-old mind and body if he had snared her too. In a moment that lasted forever, his first order was to raise a toast. While orderlies scurried to charge every glass with an expensive white wine, he stood.

'As happy as I am to have been present on a day of stunning victory, I am happier still to be able to meet, and to raise a toast, to someone I can only describe as a living legend, horrible cliché though that is.'

35

Appreciative laughter.

'And she will say she is part of a team, but we all know that without her leadership, her selfless courage, her incredible... her *unique*... skill, so many of those celebrating our victory tonight would be ashes in the wind. So, it is with the greatest pleasure that I invite you to stand and raise your glass to Naida Erivayne, first among healers.'

The scraping of chairs, the gathering and raising of glasses, and the intoning of, 'Naida. May she long walk among us,' stretched beyond forever. Naida managed to look both thankful and embarrassed, she thought, though her overriding desire was to remain conscious while her heart rate soared and heat crowded her head, threatening to rob her of control.

'Naida's exploits and abilities have been recognised at the very highest level,' said Ludeney into the lull following the toast. 'There is only one way to properly honour such extraordinary service to the great nation of Suurken. And thus, it is my unending and very personal pleasure to announce that Naida will travel to Suranhom and the Palace of Endless Spires to take her rightful position as the head of the royal medical service and personal physician to Queen Eva Rekalvian. My congratulations, Naida.'

Naida pulled herself to her feet to meet the explosion of noise that greeted Ludeney's announcement. She gripped the edge of the table, trying to smile while all around her, fists thumped down, glasses were raised and drained, and cheers and applause beat at her ears. Tears spilled onto her cheeks.

Ludeney put a steadying hand on her back and she flinched, wishing she had a scalpel with which to slit his throat. He called for calm and gestured for Naida to speak. Her throat constricted and she fed calm into her body, her Talent smoothing her tension just enough.

'I am rarely, if ever, lost for words. Any words after yours,

Lord Marshal, would be wholly inadequate in any event. So, I shall just say this: I am honoured beyond measure to be tasked with the Queen's health. She is who we all fight for and I will not let her wither while I have breath to take. But I shall miss all of you, my family, so very much, and you should know that whenever battle is joined again, I will seek leave to be here to keep you careless buggers alive.'

Naida sat rather heavily, another wave of noise rolling over and through her. She tried to keep the smile on her face, reaching a hand towards Elmridge, who squeezed it.

'Well done, you,' he said. 'I am so proud of you.'

'Promise you'll visit?'

'Have my rooms prepared.'

She glanced across at him. 'Thank you.'

Once everyone had retaken their seats, Ludeney favoured her with the sort of look that would accompany broken glass rubbed slowly and deliberately into flesh. She met his gaze with as outwardly warm a smile as she was able, and nodded her thanks for his toast. Everyone was watching.

Ludeney's voice was quiet when he spoke, leaning in close as if to give her a personal and private thanks, pitched carefully, to defy the finest-tuned of ears.

'I had not thought to see you again, Lady Esselrode,' he said.

'You have me confused with someone else,' said Naida, matching his pitch.

Ludeney smiled. 'I understand you had to try but, please, you are Helena Esselrode. Let us respect one another enough not to pretend otherwise.' He was no longer looking at her. 'We both know what you are.'

'And what is that?' she asked, putting one trembling hand around her goblet of water and wondering if she would need both to bring it to her mouth.

Ludeney raised his eyebrows and gave a tiny smile. 'They

love you, these people, don't they?' he said, favouring the room with a warm smile.

'Not letting them die on the battlefield if I have the merest chance to save them does the trick on the loyalty front. What did you do fifteen years ago to persuade otherwise ordinary soldiers to hunt a fourteen-year-old child?'

Ludeney's face darkened but his words were lost when flaps opened all around the pavilion to allow orderlies to serve the first full course of delicacies. Naida leaned aside to allow plates to be set in front of her and Ludeney. She saw Elmridge, who looked worried, and gave him an affirmative smile.

'Tell you all about it later,' she whispered.

'Talk louder now and I won't have to wait up,' he said.

'Funny.'

'Now these marinated and devilled corvid sweetbreads are from the northern steppes of Pargoan, and their exquisite taste and texture awaits you,' said Ludeney, reclaiming her attention. 'Many things await you.'

Another grind of the glass. Naida wrinkled her nose. She took a piece of meat, intending to savour its mix of spices, spectrum of flavours and interesting texture. It was revolting, clinging to her palate and throat like pond algae to a rock, and she clutched at the dream of eating rabbit stew with the infantry so she didn't choke.

'Go on, then. Denounce me. See how it plays out for you.'

To his credit, the Lord Marshal didn't let her challenge interrupt his mouthful.

'Denounce you?' he said, once he'd dabbed his mouth with his pristine red linen napkin and taken a sip of the accompanying sweet green wine. 'Now that would be a careless thing to do, wouldn't it? Having just announced you as the Queen's new personal physician. No, no, I have far more use for you than as a mere token of past evil.'

Naida's world closed in around her once more, this time with a constricting tightness that fed pain through her chest. But she had learned in the last decade and a half, while developing a consistent and impenetrable persona for her own survival, that giving up to the forces ranged against you was never an option.

'Oh, do you have an illness I can encourage to be fatal?'

Ludeney was the consummate diplomat. His smile was benevolent to the onlooker, and so warm when directed at Naida.

'Following this dinner, you will attend me in my pavilion,' he said.

'Lay one finger on me and I will educate you in all the places a man can feel the most extreme pain,' said Naida, her smile equally beatific.

Ludeney laughed, the sound booming across the grand pavilion and stilling all but the most intense of conversations. He put a hand to his mouth and raised the other in brief apology.

'The Lady Naida is a gifted conversationalist,' he said by way of explanation, and he raised his glass to her in a, perhaps, over-extravagant gesture.

There was a backdrop of polite laughter as he returned his attention to her.

'I have never had to either beg for, nor coerce, the attentions of a woman,' he said. 'Give me my due: I am not starting with you.'

'You facilitated the murder of my parents. You are due nothing,' said Naida. 'Now, I will speak with my friend and you will not even breathe in my direction for the rest of this dinner.'

Ludeney said nothing, merely turning to his right to speak to the victorious commander-in-chief who was surely desperate for some of the Lord Marshal's attention.

'He seems a decent sort,' said Elmridge, the warmth of his expression restoring some of Naida's balance.

'Seems that way. Yeah.'

39

'What were you two talking about?'

'My past and my future,' said Naida and, dammit, she could feel tears in her eyes.

Elmridge studied her. 'There's more to all this. I don't know what or why, but it's got to you. We've won, you're being honoured beyond measure. This should be joyous. What's wrong?'

'I hate finger food.'

She probably shouldn't have said that so loudly.

★

Her meticulously built and carefully curated second life had been fifteen years in the making. Her friends and allies had paid in shame, often in blood, while protecting her. Naida had hidden so well for so long but now she stood outside the pavilion of her nemesis, a chance meeting having dismantled it all.

Yet she felt no fear; part of her was even relieved that someone else knew who she was. Even if it was the man who still visited her in her nightmares. When she walked into his tent, though, she could not shake the thought that a cell door was slamming shut behind her.

Lord Marshal Ludeney was no stranger to luxury. Nor to what he evidently saw as home comforts. His pavilion was like a glimpse into another world. Not for him the sparse, efficient furnishing of a battlefield medic or a ranking officer. Naida wondered if he'd done it because he wanted to impress, or maybe he intended to intimidate with his authority. Was he genuinely uncomfortable without a considerable number of favourite things from home? Or did he not realise how grotesque it all was, shoved into a tent in a field seven days' ride from Suranhom, capital city of Suurken?

Not a stitch of canvas wall was visible, hidden as it was behind tapestries, flags, and expensively framed landscapes of anywhere-but-here. A huge, four-poster bed sat in the exact centre of the pavilion, draped in deep blue cloth, the sumptuous mattress covered in blistering white bed linen and enough pillows to sleep a battalion. Its headboard was painted with a depiction of the Shattered Throne, the seat of Suurken's monarch, a piece of furniture with an extraordinary history. Naida's eyes lingered on it a moment.

Trunks, chests, drawers and dressers ringed the tent's circumference, and an exuberantly carved desk and large leather chair stood to the right of the bed. At its foot, a sprawl of sofas, chairs and cushions surrounded a low wooden table, suffocated by the weight of fruit, covered platters, jugs and goblets resting atop it. Rugs obscured the grass and dust below. Lanterns set on poles in a dozen places cast a firm light across the whole ensemble, which was drenched in scent from gleaming brass incense-burners.

Ludeney was standing by his desk, brass goblet in hand. He had taken the time to change from his dress uniform into a collar-to-floor deep grey robe, edged in gold thread and cinched at the waist with a plaited leather belt. Naida had been offered no such opportunity and her ridiculous dinner garb hurt her all over. And she was starving. But all was eclipsed by a sick sense of anticipation.

He gestured at the laden table.

'I noticed you ate rather sparingly,' he said. 'Feel free to help yourself.'

That cured Naida of her hunger at a stroke.

'What do you want from me?' she asked.

'What was it like, lying to all these fine people for so long, hiding yourself… fearful every time you used your gift? I must say, I'm almost impressed. You've saved hundreds, thousands, of lives without once making a misstep. That is quite the deception.'

'Get to the point, I have rounds to make.'

'Not anymore,' said Ludeney. 'Can I get you something to drink… water, perhaps? You're looking a little pale.'

She drew herself up, walked to the table and poured herself some fresh juice with a, mercifully, steady hand.

'I'll never take anything from you,' she said.

'What if I were offering you your life?'

Naida almost spat out her juice, which would have been a shame as it was a glorious apple and wild berry mix.

'Shattered throne, do you really live your life in clichés?'

Ludeney's face tightened and he placed his goblet carefully on his desk before turning to her.

'You have a sharp mouth, Lady Esselrode, and you must think it fun to ridicule me.' His eyes never wavered from hers. 'That will stop immediately. I have your life in the palm of my hand and I can choose to crush you at any moment. I *own* you. And you will do as I say without question.'

'No one owns me,' said Naida, despite the weight of dread certainty on her soul. 'And I do not fear you or whatever fate you think you can visit on me.'

Ludeney chuckled, picked up his goblet, drained and refilled it. 'It's funny… no, it is, because I came here to honour a great battlefield surgeon, and now I have the solution to my most challenging problem.'

'I'm incredibly happy for you,' said Naida.

'I have work for you. Vital work that your particular, peculiar skills will allow you to do in so much more effective a fashion than I had envisaged before I found you so… fortuitously.' His cruelty had dissipated and Naida found herself comforted, and hated herself for it, knowing it to be a trap. 'The Queen needs a physician. The best. And you are undoubtedly that.'

Naida felt flattered, and her self-loathing deepened.

'Hence you will depart immediately to take up your new role. Once in the Queen's confidence, and I have no doubt that you will get along famously, you will ensure that she contracts a serious illness and, tragically, dies as a result.'

Chapter 5

Naida recognised the symptoms of her occasional panic attacks but this was something else. The physical symptoms were similar: weakness in the legs, pulse so strong it pained her throat, a tunnelling of her vision, heat flooding her face, stomach cramps. The whole set.

Now it was compounded by absolute confusion, and it felt like an age before she was able to question what she had heard. Her mind was a morass of conflicting thoughts and images, all trying to rationalise why anyone would want the Queen dead.

Ludeney had been a loyalist all his life. It had *been* his life. And the Queen … she was the living embodiment of a desire for a better future for the whole of Suurken … the warrior who wept when she sent armies to battle and who mourned for the families who would suffer grief and loss. A Queen who stood shoulder-to-shoulder with every sword-carrier, every archer and every rider, ready to hoist them on her shoulders in victory.

She was a monarch for all the people. A break with the elitism of the past. A unique opportunity to advance the cause of every citizen, not just the rich. She was feted and lauded. Even Naida, whose parents had been killed during the reign of King Pietr, the Queen's father, could see a brighter future in Queen Eva, who had ascended the throne very soon after her family's death.

'...and yet you want her dead?' said Naida, responding to her own internal monologue.

Ludeney had been watching her with considered contempt.

'Almost everything you have been told about her is a lie,' he said. 'And you will be so much more subtle than the assassins that I was being forced to consider. After all, I can rely on you not to talk afterwards because no one will believe you.'

Another twist of the knife. Naida squeezed her eyes shut, choosing her next words precisely, to make sure they were talking about the same thing.

'You are plotting treason.'

Ludeney raised an eyebrow and shrugged. 'That term is muddier than you think.'

'It's generally understood to have a pretty tight definition.'

'Then the term is incorrect. How do you define acts that will tear apart the foundations upon which our country is built and plunge us back into the dark days of superstition, division and civil war? And how do you describe those seeking to stop this disaster unfolding?'

'I'm not arguing semantics with you. You've ordered me to kill the Queen. I am, obviously, refusing.'

Saying it out loud didn't make her feel any better. Naida shivered.

'You speak as if you have a choice in the matter.'

'I cannot kill. You know what it means, if you believe my parents were evil and that same evil lurks within me.' She paused. Ludeney stared at her, unmoved. 'But it doesn't lurk anywhere. I have spent so long searching within myself for ways that the Talent could be bent to evil and there was nothing.'

Ludeney gave her an indulgent smile. 'Perhaps it is hidden.

45

Your parents betrayed no sign of their true nature until... Anyway, it changes nothing.'

Naida felt hollowed out. 'How can it change nothing? Do you believe there is malevolence within me or not?'

Ludeney leaned back in his chair. 'It doesn't matter what I believe. It doesn't matter what is true. Your parents were portrayed as the embodiment of evil; an evil to which tens of thousands lost their lives. You can argue it isn't your fault, yet you are assumed to have the same dreadful flaw. You are family. So, you will do as you are ordered because the alternative for you is unthinkable: I will reveal who you are. And while you suffer the same protracted torture as your parents, I will hunt down all those you have tainted with your touch and execute them in front of you.'

Naida shuddered and her hatred for Ludeney deepened. So arrogant in his power, so righteous. She reminded herself she was not trapped. She could step outside right now and denounce herself; tell the whole camp that she was the one the country sought, on whose head the largest bounty sat and who visited them all in their nightmares because she could do to them what her parents had done to others.

She smiled. Perhaps she should surrender herself to Willan or Elmridge... or Drevien. Her friends, her lover, could benefit from her revelation. But then she looked back to Ludeney, whose face was impassive. He'd just go back to his original plan.

Naida considered telling the Queen the truth. But he was right. No one would believe her about his treachery, only about her identity.

So, it was true she had no choice – but not for the reasons he thought most compelling. She'd go. She'd become the Queen's physician. Not to kill her, but because saving people was, after all, what she did. And he had unwittingly given her someone to save.

'How immediate is "immediately"?' she asked.

'Tonight. I have your order papers here. One does not keep the Queen waiting,' said Ludeney.

'I want my core team with me or I'm going nowhere.'

Ludeney shrugged. 'As you wish. Leave their names, I'll see they follow you shortly but you're leaving now. Your possessions are already being packed. I have travelling clothes laid out for you in my dressing area.'

Ludeney gestured past the headboard of his bed.

'My—?' began Naida, half-standing, staring again at the painting of the Shattered Throne.

'You will travel in the comfort and security befitting your new position. I will be a day behind you.'

'I have to say goodbye to my people.'

Ludeney spread his hands. 'Only a monster would deny you a tearful farewell. I will have one of my council accompany you on your final rounds.'

'Naturally you will.' And so it began; the curtailment of her ability to speak her truth.

'You're doing the right thing.'

'I'm doing the only thing.' Naida drank her juice and set the goblet down. 'Let's get this done. I find your company sickening.'

'Then I will ensure we meet often in the days to come.'

The bastard was beginning to enjoy it. Naida let him. After all, it was fun to let men like him think they were in charge right up until she pulled the rug from beneath them.

'I can't wait.'

'You'll find, Lady Esselrode, that I can be a very useful ally.'

Naida paused on her way to the dressing area. 'My parents died in the most brutal, drawn-out executions in history. You have hunted me since I was fourteen for crimes I did not commit, nor will ever commit. You will never be anything other than a sworn enemy of mine, and if I ever stoop to kill, with whatever dread power you think I harbour, you will be my first victim.'

'I—'

'You want me to do your work? Stay away from me. Forever.'

Chapter 6

By the time she was walking to the carriage, the news of her departure had spread more surely than the most virulent of plagues, and everyone but the bed-ridden had walked with her, their best wishes and deepest fears echoing up into the empty sky. A swell of noise had erupted into a roar when she'd climbed the steps and turned at the open door to wave, to clench her fist in solidarity and to blow them all her last kiss with both hands.

Naida had held herself together for as long as she could. She had known where Ludeney was at all times. She'd let her gaze travel across the moon- and torch-lit army in front of her until it had reached him. He had met her gaze, as he was obligated to do. Naida had brought her fist to her chest, mouthed the words, 'my people', and ducked inside the carriage.

Drevien was waiting inside for her. Their embrace was long and their kiss longer. Naida's tears fell unrestrained.

'How did you get in here?' Naida asked, breaking to look at her and smooth strands of hair from her face.

'Willan,' said Drevien, explaining everything. She was shaking and pale in the gloom of the carriage. 'I'm never going to see you again. Am I?'

'What? No, Drev, no.' Naida kissed her. 'Why would you think that?'

'You're disappearing to the palace. I'm an army medic. That's the end, isn't it?'

'No. I've told Ludeney I need you. The whole team but really it's just you,' said Naida, pulling her close again. 'I can't do this without you.'

Drevien relaxed in her embrace. 'I'm not that great a ward-lord.'

Nadia squeezed. 'That's not what I mean.'

'I know.' Drevien eased Naida back. 'Do you think Ludeney will send me? Us?'

'I'll ask the Queen too,' said Naida, realising she meant it.

'Then this isn't goodbye.' The tears spilled from Drevien's eyes now.

'No,' said Naida.

There was a knock on the carriage door.

'Come on. Time to go,' said Willan. 'This side, Drev, away from the crowd.'

'Go on,' said Naida. 'I'll be all right.'

'I won't.' Drevien crumpled and Naida took her hands, stroking them. 'You're the heart of this place, of us. Of me.'

'Drev...'

'I love you.'

'And you can tell me again in a few days. I will not lose you.'

Drevien drew a long breath. 'Be safe.'

'Look after Hazza for me.'

'You ask the impossible.'

They kissed again and she was gone. Naida kept the ventilation shutters closed. She had no desire to watch as she was taken from her home and family.

They were so proud. The army served the Queen and Naida was being tasked with her health and long life. Honour did not come higher than this and it had reflected from every face. It was the betrayal of their pride that broke her; the best wishes that followed her, the desire for her to succeed... if only they knew what they were really cheering on.

Naida slumped back when the carriage moved away to more shouts of good luck. Tears fell down her cheeks. She was already aching for Drevien and feeling vulnerable without the comforting presence of Willan.

Plain though it was, the carriage was comfortable. The three cushioned seats were upholstered; a small cabinet was stocked with water, wine, fresh and preserved foods; and there was a small, fold-down table above a cubby-hole holding ink, paper and quills. All very nice, but the tracks to Suranhom would turn any attempt at a letter into an illegible scrawl.

A small chest pushed under one of the seats held pillows and a soft blanket, and it was to these she turned, hoping that when she awoke, she'd be back in her pavilion and able to conduct the rounds of those her team had saved from death.

A final single tear squeezed from beneath an eyelid as sleep took her.

★

'Naida?'

The knock and sound of a familiar voice gave brief life to hope. Reality was a tight ball of anxiety in the pit of her stomach. And yet...

'Yes. Yes, I'm here.'

Still clinging to the tendrils of sleep, Naida had to take a moment to work out what was happening.

The carriage had stopped and the clanking and crackling sounds she could hear told of a meal being prepared. There were voices too, neither happy nor sad, just dealing with the business at hand. Light was streaming in through the shutters, telling her they had driven through the remains of the night.

Naida wondered how far they had travelled, and it brought

fresh pain to her mind and her heart. She straightened her clothes and opened the carriage door upon which the respectful knock had been delivered. The sight gladdened her so greatly she all but cried.

'Willan!' She couldn't help it. She leapt from the carriage and threw her arms about his neck. 'Dear Willan, how can you be here?'

The sergeant-at-arms, a little surprised and discomforted by Naida's embrace, nonetheless managed to return a part embrace, part pat on the back.

'I have often told you I know everyone,' he said. 'Someone has to be your protector, official or otherwise. Nothing would stop me being that someone.'

Naida's smile widened and she felt a rush of warmth, a comforting wave. Security. Trust. When she'd been driven away last night she'd believed she'd left those qualities behind, but they'd ridden up to join her.

'If you've deserted...'

'Lady Naida, that idea is unworthy of you.'

Naida's face flushed with shame and she put her hands to her mouth. 'Oh, shattered throne... I just... I didn't... it's just that...'

Willan raised a placating hand and his smile drained her tension. 'It was a logical conclusion, but you know me better than that.'

'I know...' Naida glanced to the carriage drivers, who had finished seeing to the horses and were gathered around the cook fire with the three riders offering the Crown's protection on the largely safe road to Suranhom.

'I petitioned the commander-in-chief for a leave of absence. We're marching to the muster camp tomorrow anyway; there's no fighting to be done for thirty or forty days, even if we're sent to the islands or the eastern marshes. Rumour going round camp after you left was that the Queen'll go all out for peace now we've taken down the Haronics.'

'I'll be sure to ask her,' said Naida and the thought of her destination sparked a rush of heat through her skull and down her spine.

Willan raised an eyebrow. 'Bloody hell. You'll meet the warrior queen... to look after her health and bring us all the mercy of her long life... to be able to speak to her like you and I are speaking now...'

There was very little that rendered Willan awestruck.

And Ludeney wants me to kill her.

'Still doesn't really explain how Ludeney has allowed you to be here. He was pretty clear that I had to leave everything except my team behind.'

Willan's grin was conspiratorial.

'Ah... he doesn't know, does he?'

'I can neither confirm nor deny,' said Willan.

'And so, to which of these fine servants of the Endless Spires did you whisper your entreaties?'

Willan pointed at the cook fire where whatever stew they'd concocted was being ladled into bowls.

'See that massive bear disguised as a soldier?'

Naida laughed. 'Elias? Yes, he has introduced himself to me. They all seem unnecessarily deferential.'

'You are on your way to tend to the Queen. They're terrified that any harm might come to you.'

'I've spent my adult life kneeling on blood-soaked battlefields, Willan. I think they can relax on a carriage ride through our own country. Anyway, what about the Bear?'

'He's my cousin. And the rider next to him, that's Adeile. I served with her in the archipelago five years ago – remember that one?'

Naida nodded, recalling the moment with complete clarity. A

torrential downpour, a chaotic battle on the shores of the most beautiful island she had ever seen. Invaders streaming off boats, their blood washing up on the sand. Sharks gathering, hunting. And Willan, shield raised above his head, charging across the shallows, hacking a path through enemies and hauling injured comrades up the beach before standing in front of her while she fought to stem the flow of blood from a fallen rider's throat.

'It was quite the introduction,' she said.

'Well, the woman who dismounted to pick up the stretcher pole when the first bearer took an arrow in the heart was Adeile. She's too humble to tell you herself.'

Naida looked at Adeile who, evidently feeling Naida's eyes on her, glanced up and smiled.

'She saved a life that day,' said Naida.

'Not as many as you,' said Willan. 'There's not one among them who hasn't been touched by your work, directly or in-directly. But they'll have to report back to Ludeney's people at some stage after you get to the Palace of Spires. I don't.'

'But you have no official order papers.'

'You are mistaken,' said Willan.

Naida touched his arm. 'Thank you, Willan. Having you here gladdens my heart. Time for breakfast, isn't it?'

Chapter 7

Suranhom. It translated from the old dialects, rather roughly, as 'ancient home', or 'first home' if you took a more absolutist view.

Technically, it wasn't the first settlement in what became Suurken, the 'ancient kingdom', but it had the location to draw people in: straddling the great Palean river, which flowed from the Bloodmoon Mountains in the far west of the country, down to the Kyrani estuary a day's sail downriver. Arguments continue over which bank of the river was first settled.

From a rise where they'd paused for the breathtaking view, Naida wrinkled her nose. When she'd admitted, the evening before, that she'd never seen Suranhom before, they'd all said she'd be awed by the view. And they were right, because it was vast and it rose from flatlands that fled in all directions for mile upon mile; and in the mid-morning sun, the standing water sparkled and the tallest and whitest buildings glinted.

'Bit tatty, though, isn't it?' she said.

'I think it's more normally described as organic growth,' said Adeile, who had overcome her initial shyness (and perhaps been a little awestruck) and had proved herself to have a sharp mind and wit.

'Infections grow organically too,' said Naida. 'Perhaps "tatty" was unfair. It looks like someone dropped a massive spider and it's struggling to get its legs back under it.'

They all looked back at Suranhom, presumably trying to shoehorn her description into their lifelong romantic bias towards the great capital city rising majestically from the Palean plains. There was a breeze-blown silence, punctuated by the snorting of one carriage horse and the thrumming sound of another urinating on dry earth.

'Some of its legs must have fallen off, then,' said Willan eventually.

Naida rolled her eyes. 'Come on, at least get on board with the spirit of my tortured analogy.'

'Still think you're being unfair,' said Willan. 'It's beautiful. A triumph of society and civilisation. The seat of the great kings and queens of the world.'

Naida felt a pang of regret. The others took pride in this great city. She could see it in the set of their bodies and the shine in their eyes. It was the seat of the Queen, after all; the place they imagined they defended as they fought. If she'd been feeling unkind, she'd have accused them of having their brains so filled with stories of glorious endeavour their eyes were blind to what was right in front of them.

But she wasn't.

'It is the greatest feat of architecture and population management in history,' she said. 'I don't think anyone would dispute that.'

Naida could sense their disappointment. They'd expected her to make all the usual noises of amazement and wonder and she'd told them it was a tatty spider that had lost a couple of legs, so fair enough. But her latest utterance had at least led to a concerted series of nods and grunts of agreement, so she left it at that.

On the ride into Suranhom, where they'd arrive for a lunch

that had not been scorched over a campfire, Naida sat with the carriage drivers, taking her turn when they'd let her but otherwise staring out at the city.

Starfish might have been more apt than spider.

In some ways it was obvious why Suranhom had developed the way it had. Good farming, rivers running with fish, and ideal building lands had driven significant development since the city had been founded. It had grown quickly from its tiny beginnings to become dominant, and was adopted as the capital when the first king had chosen it for the site of the Palace of Endless Spires.

There was nothing particularly unusual in the city's development. The palace was absolutely dead-centre and placed on a rise in the ground that gave it a nominal overlook on its citizens and their lives. From there, buildings crowded around the rise and overflowed in every direction, an avalanche of life and endeavour.

And beyond the vast, sprawling body, those spider legs... starfish... whatevers... had crept out and inched their way along two other, more minor rivers, both tributaries of the River Palean, forming two major trade routes that ran through prime arable and livestock farmland. From the legs, little strands of habitation leaked onto the plain. Naida might have likened them to the tiny hairs on an arachnid leg... but you could push an analogy too far.

The great rump of Suranhom was, she could see as they neared, dominated by timber and stone structures, mainly single storey, but where skill, money and ostentatiousness were plentiful, striking buildings of three and four storeys rose from the sludge of the ordinary. One thing was for sure, she wasn't going to change her opinion in a hurry. It was tatty. A tatty spider. Without enough legs.

And where to start with the Palace of Spires? From their

first vantage point, it had looked a stunning structure with its forest – well, small woodland anyway – of spires. One for each monarch since the Founding, almost exactly three hundred and sixty-five years ago. A time of some bloodshed, so she'd been taught.

As an idea to commemorate, and inter, deceased monarchs, spires weren't a bad idea as such, but the problem – one of several problems to her eyes – was that no one had ever set out a system for determining any limits to the architectural design.

Naida didn't want to provoke any more discord among her travelling companions, with whom she felt great kinship after the long, dull days of the journey, but she was nevertheless desperate to discuss how the tradition of each monarch design-ing their own spire had led to a right mess at the very centre of the city and the country itself.

Instead, she confined herself to the other question nagging at her.

'What happens when the current monarch looks about for a site for their spire and there's no space for the footings?' she asked, looking right to her two companions: Aryn, the current driver, a stick-thin man with an incredible way with horses; and Katarine, a soldier with a steel glint in her eyes and the dirtiest laugh Naida had ever heard.

'I think they pick a site and it gets cleared,' said Aryn, his gentle tone accompanied by a shrug. 'I mean, they're royals, aren't they?'

'Right.' It made Naida uncomfortable. 'And what sort of sites get cleared? Old buildings within the palace walls?'

'Hah,' said Katarine. 'Hardly. Can't have historical buildings and ornamental gardens crushed under the weight of a new spire.'

'So what do they do ...?'

Aryn frowned at Katarine's cynicism. 'The last two were built just to the west of the palace. Queen Eva is planning hers there too, I think.'

'And what was there before?' Naida already knew the answer. Aryn confirmed it.

'Houses. Tenements, mainly, I think. Servants and clerks, all honoured to leave their homes at the humble request of the monarch.'

It was a good thing that Aryn had chosen to gaze wistfully towards Suranhom because the look Naida and Katarine shared would have scorched the skin from his face.

'How is it honourable to become homeless so someone entitled can build a personal, permanent shrine to themselves on your bed?' she asked.

Aryn didn't understand. 'Soldiers lay down their lives for their monarch on the battlefield every day. To lose one's house seems a small sacrifice by comparison.'

'I joined the army for the money,' said Katarine. 'I'm not fighting for my monarch. I'm fighting for my family, for my country, and for other carriage drivers. All the Queen does is tell us where to set our lines.'

'Do these clerks get a choice when the Queen comes knocking?' asked Naida.

Aryn laughed. 'Well, of course not.'

'Acting with honour is a matter of choice,' said Naida quietly.

★

The riders and carriage entered Suranhom under the monarch's flag: a silver crown flanked by rearing horses, piped in silver, backed in deep green and stitched with gold. It guaranteed them uninterrupted passage to the palace gates and attracted curious glances from everyone they passed.

And they passed so many of every hue and heart, every standing in life, young and old. From her position with the drivers, Naida tried to take it all in. The scattered outlying farmsteads and land workers' terraces, and the net-strewn fisher huts and smokeries with their wonderful aromas, gave way to the claustrophobic press of the city proper.

They passed through markets selling every commodity a bright imagination could muster; spacious parks bordered by expensive houses and stables; working communities with hubs for their chosen crafts; and terrible slums. Naida was full of wonder one moment and sadness the next, and questions about the stark contrasts crammed her mind.

But whatever the sight, the sheer noise of the city enervated her, made her shrink, unable to escape it. And even the glorious odours of spice, fresh produce, exotic cooking, or the hideous stench of excrement and decay that might dominate round the next corner could not distract her for long.

Perhaps she would get used to it. Perhaps Suranhom quiet-ened at night and allowed the birds their voices and the trees to speak in the language of the breeze. She doubted it. The already raucous sounds from some of the inns, bars and brothels spoke of a night-time economy that defied silence during the dark hours.

It was as they turned out of a densely packed cobblestone street, with houses leaning in on both sides, that she got the first view that genuinely stole her breath.

Across a broad, fountained and paved square, edged on three sides with colonnaded buildings boasting eateries, shops and, above, dwellings for the rich and privileged, rose the Palace of Endless Spires. It sat behind towering, ornate, gilded-iron gates and, equally towering, bright white stone walls.

'That's the ceremonial gate,' said Aryn, having been silent for a good part of the ride through the city. They had slowed to a walk, the curious glances coming now from tourists hoping for a sighting of the monarch. 'I mean, it's the front of the palace, but the Queen doesn't use it except for official engagements in Founding Square or to be seen by the masses from yonder balcony.'

You'd need a telescope to see the Queen on 'yonder' balcony as indicated by Aryn's jutting chin. Beyond the gates, which were being opened in readiness for their arrival, a long tree- and gaslight-lined avenue opened onto a circular courtyard where a complex fountain threw its water in beautiful patterns into the clear sky.

Beyond that, the palace gatehouse rose three storeys, boasting a guard rampart lined with soldiers and trumpeters. Flagpoles displaying the royal colours stood at either end, and the great iron-banded wooden gates, granting access to the inner court-yard, would remain shut until the first gates were closed behind them.

Above that, and a further two storeys up, was the ceremonial balcony. Naida had seen paintings of it in her school years and knew the stone walls were carved in extraordinary detail, depicting ancient battles fought during the bloody years of the Founding. It was a history book in stone imagery, all so high up that no one could see its full glory unless they were lowered down from above or laddered up from the gatehouse. Daft, really.

Behind the walls, and with the iron gates closing behind them, the sheer scale of the palace building was revealed. Once in the courtyard and trotting around the fountain while the gatehouse forecourt filled with soldiers in ceremonial uniform – deep green and white, with rank insignia in gold and red – Naida tried to fathom the size of it, and failed.

It climbed in ascending terraces, window on window, rampart upon rampart, in towers and, inevitably, spires. She could count the tops of eight of them. They'd be the earliest monarch's graves, when the spires could be woven into the developing architecture of the palace buildings. More recently, they had been gathered in four locations around the palace, and now dwellings within the wider palace boundaries, but beyond the sanctuary of the inner walls, were falling prey to the whims of the sitting monarch.

Balconies, gargoyles, chimneys, curated ivy and wisteria, carvings about every window, army crests, cavalry pennants rendered in iron or stone. Four hundred years of changing ideals, designs and visions were played out and should have created nothing more than a horrible architectural mess.

But it was beautiful. *Beautiful.* Regal and awe-inspiring, the grandest statement of power and unshakeable authority.

Naida had hoped it might be an oasis from the din of the city but the inner courtyard was the city in microcosm. Aryn parked the carriage over on the left by the stables and blacksmith as directed, and Naida could feel every eye turn their way. Her blissful anonymity was about to end.

The riders moved to surround the carriage as best they could. Adeile, Willan and Elias dismounted immediately, calling for the attention of the Queen's guards. Meanwhile, Naida stared at the hubbub of the courtyard, with the backdrop of the ringing of blacksmith's hammers and the rasp of carpenter's saws.

Everywhere, it seemed, someone was carrying something somewhere, be it a barrel, a box of food, a pile of clothing, a bucket of paint and a ladder, or a bale of hay. There was an eatery that ran down the right-hand side of the courtyard and it was packed with people seated under cover, or at tables spilling into the open.

And now all of them had something to look at: Naida. Battlefield surgeon of legend and now chief medic to the Queen. How she longed for the camaraderie of the open road. Next to her, Katarine could feel her discomfort.

'I'm not being cruel or anything, but for the shattered throne's sake, don't look up.'

Naida looked up. The courtyard was ringed by three storeys of palace building boasting rooms, galleries and passageways from what she could see. But it was difficult to be sure because every opening and window had a face, or multiple faces, pressed against it or leaning out of it.

'I didn't think I'd be this big a deal,' said Naida, feeling an odd mix of anxiety and pride.

'You're joking, right?' Naida shook her head and Katarine gave voice to that extraordinary laugh, bringing heads swinging her way. 'You really have no idea how you're portrayed here?'

'No. I've never been here, remember? I've worked the battle-fields most of my life.'

'I'm not telling you about the paintings and memorabilia hawkers, then.'

Naida began to realise that she would look back on her time as a surgeon in the midst of battle as a quiet period of her life.

She felt very far from home.

Chapter 8

The chatter was increasing, and more people were finding their way into the courtyard to try to catch a glimpse of Naida. Queen's guards marched from a set of rather plain-looking doors that presumably led into the palace proper. They looked to her like an official delegation, given the smartly dressed trio of men walking between the dual ranks of ten guards.

Naida jumped down from the driver's seat and stood next to Willan and Adeile, hoping to somehow remain incognito. It worked for a while. The officials, or dignitaries, or whatever they were, walked with absurd self-importance to the carriage door and one of them indicated a guard open it.

Naida wanted to stop them but Adeile caught her arm and shook her head, enjoying the thought of the embarrassment about to be visited on the haughty delegation, all three dressed in high-collared, green topcoats, deep red shirts and three-quarter length white breeches buttoned into polished black boots.

'Lady Naida,' began one. 'It is my great pl—'

His face, already ruddy, reddened with ire to find the carriage empty, not aided by Adeile's sniggering or a guffaw from Katarine.

'My humble apologies, sir,' said Naida, stepping forwards. 'I was saying my farewells to those who have kept me safe and sane on the journey here. I am honoured and awed to be here and I thank you for coming to welcome me.'

To his credit, the dignitary recovered himself and extended a bejewelled hand, which Naida took between both of hers as protocol demanded. His eyes, though, showed a pique that might well lead to spite.

'The honour is mine … ours.' He gestured to his colleagues. 'I am Vinald, Senior Aide-to-Court to Her Majesty. Along with Aides, Panoa and Kastel, I will be facilitating your time with us, which I hope will be long and happy.'

'So long as I keep the Queen alive, eh?' said Naida, winking at Kastel, a gaunt, ageing man who looked like he could do with some cheering up.

She didn't get a reaction.

'Quite so,' said Vinald. 'If you would accompany me, the Queen is expecting you.' He and Ludeney must have been cut from the same cloth. They had the same ability to cause the greatest of ripples with the simplest of things.

'Now?' Naida felt frail. Not just frail. Inadequate, filthy, unready, and unworthy.

'Your reputation precedes you,' said Vinald and his lip curled just ever-so-slightly. 'Your rooms are prepared for you and your baggage will be taken care of.'

'Thank you,' said Naida.

With the slightest of shrugs, Vinald indicated she should walk with him. The crowds were pressing a little closer now and she could hear her name spoken amid the rising noise.

She looked over her shoulder.

'Hey, Will. Let's all meet later, have food that has to be better than Adeile's and eat it somewhere which serves wine worthy of the name.'

Willan nodded but his smile was sad. He clearly thought

this was the end of their friendship, except from a distance, and Naida was trying to work out how she could keep him close. She needed a friend. Someone she could trust without question.

'We'll find you,' said Willan.

'See that you do.' Naida smiled. 'Have fun, you lot. And thank you. You made the miles bearable.'

Vinald walked at her shoulder, between the firm lines of the flanking guards. Naida couldn't understand why people's curiosity about her hadn't already waned now they'd seen she was as ordinary as they come. And she was glad of the guards every step of the way to the doors into what Vinald told her was the grand reception hall.

'It might be harder for your friends to find you than you think,' said Vinald. 'Perhaps it is better that way.'

'I beg your pardon?'

'The palace has strict rules about who you may and may not fraternise with.'

Naida didn't break stride. 'I'll just take it up with the Queen, then.'

Vinald cleared his throat. 'Her Majesty does not deal with such trifles, Lady Naida.'

'Trifles like keeping the woman who's keeping her alive happy, you mean?'

A sharp intake of breath at that. 'Court etiquette is … complex, my lady.'

Naida had made him uncomfortable enough. Well, almost. She gave him a hefty clap on the shoulder and laughed.

'Tell you what, Vinald … Vinny? Anyway. Tell you what: let's have a wager. Name some menial task of yours you hate. If I don't manage to eat with my friends tonight, I'll do it for you for ten days.'

Vinald favoured her with the thinnest of smiles. 'Vinald. Always Vinald. Tell me, what do I forfeit if you should win?'

'Oh, no forfeit, Vinny. I will have made my point.' She locked eyes with him. 'I'll be doing things my way, or not at all.'

The wisdom of picking a fight with a close employee of the Queen, the moment she arrived, was debatable but Naida had little time to worry. The doors of the reception hall were opened and the full force of the royal and legislative courts of Suurken was unleashed on her, and Vinald was nowhere to be seen. She reckoned she deserved that. Not knowing which way she was supposed to go, Naida decided to stop right where she was and wait.

While most of the press of the well-to-do, or at least, well-connected, was curious and good-natured, and even avoided jostling the serving staff threading the room with trays of food and drink, some were less polite. Mixed with the questions she expected, others were raised with barbed intent.

Everywhere she turned, each time she tried to speak – to thank someone and say that the honour was all hers – she was confronted by another agenda, another courtier seeking to ally with her, or to undermine her appointment, and sow doubt and suspicion ... as if, like Ludeney, they already knew the truth. Though that was not possible, or she'd be in irons already.

'Do you think it odd a battlefield surgeon is suddenly the arbiter of the Queen's health?'

Naida turned to find the woman who had spoken, but she was lost in a sea of faces, colours and ridiculous headgear, and a wave of expensive odours – not all of them worth the money. A question to be heard, not answered.

'I hope we can return the honour you show us by coming here to look after our Queen.'

Another woman's voice, this one cracked with age; a withered hand touched Naida's wrist. Naida looked down. The tiny woman was veiled and dressed in a rich, deep red. Fine lace detail and embroidery were a delight to the eye. It was needle-work accuracy Naida would have been proud to call her own.

'There is no need,' she said, placing her free hand over the old woman's. 'All I need is a little understanding while I come to terms with my role and responsibilities here.'

'A woman with no history, rising through the ranks in the blood of war, and transported to the highest rank of her profession. What friends you must have.'

This was from behind her, a man this time, hissing the words to carry across the heads of many and land in the ears of many more. It hurt, this one.

'I left all my friends on the southern front,' she said, louder than she intended, then dropped her voice to a whisper. 'I'm alone in this crowd.'

The elderly woman was still by her, still gripping her wrist with mouse-like bones.

'There is more poison here than honey,' she said. 'But no one is ever quite alone.'

Naida lost interest in the rest of the crowd. They were hawks and voyeurs of no consequence. She dropped to her haunches so that this warm heart, this oasis of sense, could look down on her. Naida couldn't help it, she gripped the woman's hand a little more firmly and fed in her essence passively, seeking her weaknesses and illnesses and hoping she could find cures, or alleviations for it at the very least.

'Perhaps you can guide me,' said Naida, seeing nothing through the veil but wispy white hair and a gaunt face, breath hardly rippling the gossamer cloth. 'Might I ask your name?'

Now she had disappeared from easy view, the crowd pressed in a little further, craning to get a glimpse of Naida's new focus, sensing something was happening. And something was. The old woman was warm. Not yet hot but the infection was there in her urinary tract and would overwhelm her if she was not treated in the next few hours.

'I am of no consequence, just one whose life has been spent in joyous service of our royal family and who is so grateful for your attendance on Queen Eva.'

Naida smiled. 'Then you qualify as my first patient. You need attention immediately.'

Beneath the veil, her head shook but there was relief in her body and Naida could feel it.

'No, no, no. I have some small discomforts, but I am old. Such things are a daily reality.'

Naida reached under the veil and laid her hand on the woman's brow. It was covered with a thin sheen of sweat.

'As head of the royal medical service, I am advising you, strongly, to accompany me to the surgery and dispensary, where I can treat you.' Naida withdrew her hand and smiled. 'Though you'll have to show me where these rooms are.'

The old woman was trembling. 'I am Misha.' And her last words were all but inaudible. 'Thank you.'

Now help was at hand, Misha's façade of strength could crumble, and she wobbled. Naida stood up to call for assistance, drawing Misha close to her, holding her upright. But no one was paying her attention any longer because soldiers had gathered at the grand doors opposite those through which Naida had entered. Atop a wide, shallow quintet of marble steps, the green and white-painted doors opened inwards and there she was, walking forwards with the sunlight of an open courtyard in her wake and commanding absolute silence and reverence.

Misha tried to move away but Naida would not let her go; and so they stood together, the trail-filthy battlefield surgeon and the ancient, veiled and beautifully turned-out royal servant, while Queen Eva of the family Rekalvian, monarch of the wider territories of Suurken, Evontide, and the greater archipelagos of

Northern, Western and Central Gerestova, its oceans and rivers, walked towards them.

Naida stared while her doctor's mind calculated how long Misha could hold on, and what she needed to treat her. Given her physical frailty, it wasn't long. She should be in bed under treatment right now, though her mental strength might well be her salvation. How far were the medical facilities? Who could tend Misha if the Queen delayed Naida?

She stared because she had no choice, even while the combined distractions of the stomach-baiting scents of food and alcohol, and the beguiling wisps of drug smoke, fought to distract her. The fascination of power, of effortless charisma and, yes, of *majesty* gripped her. Queen Eva was born to it, schooled in it, knew no other life, and so wore it as naturally as Naida did her surgeon's robes. No child who dreamed of becoming a prince or princess could ever hope for such effortless grace.

And yet, in Queen Eva's eyes, the arrogance and condescension Naida expected was absent. In their place was the brightness of intelligence and curiosity. Her advisors and security detail trailed in her wake, ordered from her path by a flick of her hands. The crowds parted for her, heads bowed, and Eva flowed forwards, her long, deep-green skirts designed to give the appearance that she floated rather than sully her feet with the ground.

Eva wore an exquisite, embroidered and ruffled, white shirt, with a neckline designed to frame the chain of state, a huge emerald in engraved gold that hung from a thin cord of steel at the top of her breastbone.

Yet, however the cord might chafe her shoulders, Eva's face betrayed nothing but a welcoming smile. It shone from a face dominated by strong cheek bones, large brown eyes and gorgeous shoulder-length black hair, strung through with gold braid and green threads.

The Queen had a dark green velvet cloak about her shoulders, and she gestured for it to be removed when she was a couple of paces from Naida and Misha. Naida didn't know what to do so took her cue from Misha, whose temperature was still rising. The royal servant inclined her head. Not an extravagant gesture but one conveying respect, one that didn't assume the Queen would favour you with her gaze.

Eva did far more than that. She touched them both on the shoulder.

'Neither of you need ever avert your gaze on my approach,' she said, her voice clean, crisp and affectionate, her accent a flawless central Suurkene. 'Misha, you really should know better.'

Misha chuckled. 'I sought to lead the Lady Naida in the correct bearing, my Queen.'

The Queen favoured Naida with a look full of warmth. 'Welcome, Naida. You have earned quite the reputation. Hopefully, you will not have to conduct emergency surgery on me following a battlefield injury.' Sycophantic laughter glittered briefly. 'I hope keeping me hale and healthy will be a more straightforward task.'

'I am honoured to be joining your service, Your Majesty,' said Naida, her heart clattering so hard she thought it might drown out her words. 'I hope to be able to extend my care to others in the royal household and service.'

Naida tipped her head in Misha's direction and raised her eyebrows minutely. It was not lost on the Queen whose expression didn't falter but who waved over an attendant with the merest flick of her left index finger.

'We have extensive facilities for that exact purpose,' said Queen Eva. She beckoned Naida come closer and pitched her voice low, defeating all but the most ardent neck-craners in the vast hall who sought to eavesdrop. 'What does she need?'

Naida flushed with relief. 'Immediate bed rest, and ginger-blended Gorsin with turmeric and basil in a ratio of one to one for all ingredients. Peace, quiet and darkness, and fluids whenever she is awake. And the touch of the Gifted to kill the fever.'

The Queen tensed at the mention of the Gifted and looked at her attendant. 'See it done, as well as you are able.'

'Your Majesty.' The attendant bowed his head and Naida released a trembling Misha to him. 'You must take better care of yourself, Misha.'

'I had no idea I was ill,' she said.

Both Queen and attendant glanced at Naida, who blushed.

'I will check in on you later,' said Naida. 'Lovely to meet you, and thank you for guiding me.'

With Misha helped away through the crowd, the Queen showed Naida to the stairs, turning as they reached the top of them.

'Sorry in advance, this is the embarrassing bit for you,' she whispered before turning to the crowd.

Naida tried to look honoured and grateful in advance of the cascade of compliments she feared was about to come. The Queen held up her hands, as if she needed the silence to be any more complete. Even the rustle of expensive cloth was stilled.

'My friends. I'm delighted so many of you are here to join me in welcoming a woman who is, quite simply, the most brilliant medical professional in Suurken and, I am sure, the world.

'There is not one among us who has not heard tales of Naida's heroism. Saving the wounded from the battlefield as enemies surround her. Performing extraordinary, delicate surgery while the catapult rounds rattle into the ground around her operating theatre. Inspiring even the most frightened soldiers to stand tall and risk themselves for Suurken, because she will be there should they fall.

'We all have our favourites.'

A line of laughter and chatter ran around the room and Naida could feel the lights of glory and envy shine on her. Eyes fixed on her, the woman standing next to the Queen, where so many would give so much to stand, and being showered in accolades by Eva herself. Naida's eyes were bright with tears of embarrassment and her anxiety grew.

Out there in the crowd, as Eva continued to embellish Naida's record . . . she couldn't ride a horse, so the one about her scooping up a fallen soldier from her saddle was a stretch . . . were those who considered themselves perhaps only one or two steps from the inner sanctum of privilege and influence.

Naida wondered how many of them were already calculating how to use her to get close to the Queen. She was surprised half of them weren't already salivating at the prospect of their new opportunity. Perhaps they were.

'. . . and I want you all to make Naida as welcome as I do. To bring her into the family that is the Palace of Spires and its circle. To offer her the help she will need as she finds her way around the labyrinth my forbears have constructed here and, please . . . to not plague her with too many questions about your sore arms or warts.'

Laughter, some genuine, most horribly forced.

'Welcome, Naida, welcome to my home.'

Applause, and cheers.

Naida didn't know what to do. The Queen was standing still, letting the applause wash over her the way only someone used to receiving it could. Naida considered running, but instead clasped her hands in front of her chest and nodded her thanks, feeling genuine gratitude when there was a touch on her shoulder from a courtier, and she was invited to turn and walk out of the reception hall and into the open courtyard.

The peace that descended once the doors were closed left

her ears ringing from the noise inside and her eyes struggling to focus on the beauty and tranquillity before her.

It was a study in manicured magnificence. It was huge, presumably the original core of the palace, which had sprawled in every direction over the succeeding centuries. The open area boasted four themed flower beds, edged in stone and with paths running through them and containing a water feature. And in the exact centre of the courtyard, a remarkable fountain depicting a horse rearing atop a mountain. Water tumbled and sprayed from too many outlets to count, splashing into the wide, circular pool at its base or trickling down the finely detailed carving of the mountain sides.

Lawns, benches, borders and rockeries formed secluded areas, and at ground level the courtyard was surrounded by an arched walkway, formed in cool stone and marble, dotted with benches set in alcoves, and with doors leading off on all sides to who knew where. Above the walkway were three stories of corridors and rooms, finishing with peaked roofs with crenulated edges. She could see the pinnacles of three spires from here, each of similar design and flying the pennant of its fallen monarch.

'This is a real oasis,' said Queen Eva, making Naida start. 'Whenever the rest of the palace feels too much, when the walls of the massive rooms are closing in, this is where I come. You'll no doubt find your own quiet place, but this is a good start until you do.'

'It's beautiful.'

The Queen was walking towards her, a smile brightening her face. Naida became aware of other people with them too. Guards stood at the base of every arch. Royal staff flitted here and there, and aides and senior courtiers hovered around the Queen, plus a lady-in-waiting who appeared desperate to re-arrange the one hair on the Queen's head that had escaped its chains.

'How do you find peace?' asked Naida. 'Real peace. Solitude.'

'Ah,' said Queen Eva, linking an arm through Naida's and inspiring many an eyebrow to rise at the apparent breach of etiquette. 'I cannot divulge such secrets in such a public forum. Tell me, my doctor, what happens next?'

The Queen was walking them through the courtyard where the sounds of water were mixed with the fluttering and calls of birds, and the delicate clack of the royal shoes on stone flags. Naida didn't know how to respond.

'I'm not...' she began.

'I'm your newest patient,' explained the Queen. 'What do you need from me?'

'Oh, I see, thank you,' said Naida. 'Well, if I am allowed: access to any medical records so I can understand your health history and treatments. To complete the picture, I perform a basic physical examination but, in your case—'

'Of course,' said the Queen gently, flapping a hand. 'You must examine me. And you will, the moment you have had the opportunity to bathe, eat, rest if you so desire, and find some clothes not thick with trail dust.'

She summoned a member of staff with a flick of her fingers.

'Aide-to-Court Thierrin will see you to your rooms, will answer your questions, and see to it that anything you need is provided to you. He will bring you to my dressing chamber in two hours.'

And with that, she was walking away and through a door which opened on her approach, pulled by unseen hands. Naida caught a glimpse of rugs, tapestries and a silver-adorned table, before the doors closed, and Eva was gone.

Naida stared after her at the closed doors, numb, until Aide Thierrin cleared his throat and she turned.

'My lady Naida, if you would follow me. It's not too far.' Aide

Thierrin indicated the far end of the courtyard and stalked away without checking if she followed.

Oh, good, another enemy in the making. Naida blew out her cheeks and trailed after him.

Chapter 9

Not too far was a phrase Naida had, apparently, misunderstood all her life. Or it might have been that, now the adrenaline was draining away, she could feel the full scope of her exhaustion, and any journey greater than thirty paces was an impossible distance.

Either way, once Thierrin had taken her out of the courtyard and into an impressive hallway dominated by two sweeping staircases leading up in a horseshoe, then turned sharp right through a door onto a dingy staircase down, Naida was starting to lose all sense of relative direction.

And by the time they'd toured what felt like every servant's passageway and room, with fleeting glimpses of palace splendour and occasionally an ephemeral breath of fresh air to replace the pervading odours of rot and damp, Naida knew the roundabout route was deliberate. The answer to the obvious question was not long in coming.

Reluctantly, it seemed, Thierrin returned to corridors and halls with decoration. Places visiting royalty and other important folk might sometimes frequent. The décor and furnishing in the nooks and alcoves wasn't over-opulent, and the corridors were not very wide, but the floors were polished, and large windows gave tantalising glimpses of the sprawling city beyond.

Reaching a set of double doors, Thierrin paused to give Naida a disdainful look before opening them and standing aside. A small entrance hall was hung with paintings and populated by three doors, two plush chairs and a small table. Naida raised her eyebrows, drinking in the fresh air and incense and trying not to tip her head back as she gauged the height of the ceilings.

Walking in, she nodded politely to Thierrin, and turned to find the first door opened into a marble and wood-panelled bathroom where a bath filled with hot water awaited. A ceramic basin on a wide table had soap, brush and cleaning cloths laid out beside it, and a luxurious-looking commode finished the furniture.

Next door, a bedchamber four times the size of her tent boasted a bed larger than the one Ludeney had brought with him; rugs she could lose her feet in; wardrobes along the whole length of one wall; paintings and tapestries on two others; and views of the bustling city across formal gardens from the fourth.

Finally, there was a drawing room complete with a fireplace; seating for about ten people; and the carved desk and leather chair of her dreams. The whole of it was far more luxurious than anything she had experienced since she had fled from her family home. A sealed file lay on the desk, marked as most private and for her immediate attention, topped by an ornate-looking key.

'I don't know what to say,' she said.

Thierrin shrugged. 'Every other servant of the royal house-hold lives in windowless twilight. Not you, apparently. Make yourself comfortable. The set of files in your drawing room describe your job and some confidential information. The key is to your offices in the Crucible. Avail yourself of the bath and I will return as the Queen has bid me.'

'I'm sorry,' said Naida. 'I didn't ask for any of this.'

'Nevertheless, you have it.'

★

The bath, though ... *shattered throne, the baaaaath.* Deep, hot, and laced with the most wonderful-smelling salts. Naida could feel the grime falling from her body and the deep aches of days of carriage travel on rough roads easing. Every movement she made sent eddies of hot water sloshing across her body. Using a rough sponge, she rubbed the dry skin away and time and again, she relaxed her legs and let her head sink beneath the water.

There was release here, submerged, with the warmth flooding her ears, reaching the roots of her hair and caressing her face and neck. It seemed a shame to have to breathe and spoil the moment so she stayed under as long as she could, knowing that, having read Queen Eva's medical file before she'd bathed, their meeting should be uncomplicated.

Naida surfaced and sighed. From battlefield to battlefield, tent to tent, it had to have been over a year since she had enjoyed a bath. Washing in a stone-cold river or shivering under an icy shower had its own perverse pleasure, but she'd been yearning for this indulgence a very long time. How she wished Drevien could share it with her.

But eventually, the water cooled and, worse, was grey with dirt. Still, it was with reluctance that she heaved herself out to stand on the deep-piled mat and reach for the topmost green towel. The bathroom was cold after the warm cloak of the water and Naida wrapped the towel tight around her and picked up another to rub the worst of the wet from her hair.

The mirror above the basin was fogged over and she wiped a clear patch. The face that stared back at her was a gleaming pink, clean like she'd forgotten she could get. She started at a gentle knock at the bathroom door.

'Oh! I mean ... yes?'

'Sorry to disturb you, ma'am?' came a woman's voice, young and nervous.

'Have I overstayed my time in here?' asked Naida.

'We are somewhat behind hand.' This time it was Thierrin.

Naida opened the door and he averted his eyes. 'I am wearing a towel.'

'Cerrie will help you dress.' Thierrin, blushing and not lifting his head, gestured at the young woman before adding, unnecessarily. 'I shall wait here.'

'I have become quite good at dressing myself over the years,' said Naida, smiling at Cerrie who was wringing her hands and trying to smile through her mixture of awe and anxiety. 'And I am no one's ma'am. I'm Naida.'

'Ummm...' The poor woman was no more than twenty, face bearing the pockmarks of a cruel adolescence, black hair tied back in a tight bun, and dressed in a deep grey skirt and jacket over a pale green shirt. She managed to point at the bedroom. 'In here, ma'— In here.'

Feeling guilty for causing her such confusion, Naida grabbed her hand and walked the pair of them into the bedroom and closed the door.

'I am so sorry, Cerrie, I am a fool.'

'No...' began Cerrie, looking close to tears.

'I am. I know you have your instructions about how to address me. Tell you what. When it's just you and me, call me Naida. Out there, in front of stiff-collars like Thierrin, address me as you have been told.'

Cerrie put a hand to her mouth, and she relaxed. 'May I show you your clothes... Naida?'

'Please.'

'We took the liberty of taking all of your current clothes to the laundry.'

'Some of them are only held together by muck and blood, you know,' said Naida. 'So, what am I left with?'

Cerrie opened the doors to a huge wardrobe. On one side hung an array of dresses and skirts, plain and bright-coloured. Some shirts as well, at a quick glance, mostly white with some blue and red. Drawers filled the other side and Cerrie opened a couple of them while Naida stood and stared.

'I'm not great at dresses,' said Naida.

Cerrie ignored her. 'We had to guess the sizes of everything. Undergarments are in the third drawer here and there are some trousers in the top two drawers. What would you like? Should I suggest?'

'Trousers and shirt. I'm going to work, not to a banquet. Where did all this stuff come from?' Though from the opulence of some of the fabric and lace work, it was pretty obvious. 'Please say you haven't thrown away my boots.'

Cerrie appraised her briefly, visibly growing in confidence, before selecting white linen undershorts and a slender under-shirt, a pair of grey woollen riding trousers and a dark blue overshirt.

Naida chuckled. 'I can see we're going to get on.'

'Shall I help you?' asked Cerrie, blushing afresh. 'It seems to me you'd be more comfortable in what you've been most used to recently.'

'I'll do this bit myself... boots?'

'Oh, yes... they went to be polished and stitched. I'll fetch them.'

'Thank you, Cerrie.'

'Not at all ma— Naida.'

Cerrie bobbed her head and hurried out of the bedroom. Naida heard Thierrin asking some curt question or other as the door closed. Naida sank on to the bed, feeling the quality of mattress and bedlinen and desiring nothing more than to fall backwards and wake up in about four days' time. Instead, she pulled on what she suspected were the Queen's cast-offs, finding them a little loose on the waist and shoulders but nothing embarrassing, and went to explore her rooms a little further until Cerrie returned.

Thierrin was nowhere to be seen, which was a blessing. She towelled her hair in front of the bathroom mirror and combed it flat and neat before going into the drawing room, which boasted tall windows with the same glorious view over the city and palace's formal gardens as the bedroom.

At last, she found something that was hers. Her trunk, containing her papers, quills, inks, her few books and the odd keepsake, was sat at the side of the leather-topped desk. She opened it and pulled a few bits out to join the oil lamp and polished stone paperweight already there. Tonight's journal entry was going to be a long one and would mark quite a stark change of circumstance.

Elsewhere in the drawing room, the fire was made up and unlit, the carved marble mantelpiece was bare but for an ornamental blade that sat on a wooden stand. Its leather grip was worn smooth and the blade was nicked and scratched with the memories of all whose flesh it had pierced.

It dripped with history and she promised herself she'd study it later. Moving onto the bookcase, Naida had just begun to let her eyes trail over the priceless works sitting there when she heard footsteps behind her.

She turned to see Thierrin holding her boots, which shone like new.

'The Queen is waiting for you.'

'Thank you. I—'

But Thierrin had already spun on his heel and walked out. Naida felt slighted, which was presumably Thierrin's aim. She had work to do in more than one arena, it seemed. She pulled on and laced her boots and decided attack might be the better form of defence.

She strode past the aide and his dour expression and pulled open the door to the corridor.

'Let's not dawdle,' she said. 'And perhaps we could take a more direct route this time. This way, I'm guessing.'

Naida pointed to her left and set off, Thierrin scampering after her, the irritable clearing of his throat music to her ears.

★

Where Naida's rooms were generous and well-proportioned, the Queen's were rightly enormous, and must have occupied a large proportion of the first floor where the ceilings were high and every window looked out over beauty.

Thierrin, who had now adopted a pompous demeanour, marched her down wide corridors bedecked with paintings and treasures in cabinets, past doors to rooms she'd never see, and through dining and reception rooms and up to the doors of a vast dressing room. He knocked for admission into a hubbub of low conversation and frenetic activity.

In the centre of it all, the Queen was relaxing on a sofa in a silk robe, looking at a tray covered with fabrics. Tailors' dummies in various states of undress stood around the room, which was bright, warm and covered in mirrors, wardrobes, and pearl white rugs. An impressive seamstresses' station was at the far end.

'Excellent, you're here,' said Eva, taking a long sip from a wine cup and standing up. 'Save me from yet another dress design for yet another gala showcasing the many glories of Suurkene culture and cuisine.'

'Our worlds could scarcely be more different, Your Majesty,' said Naida. 'Are you ready for your examination?'

'I am,' said the Queen. 'That is, after all, why I had you brought here.'

83

Naida smiled, chided. 'Of course. Silly of me.'

The Queen snapped her fingers. 'Clear the room.'

With little more than a few hurry-along gestures, maids, seamstresses, tailors, dressers, attendants, servants and three ladies-in-waiting vacated the room, and a version of peace descended. But not everyone had left, and the Queen seemed oblivious, or rather, uncaring.

'Her Majesty asked to clear the room,' said Naida to the six men and three women who had not moved a muscle.

There was some indulgent laughter. The Queen sat up a little straighter, a sparkle in her eyes and a smile on her lips.

'I've missed the joke,' said Naida, feeling she was the butt of it and letting her ire rise because she knew it made her face cold. 'Perhaps someone will enlighten me.'

'Surgeon Naida,' said one man, white-haired, and with a paunch at odds with the skeletal look to the rest of his frame. 'The order required the common staff to exit. We are those on whom the Queen must rely, whom the Queen determines to be the most trustworthy, the most loyal of the houschold. Those who must, therefore, know everything.'

Naida shrugged. 'I'll write you a report.'

'That is not sufficient, nor would it necessarily be wholly accurate.'

'I'm sorry, you are?' said Naida. She smiled pleasantly, allowing him to walk into her trap. Dealing with superior, arrogant, old and privileged men was a speciality of hers.

'I am the Lord Eldon Denharl, Master of the Spires and head of the Queen's Council, the members of which are all present.'

'That's nice. And can I come to your next council meeting?'

'Don't be preposterous.'

Naida shrugged again. 'Until I am welcome at your meetings, you are not welcome at my medical examinations. Leave. Please. All of you.'

The ensuing outraged silence was punctuated only by the rustle of cloth, and a few eyes darting a glance at least once towards the Queen, hoping for support. But Eva was engrossed with her swatches of fabric and paused only to pour herself another cup of wine since there was no servant to do it for her.

'Do you realise who you spoke to in such tones?'

Naida, realising she was in a fight whether she wanted one or not, swung round to face the woman who had spoken.

'Not really, no. Who are you?'

The woman rose theatrically to her full height before she delivered the words she obviously assumed would destroy Naida's nascent power.

'I am Ianna Velez, the Minister of State for Royal Affairs. I am the critical conduit between the palace and the legislature, and I do not take orders from mere doctors.'

'That's nice.' Naida turned her back on the bird-framed woman. She could feel the weight of power and authority in the room – assumed or actual, it didn't matter. 'Anyone else want to share their job title and lack of medical understanding?'

'Enough of this!' a male voice, strident and frustrated. It belonged to a great barrel of a man with an untidy beard. 'There are protocols that must be adhered to at all times until they are changed by the Queen's Council. And if you must know, medic, I am the Lord General Jaren Kerslan, the Queen's Personal Private Secretary.'

'As a Personal Private Secretary, I'm sure you understand I'm asking that you respect me as a medical professional and, more importantly, the Queen's modesty. Privacy is not too much to ask.'

'My dear Naida,' said an ancient woman, peering at her over an equally ancient set of spectacles. 'The Queen's Council, or a quorum of it, is present during every medical consultation or procedure. Our advice, you will find, is oft-times apt and wise.'

85

'When I want medical advice, I'll ask another doctor for it.'
A hiss of indrawn breath.

'Many of us were present when our Queen was *born*,' said Velez. 'And will remain so throughout her life until death takes one of us and we are replaced by another. These protocols are vital.'

'*Protocols.*' Naida loaded the word with the maximum contempt. '*Infection* does not respect protocol. Cancer and poisoning and neurological diseases do not respect *protocol*. When a general of your armies comes to me with an intestinal worm eating her from the inside, she does not have to endure an audience while I flush her with spices and pull the creature out of her rectum. And so none of you will *spectate* while I tend to Her Majesty on medical matters, which are inherently private unless Her Majesty decides otherwise.'

She looked around at the Queen's Council, noting their advanced average age and judging their capacity for change accordingly.

'I have a personal responsibility for keeping Her Majesty alive, healthy, and able to perform her duties. I am the one whose failure will be judged most harshly. So, while I am in charge here, things will be done my way. My consultations with, and examinations of, Her Majesty will be conducted in private or, if I deem it necessary, with trusted medical personnel. I do not perform in front of an audience of quill-dippers, nor will you judge and comment on my every move and decision. The reasons for this ought to be obvious. Do I make myself clear?'

Naida wasn't sure whether it was the shock at being spoken to like this, or that they hadn't heard, or hadn't listened, but judging by the silence, she hadn't made herself clear.

'I can wait,' said Naida. 'I have nothing more pressing to do. I suspect Her Majesty, on that comfortable sofa, can wait as well. Some of you, not so much.'

Frowning and shuffling of feet followed. Naida smiled pleasantly.

'I've spent my life noticing things in people that signify discomfort that they are trying to hide, for whatever reason. Three of you have problems affecting your hips or knees that need further investigation, but more immediately mean aching pain grows with every passing moment. Another two of you have full bladders requiring urgent relief. Another has a severe headache and the brightness of the lights in here is making it hard to keep their eyes open.'

They were quiet now, weighing each other up.

'Unless you get your creaking bodies out now, I will inflict upon each of you the lack of medical privacy you are happy for Her Majesty to enjoy.'

The explosion of outrage was predictable, amusing in a way, and finally provoked the Queen. She stood. It was all she had to do to bring about instant and complete attention. Oh, for such effortless authority.

'We cannot operate relationships without trust,' she said. 'I will trust Naida until she proves unworthy of that trust. Hers is a sacred position, and you must trust her too. So, you will all leave, and you will do so now, without complaint and without thoughts of petty revenge. I mean, I've just hired this woman to keep me alive, whatever do you think she's going to do while you're not watching? Try to kill me?'

Chapter 10

Naida's laughter was too shrill and her smile too bright but in the din of centuries-old assumptions being torn asunder, no one seemed to notice. She'd forgotten. It seemed ridiculous to her now, standing here in front of the woman she was supposed to murder, but in all the rush of her arrival, the attention, the jealousy and the admiration, the true reason for her presence here had slipped her mind, subsumed by her instincts as a doctor and a surgeon to save lives.

And so it was that while she watched the Queen's Council remove themselves with maximum reluctance from the dressing room, their acerbic glares attempting to burn holes in the armour of her self-confidence, Naida fought to stay upright, much as she had in Ludeney's pavilion not so long ago.

It allowed her to stare back at them with pitiless eyes, because the full force of her pity was turned inwards. She was sure they could see the tremble in her body and the hot flush in her face. Naida remembered enough of herself to turn and nod her thanks to the Queen as soon as the door had closed on the council and the irate conversation had begun without, fading away slowly.

'You aren't going to try to kill me, are you?' asked the Queen, her eyes alight with mischief.

'I've never killed anyone, Your Majesty,' she managed, her voice feeble and cracked. 'I don't think I'm capable of murder.'

And she wasn't. Now she had to work out how to avoid killing the Queen while escaping with her own life.

'Well, that's comforting,' said the Queen. 'At least I know how to react when you approach me with a scalpel.'

The Queen's attempts at humour withered Naida on the inside. She tried a chuckle, but it came out as a dry rasp. They were alone now and part of Naida wanted to throw herself at Eva's feet, confess everything and beg for mercy she was not going to get. It would end the lie before it became too labyrinthine for her to maintain without trapping herself in its darkest corner. But it would achieve nothing but her tortured execution, and she could not protect the Queen if she was dead.

'If it's all right, ma'am, I'll approach you with paper and parchment and ask you some questions,' said Naida, desperate to return to firm ground. 'And following that, if I have your permission, a physical examination.'

The Queen raised her eyebrows. 'Were you not furnished with a medical history? I understood a meticulous record to have been kept.'

'It was, ma'am but I need to understand your concerns, the things that matter to you, and those that don't, how you feel in yourself and what worries you for the future. I don't want to lead you, having read your history. I need to understand how you interpret what your mind and body tell you. Does that make sense, ma'am?'

'Yes,' she replied. The door behind Eva bumped against its frame; gently, as if impelled by a breath of air. 'They're outside, you know. All of them except the ones who needed to relieve themselves. So, don't stab me too loudly.'

Naida managed a proper smile this time, opening her bag and bringing out writing equipment. 'I'll try not to, ma'am.'

The Queen nodded her head at the door. 'It occurs to me, Lady Naida, that we should have a chat about how you might go about making fewer enemies.'

'That would be most welcome.'

'You know why they are so keen to stand in here, don't you?'

Naida shook her head. 'Beyond some notion of self-importance, not really.'

'Not so much. No. They hope you'll declare I'm fit and fertile so they can all scurry off in search of fresh suitors. Not one of them wishes to accept *I* will choose the father of my heir, and I won't be opening my legs for any of the jelly-chinned inbreds from Cantabria or Pargoan that they keep marching to the door of my bedchamber.'

Naida stared, trying hard not to collapse into helpless laughter and her urge to protect the Queen intensified.

'My dear doctor, some of them struggle to raise a fork to their own mouths, let alone coax their cocks to spill their feeble, dying seed. Now, what would you like to ask me first?'

It was a moment before Naida was able to speak.

★

When she left the Queen, two hours and more later, Naida was so full of admiration for Eva, she felt she was floating. The Queen's private residence had taken on an aspect of wonder. It was where true greatness trod, where it lived and breathed and loved, and would die, and she spread wisdom and compassion in her wake.

Naida knew that this effect was precisely the Queen's intention and she marvelled at the skill with which Eva weaved her aura. Part of it had been asking Naida if there were any favours she could do and it had allowed Naida to reinforce her request for her team to join the royal medical service and, delightfully, to get permission for a dinner with friends tonight. It was—

'Lady Naida!'

Naida paused and blinked, frowning at the intrusion. A door had opened to her right. She could see desks and clerks within. Coming out of the office was the Master of the Spires.

'My Lord Denharl.'

'Shall we?' Denharl indicated they continue along the wide corridor. 'I trust you found Her Majesty to be in good health?'

'Yes.'

He was taken aback by the brevity of her reply. 'Good... good. I had been concerned by a... a difference in her mood and I feared she was becoming sick.'

'If I were you, my lord, I would be worrying about my hip rather than the Queen. Why don't we examine it? If you'll show me to my surgery, I'll do it now.'

'Aha. Perhaps another day.'

'Don't leave it too long. It may be a consequence of age, but it may be more serious. There are cancers that attack the hip bone, and I can blunt such attacks and alleviate the pain. Have you been skipping your regular hands-on with your Gifted?'

'In a manner of speaking.'

Naida frowned. 'Is there a problem?'

'Things move and change,' said Denharl, waving a hand at the air. 'I'll attend in due course, thank you, but there is an important matter I need to discuss with you.'

'Of course, my lord.'

They had paused before the doors of the Queen's private residence. Naida was anxious to lay eyes on her surgery, any patients in her ward and, most particularly, on Misha. And then she had dinner plans, assuming her message had found Will. A meal that would mark victory over Vinald.

'The whispers have begun. They will soon become a problem for you.'

'You've lost me completely,' said Naida.

'Aha, yes,' said Denharl, indulgently. 'That rather makes my point for me. If I may: you have landed in the palace the way a tornado touches down over the dry lands of Central Gerestova. There is a delicate ecosystem here that reacts badly to being upset, and you have, as I'm sure you are aware, upset it. You need allies and a level of understanding of the workings of the palace if you are to succeed.'

'Is it too much to ask for respect and privacy for my patient?' said Naida, uncomfortable with where this was leading. 'If that flies in the face of outdated traditions, I'm not going to apologise.'

'With ... respect ... you are missing my point. The palace and legislature runs as well as it does because of its traditions and protocols and boring rules and laws, even regarding the Gifted. We all abide by them. Just as you must have done in the army. Those that don't often have their lives made very difficult – and that would include the Queen's personal doctor. You head what is, in reality, a very small section of the palace organisation.'

'So, I'll be good from now on.' Naida shrugged. 'What do you mean "even regarding the Gifted"?'

'It's just another reality among many, Naida.' Denharl moved to the doors and pulled them open. 'You might have the ear of the Queen for now, but Her Majesty is famous for tiring quickly of her new and shiny things. There are those already who mutter about your suitability for the role – you have been a surgeon for far longer than you have been a doctor – your powerful sponsor having his own agenda, and your own methods on the battlefield being questionable.'

Naida's ire was instant but the Master of the Spires raised a finger to quell her protestations.

'These are not my views, but they are circulating, and you need to be aware of the damage such rumours can do. Let me help you. Let me be your guide. We have got off on the wrong foot, but I am glad you are here and I think your arrival is a breath of fresh air – but it must be handled with caution.'

'And no doubt you want something in return.'

Denharl smiled. 'Perhaps. But mostly, I need the palace to run smoothly. Our monarch is our de facto ruler, but you need to know the people who make everything work for the palace, the city and the country. Think on it. No one survives this bear pit alone.'

With a curt flick of his hand, he urged her from the apartments and closed the door behind her.

Naida stood there for a moment, taking in the pair of guards flanking the door, their eyes staring way beyond her, their ears no doubt burning with all they had heard.

'Fun here, isn't it?' she asked them.

Not a flicker. Naida tried to remember which door she'd come through to reach this first-floor landing. It had many doors to other parts of the palace and was dominated by the grand, sweeping horseshoe stairs that led down to the hallway she'd entered from the inner courtyard a few hours ago.

'Can you point me in the direction of the surgery and the ward or palace hospital or whatever you call it?'

One of the guards adjusted his gaze to settle on her.

'The infirmary is located on the ground floor next to the main kitchens and just before the Garden of Whispers on the way to the Crucible. Quickest way is down the stairs and through the double doors beneath them, my lady. Straight on from there. If you get to the gardens, you've gone too far.'

'Thank you. And I'm "Naida" to every soldier.'

The flicker of a smile and some warmth in that expression now. 'We are all grateful for every one of us you have saved, my ... Naida.'

'Seconded,' said the second guard.

'No doubt our paths will cross again, though not, I hope, in my infirmary.'

Both guards inclined their heads and Naida trotted down the right-hand stairway, imagining all the kings and queens that had descended them in honour or disgrace. Guards opened the double doors for her, giving her access to a wide passageway, lit by an oil lamp on every pillar, roofed in timbers supporting the floors above. Flagstones led to a bright space a hundred yards away, and a warm breeze blew towards her.

She walked quickly, bag over her shoulder and bouncing on her hip 'til she rested a hand on it. Part way down on the right, three pairs of glass-and-wood doors looked out over a memorial garden holding three spires, each broad-based and towering out of sight. She would revisit it another day; it was a place for reverence when her work was done.

Down the left-hand side, door after door of identical iron-banded timber was set into the stone walls, themselves adorned but sparsely with pennants, portraits and mounted shields, as if deliberate afterthoughts. Servants, officials, palace workers and many others walked the stone flags, busy about their days. They carried papers, trays of food and drink, boxes; or pulled trolleys laden with goods. While the odd one recognised her, most ignored her and she was happy with that.

The enclosed passageway became a vaulted and arched covered walkway, open to either side, punctuated by columns and running through gardens until it met with the walls of the legislature, known as the Crucible.

Naida stopped. The gardens were beautiful. With shrubberies, rose gardens, water features and scattered seating, they were buzzing with people as well as insects. Everywhere she looked, men and women walked purposefully, stood in groups talking, or sat debating some fine point of law or other. She'd heard of this place but never thought to see it.

The Garden of the Advocates was its official title, though some wag had dubbed it the Garden of Whispers, and it had stuck. The workings of the legislature were a mystery to most who worked there, let alone those who felt the effects of its actions, or inactions, but rumour said much of the real work – the deal-making and alliance-forming, the speech-writing and discussion of tactics – happened here.

'I've come too far,' muttered Naida. She turned back though much of her still wanted to walk down to the doors of the Crucible and see the pit, the chambers and the eateries, all spoken of in tales of more violent and brutal times.

Naida saw an attendant in a long green frock coat and shining leather boots exit a door back along the passageway and head in her direction.

'Excuse me,' she said, and despite a flicker of irritation, he stopped and something resembling a smile crossed his face.

'Can I help?' he asked, voice clipped and hurried. 'I am rather late.'

'I won't detain you. I'm looking for the infirmary,' she said. 'I'm told it's nearby.'

The attendant pointed back over his shoulder. 'Through there, and head straight on. There's a sign above the door.'

'Sorry, I missed it,' she said. 'Head full of everything, eyes seeing nothing.'

'I hope you don't want to be treated. They're all cross that their new and glorious leader hasn't shown up yet. Some choice insults I didn't need my aunt hearing. She's very cross too, but even more frail.'

Naida laughed, she couldn't help it, Denharl's words ringing loud in her head. 'To be fair to me, I was attending the Queen until now.'

The attendant's hands flew to his mouth and his face drained to grey.

'Shattered throne, I'm sorry. And I'm so grateful to you for what you have done.'

'Sorry for what?' asked Naida. 'You've done me the great service of warning me what's ahead. I'll look in on your aunt too, what's her name?'

There were tears in the attendant's eyes. 'Misha.'

Naida put a hand on the attendant's shoulders. 'She'll be all right. She's amazing and we caught the infection early. What's your name?'

'Harald, my lady.'

'It's Naida and it's very good to meet you, Harald.'

'Anything you need, please just ask.'

Naida smiled. 'Thank you. I've been advised I need allies and I'd be glad to name you among the few so far. Now, I'd best get inside before the insults get louder.'

'Thank you again.'

They parted company, Harald with a spring in his step, Naida with a warmth in her belly and a smile she would need to keep in place, she suspected.

Opening the door to the infirmary, Naida was a little surprised to find herself in a timber-laid passageway just about wide enough for a stretcher. It was poorly lit and led about thirty yards to where it widened in front of some double doors.

Walking down the passageway, she passed more doors on either side. Wooden, plain and fitted with sliding plates at eye and ground level. Her heart sank. Clearing her throat, she strode on to the double doors and opened them to reveal a shocking mess, an affront to the military eye.

A low ceiling, thick with beams, was hung with pale yellow oil lamps that leaked smoke into the cloying air, unable to escape the unventilated space. The room stank of human effluent, damp stone and rot. And this was the ward. The beds were positioned haphazardly, most without proper working space around them.

She feared she had found the operating area as well. It held a single table in a tight corner, with no space for anything that might actually help during an operation. Instruments, dressings, bowls, or treatments would all have to be brought from elsewhere – where, she had no idea.

There was just one empty bed in the ward, and she saw three medics trying to pick their way among the mess of tatty blankets, frames, and suffering bodies. The low ceiling and cracked walls reflected the sounds of pain and sickness. Naida could hear raised voices though an open door at the far end of the ward and she made her way between the beds, pausing at each one to get a feel for the conditions being treated, her anger deepening with every pace.

It felt wrong; not a place of healing, more a place to wither and die. The palace infirmary lacked *hope*. She needed to know why.

Naida's heart quickened when she saw Misha. The lady-in-waiting was lying on her side, a bowl of water, cloth and a mug on a side table. She was directly beneath a smoky lamp. Naida knelt by her, refreshed the cloth and pressed it to her forehead, other hand on her neck to feel the extent of the fever's heat.

'I'll have you moved somewhere cooler,' said Naida. 'I've got space in my rooms.'

'Hello to you, too,' said Misha, voice dry, mirroring the exhaustion on her face. But her eyes still held their sparkle. 'Don't you fret, I'll be just fine.'

Naida let her hand linger on Misha's neck. She was too hot, assuming she'd been given the right fluid infusions, and there was no reason to think that she hadn't. It was this ward. How could anyone recover quickly in a place that stank of sickness? It bore poor comparison to her battlefield set-ups, and that was tantamount to criminal in the royal palace.

'No, you won't. This place will kill you. Who's it run by, a mortician looking for new subjects? Where are the Gifted? Why is your fever still so high?'

Naida invested herself in Misha. Enough to edge the infection a fraction further towards defeat; enough to ensure she wouldn't relapse. She still needed to be moved, though. When she'd finished, she saw Misha staring at her.

'There are a few you can trust here, and many you cannot,' she said. 'Be most wary of the ones who wear their virtue like a badge.'

'I'm starting to get a picture.'

'And some you think betrayers are those in whom you should place the most trust.'

'Now you're just being oblique.' Naida smiled but there was something unsettling in the strength of Misha's gaze.

She beckoned Naida in close and put a hand on her cheek.

'Don't worry, and don't be scared, but I know who you are,' she whispered and Naida froze. 'I know why you are here.'

'I don't... who do you think I am?'

Misha stroked Naida's cheek and spoke so low as to be barely audible. 'There are two reasons I am still alive, my lady. Because I listen, and because I, too, am of the Touched, though my inability to heal myself speaks of the diminution of my ability.'

'Last time I checked, we were called Gifted. Are there any others here?' said Naida, glancing around, terrified of being overheard. She was shaking like the metaphorical leaf. 'What happened?'

'To be blunt: your parents' crimes. Or rather, their manipulation. There are some powerful groups with agendas you and I should find very worrying.'

'I've been scared every day since they were killed,' said Naida.

'Very wise.'

Naida looked around her again. She needed to ask more

questions but this was not the place. She was drawing attention. Just one more.

'Misha, how do you know who I am?'

'Because, my lady, I am Lord Marshal Ludeney's spy.'

Chapter 11

'Misha needs rest, not incessant talk.'

Naida turned and stood to face a man with starched collars and a deep green apron. He looked like more like a cook than a doctor.

'She needs a great deal more than that, none of which she'll get in this bed or in this ... ward. What is going on here? I've never seen such a disastrous ward in my life, and I live on the edge of battlefields.'

'You think you could do better? Seven days ago, there were fifteen beds in here because patients were healed quickly. Today I walked in to find we have thirty beds but the same amount of everything else. Except staff and proper bedding. We have little of either.'

'And none of the staff you do have can use a mop, wash linen and blankets or bring any order to this chaos?'

The medic stared at her, and then pitched his voice low, aware of the patients surrounding them, but unable to keep the anger out of his voice.

'I appreciate your concern for your friend, whoever you are, but you have no idea what we're facing here. *I* don't have anyone who can do anything because *I* have been removed from my post. I'm only here because people will die otherwise. And in there' – he jabbed a finger in the direction of the open door at the back of the ward – 'are people who refuse to work in here at all because of the risks. So, perhaps you would like to moderate your accusations with a bit of understanding.'

Naida nodded, seeing the doctor anew. He was a head taller than her and had young eyes in a face lined with care under pressure, and hair greying before its time. 'I should introduce myself. I am Naida, head of the royal medical service and I'm here to help.'

The doctor's smile was brittle. He shrugged. 'Welcome. We've heard a lot about you. I'm sorry you've been dragged into this. I'm Brin Gorvien.'

He smiled and she couldn't help but think he was enjoying a private joke.

'A pleasure to meet you, Brin. Into all what?'

Brin gestured towards the back of the ward where, Naida presumed, the offices, examination rooms and stores had to be. 'Shall we? My colleagues await, and perhaps you can persuade them back to work.'

'Lead the way.'

'Listen to the good doctor,' said Misha. 'He has good instincts, good sense.'

'You're very kind, Misha,' said Brin, then added, as Misha clearly expected him to: 'There's a creeping chaos engulfing the city. It's taken years, but the public mood has swung against the use of the Gifted by doctors, vets... anyone. And now we are seeing the results. The Queen is standing by the people, standing behind restrictive legislation placed on the Gifted and their capacity to practise. And here, because we are the Queen's infirmary, we are expected to be the role model. It's a nightmare.'

'Why does anyone support rejecting our greatest asset, never mind the perceived crimes of the past?' Naida took a long breath as light dawned. 'It's because of me, isn't it?'

Brin raised his eyebrows. 'You are literally the model for saving the unsavable, without the interference of the Talent.'

Misha turned over noisily.

'Battlefield traditions and superstitions are one thing and even there we use the Gifted when death is the alternative,' said Naida, trying to fight off the guilt that was threatening to crush her. The deception that had saved her life could cost so many others. 'I understand them, even if I don't agree ... but here? In the capital? So many diseases in circulation ... so few genuine cures.'

'I agree, but our medical opinions on the subject don't make any difference and, soon, you'll need to be careful saying things like that out loud.'

'What?'

'The Esselrode genocide poisoned the well. It made people look twice at every practitioner of the Talent, and that trust was never rebuilt. Instead, the tales of your exploits in some of the worst places in the world over the last five and more years have been seized on. They're proof the Talent is yesterday's answer. It's not your fault ... but in there' – Brin flicked an index finger in the direction of the offices – 'are people who have seen their Gifted friends and colleagues dismissed ... hounded out, actually. So, you aren't popular and it isn't your fault. That's why I'm sorry you're here.'

The Queen's and Denharl's reactions to her recommending using the Gifted made complete sense now. Naida sighed.

'So, who's this poor person I'm *replacing*, if that's the right word?'

'Brin Gorvien.'

It was a kick to the guts delivered with such grace Naida almost hugged him to offer comfort. He had a wry smile on his face.

'Shattered throne, Brin, I'm so sorry. What happened?'

Brin gestured around him. 'The answer to that is best given in private. And don't be sorry. Truth be told, the palace medical team needs all the help it can get at whatever level it appears.'

'Tell me you're staying.'

'I'm staying.'

Naida smiled. 'First good news of this conversation. In that case, officially you might report to me, but we'll do this as partners. The first thing we need is to relocate or revive this place. I think I can swing that; the Queen seems to like me.'

'Long may that continue.' Brin's words were laced with the certainty that it would not.

'How much influence do we have over medical facilities in the city and beyond?'

'None. Each is its own little fiefdom.'

Naida shook her head. 'Not for long. We have to develop a reporting system to alert us of any significant disease outbreak. None of us can afford to operate alone.'

'It's a logical step but harder to make than it appears. When I said "fiefdom", I wasn't exaggerating ... Come on, let's go and meet the rest of your charges. It won't take long, after all, most of them have already resigned in protest.'

★

Naida had never felt so dispirited, not even on the worst day on the battlefield. Eleven staff remained ... *eleven* ... for a palace and Crucible staff of over four thousand. The military infirmaries were overflowing because citizens who would, in normal times, call on the Gifted, followed by a trip to an apothecary, were now forced to seek aid elsewhere. The situation was grave, and made worse by those that remained, Brin excepted.

She'd let them speak and had resisted the temptation to interrupt. Every concern was valid. She shared their disgust over the treatment of the Gifted and, above everything, promised she would fight their cause. Her cause. But when they had finished, when their pointing fingers had dropped to their sides and their fury had given way to sullen, angry looks, they should not have been surprised by her response.

'I hear you, and I am with you. I understand that you feel lost, overwhelmed and angry. A great wrong is being done. But I cannot, I will not, accept that you have given up, that you refuse to go out onto the ward and try to save people's lives.'

It was Naida's turn to point, back to the beds where patients lay suffering.

'While you hide in here, furious about all that has happened, the people in your care are out there dying or crying in pain. When did stepping back become a valid way to protest? And you're in here where no one can see you or hear you. Why aren't you in the Garden of Whispers or even outside the front door here letting people know? It's laughable.'

None of them would look at her but their glances to each other were telling.

'I get it. The loss of the Gifted, your friends, is a huge blow. It affects everything you do. The man you looked on to lead you has been taken from you too, replaced by some surgeon from the battlefield. And I am standing in front of you telling you that there is no greater cowardice than walking away from those who need you. That's when people die needlessly. You need to work harder to save people.'

A couple of them looked at her then, and their hatred of her, temporary or otherwise, was plain enough. She raised her eyebrows.

'Hate me if it helps but the hard part's over now. You're here and you're all healers. And I can show you some amazing things that can be achieved without the Talent. Don't get me wrong, I will fight this attack on the Gifted with everything I have, but until that fight is won, we have to do our healing differently. Will you hear me out?'

Naida saw hope kindled while she outlined a new ward rota, the herbs, leaves and roots they needed to stockpile; the large quantities of essential medicines they needed to mix up. She didn't tell them she was bringing in her battlefield team, and my, how this place needed Drevien and Kella in particular. Or that as she made her demands of the Queen maybe, just maybe, she could convince her against her anti-Talent path.

Before she left, she checked in on every patient, issuing instructions to the orderlies shadowing her. She dismissed them and came to Misha last.

'You can't stay here,' Naida said. 'I'll see to it.'

'I don't deserve more than anyone else,' said Misha, her face covered in sweat.

'Your age demands your condition be treated with a different type of care altogether. I'm not debating it.' Naida took in the whole ward. 'I'm going to change all of this.'

'Careful you don't forget your true role,' said Misha, and Naida wasn't sure if that was a warning or a threat.

'Saving lives is my role.'

'Saving the *Queen's*,' said Misha for the benefit of anyone listening. She beckoned Naida in close, her mouth to Naida's ear, her voice a whisper from a fevered frame. 'Scratch the surface of this city and you'll find all the ugly things lurking there. Don't let your guard down for one moment. You have landed in the middle of a storm, as an unwilling totem for a Gifted-free new world. You must be careful where you invest your Talent. Plenty would betray you for their own personal gain.'

'I cannot do what Ludeney commands,' whispered Naida. 'I will not.'

'Then you condemn us both,' said Misha.

'I will find another way.'

Misha smiled. 'Your naivety is charming.' She raised a trembling hand and placed it on Naida's cheek. 'You still don't understand, do you? But you will.'

'You're patronising me.'

'Maybe a little. But I'm right, too, you'll see. Make some time tomorrow, go to the Crucible. See it, feel it, taste it.'

Naida stood up. 'Assuming I have the time, I will. And I'm still having you moved.'

'Tread gently.'

Naida nodded at Brin on her way out, asking him to come with her down the narrow corridor. Once the ward doors had closed on the smell and the heat, she gestured at the solitary rooms.

'Do we have any residents?' she asked, not concealing her distaste.

'No,' said Brin. 'They're long unused.'

'Good.' Naida unbolted and pulled open the nearest door, allowing a waft of mould, must, ancient urine and excrement to escape. '*Ashes and water...*'

There was still a bed frame within, placed in the corner of the cell that measured no more than six paces by four. It was covered in broken furniture. Naida could also see metalwork, old instruments, perhaps. Strewn over the floor were piles of rotting bedding. The rats loved it. There were no windows in the room but high up on the far wall was a hole that let in some daylight.

'How many of these are there?'

'Eight.'

'Good. Boiling water, soap and wire brushes. Get them emptied, scrubbed, whitewashed and put a grill in each door. Perfect isolation rooms. My guess is we will need them sooner rather than later if we are denied the benefits of the Gifted.'

Brin nodded. 'Makes sense. Should have seen it myself.'

'Don't beat yourself up. Right. Any tips for petitioning the Queen for funds and a suspension of certain legislation?'

Brin scratched an eyebrow. 'Well, currently, Eva is, publicly at least, very much in tune with the ordinary citizen, so asking for money to improve health here and in the wider city and country could play well. As for discussions on the Talent? My advice is not to. Look where it got me.'

Naida paused in the act of opening the door to the stone passageway without.

'You challenged her on the Talent and got replaced by me?'

'Oh, it's worse than that. I lost my licence to practise. I just haven't left yet. We had a team of eight Gifted working the palace and Crucible. They've all gone. Rooms cleared, chucked onto the street. I think they've gone into hiding.'

'Still working?'

Brin shrugged. 'They dare not. I mean, with those they trust, maybe. But the anti-Gifted mood is ugly. There have been attacks, murders.'

'But there's no actual ban, is there?'

'Not yet, but does that matter? What's happening now makes the passing of the legislation simple, driven by ignorance and infectious fear. I'm scared where it will all end.'

'You're keeping your job or I'm walking from mine,' said Naida. 'I need you running the infirmary.'

'Good luck with that.'

'Don't go anywhere just yet.'

★

Naida strode back to the palace, practising the calming exercises that had given her courage and steady hands on the battle-field. The ramifications of excluding the Talent from medical treatment would be far-reaching and rapid with summer's heat on the rise. There was a general association between critical injuries and the use of the Talent – those healings made the best stories – but disease was the greater danger. The Talent could crush them all, and had done so for two hundred years ... but as a result, natural resistance to most deadly infections was minimal. No one had needed it, not until now.

She needed to know more about the situation in the city and she needed to understand the Queen's motivation, while keeping her views in check. No easy task. Naida was nodded into the Queen's private apartments by the same two soldiers who had seen her out a couple of hours previously. Approaching the Master of the Spires' office, flanked by the obligatory guards, she saw a man ahead of her and her heart sank.

'Aide Vinald, this is an unexpected pleasure.'

Vinald tugged his coat straight. His face was impassive but for a slight curl in his top lip.

'Lady Naida, what can I do for you?'

'I need to discuss with the Queen, the provision of medical services to the palace,' said Naida.

'Protocol dictates that you make an appointment,' said Vinald.

Naida shuddered inwardly. Still, she managed to add a pleasant smile to her face. 'Then I should like to make an appointment ...'

'Requested in writing,' said Vinald. 'Submitted to the office of the personal private secretary. You can expect a response with a provisional date in eight days. An urgent appointment might be granted within four days, but the circumstances would have to be exceptional.'

Naida blinked and her smile faltered. 'That's ... cumbersome.'

Vinald spread his hands in a gesture of faux sympathy.

'The Queen receives so many requests for appointments, as I'm sure you'll understand. We must filter out those whose requests are frivolous to identify those who do need her personal time. There are open petition receptions every third Faresday, but aside from that, I am unable to help.'

'Yes, but surely there are those with direct access to the Queen?'

'Absolutely,' said Vinald. 'The Queen's Council. There are a few others with preferential access but one thing they all have in common is that they didn't arrive this morning.'

A smile oozed across Vinald's face while he watched Naida digest his insult.

'And your place in this chain of obstruction?'

'I am attached to the office of the private secretary, though I work for the Master of the Spires,' said Vinald. 'Every Aide does, as Lord Denharl runs the palace on the Queen's behalf.'

Naida chuckled. 'I think we can agree I have much to learn about the workings of the palace. However, I need to speak to the Queen regarding real and present health risks to both the palace and the wider city resulting from a ... realignment of treatment options. Eight days is a lifetime to someone infected by a plague.'

Vinald raised an eyebrow and drew a hand from his left breast down to his right hip, a shocking gesture that Naida had never thought to see.

The gesture, 'my heart belongs to the earth', was a throwback to days when the Suurkene, worshipping Arbala, believed all acts of nature were either gifts or punishments, and that reaping nature's bounty required sacrifice. The Talent changed all that. It was unnatural, it was granted to a few, it was an unearthly power. It allowed humans to alter their destiny, showed that the diseases the earth sent as punishment could be thwarted.

The Talent had been embraced by King Pryan, two hundred years before. He placed this delicate magic at the heart of the royal family, and used it to cure the previously incurable, leaving the old religion nowhere to go.

The Arbalists did not go quietly. Unrest was widespread and long-lasting. But with any user of the Talent firmly allied to the King and able to act in the open, the balance of power lay with the Palace of Spires and the Arbalists were driven underground. Tolerated but powerless. The royal family even adopted its colours, rendering it stateless.

Gestures like that, in the heart of the palace, should not have been tolerated. But the guards, who had been watching the exchange, did not bat an eyelid.

'Change brings challenges,' said Vinald. 'That is why you are here.'

'Yes, and I cannot effect those changes without speaking to the Queen. So ...'

'I will do what I can to speed your request,' said Vinald and he reached into an inside pocket and produced a folded and sealed piece of parchment. 'Once it is handed to me in writing. Meanwhile, I have been tasked to give you this. I think it is more in keeping with your natural level of company.'

He handed Naida the parchment.

'Thank you ...' Naida frowned as she opened it. 'Did you *know* I would be coming here?'

'It seemed inevitable.'

'How very clever of you.' She opened the letter and reading it flooded her with warmth, laced with the aftertaste of Vinald's bitterness. 'Must have hurt, having to write this. Is that what all this is really about?'

'Words have consequences.'

'And my words to the Queen mean I will meet my friends at an eatery table reserved for us on her behalf. Not bad for someone who only arrived this morning.'

Vinald hissed a breath over his teeth. 'You misuse your influence.'

'You seem to think I'm trying to gain it, when all I want to do is my job, so people do not suffer and die unnecessarily. And yes, break bread with my friends every now and again. I'm an army doctor, Vinald. We value our comrades because they would die for us. You'll never understand that and if you get in my way, I will go around you.'

Vinald's cheeks darkened and he glanced at the guards, both of whom stared straight ahead, expressions neutral. But they had heard every word and it was he who had lost face.

'We're on the same side,' said Naida, seeing the cold in Vinald's eyes and regretting at least some of her words. 'We got off on the wrong foot. It's my fault, not understanding how things work and perhaps not respecting your position—'

'*Perhaps . . . ?*'

'Can we start again?'

'No one goes around me,' he said coldly.

'Watch me,' said Naida, turning for the Master of the Spires' offices.

'You can't just—'

But the guards did not bar her entrance and she swept in, trying to keep her anger in check as she entered and took in the four desks in two ranks of two, behind which sat four variations of studied self-importance.

'I wonder if anyone can help me?' she asked. A haze of smoke and a sweet spice scent from incense-burners crowded the stuffy air. Doors stood closed to either side of the small, windowless office.

Three of the youngish-looking men, all four of whom were dressed in dark-green frock coats and white shirts, ignored her completely, preferring to study their work yet more closely, while the fourth raised a hand but not his head while he continued to scribble. Naida was aware of Vinald hovering behind her.

Eventually, the shaven, rather beautifully shaped head was raised, pince-nez were removed from the bridge of his long nose and his green eyes appraised her.

'And you are?' His accent was faint but placed him as hailing from Central Gerestova.

'My name is Naida,' said Naida at a greater volume than necessary but getting her voice through those closed doors would be difficult otherwise. 'I am the new head of the royal medical service.'

All the heads came up now and the atmosphere changed completely. Gone was the easy pomposity that came with employment at the heart of the palace's operations and in its place, an uncomfortable air born of, apparently, the aura and glory that accompanied the utterance of her name.

One man, as hirsute as this clerk was bald, looked past her to Vinald and jerked that bearded, flowing-locked head in an unmistakeable go-away gesture.

'And how can we help you?' asked the shaven-headed one. 'I trust you are settling in?'

'Well, it's been less than a day so far … and I need to see the Master of the Spires. Urgently.'

Again, Naida spoke quite loudly, and a genuine look of pain crossed his face.

'I would love to wave you straight in, but—'

The door he had indicated with a waft of his hand was snatched open and there stood Denharl, a little red in the face and breathing as if he had just been running. Not a good idea with a hip like his.

'—it seems he's become unexpectedly free,' said the clerk so smoothly that Naida laughed and the two of them exchanged nods of appreciation. Denharl had already turned and was walking away.

'What's your name?' she asked.

'Dmitry.'

'Thank you, Dmitry,' said Naida.

She trotted after Denharl, down a short corridor. At the end,

Denharl opened another door into a large, high-ceilinged office which, from the intricate wood panelling to the cut of the drapes surrounding the windows, befitted a person of his rank.

'I'm so pleased you decided to drop in,' said Denharl. He gestured to comfortable seating ranged in a semi-circle around an unlit fire. 'Please take a seat. Can I get you a drink?'

'Just some water, please.' Naida sat in the centre of a plush, deep red sofa, relieved that she didn't sink in too far. Denharl brought her a glass of water and fetched a tankard from his desk before sitting opposite her, his hip causing him sharp pain. 'How did you know I was here? Despite my efforts, I can't imagine my voice carried all this way.'

Denharl pointed up to the corners of his office either side of the fireplace.

'Listening tubes. You should be aware they're everywhere. Always good to know who's arrived and what they are saying about me behind my back, as it were. I'm glad you were speaking, how shall I put it … very clearly … I am an old man and was enjoying an afternoon nap.'

'I apologise for disturbing you.'

Denharl waved a hand. 'Not at all. What can I do for you?'

'I need expedited access to the Queen, both now and, I'm sure, in the future. What would you need from me, that'll get me past busybodies like Vinald?'

Denharl raised his eyebrows. 'Don't make an enemy of Vinald. He's a good man, well thought of, well-connected. I can get you access. We'll discuss my needs another time.'

'We'll discuss them now, while I examine your hip and ask you some important medical questions,' said Naida.

Denharl smiled. 'Very well. Where do you want me?'

Chapter 12

The eatery was raucous and fascinating and the easy company of Naida's friends was comforting and made her wish they were still on the trail. She wanted to enjoy the dinner she'd imagined when she'd waved them all goodbye in the courtyard just a few hours before, but she had learned so much since then, and it was all vying to distract her. Worse, this dinner had another purpose now.

Naida's examination of Denharl had prompted deep concerns for the old man's health, concerns she would have raised with the Queen... but not even Denharl's letter to Lord General Kerslan, Queen Eva's Personal Private Secretary, had been able to gain Naida access until tomorrow afternoon. At least it gave her time to gather more information.

'A toast!' announced Adeile, who had changed out of her trail clothes and into a stained but clean-smelling shirt and trousers.

'To what?' asked Elias, still in his filthy trail clothes.

There were six of them around the central table, which had a view of the front door of the Melting Pot eatery in the heart of the Crucible's entertainment quarter. Famed for the five political murders that had taken place there over the decades, the Melting Pot was still *the* place to be seen and the scruffy bunch that had shown up had been given short shrift to begin with.

Naida proffering the letter from the Queen and introducing herself had wrought a remarkable transformation. Staff ready to turn them into the street in humiliation became obsequious. The owner appeared as if from nowhere to praise their bravery before making a valiant attempt to inflate Naida's ego, only to find her humility an implacable foe. He offered them free food and drink and a table any time they were passing, all of which they accepted happily.

Word that she was seated at the table spread like Deneck Fever through a colony of rats both within and without the eatery. Naida spent a good hour exchanging niceties with dig-nitaries and politicians, embellished war stories with old soldiers and had one touching encounter with relatives of an archer she had saved.

By the time the rush had died down and they could enjoy each other's company, albeit with the eyes of the Melting Pot still on them and with noses pressed against the glass without, Naida was a confused mixture of fraud, embarrassment, humility and burnished pride.

'To our friend Naida, may she return to the battlefield and save our sorry arses!'

Around the table, stacked with sharing trays of meats, fish, vegetables, breads and fruits, and strewn with bottles, tankards and glasses, her friends rose to their feet and she stood with them. Katarine, Aryn and Willan opposite her, Adeile and Elias flanking her.

'Naida!'

It was echoed by much of the Melting Pot. Naida blushed and refilled her glass, feeling the strength of the excellent Suurkene red wine make her head delightfully fuzzy. She'd only had a glass and a half.

'And I propose a toast to you lot. To Willan, who has been my friend, trainer and protector forever; and to the rest of you who made a horrible journey a delight, created memories I will treasure forever, and who I am proud and honoured to count among my friends. I love you all!'

A bit gushing but still.

They drank and cheered and sat down, tucking back into the bounty before them. No one spoke for a while but Naida saw Willan staring at her and trying to hide the fact that he was staring at her by staring at her over his tankard while drinking deeply.

'Am I wearing a crown, or something?' she asked, lifting another slice of spiced ham onto her plate to nestle next to the mounds of aromatic chutney she was smearing on almost everything. The hubbub of normal eatery discourse was rising again, making her feel less on display but she couldn't quite relax. 'You're worried. What is it?'

'You're distracted,' said Willan. 'Whatever happened today, in that rat's nest you're going to have to call home, it's burrowed deep and you aren't happy.'

'Well, you're right, as usual. While we've been away in our happy little battlefield world, our capital has become a darker place.'

Willan frowned. Everyone round the table was looking at her now.

'In what way?'

'Have you walked the city today?' she asked.

'I've been sleeping, mostly,' said Willan. 'We've got lodgings for a few days up near the cloth market. Bit close to the tanneries but the beds are clean.'

'How long are you all here?' she asked, deciding to dive in now she'd started.

'We've no idea,' said Adeile. 'We're still seconded to Ludeney as a transit team, so whenever anyone important needs taking anywhere, we're on call.'

'What about you, Will?'

'My orders mean I can stay here as long as you need me.'

'Good, because I need you,' said Naida. She turned to Aryn. 'You were born here, right?'

Aryn nodded as he arranged slices of melon on top of a breaded fish fillet and scattered over some lime juice. 'Yeah, me and Kat. When did you get here, Elias?'

Elias wrinkled his nose. 'Lived here for about nine years when I was young, after my mother died. I was ... six. A right bastard I was too, so my father said; good at finding trouble.'

Perfect.

'Are you going to tell us what's on your mind?' asked Willan.

Naida became aware of the other tables around them, full of the rich and entitled, the politicians and the sharks. Ears everywhere. She leaned in.

'I'm not sure where the Crucible and its patronage sits on all this just yet but look, you're all army, and the army has its traditions and suspicions about the Talent, and always has. I had to respect that as a surgeon, though funny how you all ask for the Gifted when you get an infection. Now the city is turning away from the Talent, renaming the Gifted *Touched* and driving them underground. I need to know how bad it is. What the mood is.'

'What's the problem?' asked Willan. 'Doesn't affect you, does it?'

'Whether you like it or not, today's medicine works hand-in-hand with the Talent. Especially here, where there are so many people crammed into unhealthy spaces, and so many opportunities for infection and disease. There are cures we haven't developed because we've had the Gifted to do it. But if they're to be outlawed then I, as head of the royal medical service and, by default, overseer of the city's health, have a huge problem.'

In so many ways, she was talking to the wrong people. Soldiers had a deep-seated suspicion of the Talent, trained into them from the day they signed up or were conscripted. Military leadership and morale relied on the visible and the shared notions of inclusivity and family, and within that the Gifted were always something *other*. Something capricious, uncontrollable. Useful but ultimately untrustworthy.

But in the most important way, she was talking to exactly the right people. Loyalty and friendship were the rocks to which soldiers tied themselves. And you never left your friends exposed.

'We'll investigate and let you know,' said Elias. 'I'll coordinate.'

'Thank you.' Naida tipped her glass at him. 'All of you. Anything you find, tell me in person. I'm not trying to be devious but information on paper can get misused.'

'Can we do stories and fun stuff now?' asked Adeile. 'All this seriousness is giving me a hangover.'

'The table is open,' said Naida. 'Who's going first?'

'Naida! Lady Naida!' The eatery doors had been pulled open and Naida swung round to see a woman covered in blood running in. 'Please. Lady Naida!'

Naida stood up before Elias could put a warning hand on her shoulder. The woman was terrified. She was wearing what had been quite a smart skirt and jacket in pale blue and grey, but both were patterned with blood. A quick assessment revealed none of it was hers but somewhere, someone had been opened-up enough for blood to spray over her. She was panicked enough to go searching for the one person the stories said could save the victim, and whose presence in the city today was known everywhere by now.

'I'm Naida.' She slung the bag she was never without over her shoulder. 'Remain calm. Tell me the situation.'

The eatery staff about to escort the woman out backed away even as Elias stepped to Naida's side, a muttered warning on his lips. The woman pushed her long dark hair back from her bloodied face and took in a shuddering breath.

'He's dying,' she said, and her panic began to overwhelm her again. 'They chased him down and cut him so deep. And there's so much blood.'

'Where is he cut? How far is he?'

'His gut and his face and his neck. Please. Not far.'

'Show me.' Naida glanced left and right, aware of the absolute silence gripping the rest of the eatery. 'Coming?'

'Well, if you think we'd let you into the night-time streets without security...' said Willan.

'What's your name?' asked Naida.

'Rachel,' replied the woman. 'Thank you.'

'We'll save him, Rachel, if he can be saved. Let's go. Run.'

Rachel ran, fear made her quick. Naida ran behind Elias, whose long strides ate up the ground, and with Willan at her side, the others in their wake just in front of about half the Melting Pot's customers, keen not to miss the drama.

The night was lantern-lit, busy with crowds enjoying a warm night and packed with the sounds of laughter, talk and song. Three turns later, with the Crucible and palace behind them, the sounds of laughter faded and most of the casual pursuit had been put off by the increasing poverty at each corner. Naida was lost and so glad for the comforting presence of her friends.

Now, faces peered from broken doorways or from the filthy steps on which they sat. Lantern light had given way to smoking torches above a few doorways and the atmosphere of frivolity was submerged by one of aggression allied with helplessness. The road they ran down was of dirt. The buildings to either side were faceless, hiding their purposes, though at one intersection they ran past a group outside an inn who stared at them with active malice. Hard to believe it was the same city.

'This way!' called Rachel and she ran under an arch into an open space, a courtyard criss-crossed with washing lines above, a broken fountain at its centre and a crowd of maybe thirty-strong in a pool of light at the far end. 'She's here, she's here!'

Faces turned and a path was created. Peripheral figures stared like those from the inn. Naida had rarely felt less safe and she'd spent years dodging flay-shot and arrows. Her friends were outnumbered five to one by the crowd and she had a fleeting fear that this was a trap.

She ran through the crowd anyway, flanked by her friends, and to the open doorway of a dwelling. A figure was lying in the hall, bloodied people around him. There was blood on the walls, and it pooled on the floor. So much of it that Naida's heart sank. She slid to the ground, pushing a woman aside from the man's head.

'You've kept pressure on his wounds, good. Let's see.'

Quiet descended while she worked, everyone craning to see what was going on, Elias and Adeile keeping people back. Naida could hear crying and it was apposite. The man was a terrible mess. He'd been beaten around his head, his nose was smashed, his eyes just puddles of blood and his jaw broken and askew, teeth kicked or battered out.

The knife wounds were many and mortal. In his stomach, across his throat, in his legs and one through a lung, which was pushing out feeble bubbles. It was incredible he was still alive. Naida felt for a pulse. It was there, but faint.

'Will, get pressure on the stomach wound. Aryn, dressings and bandages are in my bag. Let's get the stomach bound.' She looked up to Rachel. 'What's his name?'

'Litvin,' she said. 'He's my husband.'

The neck wound hadn't cut the artery but was still bleeding

freely. The chest and stomach wounds were a bigger danger. Naida scraped back some of the victim's matted hair.

'Litvin, my name is Naida and I am going to save you. Stay with me. Help me heal you.' The man moaned softly; he was a long way gone. Probably not saveable with stitches and bandages alone. 'Katarine, clean up his neck and bind it tight without throttling him. I'll take the chest.'

What she would have given for Drevien and Kella now. All she could do was hope she and her friends could stabilise him enough to get him to an infirmary.

Naida placed her hands on Litvin's chest around the wound. She prepared to push herself into him, see if she could close off the lung puncture.

'Why would someone do this?'

'He only ever wanted to help,' sobbed Rachel. 'But so many hate the Gifted now and he used his Talent on the wrong person.'

Shattered throne.

If she used the Talent to save him, Litvin would know what she was. She couldn't risk that, it would endanger so much.

'I'll do everything I can,' said Naida, unsure it could ever be enough. She probed the edges of the wound, not reaching out, finding them well-defined by a very sharp blade. Inside, though, fibres from his clothes would threaten infection unless she could operate and clean everything out. 'I've got to get him to the nearest infirmary. Where is it?'

'Palace infirmary,' said Rachel. 'Where he used to work.'

'All right. I need a stretcher. A plank of wood will do. Will, how are you doing?'

'It's a field dressing, no more.'

'It'll serve, I'm sure. I need another dressing and that stretcher!'

Elias's voice rose above the low conversation that had begun outside. Naida heard people running. After all, you didn't ignore a man who could fill a wide doorway.

'Coming, boss,' he said.

'What about his face?' asked Rachel, her voice breaking, her body shaking now that the fear had gone, replaced by misguided hope.

'Those injuries won't kill him,' said Naida. 'He has more pressing problems than his looks.'

Some enterprising individual had taken a door off its hinges and it was brought inside, where they could get him onto it.

'You should all consider transfers to the med squads. Let's go.'

Silence fell anew while all that could, watched and winced as Litvin was stretchered up and out. He made no sound, lost to unconsciousness now.

'I have to come,' said Rachel.

'No,' said Naida. 'He needs surgery and he needs sleep.'

'He's in the best possible hands now,' said Adeile and she smiled warmly enough to draw one from Rachel too. 'And he'll have quite the story to tell.'

'If he lives,' said Naida, shouldering her bag. 'He's critically injured. He should be dead already.'

'But you will save him,' said Rachel. 'You told him you would.'

'You wouldn't have me tell him anything else, would you?' She nodded to her friends. 'Four of you on the corners. One to clear our way. I'll stay at his head and we'll be quick but steady. We jerk him about too much, he'll die.'

'He's going to die anyway,' said Naida, a little breathless when they were away from the house and running down the stone passageway towards the infirmary. Willan had run on ahead to alert whoever was still at their posts to get the table ready and heat some water.

'What?' asked Adeile from her chosen corner by the victim's

left foot. They'd made quite a scene at the night guard post on the way into the Crucible proper and were being escorted by soldiers who didn't believe they were who they said they were.

'He'd largely exsanguinated before we got to him. The bastards did a good job. Ensured maximum suffering while he bled out.'

'But he's still alive right now?'

'No idea. Hard to take a pulse on the run.'

They reached the door and hurried Litvin down the dark corridor and into the furnace masquerading as an infirmary. Bright lanterns were lit over the operating table and Naida could feel the warmth from the coals heating the water.

The infirmary was full of moans, coughs and the smells of sickness. Parien, one of the medics she'd chewed out earlier, came over to help them.

'What do we have here?' she asked.

'Punctured lung, deep lacerations in his stomach and neck, lots of bruising and suspected fractures across his body and, very possibly, significant brain trauma.'

Parien stared for a moment and Naida waited for the comment she felt sure was coming. There was a puffing out of cheeks and a small shake of the head but no words.

'If your friends hold the stretcher steady, we can slide him onto the table. What's his name?'

'Litvin. He worked here, Rachel said.'

Parien jerked as if slapped and stared at Litvin, beaten so badly she hadn't recognised him. She let out a small moan and called for others, her voice breaking.

'Mayreh, Ullan! Get out here. Litvin's hurt. He's dying. We need help!'

'That we do.' Naida nodded thanks. 'We have to try. I've got to get into his chest. Anyone who can sew should work on his gut. The neck is the least of it, and then we can look at resetting his jaw. If he's still alive. He's lost so much blood.'

But by the time Litvin had been moved to the table, and his erstwhile colleagues had arrived to help him, he'd slipped away. Naida's shout of frustration, which woke up half the ward, was partly because getting to him a few minutes earlier might have made a difference but mostly because if she been able to use the Talent, he would have survived.

'We'll take care of him,' said Parien, laying a hand on his forehead. 'What are we doing to them? He'd never hurt a soul. Shattered throne, he was a *healer.*'

'You tell me. I only got here this morning.'

'Can you tell Rachel? She blames us for not helping him when he was thrown out... but there was so little we could do.'

'Of course.' Naida nodded. 'Where's Brin?'

'At home, I suppose. You do know he's ...?'

'Yes, he told me. But I'm seeing the Queen tomorrow. He's going nowhere.'

Parien's expression cleared. 'Really?'

'Yes, really. He's good, capable. You all are. We cannot give up, challenges will—'

'I get it,' said Parien and she almost smiled. 'We all get it.'

'Naida?' Willan put a hand on her shoulder. 'Time to go. Just like on the battlefield, there'll be another needs you tomorrow.'

Naida nodded but her smile was frail, and she fought tears while remembering the hope on Rachel's face.

'Got to dig further into this,' she said. 'Something ugly is going on and Litvin is just its first victim.'

'Let's take this outside,' said Elias, indicating the attention she was getting from the rest of the room.

Naida nodded. 'Good idea. Parien, I'll be in tomorrow to help with the scrub out. Meanwhile, thank you, and well, you know ...'

Parien shrugged. 'See you tomorrow.'

The six friends said nothing until they were back in the stone passageway, with a warm breeze blowing up from the Crucible and its grounds and gardens, deserted but for guard patrols.

'This wasn't quite the evening I had envisaged,' said Naida. 'I feel helpless.'

'But you're not,' said Adeile. 'You have access to the Queen, and you have us.'

'But you're not an official investigatory force,' said Naida. 'What can you do?'

'How about this,' said Willan. 'Let's get back to the Melting Pot, have a drink and relax, get some sleep. Then you and I go and see Rachel first thing, get that horrible job done. Later, you see the Queen and we all go and sample the atmosphere in the city, nothing more. Pick up whatever insights we can and then meet up somewhere ... help me, Aryn ...?'

'The Bonesaw Tavern seems appropriate,' said Aryn. 'It's down by the river next to the King Olan Infirmary. Lots of closed booths there.'

'...Great,' said Willan. 'Easy to get to?'

They walked back towards the Melting Pot and Naida yearned for the light and music and chatter.

'Every carriage driver knows it.'

'All right,' said Naida. 'Reserve something in my name if you can. At dusk. Should help you, and once we've dealt with the noise, we can get the owner to guarantee us privacy.'

'Anyone want to chime in?' asked Willan.

'I might be panicking about nothing,' said Naida. 'But this feels wrong and I'm not alone in thinking it. I want you all to be careful. We've just seen what those opposed to the Gifted will do and apparently, his murder is not the first.'

'I wonder who's behind it,' said Adeile. 'Really behind it, that is, not just picking up on the mood as Queen Eva seems to be.'

'Don't ask,' said Naida. 'Not yet. Just get the mood, like Will says, all right? Take no risks.'

'Got it, boss,' said Elias.

'Stop calling me that, will you?'

'Probably not.'

'Fair enough.'

Elias pulled open the door to the Melting Pot... and their dream of a quiet, relaxing drink to end the evening was snuffed out in the clamour for the story of a medical miracle Naida could not give them.

Chapter 13

The Crucible. The seat of Suurken's legislature, where power was brokered by myriad means, not all of them legal, and a building that crackled with energy and tension, and stank of wealth and entitlement, tainted by desperation and fervour.

In the maelstrom that was the Crucible, she was anonymous, and she was determined to revel in it for a few hours until she saw the Queen that afternoon. The Crucible was a vast, oval building with grand doors at each major point of the compass. During the day, and when the legislature was sitting, those doors were open to the public, who came in good numbers to see the sport in the pit.

Naida wanted to drink it all in. Colourful stalls outside sold everything from food and drink to spice and cloth and souvenirs – thankfully she was yet to see any dedicated to her – while inside, the space echoed with ten thousand footsteps on stone, the buzz of conversations and the rattle and stamp of printing presses.

Naida walked through the west doors, across the wide marble hallway with doors to either side leading to who knew where and into the vast atrium space that circled – well, ovalled – the pit, and from where she could already hear someone making an impassioned speech to intermittent cheers and corresponding boos. Impressive how the sound carried so far.

She wasn't sure whether to turn left or right, meaning to make a full circuit, and ended up just standing and staring at the architecture, stunned by its scale and execution. The outer wall was of stone and rose as high as the palace. It was punctuated by curved buttresses – those she could see were carved with horses, bears or trees, and they supported an extraordinary iron, steel and glass roof structure. Many of the panes were stained and it took a while for Naida to work out, being buffeted and cursed by those trying to get around her, that it represented a root system, cradling figures, presumably historically important ones. It was impossible to say from the floor.

Across the atrium, that wide enough to parade an army, was the inner wall, inside of which was the pit. This was a wooden structure, dark-stained, and rose maybe a hundred and fifty feet to the roof. From what she had read, the viewing galleries rose right to the top of the wall, so she'd get a better view of the stained glass from there.

About to circumnavigate to her left, Naida was stopped by a gentle hand on the shoulder. She turned to see Dmitry, a wide smile on his face and two mugs of steaming something or other in one hand.

'First time you come here, you have to have one of these,' he said, offering her a mug, which she took, sniffing the sweet alcohol scent.

'Have you been following me?'

Dmitry blushed. 'No ... no! I was delivering some papers to the Hound's Jaws and saw you looking a little lost – everyone who comes in here for the first time looks the same.'

'Oh yes, and how's that?'

'Transfixed, staring at the ceiling?'

'Guilty ... um, what is the Hound's Jaws?'

Dmitry smiled. 'Actually, it's a who, not a what...hey, how about I give you a tour?'

Naida reached past the likelihood that he had been sent to keep tabs on her and allowed herself to feel relieved to have a guide.

'That would be lovely, thank you. So long as you have time.'

'For you, I am assured I have all the time in the world.'

Naida appreciated the admission and took the arm that Dmitry proffered. 'Safer this way, is it?'

'Well, it means we can steady each other while we walk and drink.'

Naida laughed. He was all right, this employee of the palace. She sniffed her drink again and sipped it. The liquid fired down her throat, warming and spicy, sweet with a lingering sharp aftertaste.

'That is amazing,' she said. 'What is it?'

'It's Chrelein, a Gerestovan spiced white wine mixed with sweet berries and sprinkled with lemon zest, topped off with honey. A traditional drink of the mountain tribes. About half the stalls around the plaza will sell it to you but by far the best place to get it is Julmilla's, right outside the door where you came in.'

'I'll be sure to remember that in future.'

Dmitry chuckled. 'Too much information?'

'A little.'

'Let's go and see a debate.' Dmitry pointed away to the right where a queue of people snaked toward the pit.

They walked to the end of the queue of about fifty people who were dressed in everything from gaudy finery to dull woollen working clothes, and shuffled forwards sporadically. Naida was glad of the drink and even gladder of the company.

'Come on, you must have questions,' said Dmitry. 'I suspect you always have questions.'

'It's funny seeing for real what you've only ever seen in

129

drawings,' said Naida. 'I feel like I'm walking through someone's imagination.'

'That's not a question.'

'All right… what are all the offices for?'

Dmitry blew out a breath. 'So, that's about a hundred questions but there is a shortish answer. The ones on the outer ring are almost all petitioning agents… you don't know what they are, do you?'

Naida shook her head while sipping her drink. She felt warmed by both it and him. It was the perfect antidote to the terrible end to her night and the terrible start to her new day.

'Right… well, anyone can bring a petition to the pit to be debated and either passed into law or thrown out on its ear, but first you have to register the petition with the Hound's Jaws, basically the gatekeepers of the Crucible. And you can't just walk onto the floor of the pit and address the Uppers and Lowers… I'll explain who those are when we get in and you can see them… you have to employ an agent, who will tout the petition to their list of speakers. It's expensive, and obviously the higher grade the list, the higher the cost.'

They were about twenty from the front now. Naida could see a clerk at a desk taking names and issuing badges on lanyards. Every individual was searched and questioned by one of two guards before being granted entry to the galleries.

'Got it,' said Naida. 'And the inner ring?'

'All sorts,' said Dmitry. 'So, scattered around the ring are the presses printing the day's orders, and updates on any petitions and where they are in the process. I've already picked up this morning's. You've also got the opinion makers – Gavellers – who take your money to try to influence certain Uppers and Lowers in a particular direction. Some of them are charlatans, some of them actually have influence and, you know, money talks.'

'Bribery?'

'That's an ugly word for it. Think more of... an encourage-ment to campaign actively – cover costs, that sort of thing.'

'Right.' Naida stared into Dmitry's eyes and saw the sparkle there. 'Any other offices for legally sanctioned corruption over there?'

Dmitry half-choked on his drink. 'I think you might be quite dangerous.'

'You should see me on the battlefield.'

'I've heard plenty of stories.'

'Later on, you can run me through them and I'll tell you which ones have any basis in reality.'

'Deal,' said Dmitry. He pointed to a couple of offices that had signs hanging over their open doors and queues of people waiting to enter. 'These are fun. They're applying to join the legislature as Uppers or Lowers by joining a sort of apprentice programme, or by direct election. You need to have significant backing, proposers and seconders, a decent-sized purse, or be able to represent an area that you can argue is currently under-represented.'

'Anything else?'

'Most expensive coffee in the world. Over there.'

'How does it taste?'

Dmitry shrugged. 'I'm a clerk in the Master of the Spires' office, how would I know?'

They reached the front of the queue, and Naida was des-perate for a mug of coffee for some reason. She noticed the guards' livery. It was blue and grey but otherwise of the same cut as the palace guard and wider army. She nudged Dmitry and asked him.

'Ah, that's because the Crucible Militia is an independent force. Independent from the Crown, I mean. Sworn to defend the legislature from attack and hence protect the separation of Crown and law.'

'Dmitry, good to see you,' said the clerk, a middle-aged woman with a monocle, her hair hidden under a black scarf and a rather harassed look on her face. 'You know the drill.'

'And good morning to you, Jessica.' He leaned over to write their names on the roll, giving Naida a false name. 'I'm here with a friend today. First visit to the capital, would you believe?'

Jessica glanced at Naida and handed over a lanyard. 'Well... have fun. It's an experience, if nothing else.'

Having heard the conversation, the guards waved them both through and Dmitry pointed the way to the stairs up to the top gallery. Inside, the sound of voices from the floor of the pit was loud, carrying clear across the acoustically designed space. The conversations from those already in the galleries, punctuated by the roars, cheer and boos and the stamping of feet, felt close enough to touch and Naida felt a thrill run through her.

'So, who are those soldiers loyal to, if not the Queen?' The thought sat uncomfortably with Naida which, she presumed, was a product of her years patching up soldiers who would die for their monarch.

'Well, they're under the control of the High Gavel... stop laughing... he or she is the highest officer of the Crucible. Stop laughing.'

Naida was shaking with mirth, feeling light-headed from the Chrelein. Every time she tried to speak, she laughed some more. Drink was going everywhere.

'I'm... I'm sorry. I've just got this... image running through my head and I can't shift it. Does he sit up a ladder?'

Dmitry shook his head. 'No.'

'Sorry. Is his gavel on a shelf above his head?'

'Stop it.'

'Are there low and medium gavels?'

'*No*. Just … no.'

Naida was feeling a little embarrassed and she was relieved when they reached the head of the stairs and stepped out into the pit because it took her breath away. Dmitry steered her along a line of benches, which was a good thing because she was staring.

The colour of the clothing. That's what struck Naida first. Vibrant, unabashed, extravagant and exciting. It was a feast for the eyes, a festival of expression and every stitch of it worn by a member of the audience, contrasting starkly with the décor of the pit itself which was as dull as a winter puddle.

The floor was stone-grey, pitted and stained. Two figures circled each other on it: one was speaking, one listening and making negative gestures for the benefit of her supporters and the crowds in the galleries. At one end of the floor was a raised section on which sat a high-backed chair, with one wide arm to the right on which rested a gavel. The man – who was presumably the High Gavel – had his hand resting on his namesake. It wasn't quite as funny now.

There were three tiers of seats and benches around the floor, each raked and, from a quick count, ten rows deep. Dmitry reached the empty space on the bench he'd seen from the stairs, and they sat down. There was a roar of approval of something that had been said on the floor and the gavel slapped against the chair's arm for order.

'Check out what's in the petition,' said Dmitry.

Dmitry showed her the order paper he'd picked from the seat and tapped a line, which read:

Petition to enforce registration of practitioners of the Talent and further to regulate and oversee their practices and premises. No wonder Misha had recommended she come here this morning.

'Or just murder them if that's not enough restriction for you,' muttered Naida, noting the names listed in two columns beneath the petition and the blue stamp next to the statement. Every petition had a different coloured stamp.

'What was that?' asked Dmitry.

'Nothing. What are all these names?'

'Ah yes, well, getting a petition agent is just the start. Once the agent has found an advocate, that advocate needs to gather eight supporters, often by way of mutual back-scratching with other petitions, but it might be something more personal or financial. Then the petition is viable, and a speaker can be appointed to make the case on the pit floor.'

He gestured down to the two strutting individuals from whom Naida was hearing snatches of speech that alternately warmed and chilled her. She leaned forward to pay better attention.

'Just as a by the way, the clerks at the four desks there at the compass points? They're all pit recorders. Everything that's said, every reaction, and sometimes every gesture, is written down or sketched. At the end of the day, they compare, and an agreed text is written up for printing, overseen by representatives from both sides of each petition. The original texts are stored. This is the ultimate bureaucracy; everything is recorded. Nothing is thrown away. Makes my office look sparse and amateur. Remind me to explain the bloodstains on the floor, too. They've got a good story.'

Naida smiled and let herself get drawn into the debate on the floor. The speaker for the petition was a young woman called Francesca Oliari, dressed in many shades of blue and with jet-black hair tied back from a narrow face. Naida had noted her name from the order sheet. On the opposition side, Naida's side, Johan Temets, middle-aged with his hair greying and thinning and dressed plain but smart in white shirt, brown jerkin and black trousers.

'...he asks why must we register and regulate the Touched,

and I simply reply, why not?' Oliari was in the centre of the floor and addressed her question to the galleries, her arms spread, waiting for their approval, which she got from far too many quarters. 'Let me give you a little list:... the army... regulated! The quality of iron and steel... regulated!' She encouraged the crowd to join in with a few flicks of her hands. 'Incoming trading goods...'

Regulated!

'The interment of our dead...'

Regulated!

'The Crucible itself!'

REGULATED!

Oliari didn't need to encourage the cheers, the applause or the stamping of feet that engulfed the Crucible. She paced the circumference of the floor, egging them on until Temets swung round to beseech the High Gavel, who rapped with his hammer, the splitting noise bringing swift silence.

'Are you done with this round, Speaker Oliari?' he demanded, voice booming.

'Only to say, my honoured lord, that I have mentioned but five from a long, long list. A list designed to maintain order, keep our people safe, provide rules that facilitate sensible progress. Adding the Touched to the list of regulated professions doesn't demean it, it elevates it, brings it respectability. Keeps people safe.'

Oliari bowed to more cheers and applause, which died away as the High Gavel raised a hand.

'Speaker Temets, you may respond. Do you wish to speak now, or shall we begin to invite questions from the honoured benches of Uppers and Lowers?'

'I will take it now, most honoured lord. I cannot let her litany of obfuscation and falsehood stand.'

There was an almost comical indrawing of breath from

135

the crowd and a sense of fevered expectancy. The theatre was compelling but Naida wondered how many in the galleries understood that lives were not just at risk but being lost already.

Oliari made a face that suggested Temets was about to make a fool of himself and gestured for him to proceed.

Temets stalked to the centre of the floor, stood on the central, heavily stained stone and turned a slow circle, daring the crowd to react.

'That's where Rab Eiles died, losing the petition to end the use of beheading as a method of execution a hundred and thirty-seven years ago,' whispered Dmitry. 'Back in the days when, if there was no voted resolution, the petitioners fought to the death. Unbelievable, when you think about it.'

'Yes, how far we've come,' said Naida, the image of Litvin coming to mind all too easily.

'*Elevates … respectability … Touched …* What's wrong with these terms, do you think? Did you remember that not one hundred days ago … one hundred days, the blink of an eye … those with the Talent were referred to as the Gifted? Remember that? You should. You will all have used that term. You will all have visited one of the Gifted because of an infection, a wound that would not heal, a headache you could no longer stand, pains in your joints that gave you no peace.'

Their deliveries could not have been more different. Where Oliari was all drama and rabble-rousing, Temets was calm, even quiet, and he spoke as if each of the crowd, each of the Uppers and Lowers, were in a room with him alone. The Crucible fell silent.

'Shall we have a show of hands? Who of us has not … *not …* visited one of the Gifted to seek relief from illness or other malady?'

A hand went up right next to Naida. She stared at the woman, young, angry, dressed in dour, poor clothes.

'Really?' said Naida, staring her straight in the eyes. The woman couldn't match her gaze and her hand dropped back into her lap. 'Lying gets people killed.'

Temets looked around. 'I see a few hands went up and to each of you, I say, come down here, right now, and swear to it on the lives of all you love. I stand here and I call each of you a liar. If you have issue with that, come down here.'

No one moved. The tension in the Crucible rose.

'Another show of hands, please. Anyone who has witnessed a malevolent act by one of the Gifted towards another person, please raise your hands. False accusations can lead to imprisonment, so think before you decide to lie. I will follow up every complaint personally.'

No one moved a muscle. Temets took a deep breath and sighed it out.

'The Gifted do not *need* elevating, they do not *need* respectability, they already have these things. You've confirmed it. You've trusted them to heal you. One of them has saved the life of someone you know or love. And yet you want them controlled, regulated, investigated. My adversary's little list details professions where a lack of regulation can lead to the death of innocents. And yet none of you ... *none of you* ... can attest to a single occasion where one of the Gifted has performed anything other than an act of kindness.'

The guilt lay heavy in the Crucible. The silence when Temets stopped talking weighed on the ears.

'I do not know,' said Temets, 'why you are being driven to hate those who save your life for precious little reward. Why the single, awful Esselrode event, never repeated, which took place in another country during a war – is being used to convince you that every Gifted carries the same evil within them. It is a baseless accusation. No evidence has been provided. Why would anyone want to restrict your access to those who can heal you ... save your life?'

The question hit Naida like a hammer and she was amazed that she hadn't posed it to herself already. She glanced around the galleries and at the angry woman next to her and saw that, though they might be quiet, Temets' message wasn't making a dent.

'You are being encouraged to mistrust when it is against your best interests. Encouraged to shun and drive the Gifted underground ... even though they are your best chance of surviving many of the diseases that commonly threaten this city.'

Naida took the order paper from Dmitry and studied the names on the petition.

'Who proposed the petition?' she asked, pushing the paper under his nose.

'None of them,' he said. 'They can remain anonymous if they want.'

'Huh,' said Naida. 'Can we find out?'

'All the records are kept in the archives below the pit,' said Dmitry. 'But why do you want to know?'

'Idle curiosity,' said Naida.

Temets summed up. 'So, I urge you all, in the galleries, and you, my honoured Uppers and Lowers. When you consider where to lend your support, think on two things. One, who stands to gain from a restriction of the practices of the Gifted? Because someone must. Why else support the restriction of our greatest healing resource? And secondly, where does this lead? Because it may be registration and control today ... but tomorrow? When the Gifted are being tagged and watched in their homes? It will be criminalisation and prohibition. Do not take the first step down this road. Thank you.'

There was concerted and generous applause, and no booing, but neither was there the cheering that Oliari had enjoyed.

'He's good, isn't he?' said Naida.

'Outstanding, and very expensive. There's a lot of money behind the opposition.'

'What happens now?'

'There's a break and then open questions from Uppers and Lowers and perhaps one or two from the galleries.'

'Hmm,' said Naida. 'Can we leave? I have questions of my own.'

'Sure.'

'I'll buy you a coffee.'

Chapter 14

They sat in the Garden of Whispers to drink the most expensive coffee in the world and concluded that, although it was good, it wasn't worth the money. Their bench was quite near the infirmary and they sat with their backs to it, watching deals being done and side debates being had.

'Think the petition will carry?' asked Naida.

'It's hard to say. Famously, Uppers take the mood of the galleries and go with it because they want to be seen as men and women of the people; while Lowers have minds of their own, or large purses they want filled to lean one way or the other. These are all gross generalisations, mind you. What do you think?'

'I think it'll pass, and I think, like Temets, that it's a step down a very dark path. It's a path we're already on, though.'

'What do you mean?'

'A man died on my operating table last night,' said Naida, remembering his ruined face. 'Murdered for being one of the Gifted. He had worked in the Queen's infirmary.'

Dmitry studied the dregs of his coffee. 'I'm sorry.'

'Where does the palace stand on this issue?'

'It has no official position. It tends to support the decision of the Crucible, but that's not a matter for a clerk.'

Naida patted his hand. 'Sorry. All right, let's get away from the uncomfortable. So who are the Uppers? Can I become one?'

Dmitry laughed. 'If you struggled to afford that coffee, you'll never get close. Unless you marry a senior soldier or perhaps one from our more prominent landed and privileged circle. Preferably someone already with influence over the arcane and impenetrable system of appointing Uppers.'

'Another dream crushed,' said Naida.

'I mean, basically, Uppers are society's rich and powerful, and Lowers are ordinary folk, so your best bet is to find a constituency among them.'

Naida drained the rest of her mug. 'This has been lovely.'

'But...'

'But nothing. I have to check in at the infirmary, help clean up, then I see the Queen.'

'Fair enough. Give me your mug, I'll take them both back.'

Naida handed it over and stood up, feeling a little sad to be parting from Dmitry. 'Thank you.'

'Dinner sometime?' he asked.

'Love to.'

He grinned. 'Great. I'll be in touch.'

Naida reached up and kissed his cheek. 'Do that. I still need to hear about petition opposition.'

'Well, that crackling conversation will have to wait.' Dmitry began to walk away. 'Any other fascinating facts you need to know, my office door is open.'

Naida waved and turned for the infirmary, her mood cooling and her shoulders beginning to hunch with a familiar tension. She paused outside the door to adopt an expression of positivity and determination, and the first face she saw was Brin Gorvien's as he backed out of one of the cells with a pile of filthy sheets in his arms, gloves up to his elbows. The stench was unique and repulsive.

'Where do you need me?' she asked.

'Bucket, boiling water, soap and brushes out the back. Help yourself and get started on this one. I'll be back when these are burning.'

★

The Queen seemed distracted when she met Naida in a suite of reception rooms close to the Master of the Spire's office. She kept Naida waiting over an hour, which at least gave Naida time to examine the room. First-off, she checked for listening tubes, feeling uncomfortable that anywhere she was, she might be overheard by Denharl or anyone else with access to what could be a palace-wide system.

After that, though, she was able to relax, enjoy looking at the multiple hangings of landscape art while drinking more coffee that was not as good as, but probably more expensive than, the most expensive coffee in the world. The main room, from which ran a bathroom and privy and a short corridor to a small kitchen, was typically high-ceilinged, with towering windows overlooking an inner courtyard. There was a massive fireplace and mantle in black marble, and a central setting of four sofas around a large square table.

Every surface was covered in ornaments, mostly museum pieces but also a hilarious clay model of a duck that the Queen had made when she was four, according to the mounting card. Naida thanked the card for telling her it was a duck. There was precious little other supporting evidence.

'I wasn't very good with my hands,' said the Queen, catching Naida looking at her effort when she sailed in, dismissing her attendants with the waft of a hand. 'What do you think of it?'

'It's awful, Your Majesty, even for a four-year-old,' said Naida, bowing. 'Can I get you a cup of coffee or tea or something else?'

The Queen said nothing, preferring to walk over to a window and peer out, huffing while she tried to spot someone or something. Naida almost asked if she should leave but remembered why she was here and kept quiet, choosing to wait by the sofas in the centre of the room, studying the rug under her feet. It was bland, worn and fraying at the edges.

'Tea,' said the Queen. 'I think we might end up being very good friends.'

Naida poured the tea, a sweet-smelling basil and mint infusion and carried the cup to the Queen.

'Thank you, ma'am. Might I ask why?'

'Because you're not a tiresome sycophant.' She pointed at her duck. 'You're the only person who has been honest about that monstrosity. It's why I keep it there, obviously.'

'I hope you'll appreciate my honesty going forward, ma'am.'

'I'm sure that I won't,' said the Queen and she waved Naida to a sofa and sat at right angles to her. 'And in private, you may address me as Eva. I find all this *majesty* and *ma'am* stuff elongates conversations terribly and hearing it thousands of times a day is excruciating.'

Every time the Queen spoke, Naida's respect for her grew.

'I'll do my best, Y— Eva, but I may need some practice.'

'You'll get plenty, I'm sure. Now, I hear you had a busy night last night. Did you enjoy the Melting Pot?'

Naida was put off her stride again and took a moment to compose herself. She took a sip of coffee.

'We were honoured and humbled you made such a gesture on our behalf, ma'am… Eva. Dammit. It was a remarkable place. Beautiful food and a very friendly clientele. But…'

'Yes, hard to retain good memories when the night ended in blood and death.'

'Quite,' said Naida. She took a deep calming breath and clung to her courage. 'The victim, Litvin, was Gifted and murdered

143

because of his Talent. He used to work at the palace infirmary before he was dismissed.'

Eva nodded and stared at the table. 'It is regrettable, and we will leave no stone unturned tracking down his killers. He was a good man, undeserving of his end, and I shall see to it his dependants are well-cared for.'

Naida forced a smile to cover her disappointment. 'A generous gesture that I'm sure will be appreciated. I'm not here to discuss the merits or otherwise of the Talent, but rather the consequences of its absence on the delivery of medical services.'

'We need more like you, eh?' said the Queen, her own smile fragile, uncomfortable with the conversation. Naida felt a moment of fear before she realised Eva was speaking of her as a non-Gifted healer. 'And perhaps you should focus more on your core role, which is keeping me alive, and leave others to attend to the wellbeing of my subjects?'

'I'm delighted to say your state of health is such that I have a great deal of spare capacity. And, if I may, Eva, I had plenty of time to study the scope of my role on the way here, which is to manage all medical facilities across Suranhom. It's my job and the exclusion of the Gifted will create significant challenges. A hundred more people like me won't be enough.'

Eva looked at Naida over the rim of her cup while she sipped slowly.

'So, you're going to tell me what will be enough, and that it's going to cost a lot of money,' she said eventually.

'Well, yes I can and yes, it will, but before that, I need you to understand the scale of the risk we're taking by barring the Talent from medical—'

'That isn't what is being proposed in the Crucible, surely?' said Eva.

'It's what's already happening. Litvin is tragic proof of the hatred that's been generated. It doesn't matter what legislation is passed. Your own infirmary has dismissed its Gifted.'

'They call them Touched now, you know.'

'Yes, I do. It merely feeds the narrative of mistrust. It's very dangerous. All it's going to take is an outbreak of any one of twenty highly infectious diseases in a slum, and this city will be engulfed because we will not be ready or prepared to deal with it.'

'The T—, Gifted, could help.'

'They're hiding in their homes, terrified for their lives. But you could calm the situation. Speak out. Make known your dismay at the aggression and suspicion of people whose sole desire is to heal, to help. They are not subject, yet, to any restrictions; they are not acting illegally if they treat people – yet they are already being judged and found guilty by association with a single event that happened fifteen years ago. Surely you champion fairness? You cannot just sit by.'

'Cannot?' Eva's gaze was cold and Naida's gut clenched. She'd gone too far, forgotten who she was addressing. 'Not a word I hear, Naida, as Queen.'

'Yes. And a great Queen. Loved from the most hard-bitten soldier to the most privileged lordling. What you choose to say, how you choose to act, has enormous influence and this country is blossoming under your rule.'

A smile at the flattery, there and gone.

'I think you have it the wrong way around. I do not influence the people, I reflect the people. The people do not want the Talent. They mistrust the base motives of the ... Gifted ... what do they learn, each time they touch a human body and discern how to treat it? What if more of them could harm, not help? That is where the people's minds lie.'

Naida put a hand to her mouth, as much to stop herself speaking as to represent her concern.

'People are reaching out to the land once more. Arbala, Eremene, Heliolus … none of the old Gods ever died, did they? Many still worship though their influence has diminished over the decades. The gods were testing us and we … the people … have returned to them. We are turning our backs on the temptation that the Talent represents. It is the pursuit of convenience, which has made us weak, and life is not convenient.'

Well, it is for you, thought Naida. *Not so much for the poverty-stricken sleeping in filth.*

'With respect, Eva, the Talent is not a convenience, nor is it a temptation. It is two hundred years of progress, which has overtaken the research that might have been done otherwise to provide treatments and cures. Those turning their backs on the Talent and embracing Arbala and Her minions instead will die wondering why She has let them down.'

'The Earth provides. And it takes. We exist at its mercy and at the mercy of the gods who provide its bounty for us.'

Naida wanted to stand and scream: *No, we don't! Not anymore.* The Gifted had freed them of the terror of Shine Fever, or Garrat's Disease or Red Spot.

'After all that the Gifted have given us, can that really be what you believe?'

'It is what the people believe,' said Eva calmly, and there was no sign that she felt trapped by it.

Naida felt a chill as Eva's words rolled over her. All the warmth and respect she'd had was draining away. It was hard to marry the strong-minded woman she'd first met with the one who had explained the return of dangerous beliefs and prejudices. What might come back with those beliefs didn't bear contemplating.

'I don't understand …'

'You are not Queen.' Eva shrugged. Her position was contradictory. She wanted her subjects to be protected and feel safe but was failing to protect the most vulnerable and, by extension, everyone and anyone who got sick once the Gifted were gone, as Naida feared they soon would be.

Naida bit down on her argument and changed tack. 'Should this exclusion of the Talent continue, or indeed be sworn into legislation, we will need to train hundreds, thousands more doctors, surgeons, and orderlies to work in redesigned, expanded, and in many cases entirely rebuilt, infirmaries across the city. The infirmary that bears your name is a case in point. It is not fit for purpose without the Gifted treating infectious diseases.'

Eva frowned. 'Why must this happen?'

'The Gifted have become essential in treating infection; they can affect healing from injury deep in the body where few surgeons dare go, and in all cases speed up recovery, meaning beds are not occupied for so long. Without them we will need more beds in better ventilated buildings designed to accommodate strict cleanliness regimes and partitioned operating areas.'

'Expensive.'

'We can help defray costs by not losing any people who already have the skills we need.'

Eva was alert enough to know exactly to whom Naida referred.

'Brin Gorvien trod a precarious path. On the other side of dismissal was imprisonment. Our final conversation was not witnessed, which is to his eternal good fortune.'

'I don't know what was said.' Naida thought for a moment. 'But I do know he's passionate about his work and had friends who were dismissed to show the Crown is in tune with the mood of the people.'

'Modesty and decency forbid me to repeat his words.'

'I need him, Eva,' said Naida. 'The remaining staff respect him, and they want to work for him. They don't for me – at least, not yet. Please, revoke his dismissal. I will vouch for him. He is *such* an asset in a post–Talent city, and I need him.'

Eva sighed and got up. Naida made to rise but was waved back down.

'Reinstating him would be an unthinkable loss of face.' Naida swore under her breath but the Queen wasn't finished. 'However, I understand the difficulties our current situation presents, so I am minded to write to the Exchequer and the Master of the Spires, placing you in charge of the budgets that ensure the continuity of our public health duties. No requests will be refused, though they may be challenged.'

She turned back to Naida.

'You may hire whomever you deem most suitable for the roles you need to fill. I need not be aware and perhaps, in certain cases, should be kept unaware, of your staffing decisions.'

Naida felt some light edge around the drapes of a very difficult conversation. One that had thrown up so many questions.

'That is very generous, and I understand entirely, Your Majesty.'

'Good,' said the Queen peremptorily. 'Anything else?'

'Nothing, thank you.'

'Good. You may go. I would advise you to be accurate in your budgetary requirements. The Exchequer is a bastard, exactly as you should hope and expect.'

Naida smiled. 'Thank you, Eva.'

'We need to be friends,' said Eva. 'We will discuss the most delicate and intimate of matters, after all, and you are honest, and I need honesty.'

'To be considered your friend would be an honour.'

Eva waved a hand. 'Honour implies a reward and rewards have no place in defining friendship. We should eat and get awfully drunk together. I'll arrange it.'

She turned her gaze back to the window and Naida was dismissed.

Chapter 15

She went and bought another cup of that coffee and sat on the same bench she and Dmitry had shared earlier in the day. Less than two days in Suranhom on her supposed mission to kill the Queen, and the means to do it was being handed to her, if she was so-minded.

All she had to do was wait, and infection would come calling. It would be simple to bring contaminated material into the Queen's private chambers and let it do its work. Naida even questioned whether it would trigger a darkness within her. After all, she was inducing nothing. She wasn't introducing disease through surgery or examination, both options she had feared she might have to consider. Leaving a bloodied towel contaminated with Garrat's under a bed would do all the work. All she would have to do is fail to cure the disease.

Yet she would still be a killer. She would have delivered the infected material, and then have withheld a cure from the Queen when she had the means to stop the infection dead in its tracks.

Would that unleash the darkness that had allegedly engulfed her parents? Would it make her capable of, and willing to commit, genocide? Would the power that she had been told had smothered her mother and father also dominate her so completely?

It wouldn't, she thought, because it didn't exist. Last night she had chosen not to use the Talent to save Litvin and he had died. As far as she could tell, she was not now possessed of a dread power she would unleash on anyone who dared stand in her way. She'd never really believed in a darkness on the edge of the Talent, and last night was accidental proof she was right.

Anyway, she wasn't going to contaminate the Queen's bedroom with Garrat's or with anything else, so did it really matter? And should the Queen fall sick, Naida would move the earth to treat her successfully, and use the Talent to do so, because Eva would never know.

Naida put her coffee mug to her nose and breathed in deeply, letting the strong roasted aroma flow around her. Of course it mattered. It meant everything and nothing simultaneously. It didn't weaken Ludeney's hold over her, because she remained the daughter of monsters. But it raised so many questions about her parents and why they ended up in Traitor's Square suffering long days of torture before being burned to ash in the cage.

Her parents had been accused of using their Talent to actively propagate a disease that had run unchecked through vast swathes of Cantabria's capital city's population. Genocide. She had never believed them capable of such an act and now here she was in a place that could provide all the answers. She might even be able to prove the belief she had clung onto through all the years of being schooled in their evil: that her parents were innocent.

It was a difficult path she was considering, and she needed a distraction while she gathered herself. Gazing across at the Crucible and watching the steady flow of people in and out, the gaggles of conversation, the arguments, the dealing, the pressure being applied one way or another, she wondered what the result of the debate was.

'Why wonder?' she said out loud and got up, draining her mug and thinking to drop it back at the stall on her way to learning results and ongoing processes. 'Where's Dmitry when you need him?'

With the day beginning to wane towards another warm evening, the crowds inside the Crucible were thinning. The queue at the coffee stall was gone and she placed her mug on the counter, earning a nod of thanks from the grey-haired man behind the counter. Outside, she'd noticed children scurrying about, picking up abandoned mugs.

'I guess I'm denying some enterprising child a coin for collecting this?'

The man smiled. 'I'm grateful to you for thinking to return it. Here's your deposit back.'

He pushed a small copper coin across the counter, which Naida put in the tip jar.

'It's good coffee, served lovely and hot,' she said.

'Thank you.' He stared at her. 'You look familiar. Have we met before?'

'I bought the coffee that was in that mug, if that helps?'

'No.' He chuckled. 'I have a terrible memory for customers' faces.'

'Well, there's a souvenir stall or two in this city with my face painted on mugs and plates, I'm told.'

'Well, naturally,' he said with a snort. 'All right, let's do this properly. I'm Sammel.'

'Naida. Glad to make your acquaintance.'

Sammel's face pinched with embarrassment. 'Oh ... well perhaps there is a stand after all. Sorry.'

'I'll forgive you if you tell me where to learn the results of today's debates.'

Sammel relaxed. 'Your best bet is to head round to the left. About six offices down is the official recorder's office. They update results as they happen on a blackboard, with summaries of debates the following morning.'

Sammel had been making coffee while he was talking, and he pushed the full mug across the counter.

'Here. This one's on me. Keep the mug.'

Naida smiled. 'Thank you.'

'Be sure to be the one to stitch me up if I get cut,' said Sammel.

'Deal.'

Naida raised the mug and wandered round to the recorder's office. It was a tiny little space, wood-panelled, airless, boasting two back-to-back desks, two harassed-looking staff and a venerable printing press designed to produce single copies of individual pages. Naida saw trays of letter blocks stacked up to its left and a page-making table in the left-hand corner.

To the right was the promised blackboard, but if she was looking for clarity, she wasn't going to find it there. Columns and rows boasted figures, arrows, ticks and crosses.

'How do I work out the results of today's debate?' she asked the room, hoping any of the five people looking at the blackboard or the two blue-shirted clerks with their heads down, making marks in books, could help. 'Anyone? Diamene, can you help?' Naida read the nameplate on the nearest desk.

Diamene looked up, face thunderous at being interrupted.

'It really isn't that hard,' she said, accent thick from a childhood in the northern archipelagos.

'Then it won't take you long to explain it.'

The air crackled with tension, but Naida had stared down generals on battlefields and so there was only one winner.

'Left-hand column is the petition code from the order paper. Next four columns detail Upper and Lower voting, for or against – I trust a tick or cross is self-evident enough, even for you – and the arrow indicates whether the petition is moving up to the approvals committee, down to the amendments committee or is returning for further debate. The whys and wherefores will be in tomorrow's record papers. Is that clear enough?'

Naida smiled. 'Perfect, thank you. Do you like coffee?'

'Yes.' Diamene snapped.

'Have mine,' said Naida, putting the mug on Diamene's desk. 'I haven't touched it. And you look like you've had a far harder day than me. Sammel says you can keep the mug too. If you want.'

Diamene stared. 'That's ... incredibly kind of you.' Her tone had softened, though she couldn't quite manage an apology.

'Anytime.'

'Which result were you interested in?'

'The one about the registration and restriction of the practitioners of the Talent,' said Naida, feeling a change in the atmosphere around her as people wondered, she assumed, where she stood on the issue.

'It's the second one down. Carried, very comfortably, straight into approval committee stage as a result.'

Naida felt deflated but not altogether surprised. She glanced at the numbers and could see a four to one majority in favour of regulation.

'I was there this morning,' she said. 'I thought Temets spoke very well. Truthfully.'

'Like that makes any difference,' said someone standing near her, also studying the blackboard.

'I'm sorry?' asked Naida.

'It's already decided, isn't it?' he said. He was a young man, smartly dressed, who had clearly enjoyed a glass of wine or two that afternoon. 'Temets speaks well on all sorts of issues, it's why he's on the floor so much. Sometimes it makes a difference but he, like everyone else involved, knew this one was just for show. I mean, having Oliari down there says it all, right? Are you from out of town?'

'How did you guess?'

'You aren't cynical enough. Don't worry, it won't take long.'

Naida shared a glance with Diamene, who said all she needed to with a lift of her eyebrows.

'Thanks,' said Naida, feeling out her next question. 'So, if I wanted to learn who proposed a petition and who funded the opposition, how would I do that?'

'An archivist might release that information to you, but there's no requirement to make it public if you raise a petition,' said Diamene. 'Why would you want to know?'

'Why don't you?' asked Naida. 'How can anonymous interests be allowed to drive legislation? How is that helping the ordinary subject?'

'You think the Crucible is about helping the ordinary subject?' The tipsy man rolled his eyes. 'Don't add naivety to your lack of cynicism.'

It was a fair point. But the nagging worry lurking in the back of her mind pushed its way to the front. This wasn't some organic groundswell of opinion against the Gifted that had run out of control. This was deliberate. Someone, or some group of interests, was driving the notion that the Gifted should be restricted and, given how they were being discriminated against, criminalised. What she couldn't work out was why.

Knowing who was behind the petition would help. She was taking this personally ... but it was personal. The fear of the Talent was being drummed up using her parents as proof of all that was evil in the Gifted. In her.

'Are you all right?' asked Diamene.

Naida snapped out of her thought bubble to see three or four people staring at her and felt herself blush.

'Yes, yes I'm fine. You have given me a great deal to think about. Thank you for your help. Both of you.'

Back outside, Naida began walking, meaning to get somewhere

quiet while the growing anger inside her resolved itself. She'd stumbled into something more complex than Ludeney's desire to replace the Queen once Naida had murdered her, though that was complex enough.

Every time she answered one question, another ten presented themselves. Like: why did Ludeney, who had overseen the arrest and execution of her parents, want the Queen removed if she was going along with the anti-Talent movement that, surely, he agreed with? Especially when she was on the cusp of being able to declare peace from a position of military dominance.

Naida couldn't help but feel that a concerted attempt was being made to shift the tectonic plates of power by upsetting societal norms and persuading people to clamour for change against their own interests. Worse, if she did manage to kill the Queen, no doubt Ludeney would unmask her as the daughter of the genocidal Esselrodes and the move against the Gifted would be complete.

But that hadn't been Ludeney's original intent when he came to announce her appointment. At that time, he'd had other assassins in mind, he'd said as much. Ludeney's fortune in seeing Naida for who she was gave him a means to kill the Queen while making it look like an accident. Unmasking her to cover his tracks was the obvious self-preservation move, and that meant the effective end of the Gifted would be collateral damage.

It led back to the core of the issue: who benefited from removing their greatest weapon in the war against disease and infection, and how? And why did she feel this whole conspiracy, if such it was, had begun with the execution of her parents?

Naida had to get access to the archives and, though she hated to admit it, she needed to talk to Ludeney too.

Chapter 16

'You and I need to talk.'

Misha, who had refused to move from the infirmary, was making a solid recovery, no doubt aided by a little of her own Talent now she was able to direct it herself and to do so without drawing attention.

Naida hadn't managed to get the infirmary relocated but the whole place smelled cleaner, looked brighter, and had a more positive atmosphere since it had been scrubbed raw and painted white. Holes had been knocked high up in the exterior walls to aid ventilation. The beds were laid out in rows, with a good distance between each pair and the whole place was orderly. Almost military. Drevien would approve and Naida looked forward to showing her.

But the smiles Naida was seeing now were all because she'd pulled off the impossible and retained Brin Gorvien. Naida wasn't feeling much like smiling though. Too much was wrong, and she was right in the middle of it.

'It is always a pleasure to talk to you,' said Misha, the glint back in her eyes, the strength in her aged body – and in her voice – returning. She was sitting up, reading a book, glasses perched on her nose and a cup of mint tea on a side table by her bed. She had been moved away from the heat of the lanterns, which still hung from the low ceiling. 'We'll soon be able to do so in the comfort of my rooms.'

'Can you walk?'

'I'm told that I can.'

'Good, let's get a little sunshine.'

If Misha was unsettled by Naida's curt tone, she wasn't showing it. She smiled, pulled away her blanket and swung her legs out of the bed. She was wearing a thin but expensive nightdress and pointed at a robe hanging at the end of the bed.

'Would you?'

Naida helped her into it, and saw that Misha was surprisingly steady on her feet.

'I'm pleased you're getting better.'

'Not as pleased as I am.'

Naida couldn't help but smile. 'No, I don't suppose I am. Come on, I found a back door into a little private garden. Ready for some fresh air?'

'Practically salivating for it,' said Misha.

They managed a few pleasantries on the short walk past the infirmary's offices, the new operating room and the stores, all of which sparkled with order and fresh paint. Naida was being assessed, or rather her mood was, and Misha was sifting through the reasons she might want to speak in private, and planning responses.

They walked into the garden. It was a small but pleasant affair: mainly lawn, with cushioned benches on each side, a fountain with wildflower borders, and plenty of bees. The garden was walled, studded with trellises upon which were climbing flowers and there was only one other way out: a wooden door in the far wall which, Naida had been told, led into a groundsman's plot.

They sat in the shade along the left-hand wall. One of the orderlies brought them tea and withdrew. The garden was beautiful, full of scents and colours.

'They should have a dog in here,' said Misha. 'They are a comfort and a healing aid, you know.'

'I'll mention it to Brin.'

Misha clacked her tongue. 'No, you won't, but it's fine, humour an old woman.'

Naida felt stung and it was a moment before she realised Misha, whose depth of experience became more apparent with their every meeting, was trying to throw her off her stride and take over the conversation.

'No, I won't humour you, Misha. I reckon you already know why I'm here.'

'You want to know why Ludeney wants the Queen dead, despite them both apparently wanting peace and an end to the evil scourge of the Talent?'

'That's part of it,' said Naida, grimly. 'And I want to know who's behind this fear-mongering against the Gifted. I mean, if you want to kill the Queen, you don't need me. Just keep advancing the anti-Gifted rhetoric and she'll die from cutting a toenail.'

Misha looked at her steadily. 'Not everyone will lose access to the Gifted. Surely you realise that?'

Naida closed her eyes, cursing her stupidity ... her naivety – a popular word to describe her today. Misha put a hand on hers.

'I can't imagine why the Queen hasn't introduced you to her personal team of Gifted, can you?'

'All right, you can stop now.'

'The Queen follows, she does not lead. And like all of her kind, she is nothing if not a hypocrite of staggering proportions. Her generals tell her when there will be peace, her donors tell her how she should feel and what she should say in public. She's cast her glamour over you, I'm sure. She's good at that. But there is no substance behind it. Does that answer your questions?'

Naida watched a bird land in a rose bed and jab at the topsoil, looking for worms and insects.

'So Ludeney wants to install his own puppet instead, and you don't see any hypocrisy there?'

'Who says the new monarch will be a puppet?' asked Misha. 'Any pretender must remain in the shadows while the path is cleared. Come on, Naida.'

'So, what does Ludeney want? Peace? An end to the Talent? I should at least know what agenda I'm serving, don't you think?'

Misha shook her head. 'It's no concern of yours, unless the Lord Marshal decides otherwise.'

'I've already been clear about this: I won't kill her, nor will I oversee her death. I'm not a murderer, and threatening to unmask me won't make me one. Do it. Until then, I'll carry on trying to fortify the city against the madness of removing the Gifted from it.'

Naida was ready to go but Misha squeezed her hand.

'I told you I was a friend and I mean that, never mind who I work for. I can tell you for certain: Ludeney does not want you dead.'

'I don't believe you,' said Naida. 'He had his soldiers chase me through my home to murder me. I was fourteen and it still gives me nightmares.'

For the first time, Misha looked uncomfortable. 'We all have things in our past we are not proud of.'

'I don't,' snapped Naida. 'What have you done that's so awful you wish it hadn't happened?'

'I'm on your side,' said Misha quietly. 'We are both of the Gifted. We both want to survive. Believe me when I say I am trying to plot a path for us to survive the mess being created around us.'

'I want to see Ludeney,' said Naida. 'He's pursuing the wrong path. Killing the Queen won't help, it'll send the city over the edge. Everyone loves her. If he wants her removed, maybe we can find another plan. After we've changed her mind, got her on the side of the Gifted.'

'It's gone too far,' said Misha.

'Set up a meeting. Meanwhile, I have other avenues to pursue, and if you're smart, you'll aid me.'

Misha pulled her robe more closely around her and Naida thought perhaps they had been outside for long enough.

'There is so much of your parents in you — your mother, in particular.'

Naida gaped. She felt a little faint, and her hands trembled about her tea.

'You *knew* them? How?'

'My dear, I was sent in to treat their wounds every night when they were returned to their cells. Their burns, their lacerations, their amputations. I eased their pain and listened to them insist on their innocence. They were always calm, measured and determined — once their scream-drawing agony had subsided and the memory of the day's baying crowd had faded to silence in their minds.'

Naida placed her mug on the ground and her face in her hands while she tried to hold herself together. This was too much. She had never been shielded from knowing her parents' fate: they had been tortured publicly every day and healed overnight, for day upon endless day, to atone for the pain they had caused and the long days the plague had ravaged Cantabria. The nation had flagellated their bodies to purge itself of guilt.

But this was new, an insight into their dying days. The knowledge that they had always insisted on their innocence. And it was Misha's shame.

'You were the one who kept them alive,' said Naida. 'To face further torture.'

'Those were my orders, but that is not what I did. It was

my honour to serve them, to follow their wishes,' said Misha. 'I offered to do nothing, let them die quickly. I even offered to help them on their way. But they asked me to ease their pain, and I did.'

Tears were on Naida's cheeks. 'I don't understand. Why would they want to stay alive in order to suffer? Why wouldn't they just want it over?'

'I don't know how they lived so long, even allowing for their Talent, when their injuries were so severe. Perhaps it was their determination to prove their innocence. They never wavered from their conviction.'

Naida had been taught they were guilty and that the evidence had been incontrovertible. Everyone knew *that* truth. But they were her parents even so and while nodding along, she had always refused to believe it. Yet the belief they had to be guilty was so hard to resist. The internal war had never been resolved.

Misha could see her struggle. She sighed. 'I know your protectors told you what they understood to be the whole story, but I was there, in their cells. Their stories were consistent. They were holding on for a specific piece of evidence to exonerate them. To allow their family name to be reinstated and for you to be freed from a life in the shadows.'

Naida felt sick and faint, her thoughts muddled. Every time she turned a corner, some part of the fabric of her life dropped away, leaving her further and further adrift.

'What ...?' Naida could barely frame her question into words. 'What did they say to you?'

'It isn't what you'd assume. They never begged, they never asked me to help them escape. They trusted that the truth ... the truth *as they saw it* ... would come out. They wanted to be alive to hear it.'

So, she'd inherited her naivety from her parents, then. 'I meant, what did they say had happened?'

'They didn't know. But they insisted they hadn't caused it. They were there to heal, they said, not to kill.'

'What piece of evidence, did they tell you? Did it even exist?' *Does it exist...?*

'I don't want to add to your pain, but it became ever more difficult to know where belief and coherence ended and mental incapacity born of exhaustion and torture began.' Misha studied Naida. 'They claimed all sorts of things towards the end about their links to the monarchy and plots against them, and I think they were hoping King Pietr would ride to the rescue, speak up for them. But the poor man was already lost.'

'Obviously their links to the monarchy weren't close enough,' said Naida, angry that when it came to it, the King, who had been such a friend to them, had cast them aside.

'I don't mean being close to the royal family, I mean they claimed they should have *been* the royal family.'

It was so ridiculous, Naida almost laughed but that ephemeral feeling was overridden by sadness at the desperate state of their minds towards the end. Naida didn't want to ask her next question. Nor did she really want an answer. There was no answer that could satisfy her or bring about any sort of closure to this traumatic turn of subject.

'Did you believe them? About their innocence, I mean.'

'I have wrestled with that question over and over,' said Misha, the memories distressing her. Her eyes, like Naida's, shone with tears.

'It's understandable,' said Naida.

'Everyone knew what had happened. *Everyone* knew that they were guilty. There was no other explanation. The trial stopped the whole city. People poured in from surrounding regions to be here, and the presses ran day and night to copy the transcripts and sate the appetite for information. The trial was public, nothing was hidden, and the outcome was clear.'

'There's a "but" coming, isn't there?'

Misha nodded. 'There was never a confession. The Esselrodes were found guilty despite maintaining their innocence in the face of the mountain of evidence against them. Like everyone else, I never doubted... not until I met them for myself, when they were at their most vulnerable: alone in their cells, in excruciating pain and with nothing to look forward to other than another day of sickening physical torment.'

Naida pulled her head out of her hands. 'Did no one stop to think why they would inflict that on themselves if they were guilty? There was never going to be a rescue, was there?'

'Yes, they had every reason to confess – it would have made their deaths quicker. But they didn't, and I swung between being sure they were so lost in their madness that they believed they had done nothing wrong, to thinking they must be innocent.'

Here it was: the notion that her parents, her childhood, and her identity, had been stolen by whoever had been behind the plague that had ravaged Cantabria and blamed her family. It was precious little comfort to realise others shared her belief.

'In those moments that you thought them innocent, what did you do?'

'Nothing, Lady Naida. What could I do? When I asked if I could help them, they told me to keep quiet. At the time, publicly believing them was a death sentence, as so many of your household discovered. The mood was that ugly, the crime that unforgivable.'

'Why now, though? I don't understand what has reawakened it now?'

'That is the key to the lock of all this, isn't it?' said Misha sadly. 'And it is a key that we will never find.'

'No—' said Naida, but her mind was racing.

'I'll get you your meeting with Yavin Ludeney. He'll delight

163

in talking to you, I'm sure. But his time is short, and so is his patience.'

'Thank you, Misha. Sorry for my tone earlier.'

'I'm surprised you weren't angrier. You're just like your mother: always in control.'

'I need to go; shall I help you inside?'

'No, dear, I'm enjoying the fresh air. I'll get myself back to bed when I need to, don't worry about me.'

Naida kissed Misha's cheeks and hurried back through the infirmary, instructing the orderlies to keep an eye on her.

Chapter 17

'How long have you been here?' asked Elias.

'Same as you. Almost two days,' said Naida.

'And you're already planning to commit a capital offence.'

'Are you sure you're not straying off-brief a little?' asked Adeile.

The Bonesaw Tavern was a lively affair. A big open bar area had music from a three-piece fiddle and drum band, and dancing, table service, and a separate bar serving an array of stews – not all of quality provenance if the prices were any guide. Around the edges of the bar were semi-private booths for hire, and most were full of couples, dealers, card games and one group of doctors from the King Olan Infirmary next door, judging by the snippet of conversation she overheard.

Smoke hung heavy in the air, scented with stale alcohol and sweat. Myriad conversations played out, some punctuated by the overloud laughter of the inebriated. There'd been one fight, over almost before it started, and Naida, who'd been recognised by an ex-army medic the moment she walked in, had checked the bruised party over, sent him back to the bar and had since been largely, and happily, ignored.

'I just want to get to the bottom of what's really going on.'

'I'm not sure why we should care, beyond the basics of fair treatment for all,' said Willan.

'You don't have to,' said Naida. 'But I do. You'll not find a medic in this place who isn't terrified at the prospect of medicine without the Talent. This is a densely populated city with large areas of poverty and poor sanitation. So no, Adeile, it isn't *off-brief* to find out why medicine's most useful tool is being removed.'

'So, we need more doctors, then,' said Aryn.

'Thousands and thousands of them, and all the best surgeons and their teams are already seconded to the army. There's no quick or safe way to cover the Talent gap. And no one but me, apparently, gets it.'

'Gets what?' asked Elias.

'If something like Shine Fever takes hold in the city, for example? It's easily curable with the Talent. But there aren't enough herbs and flowers in the city – maybe in the country – nor enough people to prepare and administer them, to save lives without it. One case on the first day is a hundred the next and tens of thousands a few days later, the majority of whom would die. That's why the Talent is so critical.'

'Would it really be that bad?'

Naida shrugged. 'Yes. Look how fast the plague in Cantabria spread after the ... it was triggered, and there was no Talent to stop it. The mortality rate was horrific. And now, they're using that very event, which the Talent could have prevented, as a reason to persecute the Gifted. It is perverse and disgusting.'

'Who is *they*?' asked Adeile.

'If I can get into the archives, I might be able to tell you ...' Naida spread her arms. At the same time, three serving staff appeared with trays of food and drink. A heady mixture of scents from meat, roasted vegetables and stewed fruits filled the booth. After being given fulsome thanks, the staff withdrew. 'Wow. This is some spread. Look, enough of my talking. Tell me what you saw out there today.'

Naida heaped her plate and let Willan refill her cup with chilled spiced wine. But she ate and drank very little as they talked, hearing more pieces moving into logical and worrying place on the political gameboard she'd fallen into and would, hopefully, mess up for those pulling the strings. Naida had never been good at metaphors.

'It's febrile down in the Fishooks and along the docksides to Ropers and the Old Landers,' said Elias.

'You're going to have to help me out. Where are they?' said Naida.

'Dockland slum areas, mainly. Places that used to be well-to-do until the trade dried up. I mean, it's not total destitution, but much of the housing is squalid tenements. Few Gifted will go there now, I heard. Not with vigilante groups trying to sniff them out. Known associates, whether Gifted or not, are being targeted too. Feels like battle lines being drawn up. The medics working down there are worried, like you. Getting into hot season now, too. Ripe time for disease.'

'How far are the docks from here?'

'Twenty minutes on foot to the river, then along the docks into the riverside slums beyond. It's a big area, rubs shoulders with the southern borders of the fish, fruit and cloth markets, which are frequented by rich and poor alike.'

'High-risk, then,' said Naida. 'Any other infirmary closer than the King Olan?'

'No.'

'So, I need teams from Olan to get into those areas daily. Thanks, Elias. Aryn?'

'I was up in the west. Fieldswalk, Hinds Row, Kingsmeadow … I mean, by their names we should judge them, eh? An hour on foot from here, Naida. Well-lit, tree-lined, cobbled streets and fancy houses. You get the picture. Now up there, there were never Gifted clinics, it was all home appointments. Doesn't seem to be too much change. They've seen extra military patrols in the area, and a clash with a gang looking for Gifted, but I didn't see too much fear. Not the tension Elias saw. In fact, I'd say they're keeping their Gifted close, protecting them.'

Naida nodded. She'd wondered if it was as stark as comfortable-and-wealthy versus poor-and-hungry and as the anecdotes came in, it became clear that it was. She wasn't surprised, given what Misha had said. But where was this anger, being deliberately generated, going to be directed? There was nowhere obvious for it to go. Once the Gifted were gone, what then? It begged the question, again, why the Queen would do nothing about it. But the Queen might only be hearing one side of it.

'Can you explore again tomorrow?' asked Naida. 'I'd like to plot it all out on a map, see where the lines are being drawn, if we can. Got to know where to direct resources.'

'What are you going to do?' asked Adeile.

'Well, in addition to doing the job I was brought here for, I need to find a way into the archives without getting myself burned in Traitor's Square for it.'

Naida stared at Adeile, who was beaming in a manner so unbearably smug it hurt her eyes. 'What?'

'I know how you can do both,' she said. 'You're going to call me a genius and love me forever.'

'Pretty bold statements. This had better be good,' said Naida.

'Well, you're the Queen's personal doctor, right? And it seems to me, you need to know her full medical history, and perhaps anything hereditary, in order to be able to treat her, right?'

'Can't argue with that.'

'Just thinking where all that very sensitive information might be kept, is all,' said Adeile.

Naida stood, leaned across the table, put her hands firmly on Adeile's cheeks and gave her a long and loud kiss on the lips.

'You are a genius and I will love you forever,' she said,

thinking she needed to find Dmitry as soon as possible the next morning.

Everything is recorded, he had said. *Nothing is thrown away.*

★

Any place described as a warren was, generally speaking, nothing of the sort. The records and archives beneath the Crucible, however, absolutely was a warren. So much so that anyone granted access needed a guide to navigate the unmarked corridors, rooms, alcoves and halls. All were home to shelves heaving with boxes; stacks of paper, rolled, flat and folded; tied and tagged bundles of files; glorious leather-bound books sorted by size or spine colour; and great rolls of tapestries.

The smells of old paper, wood and stone were redolent of history. It was all here. Somewhere. Walking the archives with her guide, a round-shouldered, middle-aged man with a pale complexion, what surprised Naida most was the ease with which she had been granted access.

Dmitry hadn't been in the Master of the Spires' office when Naida had dropped in but one of the other clerks had been more than happy to sign a standard form, authorising her to access the royal medical records. All the clever lines she had prepared were made redundant in an instant and she'd presented herself at the entrance to the archives, down a well-guarded set of stone steps set into the north wall of the Crucible, feeling obscurely disappointed.

There seemed to be a central path, a spine if you like, or perhaps a trunk was a better word? Yes, a trunk, from which branches sprung, from which twigs sprung. Some of the branches and twigs meandered until they joined others, some looked, from her glances as they passed doors and passageways, to be dead ends stuffed with paper.

'How big is this place?' she asked.

'Everyone asks that,' said the archivist, whose name was Stabile and who spoke in a dreary monotone.

'Probably because it's an interesting question. I mean, maybe not for you but for me ... so, what's the answer?'

'No one has measured it, so far as I know, because the information serves no purpose beyond satisfying the idle curiosity of tourists.'

'That's me told,' muttered Naida as another conversational gambit died.

It was warm and dry down here where she assumed it would have been cold and damp. It couldn't possibly be natural. And now she considered it, there was a gentle warm breeze caressing her ankles. Naida smiled.

'As a medic,' she said, 'I'm fascinated how you're managing to control the atmosphere down here, both temperature and humidity.'

Stabile turned, in the act of unlocking a door, and his eyes sparkled behind his specs.

'Now that *is* a worthy question. Let me show you.' So animated did he become as he strode back to the hall, beckoning her to follow and quickening his pace, that she worried for his hitherto stiff frame. 'In here: it's the easiest place to show you.'

He bustled between two sets of wood-framed shelves which, unusually, stood empty.

'We're just building better storage,' said Stabile, waving at the shelves. 'This will double the capacity, you know.'

The hall, lit by pipe-fed oil lanterns, rose four or five times her height above her head. She wouldn't describe it as bright but there was enough light to find what you wanted and for study: desks had their own free-standing lights, flint and steels.

'Down here, see?' Stabile pointed at a grille set in the wall at floor level. It was more than two feet on a side and a steady pressure of warm air flowed from it. 'Hot air system. I designed it. It's amazing, even if I say so myself.'

Naida's smile broadened at Stabile's justifiable pride. 'So, how does it work?'

'It all works on convection. There is a network of flues that service the entire archive system, and we're still building. They all lead back to a series of furnaces that heat the air inside narrow pipes that run across them like veins on the back of your hand. We use a system of shutters to produce convection currents that drive the warm, dry air into the wider flues and, ultimately, through these grilles.'

'And this system reaches every room? Wow.'

'Almost. We're connecting those that remain as fast as we can. There is so much history down here, we cannot risk losing it. It isn't a perfect system, but it keeps the archive from the ravages of mould for the most part. Come on, I'd better get you to where you need to be.'

'Thank you.' They retraced their steps. 'Why are the grilles so wide?'

'We need the heat to be gentle and spread evenly,' said Stabile, his lips very much loosened now. 'With narrower outlets, the spread is uneven. Larger outlets in walls and floor – and roof, where we can put them in safely – work far better.'

'Fascinating,' said Naida, hoping that he would keep talking. 'Presumably the furnaces are pretty close by?'

Stabile unlocked the door to the royal health archives and ushered Naida into a room packed with over four hundred years' worth of records detailing every malady to afflict every monarch and, he assured her, many others of the royal household staff.

'They are indeed. There's a series of administration and servicing buildings at the western end of the Crucible. It's all in there.'

'Have you ever crawled the flues yourself?'

171

Stabile shuddered. 'No. It may seem odd, given I work down here, but I'm claustrophobic. I leave that to the engineers.'

'This place ought to be a claustrophobe's worst nightmare, though,' said Naida. 'How do you survive it?'

'One cannot be fearful when one is surrounded by history, my lady.'

Naida felt the prick of tears. 'Oh. That's beautiful.'

'The truth always is,' said Stabile. He reached for a box and laid it on the desk in the centre of the room, which measured twenty by twenty feet, much of it occupied by shelves and cabinets. 'This is the index, as far as it goes. You'll find it filed by name of monarch; I'm not about to guess what you are looking for, but it shouldn't be too difficult to search. I'll check in with you periodically. Is that acceptable?'

'Yes, thank you.'

Stabile withdrew and Naida felt the weight of history bearing down on her. She lit the lantern on the desk, glad for the already-bright light from the ceiling but hungry for more. The warm air ruffled her hair where she stood beneath the grille. She wanted to head straight back to her friends and tell them of the ludicrous plan she had hatched ... but while she was here, she thought she might as well avail herself of the information about her key patient.

As it turned out, the ultimate bureaucracy was a bit light on details of its current monarch's health, which didn't surprise Naida at all, but what was there was fascinating and, for the future of the Rekalvian dynasty, made very unhappy reading. Small wonder Ludeney wanted her dead: she had no heir, her extended family was thinning out with age or had no claim to the throne, and the notes suggested she was infertile and that there was considerable work underway to find a cure. Work Brin Gorvien had been spearheading, making it all the more surprising he had been dismissed... unless he had failed in this task.

Glancing through the notes, some scrawled, some in impeccable script, Naida's eyes were drawn to the date on a piece written in a faint hand with many long letter tails and serpentine coils. On that date, placed in the margin, Eva would have been sixteen and Naida's parents would have been suffering their awful, prolonged execution. As she read, her heart went out once more to her Queen.

I have noted a deterioration in the mood of the young princess, as if she were suffering from what might be called a malaise of the spirit. I know it is not. The events of the day are weighing heavily on the young mind of a princess who can see the future and the central role she will play in it and is already struggling with how she might confront it.

Eva has always been active in the affairs of the palace and has always had the ear of her father, His Majesty, the King Pietr. With the slow despatch of the Esselrodes being played out in Traitor's Square daily, the King is necessarily diverted, and is in poor health himself, hence many of his duties have fallen on Eva's inexperienced shoulders.

While she has a strong mind and a powerful sense of duty, this is an unfortunate confluence of disaster, death and duty that may mark Eva forever. I recommend that her mind, mood and wellbeing be monitored closely in the days to come until she ascends the throne, and indeed beyond.

The signature was illegible and Naida tried not to judge, knowing hers was no better. Interest piqued, Naida fetched every box and sheaf of paper she could find on Eva's father, a dread fascination gripping her. There was scant information about him, which seemed wrong.

The events in Cantabria, leading to the arrest and execution of her parents in the midst of an exhausting war, would place tremendous strain on any monarch; particularly when they were such close friends. But what illness had he suffered? She had to know.

Pietr had been victim to very little, it seemed, and the meagre notes detailed his treatment by one or other of the Gifted in his service. That was, they were scant until a year before the genocide. From a slim, ribbon-tied file, Naida pulled out a series of notes written in a close script and detailing a series of discussions Pietr had with a member of the royal medical corps specialising in matters of the mind and mood.

Much of it was transcript and of little interest. Naida flicked through it, looking for analysis, diagnosis and any treatment that had been given. There were all sorts of concoctions that were a tonic for the mind, or could sharpen focus and lift moods, but there was little sign he had been prescribed any of them, barring a sign-off which read:

It has been concerning to see His Majesty misplace words, struggle to recall recent events and even forget the names of some of those close to him. But between these moments, the sheer depth of the King's involvement in day-to-day affairs is unsustainable. It has been very encouraging to see, through the peace and relaxation, the music and reading that has interspersed our conversations, that the King appears to have recovered much of his former sharpness and ready wit.

I strongly recommend that the King's Council review the King's workload and delegate as many tasks as can be countenanced to other, trustworthy, individuals and the Princess Eva, where applicable. I shall be speaking to the Master of the Spires at the earliest opportunity.

It was unsigned.

Naida sat back, feeling that this information was both important and insufficient. She had come in here to learn where the petitioners' records were kept, and that remained a mystery. Now, beyond the information that the Queen, apparent infertility aside, had enjoyed good physical health throughout her life, Naida had to find more evidence concerning both the Queen's and her father's emotional and mental states during that awful time.

Not just because it involved her family, she told herself, but because everything that was happening now had its roots in those events. If she hoped to push back against the tide of anti-Gifted sentiment, she had to understand the originating events. And that, she guessed, would require the minutes of King's Council meetings.

'Naida.'

'Shattered throne!'

Papers scattered to the floor from the desk. The lantern teetered on the edge. Naida tried, belatedly, to snatch paper from the air and maintain her balance on her chair. A hand reached round and caught the lamp, replacing it on the desk. Naida looked to her right.

'Dmitry ... ash and water, you scared me.'

'I rarely have that effect on anyone ... lost in your research, were you?'

Dmitry was looking at the few papers left on her desk and she gathered them up, unsure why she didn't want him to see what she'd been studying.

'Just catching up on Rekalvian medical histories,' said Naida, dropping to her haunches to start collecting all she had spilled. 'What are you doing here?'

'I thought you might want some company.' Dmitry knelt

down to help her, his eyes roving over every page he touched before placing them on the desk. 'Can I help you refile this?'

Naida wanted to say no, but it would be suspicious and anyway, why shouldn't she look at all this? It was her job to know.

'You do know King Pietr is dead, right?' said Dmitry, smiling.

'Very funny.' Naida's heart was still rattling away, making her breathless. She wanted nothing more than to be away from here. 'It's important to be alert for hereditary conditions.'

Dmitry lifted his hands in a gesture of peace. 'You don't have to explain yourself to me. Find anything interesting?'

'Nothing to worry any of us where the Queen is concerned, you'll be glad to know,' said Naida.

Her hands were shaking, and she was struggling to rearrange the stack of notes about Pietr's state of mind. She hated that she had become so flustered and embarrassed. It was not a ringing endorsement for her as a surgeon.

'It's a relief that you've found nothing to worry anyone,' he said and consulted the index file. 'Right, let me get this stuff back on the shelves . . . is there anything here you needed?'

'No, nothing, thanks. Are you good at getting out of here or do we need the eventually loquacious Stabile to make our escape?'

Dmitry laughed and it broke the tension. He placed the sheaves, files and boxes back in their places.

'He's quite a character, isn't he? I presume you got him going about his ventilation system.'

'It did seem to unlock him,' said Naida, hoping she wasn't blushing. 'And to be fair, it is pretty amazing.'

'That it is. And yes, I know my way around here. Come on, I'll buy you a drink.'

Leaving the room and moving back into the hall after Dmitry assured her Stabile would lock up behind them later, Naida shuddered, imagining how their meeting might have gone had she been reading something she shouldn't.

'So much paper,' said Dmitry. 'And to think that, once it's down here, ninety-nine point nine per cent will never be touched by human hand again.'

'So why doesn't it get burned? I mean, it's sitting down here, below the Crucible, as a massive fire risk anyway. Better to take it outside and be proactive?'

While she walked, Naida tried to remember every turn, every branch passage, every solid or iron-grill door, so she could scribble a map later. The scale of the place gave her shivers and the lack of any signage to indicate the location of the information she wanted would give her sleepless nights.

'Ah, but who decides what gets destroyed? Actually, I'll tell you: the archive is managed and operated by the legislature and all its many bureaucrats, alongside the Master of the Spires' office. There is no committee that oversees the content. If you want something removed and destroyed, you can petition for it through the Crucible. Who in their right mind would bother? All it does is draw attention to the documents in question. Better to let them be lost down here.'

'Does anyone know where everything is kept?' asked Naida.

'No.' Dmitry chuckled. 'Wouldn't be safe, would it? Most archives and records come down here unmarked. You're lucky there's an interest and value in keeping medical records available.'

'Such as they are...'

Dmitry glanced at her. 'Oh, scarce, were they?'

'That's a generous way to describe it,' said Naida. It was an answer that seemed to please him, for some reason. 'But some of it is behind locked doors and some of those locked doors are pretty sturdy. So, some people must know where to put the, presumably, most sensitive material.'

'Best not to prod too far in that direction,' said Dmitry. 'What is hidden is hidden by those with the power to keep it so and punish those who try to uncover it.'

'All right, Dmitry ... just making conversation,' said Naida, a little taken aback by the ire in his tone. Dmitry waved his hands irritably and increased his pace.

'I'd just rather not be drawn on the subject. People hear what they want to hear.'

'Who would hear?' demanded Naida. 'There's no one down here but Stabile and us. And it's fascinating, isn't it? Think about it. There's stuff down here that is, presumably, damaging to the reputations or even freedom of powerful people. How could they allow it to be stored down here, like a plague boil ready to burst? Do they not know it's here?'

'I've really no idea.'

'Dmitry, stop!' Naida stopped and waited for him. He walked on a few paces, realised she wasn't with him and turned. 'What's going on? Why are you really down here? It wasn't to keep me company, was it? Why are you watching me?'

'What are you talking about? I'm here because I want to help you. There's nothing sinister about it.'

Dmitry began walking back, a look of hurt across his face.

'Until I ask the wrong question.'

'Some questions carry more risk than others and I'm trying to stop you getting yourself into trouble.'

'With who? You?' Naida jabbed a finger at him. 'How can there be *wrong* questions?'

Dmitry stopped a few paces away and sighed. 'No ... look, I think we're at cross purposes here.'

'You're telling me.'

They were standing in a passageway with alcoves on one side, and a series of well-spaced doors, most iron-banded or made of heavy oak, on the other. Their voices, never loud but raised, echoed along its length to be swallowed by the deadening weight of paper in one of the halls.

'Down here lies the history of Suurken, of the monarchy and people of circumstance and influence across the centuries. Some of it is dark and ugly, but it's still ours. Some of it requires context for the actions and decisions to be understood, and if it became public without that, it would be to the detriment of us all.'

'So, the truth doesn't matter?' asked Naida, wincing inwardly, knowing that her life from the age of fourteen had been an intricate lie.

'When the truth can do damage greater than the perpetuation of an assumption, or the propagation of a lie, then a judgement should be made.'

'I'd absolutely say that if I was guilty of something I was desperate to hide,' said Naida. 'Wow, this isn't what I expected when I popped down here to check on the Queen's medical records. Anything I should know about them?'

'Nor me,' said Dmitry, and he smiled at last. 'And I've no idea. The medical archives are the province of the head of the royal medical services. You know: you.'

'Oh. Good to know.'

'Are we done?'

Naida shrugged and they began walking again. 'All I know is, if I was aware that compromising records existed concerning my actions, I'd be desperate for them to be destroyed.'

'Hence the very heavy doors, guarded every moment of every day by the Crucible militia,' said Dmitry.

'Everyone can be bought, can't they?'

'You still have much to understand about how the legislature and Crucible systems operate. I don't mean that to sound patronising, sorry.'

'I'm sure you're right.'

179

'So, is it wine or coffee?' asked Dmitry.

Naida shook her head. 'Another time, eh? I need to make notes before I forget it all.'

'That does rather sound like a brush-off.'

'I leave it to you to decide whether I'm speaking the truth or propagating a lie.'

Chapter 18

Back in her rooms, Naida snatched some paper from the writing desk and sketched what she could remember of the archive layout. But she couldn't concentrate. Every time she told herself she was overthinking it she recalled her unsettling encounter with Dmitry, which read as both a warning and proof that he had been tasked to watch her. But by whom, and what had she done to make them worry about her so much?

The list was short. The Queen? Maybe she had everyone watched until she felt she could trust them. Denharl? He seemed the most likely candidate because he clearly felt he could use her. Ludeney? Maybe. But it seemed unsubtle for him.

In some ways, 'who' didn't matter, the fact it was happening did. She'd done nothing problematic so far, beyond protesting about the persecution of the Gifted. But, if she could persuade her sceptical friends to help her, that was about to change.

Naida looked back at her sketch, wondering how long it would take to find the information she needed to begin to unpick the mystery she hadn't realised existed until Misha's astonishing testimony. She chuckled. Misha's words had not been uttered by chance. She, and perhaps Ludeney, had wanted her to know. And now she wanted to know why. What exactly had happened during that grim time?

There was a knock on her door, and she jumped out of her skin for the second time that morning. She called for whoever it was to come in while she stowed her embryonic map at the bottom of the paper drawer in her writing desk. She turned to see Thierrin waiting for her.

'The Queen will see you now,' he said.

'But I'm not...'

'The Queen will see you now.' Thierrin was enjoying her discomfort. 'She is waiting in her private reception chambers.'

'I... Well, of course. I'm at Her Majesty's disposal.'

'Indeed, you are. Follow me.'

And Naida did, because walking next to the smug royal official might involve talk and she'd rather gnaw her own foot off than engage him in conversation. Thierrin did not walk fast, but neither did he take the circuitous route he'd enjoyed so much the first time, and within minutes he showed her into the reception rooms, unhappy at the respect shown to her by the guards on the doors. Naida's smile was wider than normal.

The Queen was standing at the side table that displayed her appalling duck. When the doors closed behind Naida, Eva turned, and her expression was unreadable. Others might call it carefully neutral, but Naida could see the tension in her body and the very slight tremble in her hands. She was angry. Naida would have to tread carefully.

'You've been busy this morning,' said the Queen.

'Yes. The archives are amazing – quite the experience, and not one I'd choose to relive.'

'The shelves holding the weight of so much recorded history by default also hold the weight of so much recorded death. It is a burden that oppresses the atmosphere.'

'You've been down there?'

The Queen's expression lightened for a moment. 'For a young princess who could go where she pleased, it was the best place for hide and seek. Though I was never allowed behind any locked doors.'

'Your and your father's records are happily unexciting for the most part. I saw there was one area in which treatment was being investigated, which had not been mentioned in my examination, and I am happy to continue it.'

'The issue is that you should never have been allowed down there without a briefing, and preferably not allowed down there at all.'

Naida breathed easy. This was about the Queen's lack of an heir that she'd alluded to during her examination, and she was not angry with her new head doctor. On the other hand, someone in the Master of the Spires' office was in for some career-limiting trouble.

'It was important that I read the medical histories,' said Naida. 'In addition to your excellent responses to my questions, old notes often reveal things that should not be forgotten.'

'And sometimes they reveal things that should. It's lunchtime, shall we eat?'

'I ... yes, I'd be honoured. Are you sure you can spare the time?'

Eva laughed. 'I'm the Queen.' She walked to a bell pull and gave it a single tug. 'And I have the perfect place.' The door to the reception room opened and a palace maid and a lady-in-waiting entered.

'Your wish, Your Majesty?' asked the lady-in-waiting.

'Lunch, Olga. In the Garden Room. For two.' She indicated Naida. 'We will have the dishes Cook Roan and I discussed just yesterday. I think the marinades will have had enough time. And bring wine. Lots of wine. Oh, and Olga?'

'Yes, Your Majesty?'

'Inform the infirmary that Lady Naida is attending me this afternoon and will not be making rounds today.'

'Your Majesty.'

Olga shot Naida a look of pure envy and withdrew, hurrying the maid out with her. Naida caught the Queen's eye.

'Yes, she'll hate you and she'll tell everyone that I'm wasting my time with a mere doctor when I have affairs of state to deal with but—'

'You're Queen.'

Eva smiled. 'Precisely. Shall we?'

The change in Eva's mood was startling and this was not the first time her mood had turned on the point of a scalpel. Naida reminded herself she was about to spend the afternoon with her Queen, not a friend, no matter how much alcohol was consumed.

Traps lay ahead.

★

'This is where I come when I don't want my conversation overheard, but where I can be sure my laughter will carry, and everyone will wish they were here,' said Eva.

Naida wasn't sure whether to be honoured, excited or terrified. But the Garden Room was beautiful and tranquil. A set of double doors opened off a tapestry-hung corridor from the Queen's dressing room and bedchamber into a garden built, Eva said, above the Throne Room. It was filled with flower borders and beds, and pretty stone pathways.

Benches sat around simple fountains at either end, and at its centre stood an iron and stone pagoda covered in manicured bougainvillea, clematis and rose. Pillars stood at each corner and lace curtains were attached to each one, ready to be pulled across the otherwise open structure if desired.

Much of the perimeter of the garden was stone covered in trellising and a gorgeous display of climbing plants, perhaps even more impressive than that occupying the pagoda, but there were windows here and there, and two other sets of doors. Plenty of places for the voyeurs to cluster.

A circular table had been covered in a pristine white cloth and laid with two settings involving an impressive volume of cutlery, suggesting more courses than Naida was used to. A servant stood by a side table upon which stood three flagons and several pairs of wine glasses and goblets. The Queen waved him to pour a deep green wine into two goblets and then dismissed him with a second, almost identical wave. She scooped up both and handed one to Naida.

'To friendship, honesty and trust,' she said.

'Friendship, honesty and trust,' Naida repeated.

They sipped and Eva indicated they should wander through the rose and wildflower beds towards one of the fountains. She sat them on a cushioned stone bench where they could both see all three sets of doors and had a blank wall behind them. Before Eva spoke, Naida realised the fountain water would mask their words. Nothing the Queen did was by accident.

'I am not infertile,' said Eva.

Naida, whose glass had been halfway to her lips, found herself so comprehensively surprised she was grateful she was already sitting down. She froze, trying to shoehorn her thoughts into some form of coherent order, failed and took a sip of her drink. Well, more of a gulp because when she was done her glass was empty.

'That's ... quite a piece of news, given what I've read today,' said Naida.

'Well, that depends on your point of view. Why don't you get yourself a refill?' Eva's eyes sparkled and she patted Naida on the knee when she sat back down. It should have been condescending, but Eva was being genuinely sympathetic. 'I want to be clear about this now because once I've drunk my share of all those flagons, you may not take me seriously anymore.'

'I'm listening. Tell me about *the treatments*, and the Queen's Council's surely ever more volcanic concerns that you have not yet produced an heir.'

'You have a delightful turn of phrase,' said Eva. 'I have undergone a number of well-intentioned treatments, which have been formulated to address a fertility problem it was wrongly assumed I had. No statement made to the then-chief medical officer by my team of the Touched ... the Gifted ... would dissuade him of his diagnosis.'

'So, what was the problem?'

'I don't want children. Therefore, I'm not having them.'

'How—' Naida stopped. She wondered if any monarch had ever decided to end their family's direct line of succession. 'I hesitate to be indelicate, but have you attempted to conceive?'

'That's a terribly polite way of phrasing it,' said Eva. 'I am impure in all the most wonderful of ways.'

'That wasn't quite—'

'I fell in love once, too,' said Eva and the catch in her voice broke Naida's heart.

She wanted to reach out a hand in comfort but the Queen withdrew fractionally, needing to say what she wanted to say independent of any support. Her faint smile was tinged with such terrible sadness.

'I was sixteen. Too young, you'll say, but I'd been presented with suitors since I was fourteen. Thought I knew it all and I have still never again experienced the ... lightness ... that came with his attention, his touch, his love of everything that I was. And I was awakening and we stole away, in secret, I thought, and I was pregnant and engaged to be wed and my life was pure joy.'

Eva laughed and tears spilled on to her cheeks. 'Oh, just look at me. Fifteen years ago now and still I'm a mess.'

'You don't have to tell me anything more.'

'Oh, I do, because everything stemmed from this. And it's all been inside me for so long.'

Naida nodded, trying not to take too big a breath at the honour bestowed on her.

'I should have known that nothing happens without a plot behind it,' said Eva. 'There was I, a princess in love, rushing to tell my father the news but he'd got there first, my Haronic prince. My betrothed was already enjoying his King's favour and there they sat, discussing his adoption of the Rekalvian name, the design of his cushion on the Shattered Throne and how far my lesser throne should be placed from his when he became king.'

'I am so sorry,' said Naida. She took Eva's hand, aware it was a terrible breach of etiquette, but Eva was trembling. 'I should never have asked.'

'I lost the baby.' The breeze stopped blowing a moment, it seemed, and heat flushed in. Naida squeezed her hand even harder, and Eva squeezed back. 'I thought it was a blessing at first, stupid me. Instead, when I refused to lie with him again my father said it didn't matter, the prince could father bastards and the wedding would proceed. Sadly, the Haronic prince met with an accident.'

Naida tensed and withdrew her hands. Eva stared at her a moment.

'Well, what would you have done?'

'Probably the same,' said Naida. 'It's a horrible story.'

'It gets little better. After the Haronic, he promised me to all sorts of suitors if they could impregnate me. How's that for paternal love? Funny how mentioning the fate of the Haronic withered their lust and their faux romance. That's when they decided I must be infertile. After all, how could I not be preg-nant after meeting all those lovely young men?'

'But the risk you took was enormous,' said Naida. 'And I

presume you knew what the ramifications of apparent infertility were for you.'

'My very own gilded cage,' said Eva. Her voice had never broken. There was no self-pity. Her strength was remarkable, formidable. 'There were times I thought death might be the best way out. As an only child, that would have been a mortal blow to my legacy-obsessed father, but I wouldn't have been there to see his face when he realised it was all over.'

'To see what was all over?' asked Naida.

Eva smiled. 'Why, the monarchy, of course.'

The doors on all sides opened and servants walked in with covered trays. Naida was still reeling and didn't notice until Eva began pulling her up by the hand. She wasn't just talking about her line, but of the monarchy as an institution.

'Come on,' she said. 'Enough of this seriousness. Let's sit down, eat, drink, and tell stories. I'd love to hear the truth of all the tales told about you.'

Naida gave a thin smile. 'I'd be delighted.'

She was neither hungry, nor in the mood to drink, but no one denied a Queen, and certainly not one who had been through such trauma. This Queen deserved anything she wanted, if it distracted her from her memories.

They sat, toasted one another again and Naida let the glorious scents of the perfect lunch wash over her. Eva dismissed the servants, then bade Naida forget herself, and the world, and relax.

'Tell me,' she said. 'Is it true that you saved a cavalry officer who had lost both his legs and had him back on a horse to lead the victory charge?'

'Partially,' said Naida. She took a long swallow of some smooth fruit-laden white wine. 'So...'

★

Naida was drunk. Eva was drunk. Dusk was creeping up on them, and the heat of the day was dissipating. Lunch had become dinner and neither of them wanted to call time. But Naida had not forgotten the Queen's last words before lunch had arrived, all those hours ago, and try as she might, she couldn't let it go. She needed a way back in and it would be tonight, or the moment would be lost forever.

'…no, what you said was *I don't miss the battlefield* and then you talked for almost ever about how much you missed the battlefield,' said Eva.

'Point of order!' Naida put her hand in the air. 'Your royal highness of highness.'

'Granted, minion.'

'I did not talk about how much I missed the battlefield, but how much I missed the people I worked with on or near the battlefield. I contend that there is a difference.'

'Pedantry and hair-splitting,' said Eva. 'Drink.'

Naida did and Eva filled her goblet with more of the black-currant wine.

'It remains true.'

'Is that why you've asked for so many of those people to come and infest my palace?'

'Three of them. And thank you for agreeing to my request.'

'Is that a point of order?'

'No, because you'll rule that three is an infestation. Drink!'

Eva drank and refilled her goblet, her hand still rock-steady. In front of them lay the wreckage of a great meal. There was still some fruit, cheese and sweet biscuits left, but mostly it was a scene of culinary devastation, and it had been wonderful. Briefly, Naida had been transported back to the longest dinner of her life – the night she'd met Ludeney – and remembered how each flavour had contributed to her nausea.

This afternoon, though, in the company of a delightful

woman and blessed by sunshine, warmth and birdsong, that memory was a world away. Though she thought she knew why Ludeney was so desperate to kill his Queen and have it look accidental. And indeed, why he thought she might want to help him.

The city was being brought to fever pitch – a state which could so easily spread. The overt assassination of a popular monarch would provoke widespread unrest, even civil war. Ludeney had to act from the shadows, putting his man or woman in place as the natural successor to carry on Eva's great work – or something – before her tragic demise.

Naida wondered again who Ludeney wanted on the throne, and what would happen if she told Eva why she was here ... and who she really was. And though she was beginning to understand Eva, and marvel at the Queen's strength of character, she did ask herself whether she was the right person to be on the throne.

The question was easy to dismiss, if you wanted to. After all, she *was* Queen. For good or ill. And her disastrous path of restricting, and inevitably outlawing, the work of the Gifted aside, she was the Queen about to end a war that had dribbled on for three decades, draining Suurken of the best of its people and its potential to advance. She was a good Queen. And yet ...

'You know they all want me dead, don't you?' said Eva.

She'd done it again. That combination of mind reading linked to verbal flay-shot, designed to provoke an unguarded reaction. Naida started and spilled wine over her hand. She looked up to see Eva staring at her, that anger burning in her face again. She was sizing Naida up, trying to assess if she was one of *them*.

'Who do?' asked Naida.

Eva shrugged and waved a hand. 'Everyone. Well, nearly everyone. Most of the Queen's Council, I think. The generals who worry what they'll do if they aren't sending young men and women to die over long-forgotten sleights. Take your pick: if they rely on the continuation of the monarchy or war for their livelihoods, they want me gone.'

'Or are Gifted.' That stopped Eva in her tracks, and Naida feared she'd gone too far. All the goodwill of the evening might be about to burn like paper in a furnace. 'These are enemies you don't need to make.'

'But my people are the only allies I have. If I lose the support of my subjects, I'm as good as dead.'

'You really think someone will try to kill you?' asked Naida, impressed by the genuine surprise in her voice.

'Maybe not immediately, but when they realise the extent of my intentions ... well. I have you to save me, so that's a start.'

'And what do you intend? Tell me it's none of my business, but I'd love to know when to stand by with the bandages.'

Eva laughed. 'Thank you for not being afraid of me.'

'A life spent hoping a catapult round won't squash you will do that to a person.'

'I have no doubt,' said Eva. 'I've been Queen for over a decade, though it feels like a lifetime. Maybe because my father lost his mind in the last two years of his reign, and I was pretty much in charge. That was a blessing, in a way; at least he didn't have the wit to find new suitors for me, and those sycophants who still tried had a tendency to end up dead like the Haronic.'

Naida took a long, slow drink. Every statement about the brutality of her life before she ascended the throne was more tragic. It said much about her clarity of thought. Perhaps she did know Naida was here to kill her.

'Have you ever been able to relax?' asked Naida.

'You see, you do get it,' said Eva. 'I'm so glad you're here. I wanted the best doctor possible, and I got a sister, too. Thank you.'

It was probably the wine talking but Naida's heart swelled

with pride, and opportunity. She refilled both their goblets, pleased to see her hand was as steady as the Queen's.

'You'll never be alone while I work for you,' she said.

'The Queen is never alone,' intoned Eva.

'You know what I mean.'

Eva smiled and a tear spilled from her left eye. 'What do we do now?'

'Keep you healthy, keep those who would do you harm from your door. Buy you the time to do whatever it is you need to do.'

Eva made to speak then closed her mouth, evidently thinking better of it. She let her gaze drop to her lap, considered her words, nodded and began again.

'I intend to leave this country a better place than I found it. A country at peace. With its sons and daughters returned to their mothers and fathers; with the whole of our people working for the whole of our country. Where the people decide how the country runs. Where the monarch is made redundant, consigned to history as part of the journey the country had to make. And that's because no princess ten generations from now should suffer betrayal by her own father. Sick systems need to be excised.'

Naida found it impossible to believe that any monarch would give up their power, influence, and all the riches that went with it. Even Eva, who seemed desperately unhappy to be Queen. But she'd said this twice now and there was no lie in her that Naida could see.

But her apparent naivety worried Naida. At once saying people wanted her dead and at the same time claiming none knew of her plans. Her determination to remain childless would be enough to spook some into looking elsewhere for a royal line. Naida wondered how much Ludeney knew.

'It's quite some dream. Is it really your goal, to remove your own authority? If I may, seeing the people determine that the Talent should be restricted or outlawed makes me question whether they are ready for more responsibility.'

'Everything will be done at a pace and a time of my choosing. There will be no cliff from which we step, but a gentle set of stairs we ascend to a brighter future.'

Eva giggled, pleased with her prosaic statement. She toasted herself.

'I can help you. If you give me the tools,' said Naida.

'The tools cannot be the Touched.' Eva refilled her goblet once more. 'But eventual rehabilitation for those who have transgressed is always possible.'

Eva waved a hand and the doors opened to disgorge servants who cleared away the debris of their meal and brought fresh flagons of wine.

'Let us toast us,' said Eva. 'Sisters by the bonds of trust and friendship, never to be broken.'

Chapter 19

Sleep had been fitful and unhelpful. Dawn had arrived with unseemly haste and now Naida was being dragged from her bed by an urgent hammering on her door. Her stomach was threatening to empty itself violently and her head was a thundering reminder of how much fun she'd had yesterday.

'All right, I'm coming.'

Naida dragged off her night shirt and found her clothes from the day before in a heap. They'd do. She pulled on her undergarments, shirt and trousers on the way to the door, and pulled it open knowing she must look like she'd just stepped out of a hurricane.

'The Qu—' Thierrin, impeccably turned-out and as fresh as a morning breeze, took one look at her and couldn't suppress his smile. It was the first breach in his haughty persona. 'Oh, I see you already know how she's feeling. Sadly for you, it's your job to cure her and her job to complain about how terrible she's feeling.'

Naida pushed a hand through her hair. 'I'll get my bag.'

'You've time to wash your face and tuck in your shirt,' said Thierrin. He sat on one of the chairs in her hallway. 'But not for much else.'

'Great.' Naida walked as gracefully as she could into her

bathroom, splashed cold water on her face, dragged a brush across her head and straightened her clothes as best she could. 'I'm good to go.'

'Your bag?' said Thierrin, and the humour on his face was good-natured.

Naida blushed scarlet. 'Nearly good to go.'

Thierrin hurried her to the Queen's apartments, down the now-familiar corridors and along to her suite of private rooms. Before passing the inevitable guards, Thierrin opened a couple of doors on the left-hand side of the cabinet-lined hallway. Naida stopped and stared.

'These might be useful to you: a small but comprehensive apothecary and a medical facility. Specialists you can call on at any time.'

'This would have been great to know on day one.'

'I didn't like you on day one,' said Thierrin.

'Well, that's honest, at least. What changed?'

'You stopped being perfect.'

'Shattered throne, I never started being perfect!'

'Still,' he said and indicated the guards should open the double doors. 'After you.'

The taint of vomit hung in the air, as did the scent of soap and perfume. Every window of the reception room was open to the new day and a fresh breeze ruffled the net curtains and disturbed the pages of an open book lying alone on a low wooden table.

White-painted and high-ceilinged, the room was bedecked with portraits of past monarchs and of royal families at play, chasing through gardens, playing racquet sports or enjoying picnics. Apparently, summertime was eternal back in the old days. But this was a deliberately happy room and Naida had no doubt that Eva had made it so.

'Where is she?'

'In her bedchamber, I suspect,' said Thierrin. 'I may not go in there, but as her physician, you do have access.'

'Thank you, Thierrin.'

'My pleasure. I hope your hangover dissipates quickly.'

Naida walked into the shuttered room and found she was not the only one with access to the Queen's bedchamber. Three servants stood at the side of the room with bowls, fresh sheets and towels at the ready while, surrounding the impressive bed itself, were about half the Queen's Council, affecting concern but in fact muttering disapproval.

'Yes, yes, yes,' said Naida with as much bustle as she could muster. 'The Queen is feeling a little fragile this morning but it's nothing I can't alleviate. You can all go now, thank you for your concern.'

The ire that was turned her way was impressive in its suffocating power. In the merciful gloom, to which her eyes were adjusting quickly, Naida saw Denharl, Velez and Kerslan glaring, alongside some of the others whose names she hadn't cared to ask for.

'It is a serious matter that Her Majesty is in no fit state to attend no less than three meetings of state this morning. Her presence at the people's petition round table late this afternoon is also in serious doubt,' said Denharl.

The taint of vomit was stronger in here, emanating from the bathroom but also rather closer to the Queen's head.

'Those important meetings of state slipped my mind while I was having an important meeting of state yesterday lunchtime,' said the Queen.

'Your Majesty, I'm not sure an afternoon with your doctor has quite the same import as a meeting with the ambassador of Greater Perroda,' said Ianna Velez, the Minister of State for Royal Affairs.

'I'm not sure anything is more important than improving the

health, and hence life, of the Queen of Suurken,' said Naida, prompting some sharply indrawn breaths.

'Oh, well played,' said Eva, adding a rather weak clap to her inflammatory words.

'Your Majesty is too kind,' said Naida, mentally adding all of the Queen's Council present here to the list of people who already thought she was far too close to the monarch. 'But we are getting distracted. I need to be alone with the Queen to begin to ease her malady.'

'A malady you saw inflicted upon her and did nothing to prevent,' said Kerslan.

'Had I been made aware of the Queen's agenda for today, by you or by any of the staff to the personal private secretary, I would perhaps have recommended more water.'

'Oh, you're good,' said the Queen. 'Clear the room. I think I'm going to throw up again.'

Without the Queen's Councillors in the room, it felt cooler. Naida walked to the head of Eva's bed. Even in the gloom, she could see the Queen's complexion was grey.

'Oh dear,' she said.

'I think you're supposed to be positive about my condition. How do you feel?'

'Terrible, thank you for asking but, really, we need to get you ready for the day, don't we?'

'We do.'

'Are you about to be sick?'

'No, there's nothing left to eject.'

'Well, that's a start,' said Naida.

'You'd better have some amazing potion you can mix up,' said Eva. 'Some army thing you all swear by. That is why I hired you, after all.'

Naida chuckled. 'Well, if the apothecary has turmeric and nettle root, I might have just the thing.'

'Good. Mix it up with all speed. And make one for yourself. We can toast yesterday in a slightly more sober fashion.'

'I'll be back soon.'

'I'm so glad I can trust you,' said Eva. 'I set such great store in trust. Life is unbearable without it.'

★

Naida was sitting in the shade on a small private roof terrace accessed from near her rooms, considering Eva's not-very-well-veiled warning while her internal voice berated her for her stupidity in getting so very drunk.

It was entirely in keeping with her mood and physical state that the door should open to admit the person she least wanted to see in all the world, despite having asked to see him. What was the opposite of serendipity? *Unfortunate timing* really didn't cover it.

'Quite the life, my lady. I used to enjoy this terrace myself before taking rooms a couple of doors along from Lord Denharl. I rather wish I hadn't moved.'

'The city of hate ruled by the Queen of love,' said Naida, not rising as Ludeney approached. 'It's been *such* an experience so far.'

'An extreme take on both counts,' said the Lord Marshal. He was wearing what, for him, must be casual clothes: a high-collared and knee-length, deep green topcoat, white shirt, high-lace boots and black trousers. Not a braid in sight.

'A paradox.'

'How so?' Ludeney gestured at the seat and Naida shrugged her reluctant permission for him to sit.

'There is so much to love about her... her strength, her intelligence, her *humanity*. It makes it all the more confusing that she appears to support, or at least not oppose, the demonising of the Gifted.'

'You have a unique opportunity to remove that support. Inaction has reigned though, has it not?'

'I've been here for three days. And if your spies are calling my work inaction, they're not very good spies, are they?'

'I don't need a spy to tell me that the Queen doesn't look particularly ill.'

Naida laughed before she spoke. 'She's got a cracking hang-over today, as it happens.'

Ludeney remained impassive. 'Time is short.'

'Glad you're aware of the looming health emergency too. I need serious resources and a reversal of the anti-Gifted rhetoric.'

Ludeney's nostrils pinched and he exhaled irritably. It was a small victory.

'You're here to achieve one task. You asked for this meeting and here I am to hear about your progress. Progress that has been insignificant, unless you can tell me otherwise?'

Naida felt like laughing straight in his face but instead man-aged a more diplomatic approach.

'What sort of progress am I supposed to have made in three days?'

The doors to the terrace opened again and servants walked out bearing trays of tea and fruit, placing them on a low wooden table and withdrawing.

'That was good of you, thank you,' said Naida.

Ludeney smiled. 'I am not without humanity, as you will discover in these coming days and seasons… I have been briefed; I know how you and the Queen spent yesterday afternoon.' He paused, but she said nothing. 'I know you have retained your predecessor to continue doing much of the work, and have spent most of your time, when not drunk with the Queen, refitting the infirmary, eating out with friends and visiting the Crucible. These don't constitute a plan of even the vaguest outline.'

Naida shrugged. 'You missed the bit where I left an eatery to try to save a life.'

'Aye, and failed because you were unable to reveal your Talent.'

That stung.

Naida poured some tea into the tall cups, and the aromas of fresh mint and ginger were most welcome. She took a sip, the liquid firing her throat.

'But not because of events in the city. Because of the disguise I have taken and must maintain. And even if it was because of the anti-Talent surge, killing the Queen is not the answer, changing her is. I have told you I will not kill her – I won't kill anyone – but I will work with you to set her back on the right path. I know it can be done.'

'Ah.' Ludeney tipped his head back. 'So, your plan is naivety: assuming you can change a queen's mind. That is idiotic on so many levels and even if it were possible, you cannot change her infertility, can you?'

'She's n—'

Naida didn't quite catch herself in time. Ludeney's face registered her failure.

'Go on,' he snapped, his cheeks colouring.

Naida felt herself calm completely, her battlefield surgeon training kicking in, natural like frost in winter.

'She is not infertile, but she will not suffer children to be born into a broken and amoral system. Betrayal of your future by your father and the man you thought loved you will do that to a princess. And no doubt it was a betrayal nodded on by senior staff in the palace.'

Ludeney had nothing to say. How could he?

'People like you, Lord Marshal. Tell me I'm wrong.'

'What would you have me say?'

'King Pietr wanted to relegate his own flesh and blood to

chattel to secure the continuation of his name. Yet you think her refusal to bear children and risk seeing that cycle repeated, should her sons have daughters, makes her unfit to rule. I think it's the opposite. Let's start there.'

'He was a brutal man.'

'Yes. Look what he made my parents endure … after you caught them for him.'

Ludeney's gaze flicked away for the briefest moment and the muscles in his jaw tightened. 'Yes.' He frowned. 'Even now, that is … difficult … to remember.'

'I could not have less sympathy for you,' said Naida. But she thought there was more to his discomfort. Something painful he remembered but would not articulate. *Everything is written down*, she thought.

'I don't expect any sympathy from you. I expect you to do what I brought you here to do. It is her duty to provide an heir! It is vital for this country to have stability. And if she does not have a biological heir, it is her duty to select one from within the roll of admissible families.'

Naida rolled her eyes, but this time did not reveal the Queen's plans. 'Families who were complicit in this madness? And you're surprised? I will not kill someone because of some twisted notion of duty. I have principles. Know what they are?'

Ludeney had the good grace to look embarrassed, but it was all too fleeting. He gathered himself and the resolve returned to his eyes.

'You understand the decision before you? If you do not, you will be denounced. You will suffer the same fate as your parents.'

It should have terrified her anew. She'd heard the accounts, and no doubt the details were somewhere in the archives, every cut and burn and lash and nail and break written down in exquisite detail. But she didn't believe his threats.

'You won't do that, for the same reason I won't tell Eva her most trusted soldier and military adviser is plotting to kill her.'

'Oh, she'll believe me,' said Ludeney, the confidence that came with entitlement dripping from him. 'I am, after all, her most trusted soldier and military adviser.'

Naida smiled, knowing she was all-in now. This conversation would decide her fate, and a thrill of excitement ran through her.

'I'd love to see how that plays out. *Pardon me, Your Majesty, but the woman I hand-selected to be entrusted with your health and wellbeing is actually an Esselrode trying to kill you.* I mean, how could it possibly go wrong for you?'

Naida hadn't been sure it would be enough, but Ludeney was looking uneasy. He pushed his tongue behind his teeth and hissed, shifting uncomfortably.

'I will say I have informed her the moment I discovered the truth,' he said, but his heart wasn't in it.

Naida got up, her heart racing. 'Let's find out, shall we? Make our claims to the Queen and see what happens.' She held out a hand to him, and his expression made the thought of her impending torture and murder almost worthwhile.

'What?'

'I'm calling you out, Lord Marshal. Taking a bet, acting on a hunch, rolling the dice, turning the tables... whatever your chosen phraseology. Come on.'

Ludeney stared at her, she could feel him searching for the lie within her, the bravado, for any reason which might knock her back down. But right now, Naida would absolutely follow through and it was genuinely empowering to know it. More than that, she enjoyed the position she had placed him in.

'Sit down,' he said quietly.

'I will not kill her for you, nor for anyone else,' she said, sitting down again. A breeze blew across the terrace, welcome, though ephemeral, relief from the heat that grew by the day – by the hour, even. 'So enough empty threats. With that said, if you can prove to me that she is a genuine threat to the country, then I will help you remove her from power.'

'Her opposition to the Talent is not enough for you?' asked Ludeney.

'It is a position that she needs arguing out of, not to be assassinated for holding,' said Naida. 'Neither should she be murdered because you don't understand how deeply her father's betrayal affected her and how much she fears it happening to another.'

'I wholeheartedly agree with you,' said Ludeney.

Naida felt becalmed. 'Oh.'

'She is far, far more dangerous to this country than you know, which is a paradox given that in so many regards, she is a fine monarch.'

Naida's heart missed a beat wondering how much he knew, or thought he knew, about Eva's ultimate aim.

'I have surprised you,' said Ludeney.

'I – yes, you have. So how is someone who is, on the whole, a harmonising force in Suurken, a danger to it?'

'Because a threat to the monarchy is an existential threat to our society, and that cannot be allowed. The monarchy must endure.'

'Depose her, then.'

'*Depose?* One word but an enormously complex route to change. It is why her untimely death would be far more convenient.'

'Not for her,' said Naida. 'And who is this paragon of virtue you have waiting in the shadows to take her place? If I'm to assassinate the current monarch, I should at least know on whose behalf I am doing it.'

Ludeney said nothing, choosing to sip his tea instead.

'Well? I mean I'm not about to announce it from the floor of the pit.'

'Be assured that if I had a name, you would be the last person I would tell.'

Naida gaped, but not at the attempted slight. After all, Naida wouldn't tell Naida either. 'How can you not know who you want to ascend? What happens if Eva dies, and you still don't?'

'I know *exactly* who I want to ascend,' snapped Ludeney. 'That would be the rightful heir. Our problem is that the Rekalvian dynasty began in a slew of their rival family's blood and surviving members of that family are proving extremely difficult to track down. Not every record survived and the search for those that do is complex. There are very few leads.'

'Sorry,' said Naida, desperately trying to process all she was hearing. 'Are you implying that Eva is *not* the rightful heir?'

'I'm implying that since we discovered Eva's plans for the monarchy and hatched our own to replace her, we have discovered enough information to suggest that the Rekalvians should never have ascended the throne of Suurken.'

'Suggest? Come on, Lord Marshal, are you sure your determination that Eva is bad news is not colouring your view? It's easy to see what you want to see if you look hard enough. Bring me your proof and I will help you. Until then, I will do her no harm and I will work to change her mind. She is my Queen.'

'A respectable position,' conceded Ludeney. 'And you will just have to trust me in the days to come. After all, should the Queen die before an heir is found, I will be required to rule at the head of the Queen's council.'

Naida's first reaction was to laugh at the admission of his true motives, but she caught the look in his eyes and knew she'd be making a fool of herself. His loyalty to the monarchy was an eternal fire. A sadness overtook her.

'Strange … Misha said my parents made claims about their royal lineage when they were close to the end. Perhaps they *did* know something.'

'I beg your pardon?'

'Ask Misha. Actually, I'm surprised your spy didn't tell you this nugget of information … why are you looking like that? There's nothing in it. After so many days of torture, they would have been insane. Trust me. Doctors know this sort of thing.'

Ludeney was barely listening to her but when his attention returned there was an odd intensity about it.

'Everything is worth investigating.'

'Maybe but unless we confront the most urgent problem facing us all, none of this other stuff will matter.'

'Time is increasingly short,' said Ludeney.

'On multiple fronts, apparently,' said Naida. 'Mine involves tens of thousands of needless deaths in the next thirty days. What about yours?'

Ludeney smiled and it was the first time she had seen warmth in his expression.

'I hope we have enough tea to see us through. How can I help you?'

Chapter 20

'Good morning.'

Naida opened her eyes and found Drevien, popped up on one arm, looking at her. 'Just like old times.'

'Yes,' said Drevien. 'You can't put a scalpel between the opulence of a palace bedroom and a leaky tent on a far-flung, blood-soaked battlefield.'

Naida reached an arm out of the tangle of sheets and pushed Drevien on to her back, moving to sit astride her.

'I can always pitch an old scrap of canvas in some mud if you're feeling uncomfortable.'

'You're hilarious.' Drevien smiled. 'Still can't believe I'm really here.'

'Nor me. Good though, isn't it?'

'Can't complain. It'd be nice if we weren't buried in a crisis, mind you.'

Naida nodded. 'Is that why you're awake so early?'

'Not really.' Drevien stroked Naida's thighs. 'Are we in a desperate hurry right now?'

The arrival of Drevien, Kella and Sennoch late the previous afternoon had been the fillip Naida had needed but, after the hugs and story-swapping, the meandering dinner had been a more sober affair.

Naida had outlined her fears and promised letters of authority allowing them to operate freely in every medical centre across the city, securing supplies of equipment and allowing them to draw on apothecaries for anything that might help in the event of an outbreak. It was still essential to identify and quarantine any outbreaks quickly, but that was where her network of eyes across the city ought to help.

Naida raised her eyebrows. 'I have letters to write, the royal medical centre to show you, and teams to put to work reporting to you, Kella and Sennoch. No doubt the Queen will require my presence at some stage, and I still need to finalise plans for plague treatment centres and zones.'

Drevien glanced towards the drapes around which an early dawn light was edging. She reached up and linked her hands on the back of Naida's neck.

'So, not all that busy then,' she said. 'Nothing that can't wait a bit.'

'No,' whispered Naida. 'Nothing that can't wait a bit.'

Drevien pulled her close.

★

Only a day later, though, that morning was rendered a distant dream. While Naida had been surprised at the speed with which Ludeney had responded to her requests, she was uncomfortably aware of her continuing role in his plans. Various platoons of the city guard were mobilised to help transport medical supplies, and to organise and bolster existing quarantining equipment; including timber and bolts for street barricades, tent canvas, firewood and lantern oil.

Naida had been assured it was all very low-key, but there would be other eyes out there noting every movement, and while she was happy that it might engender some caution among Suranhom's citizens, raising unnecessary alarm was dangerous. And who knew what other plans might be afoot?

They found out, sadly, during lunch at The Bonesaw, on the purse of the head of the royal medical service because it was to catch up on progress and problems. Naida was as relaxed as she could be, given the ever-rising heat of the summer, the increasing number of anti-Talent marches and rallies across the city, and the inability of anyone barring her and, perhaps, Ludeney, to see what was coming straight at them. And he still wanted her to assassinate the Queen.

'Over here, Jess,' said Adeile. 'What's up?'

Naida turned to see a girl making her way over from the door. She was no more than sixteen, dressed in rough woollen clothes and had chubby features, blushed red from running in the heat, and lank brown hair gathered in a ponytail.

'I found out,' Jess panted.

Naida moved up on her bench so she could sit.

'Sit down, take a breath and have a drink. Ale? Water?'

'Thank you,' said Jess, staring at Naida, in awe at this honour. 'Ale, thank you.'

Naida gestured at Aryn to fill a goblet. Jess took a grateful draft and wiped a dusty hand across her mouth.

'Thank you.'

'Least we can do,' said Naida. 'So, who are you, then? Friend of Adeile's?'

'Niece,' said Jess. 'On my mother's side.'

'How lovely,' said Naida. 'So, what did you find out?'

'There's barricades gone up around Old Landers, bits of it anyway. They're saying it's Red Spot.'

Naida closed her eyes. She felt a weight pushing on her soul and she realised that despite the absolute inevitability of a disease breaking out in the city, whether by accident or design, she had hoped that somehow, they'd escape.

'It's the hope that kills you,' she whispered.

They were all staring at her like soldiers staring at their commanding officer, waiting for orders.

'We've done all the preparation we can, but if this is Red Spot, it's come far sooner than any of us wanted. So, let's put what we've done into action. Which medical centre is closest to Old Landings?'

'King Olan's, next door,' said Kat, jerking a thumb over her shoulder.

'Well, that's something. Sennoch, Drev, Kella, bag up all the kit you can. Willan, get the carts. Aryn, get word to every medical centre in the city. Go to Bryn at the royal service first – he can write you letters of authority to take elsewhere. They need to get treatments and protective garment supplies to every road border into Old Landers and the wider docklands. If they can supply staff, they should present themselves to King Olan's infirmary, where Kella will be coordinating.'

Naida scratched her forehead, trying to be sure she was covering everything.

'Containment, Naida,' said Drevien.

'Thank you.' Naida thought for a moment. 'Jess, who's put up the barricades?'

'Gangers,' said Jess.

'Really?' said Naida, and another piece perhaps fell into place. 'I wonder how they knew before anyone else.'

'Good question,' said Elias. 'Which gang?'

'I don't know,' said Jess. 'I didn't get that close.'

'Elias, can you get to Ludeney?' asked Naida.

'What do you want me to do?'

'We have to mobilise his guards to every contact point, and we have to do it now. Gang barricades will help, whether on purpose or not, but it only takes one infected and we could

209

lose half the city. They need to get their barricades prepared, if not deployed just yet. Can you do it?'

Elias was already out of his seat. 'Consider it done. Reconvene where?'

'We'll leave word here when we know,' said Naida. 'But if you hear nothing, come to Old Landers.'

Elias dashed from the inn, followed by Aryn, Sennoch, Kella, Drevien and Willan. Naida gave Kat and Adeile a brittle smile. Jess was staring into her ale.

'Can we get Gifted in, do you think?' asked Naida.

'Maybe,' said Kat. 'But they're rightly afraid.'

'Do what you can. You all right, Adeile?'

'Not really.'

'We'll get through it,' said Naida.

'Not everyone wants us to, though, do they?'

Naida looked out of the window on to a cloudy and humid day in Suranhom, and the people passing by, blissfully unaware of the horror festering on the riverside.

★

Red Spot.

It had to be Red Spot, didn't it? A summertime slum disease, occurring when the poor-quality meat and grains the poverty-stricken had to eat couldn't be stored safely. Where the drudge flies laid their eggs and left behind the faeces that provided the ideal breeding ground for the disease that passed to animal and human without pause.

It didn't help that the early symptoms – a high fever, nausea and vomiting – did not present themselves for two or three days after exposure and were similar to so many other, far less serious, maladies. Only then did the violent red spots appear behind the ears, knees and between the toes before colonising the rest of the body. As the victim was consumed from within, the cramps began, they started bleeding from every orifice from eyes to anus, and as the disease reached its final stages, they suffered in screaming agony.

Most died, if not attended by a Gifted. A few survived. The textbooks were full of ineffective treatment methods and warnings about the speed and ease of contagion. This spread was what Naida feared. Her fervent hope was that this outbreak would prove the need for the Talent.

With the carriages still being loaded at Olan's, Naida decided she could not wait and set off with Drevien, who'd been brought up in the dockland slums, to find the centre of the outbreak. They needed to be there to begin triage, organise quarantine areas, and put basic treatment in motion before the mass of supplies arrived.

Word had begun to spread as they ran through the streets towards Old Landers. Panic could move faster than the disease and it was beginning to bite. They had two sacks, filled with full head masks, gowns, gloves and two boiling pans. Naida had filled a hessian bag, with ginger and lavender tincture for the fever, and turmeric and honey balm for the red spots. Though they weren't spots. They were boils. Seeping, weeping, red pustules in which all the pain in the world was concentrated. Death was sometimes a relief.

Naida was scared.

They'd reached the river, which ran as peacefully as ever towards the sea. Soon, unless they were successful, it would carry bodies and disease downstream to oblivious fishing and farming settlements. As Naida and Drevien headed into Fishooks, the fear was palpable, hanging in the air like a thick, oily smoke. The tight streets that led away from the riverside, its banks, docks, warehouses, and jetties were very quiet for the middle of the day. Bankside, those people working the boats and offloading cargo had scarves about their faces, and suspicion in their eyes as they watched Naida and Drevien's every pace.

Drevien pointed the way along the wide cobbled street that ran right along the river, through Fishooks and into Old Landers, where the once-grand docks had long fallen into disrepair, the warehouses had been transformed into dreadful housing, and the meagre trade that crossed the river was controlled by a number of gangs that had carved up the turf between them.

Old Landers was, by common consent, the most dangerous part of Suranhom, and it was no surprise that they encountered their first barricades well before they reached its fluid borders. This one was not a secure affair, more of a checkpoint than a barricade. A few barrels, some heavy chain and rope, and five people, masked and gloved, carrying meat hooks and cleavers. Naida hailed them and they turned.

'State your business,' said one, a tall woman, heavyset, with frightened brown eyes peering out from between hat and scarf.

'Medical,' said Drevien. 'We're from Olan's.'

The woman shrugged. 'Two of you? Won't be enough. It's dreadful in there.'

'Tell me,' said Naida.

'It's worst about a mile from here, the ways in are all barred. We don't want that death here,' said another, an old man.

'Who's standing on the barriers?' asked Naida. 'Will they let us through?'

'Through, yes; back out, no,' said the old man. 'Keelers ahead, other gangers elsewhere, I heard.'

'So where are the sick? How many are there?' asked Naida.

'How many? I don't know. But there's the old tea warehouse mid-Landings, over there under the smoke cos they're already burning bodies,' said the woman. 'Think all the gangers are pushing the sick that way.'

'Not just the sick,' said a third. 'Whole families being swept up, I heard.'

'You've all heard a lot,' muttered Drevien.

The woman gave her a sour look and stepped aside. 'Go see for yourself. Don't suppose I'll see you again.'

Naida nodded. 'I hope you're wrong. Look, I don't know what communication you have with these gangs but it's imperative we keep the sick contained where they can be treated and stop the spread.'

'That's why we're here,' said the old man. 'Good luck not dying in there with them.'

'We save those we can and ease passage back to the earth for those we cannot,' said Drevien.

Two of the locals made the chest-to-hip symbol of Arbala. Naida pursed her lips and tapped Drevien's shoulder.

'C'mon, let's go,' she said. 'You should remember, folks, if you had Gifted here, you wouldn't have a problem.'

They trotted past the barricade and on into the slums.

'They're burning bodies already?' Naida felt swallowed up by the import of the words. 'Infection to death is six days minimum.'

'It's a cover-up,' said Drevien.

'This isn't a new outbreak, is it? It's already an epidemic. Don't risk yourself, Drev.'

'Same goes for you too.'

They gripped hands a moment before moving along the riverbank to the accompanying smells of decay, filth, and the occasional blast of fresh water on the breeze. It was a depressing journey through long-faded grandeur.

The wide docksides, where ships from across the trading world had moored to offload their goods before the wars broke everything, had been created with stone flags and cobbled pathways. Beautiful in their day, the stones were now weed-strewn, broken or missing. Jetties had rotted, the rusting arms of cranes leaned down to the water, warehouses were hollowed out, roofs fallen in – anything that could be taken, had been. Detritus remained: rat-run, bleak, and covered in years of water-borne slime and mould.

Beyond them were glimpses of courtyards and squares, where life had once glittered around fountains and eateries, where market stalls and hawkers had once vied for attention, now silent, echoing misery and destitution, where vegetation was tightening its grip.

They saw the odd face, either out in the open or peering from a high window in one of the tenement blocks that dominated behind the old warehouses and surrounded every open space. Unstable floor upon unstable floor, slowly being deserted by even the poorest citizen who would rather die on the street than in a collapsed building.

It was eerie. Naida had never trodden these cobbles before but she could sense the desperation of people driven beyond poverty and now threatened by a devastating plague. Heading towards the smoke smudging the sky, she and Drevien became aware of sounds growing as they approached the borders of Old Landers.

Children crying. The screams and pleas of adults in response to harsh shouted orders, all carrying down the river, growing in intensity as they neared, and increasing the dread Naida felt. This was where it was happening. And while she had to admit that the gangers were, essentially, doing the right thing, their methods, driven by their fears, would brutalise sick and healthy alike and miss critical evidence that might help locate the root of the infection. They might even be spreading it further as a result.

Ahead of them, people were being moved along the dockside. Men and women, armed and even armoured in some cases, were forcing a punishing pace from terrified people, some of whom were plainly incapable of travelling much further. They were being shown through a far more effective barricade than the one back along the way. It blocked the dockside, with two carts acting as gates within a structure of iron and wood sheeting. It had been constructed from a plan, not thrown together in haste.

'It'll help,' said Naida. 'But not if the source of the infection isn't inside it. It could still be out here, sitting and festering, awaiting new victims.'

'What a cheerful thought.'

'Let's deal with the sick we know about first,' said Naida. They'd caught the end of the procession of the unfortunate. 'Find someone that needs support and get them through. Mask and gloves first, my love.'

Drevien doled out a set for each of them, marking them out for attention from both the sick and the gangers alike. One caught Naida's arm as she made her way towards a stumbling young man, bleeding from his eyes, ears and nose. She turned and saw a scared man, whose body was packed with muscle, aggression and fear.

'What are you doing?' he demanded through his mask, gripping her arm tightly. 'You can't save them.'

'I'm doing my job and yes, I can,' said Naida. 'I'm a doctor. Let go of my arm.'

'You go in with them, you don't come out again,' he said, letting go. 'Your choice.'

Naida waved Drevien over, leaving the sick for the moment. She'd looked into the ganger's eyes and something wasn't right at all. This large man, an enforcer on a normal day, was uncomfortable with what he had been tasked to do.

'Tell you what,' said Naida. 'Give me your name and let's talk as equals. I am Naida, head of the royal medical service.'

The ganger's eyes widened, and he turned her away from the column. 'Dangerous for you to say that here.'

'More dangerous than Red Spot?'

'No, you misunderstand. The desperation down here is bad enough. If they find out it's *you*, with your reputation, in here with them, they'll mob you and infect you. You need protection in there, and no one's going to agree to give it.'

'I have some coming but thank you for the warning. What's your name?'

'Laris,' he replied, looking about him, noting the looks he was getting and the slowing of the pace in the column. 'Get them through!'

'I need to work with whoever is organising this. I have to set up proper treatment areas, separate the definitely infected from the maybe-infected. What you're doing here is consigning the healthy as well as the sick to unbearable suffering. You know it. I can see you do.' Naida shifted her footing. 'These are your people, Laris.'

'We're trying to contain the outbreak,' he said. 'What more do you want?'

'You can't contain it if you don't know where it originated. I want you to help me save as many of these people as we can. Forget your gang loyalties and orders: when I've assessed the scale of the problem, I need to get back out so I can bring in the right assistance.'

Laris shook his head. 'I can't do that.'

'Then who are you protecting?' snapped Naida, her voice hard, carrying across the miserable march and turning every head. 'Just you? Your boss? Who?'

Laris rediscovered some of the authority that came with his sheer physical presence.

'You don't speak to the Keelers like that, whoever you are. We run Old Landers our way. Don't interfere.'

The fear remained but the uncertainty had been drowned in self-righteousness. Naida hoped it was temporary.

'I'll do what I can to save your people, Laris – the ones your bosses feed on like rats off a corpse. Flex your muscles, because when I'm done, I'm coming back out again.'

Laris couldn't meet her gaze. 'I can't let you. I have my orders, and your reputation won't save you if you test me.'

'We're on the same side, Laris.'

'I don't think we are. You'd better go.'

The column of the unfortunate picked up speed again after a rasp from Laris aimed squarely at Naida's back. She and Drevien joined it, helping some of those who were struggling to get through the barricade, and urging others to help them too.

'He was right about your name,' said Drevien, supporting a frail but healthy-looking old man while Naida carried a girl of no more than eight, who had blood in her ears and a fever burning inside her.

'I know,' said Naida.

'What is your name?' asked the girl, staring straight into her, straight through her, as they passed the barricade.

'What would you call me?' asked Naida gently.

'Doctor Saveus.'

'That's what I'm going to try to do.'

'It's what my mother shouted at the doctors when they were taken away.'

Naida's heart skipped a beat. Wasn't that supposed to be a joke? The girl was half-smiling but that might have been because she was losing her sense to the fever.

'What do you mean, little one?' Naida fed herself into the girl while they walked, knowing she was too young to know the Talent was saving her, even if she were to grow up a Gifted.

'The doctors who weren't too scared to treat us were taken

away. They told us it was because other people were sicker. But my mother said it was because they didn't want us to live.'

Naida glanced around. Drevien nodded, catching her eye. The column was moving at a grindingly slow pace, and behind them the barricade had been closed. Around them, the blank faces of sealed warehouses on one side and the bass melody of the river on the other. Ahead, their destination: the warehouse at the end of the docks. Behind it, more poor housing would give way to rural and marsh land, and the tidal mudflats that gave a rich bounty of shellfish and eels.

The site chosen to corral the sick was a good one. Easy to cordon off front and rear, river on one side and barricaded roads on the other. It wasn't going to be easy to get back out, but first things first. She could hear cries of pain and desperation from the warehouse, floating on the breeze. The ambient hum of hundreds of voices. It was going to be grim.

'Who took the doctors away? Keelers?'

The girl shook her head. 'No. Strangers.'

'A rival gang?'

Another shake of the head. Naida couldn't escape it now. This outbreak was no accident.

They reached the doors of the warehouse. Just behind it, the pyres sent stinking smoke into the sky. Naida stepped inside and for one brief, awful moment, thought about turning on her heel and running away.

Chapter 21

All her years on the battlefields, all the blood in the infirmaries and surgeries, all the shock and pain of desperately wounded soldiers unable to comprehend what had happened to them… none of it prepared her for the field of misery she saw, or the stench and noise that assaulted her.

There were thousands cramming the floor of the warehouse in the stultifying heat of the day. There was barely enough room to walk between people. Naida couldn't quite see the far end in the half-light coming through the openings and broken timbers, but it was clear there was no separation of sick and healthy, no organisation of vital supplies, no water boiling. Nothing. There were some tending the sick, moving amid the mass but there was nothing they could do but offer comfort.

'This isn't a treatment centre, it's a mortuary in waiting,' said Drevien.

'So much for "no risks",' said Naida.

Drevien shrugged. 'We have to help.'

The column moved around them, as if impelled by some unseen hand at their backs. Naida turned, addressing them, the young girl now sleeping in her arms, her fever beginning to subside.

'Don't go in there. Stay out here, in whatever shade you

can find, until I can sort the place out.' She got some confused glances, but no one stopped.

'Stop! Please!' Naida raised her voice which echoed across the open space. There must have been a hundred or more in front of her and more were coming all the time. 'You'll die in that warehouse for sure if I can't get it organised. If I can, some of you who are already infected will live, others will not become infected at all.'

This time they reacted, stopping, talking among themselves, starting to look to her for help and instructions. But where to send them, she had no idea. Willan was bringing tent canvas but it would not be enough. All she could do, for now, was try.

'Thank you. All right, I know this seems cruel, but it is to help everyone. It is vital that if you are infected, you separate yourself from those not infected. Now. Seek shade outside and I will come to you. No matter how mild your infection is, I need to treat you. Those not yet infected, I need your help. I need volunteers to go and confirm where all the blockades stopping us getting out are located.'

A few hands went up.

'Thank you, it's a massive help. If we are to save as many as possible, we have to get more medics in here, along with a whole lot of equipment. For that, we're going to need a way out. If you find one, don't come back inside, I'll come out to join you.'

She turned to Drevien.

'Let's do this.'

One thing at a time, one thing at a time. Naida let the words run round her head while she surveyed the enormity of the task before her, and the enormity of the crime being perpetrated against these people. The many hundreds in here needed to be triaged and organised, and Naida needed a general. She wondered if she'd find one in here.

The girl squirmed in her arms. She was so light, malnourished. Without Naida's intervention, she would have had no chance. Naida felt a tug on her arm, and turned to see a woman of maybe twenty, gaunt and feverish herself.

'Let me take her,' she said, holding out sweat-covered arms already blooming with Red Spot. 'I'm not use for much, but I can help her go in peace.'

Naida nodded, passing the delicate child over. 'Thank you, though I think this one might be lucky. I'll find you. I can ease your pain.'

'Don't worry. Others are less far gone.'

'There is always hope. Hang on as long as you can.' A thought struck her. 'Is your head of a council, or anything similar, in here?'

The woman nodded. 'You need Tan Delliher or his wife Rosa. Fisherfolk, good at standing up to the Keelers. People take their problems to their door. They'll be inside somewhere but even they're helpless now. He's short, lots of hair, beard and big arms. She's the same, pretty much, except the beard. You'll know them if you see them.'

Naida smiled, amazed the woman could find humour. 'Thank you. Rest. Sip water, don't eat and don't scratch at your spots, it spreads the poison faster.'

'Is that why they itch?'

Naida smiled ruefully. 'Diseases are buggers like that.'

And there she stood, knowing full well that she could cure this sick woman but not daring to because to reveal herself to someone who recognised the Talent working within them was too great a risk. If she was to turn the popular mood back in the right direction, and persuade the Queen to drop her support for the growing clamour of a return to the old religions, she had to tread very carefully. But it would cost lives until they could get some Gifted here.

Ludeney's knowledge of who she really was loomed large in her mind. If she put a foot wrong, suddenly she, daughter of the perpetrators of Talent-led genocide, would be the vanguard of a move to bring the Gifted back from the shadows. She shuddered.

'Naida?' said Drevien, touching her arm. 'We need to get working.'

'Yes,' said Naida. 'Sorry. I just … we know what these people need, don't we?'

'Too late for that unless Kat can persuade some Gifted out of hiding,' said Drevien. 'We just get to pick up the pieces.'

'We have to get them in here. We have to.'

Back inside the warehouse, the stench of sweat and sickness intensified; and the noise and the fear were building in concert with the dawning recognition of their dreadful situation. Naida could see knots of people standing to one side near the doorway. Some in conversation, some just staring. But all standing apart from the sick.

Walking towards them, she could feel eyes fix on her, on the masks and gloves she and Drevien were wearing and the bags they carried. Some chatter faded and she could feel the silence spreading slowly. It would help but she could do with a whole lot more of it.

'I'm looking for Tan and Rosa Delliher,' she said into the desperate faces that had turned to watch her approach.

Two figures pushed forward, both dressed in loose shirts and trousers. Tan was heavily bearded, tattoos across much of his exposed skin and, as his name might suggest, he had a hard-baked tan. Rosa had a magnificent head of hair, black shot with grey, heaped natural curls, a powerful frame and an expression that brooked no fools.

'Who are you?' she demanded.

'Naida, head of the royal medical service. This is Drevien.'

Tan barked a short, dismissive laugh. 'All two of you? To fix a problem Queen Eva created? Get out, we don't need you.'

While Naida wasn't possessed of an ego to speak of, she wasn't used to this kind of response to her name. In fact, she wasn't sure she'd ever been received this way. Momentarily thrown, she glanced at Drevien.

'What part of that's confusing you?' asked Rosa.

'The bit where you don't need people who are here to save the lives of your friends and family is a little puzzling,' said Naida, regaining her mind. 'The idea the Queen started it is not confusing, it's just ridiculous, and anyway, she didn't send me. I doubt she even knows this is happening. Also, more are coming and more will continue to come.'

Contemptuous noises greeted her words and Rosa's expression hardened still further.

'Heard you was a good surgeon but sawbones ain't no good to us now,' she said. 'It's Red Spot: you live or you die. Ain't no saving to be done. Not without the Touched, and they were got out before the disease came in. Funny, that, eh?'

'Sorry, are you saying that the Gifted left you alone to face it?' asked Drevien.

Rosa twitched. 'No. They were taken away so they couldn't save us from it.'

'Does it matter?' Tan raised his voice. 'Here we are.'

'Yes, it does matter,' said Naida. 'And if you let me help you, I can save some of your people.'

'You aren't getting this, are you?' said Tan. 'We've all been brought here to die for the benefit of people wealthy beyond imagining. There's a redevelopment coming, Surgeon Naida. And we are an infestation that needs removing first.'

Naida was speechless as linking conspiracies came together in her mind. She had already suspected the disease had been planted and encouraged to multiply; the timing was too convenient. But that its purpose might be to effectively cleanse an area so it could be redeveloped for the rich made her feel nauseous. Raising fear of the Gifted and removing them from the area could not be ignored. But as a link to the Queen? It was tenuous at best. Eva was a monarch who wanted to be seen to support the public mood, not to destroy the public.

'I don't know where to begin,' said Naida.

'How about with why you didn't fight back?' asked Drevien.

'*Fight back?*' barked Tan. 'Yeah, we tried that. Fists turned out not to be so good against blades. Rosa, where's Kinso?'

'Here,' the voice was strained, that of a man in pain.

The knot of people parted to reveal Kinso, sitting propped against a wall. The blood had soaked through his torn trousers and his once-pale-green shirt. Stab wounds and slash wounds, Naida had seen them a hundred times, so had Drevien. Kinso's face was white with the pain, the loss of blood and the shock. He was probably unsavable but it had never stopped her from trying before.

Naida was by his side in a couple of strides, kneeling down to assess him.

'Kinso, I'm here to help you.' The man gave her a wan smile and nodded vaguely. She glanced at Tan and Rosa. 'Do you have any boiling water?'

'What would we boil water in?' said Rosa, bitterness in her tone.

'We can help you there,' said Drevien, unshouldering her pack.

'I need people to fill the pots with river water,' said Naida. 'I need people collecting wood, and searching for anything we can store more water in. Barrels, the hull of an old rowboat, anything. And I need the sick and the healthy separated. Keep the sick downwind. Well, come on, what are you waiting for? Go. Sort it out.'

224

Naida set down her bag and opened it, sorting through for a needle and thread. She turned out one of her other packs, finding clean cloth and bandages. And while she did so, she made a decision. With Tan barking orders she had some momentum. Now she needed a victory and Kinso, a would-be hero of no more than thirty, filthy and bloodied with no hope and no future, was going to be the lucky recipient.

'Kinso, my name is Naida and I'm going to save you.'

★

Nightfall. In front of Naida was a fire where her latest headgear, gloves and apron burned; and beyond it, the river that ran on unconcerned. Behind her, the warehouse and the cacophony of suffering they could do precious little to quieten. In and in came the unending column of misery, albeit less dense now that Old Landings was emptying; and out and out were carried the bodies to the funeral pyre.

They'd worked for eight hours without a break, so few trying to do everything for so many, knowing they'd fail most of the time. But at least they had a working organisation now, even if its primary function was the grimmest of triage operations. Naida took a swallow of her nettle and ginger tea, the first sustenance she'd had since arriving, and turned back to the horror engulfing them, moment by inexorable moment.

Naida should have been impressed beyond measure. Perhaps one day, she would look back and be able to feel such emotions. Multiple fires burned across the encampment, on which pots held boiling water and thin stews, and which delineated the areas occupied by the sick and the … currently … healthy, though healthy was a relative term in this context.

It was yet another hot night, and all of those infected had been moved outside to lie beneath canvas shelters that had been erected all around the warehouse and anywhere else purchase could be found over the hard-packed mud and cobbles. Blankets, matting, vegetation, spare clothing, anything that could be used to make people a degree more comfortable had been pressed into service, but in truth many of them were too far gone to care.

Willan, with some initially reluctant locals, had then marked out safe paths for the living to tread, and for the dead to be carried along to the pyres. Places had been made for contaminated clothing to be boiled clean at the border of the pyre area. Lines of wet clothes hung in the close warmth of the night.

Inside, the warehouse had been emptied, and swept, and then scrubbed clean, and scrubbed again, the volume of work made possible by the number present to help. Those not showing any signs of Red Spot were in one area, separated by the carts on which all the gear from Olan's was being unloaded as required. Seeing the haphazard way in which it was being done made Naida wish for a proper quartermaster.

The other, smaller-for-now, area was for those who exhibited what might be symptoms but might just be the effects of bad nutrition and terrible living conditions. Naida wasn't holding her breath, and neither were they. Most knew they were cases in waiting and although they were being as careful as they could not to infect others, transmission remained inevitable unless they could get out of this plague camp.

Drevien was still working. A fact that filled Naida with love, pride and terror. However careful she was, infection was inevitable. If Kat was unsuccessful and no Gifted arrived, the death toll would be appalling, the level of suffering incomprehensible. She wondered if she would intervene to cure Drevien if she fell victim to the plague. Silly question, really.

'Lady Naida.'

Naida turned, happy to be distracted from her miserable train of thought.

'Tan. Thank you. You and your community's assistance is going to save a lot of lives.'

Delliher shrugged. 'Your optimism is commendable. I guess now they'll die neat, at least. But I'm not here for thanks. Kinso is comfortable and has eaten. Given his time was so short when you arrived, it is I who should be thanking you.'

Naida held up her hands. 'I bet no one thanks you for catching a fish.'

Tan chuckled, an infectious bass rumble. 'That they don't. Do you have a moment?'

'For you I have all the time you want. I have questions, too.'

'I guessed you would.' He indicated and they walked towards the river where they would not be overheard. Naida felt a frisson of anxiety. This did not feel like good news was forthcoming. 'My people did what you asked: mapped the barriers and buildings. We're sewn up very tight. We've got people coming in from Old Landers, Fishooks and the Ropers, which tells me they're clearing right up to the marshes in the north and down to the markets that border Olan's and the Ham Yards, south. East, it's a wall of sealed warehouses with the spice and cloth markets beyond. We don't know if they're guarded, we don't have the means to break down any door.'

'Clearing?'

'Aye. This whole dockside has been cut off for days. Any that go out don't get back in. Almost before the Spot first appeared, which is when the gangers came and took the Gifted away. Some cheered. The older of us feared. And old people are always right.'

'Almost always,' said Naida. 'So, who's behind it?'

'Wait, there's more: the barriers, all seven of them, are heavy duty and packed with gangers. We couldn't see and count everyone, but you need maybe six on a barricade. There's at least three times that around each one.'

The coming of night had taken the heat from the day. Naida took in a breath of warm river air, frustrated, letting it invigorate her tired lungs. If this were a quarantine procedure, she might have been pleased they were taking such care to keep it secure. But she was increasingly sure that wasn't its purpose.

'So, they mean to keep us in.'

'That's one interpretation,' said Delliher.

Naida stared at him and, given what he believed, what he was hinting at made sense.

'A slaughter would be a high-risk strategy. Red Spot loves to spread through blood spatter.'

'That isn't funny.' Delliher scowled and scratched at his beard. 'We should be ready, but having no weapons makes it hard.'

'Tell me more about the Gifted being moved out,' said Naida, shifting the subject. 'Were they happy to escape persecution in the area? Did they want to leave, or were they made to?'

'None of them was cheering when they left, put it that way. And the Spot was just starting to spread. Only one conclusion.'

'You'd welcome them back?'

'Stupid question.'

'You'd think, but with all that's going on I feel I need to know where you stand.'

Delliher shrugged and said, 'Thought you army medics didn't like the Gifted?'

'No.' Naida shook her head. 'It's not like that at all. Soldiers have old superstitions and fear Gifted intervention upsets the natural order ... if it's your day to die, that sort of thing ... though apparently a surgeon up to her elbows in a soldier's guts is completely fine. But when there's infection and disease, it's funny how fast they change their minds. No, it doesn't make sense to me, either, but here we are.'

They turned at the sound of the bell announcing another

death, the name shouted into the night. Scant respect, but it's all they could afford right now.

'Who benefits from this, Tan?' asked Naida.

'There's a question.' Delliher's smile was grim. 'Rumours are rife. For sure, someone wants this land and don't want the problem of rehousing the residents.'

'Gangers?'

Delliher wrinkled his nose. 'No. But maybe whoever's paying them to trap us here 'til we die.'

'How do I find them?'

'You don't. You die, like the rest of us, because they're being paid a lot to keep this place sealed. You broke into a tomb. You ain't getting back out.'

'We'll see about that.' She began walking towards the wide apron in front of the warehouse, where two more open carts were trundling in. Both carried people in medical uniform, and were otherwise stacked with crates and barrels and strung with cauldrons and sacks of food.

Delliher gave her a sideways glance. 'Meaning?'

'You don't walk into an enemy camp without the means to leave.' Naida waved. 'Elias, Kat! Adeile! Over here.'

The threee of them jumped from their carts and trotted over. Naida held up her hands.

'No hugs, no touching, just in case,' she said. 'Meet Tan Delliher. He's community leader here alongside Rosa, his wife. She's in the warehouse doing the work of ten people. Run operational decisions by them. Drevien will fill you in on the system here. What did you bring?'

Everyone grunted greetings and Elias jerked a thumb over his shoulder.

'Let me show you.'

Back at the wagons, the newly arrived people were unloading and Kella, who had travelled with them, was in conversation with Drevien who was staring past her at the carts in some surprise. Naida frowned.

'What's up?' she said.

'Adeile'll tell you.'

Naida smiled and felt a little surge of hope. 'So?'

'It's not all good news ... but I've brought five with me.'

Naida almost hugged her, just stopped herself. 'How can that not be good news?' Thinking she could use the Talent herself, knowing she could hide it amid the noise of the other Gifted.

'Because they're safer in a plague zone than anywhere else in the city,' said Adeile.

Chill stole across the humid compound and the hairs rose on Naida's arms. 'What are you talking about?'

'Plague news spreads faster than the plague, right?' she said. 'Elias did a great job mobilising some of Ludeney's people to shore up access points to the dockside here, which helped calm some immediate fears, but there's always people looking for someone to blame. It got ugly very quickly. There are Arbalers and Eremines holding forth in squares and streets all over the place. Right out in the open, denouncing the Gifted as plague carriers, demanding a return to some misguided past.'

'Sounds familiar,' said Delliher, his tone grim and gruff.

Naida tried to keep herself together while she listened to brutal history repeating itself.

'Sounds organised. What's happened to the Gifted who were taken from here?' she asked, unable to raise much more than a whisper.

'Seems they were handed over to the palace guard a few days ago and are due to go on display in Traitor's Square. They're lining up another Esselrode trial, using the outbreak. But this time, they're innocent,' said Kat.

Naida had to keep a careful control over her expression. 'Who's pushing this?' she managed.

'You all right, Naida?' asked Adeile.

'Yes, just … look at where we're standing. Look at the risk of infection the whole city is taking. But rather than unleash the power of hundreds of Gifted, the population is being goaded into a mob on a false accusation, and now herded to a sham trial where the risks are even greater! No Gifted will be safe now, no matter where they live and who they know. Who's pushing it?'

'The Queen announced the trial today, and there are notices about the Gifted being banned all over the place, but in truth, there was little else she could do once word was out,' said Adeile.

'Aye, and how did the word get out?' asked Tan.

'I don't know,' said Kat. 'I'm sorry.'

'All right, all right,' said Naida, trying to organise her thoughts. 'Tan … we've got five Gifted here, ready to help. But we need you and Rosa to say it's all right for them to get to work. Can they?'

Delliher pointed at the canvas shelters. 'Get them started. I'll talk to Rosa, make sure she agrees but we have been married forty years. Reckon I know the answer on this one.'

'Sennoch?' Naida called. The surgeon had just jumped from Elias's cart. 'Gifted to deploy.'

He trotted over. 'Great. Let's go.'

The Gifted, who had been disguised as medics on the cart, headed off to begin the long process of removing Red Spot from as many as they could before exhaustion forced them to rest. They would begin with the lightest cases.

'Thank you,' said Delliher.

'Long way to go yet,' said Naida. 'Now come and see what Elias has for us.'

Elias had done far better than Naida could have dreamed. It wasn't just the Gifted who'd been disguised. And the crates of

231

medical clothing and barrels of water and food also concealed something more.

'This place is going to become a target sooner or later,' explained Elias, who had seen a quarantine go wrong before. His people levered open crates and barrels and handed round leather armour, blades and bows. Delliher was smiling. 'So, I brought some friends.'

'I have fit fishers and dock haulers aching to take a swing,' said Delliher.

Elias nodded. 'I hoped you'd say that. It's why we bought so many sharp things.'

'Are you a ranking officer?' asked Delliher.

Now Elias smiled broadly. 'The question of an ex-soldier. Where did you serve?'

'Oh, I didn't,' said Delliher. 'My eldest served in Cantabria during the failed first invasion. He ran rear guard during the evacuation. It was carnage. No wonder we didn't go back for another five years.'

'Then look what happened,' said Elias.

'I did all my fighting on the dockside during the Holdern uprising, way back when. There's plenty of us know how to hold a blade or a club.'

'I'm just common infantry,' said Elias. 'I'd be happy to put us under your command. You know what you have, and you know the lay like I don't.'

'We'll do it together,' said Delliher. 'We need to be able to react to forces coming in from multiple directions.'

'Elias,' said Naida, feeling she should have been uplifted by what she was hearing but feeling only helplessness. 'I have to get out of here. I have to get to whoever is engineering this.'

'With respect, there are more immediate problems,' said Elias.

'How can there be?'

'Our actions here have not gone unnoticed,' said Elias. 'We

got through the barrier up at Old Landers with bribery and threats. So not only are the Keelers unhappy with us, the word is already out in the city that we've brought aid ... and protection. It won't take long for someone to work out we've brought Gifted, too.'

Delliher nodded. 'You haven't grasped it, Lady Naida,' he said. 'They, whoever they are who started this, do not want us ... cannot afford for us ... to live. If we survive the disease, they will have to find another solution.'

'Who's that?' asked Adeile. She was pointing back towards the Keelers' barricade and at a covered wagon trundling in, flanked by two riders, the party rendered mysterious by tendrils of river mist muddying the darkness. 'Thought we were all here?'

'We are,' said Naida. 'Elias, Kat ... anyone who wants ... care to join me? Let us extend the hand of welcome.'

'Welcome,' muttered Kat. 'Right.'

Chapter 22

Naida walked at their centre, Tan Delliher with her, and the rest of them in a loose crescent behind her, leaving no doubt they expected the wagon and riders to stop. The atmosphere had changed. It was cloying and tense even though none of them were expecting a fight.

About halfway between the Keelers' barricade and the row of fires marking the border of the camp, Naida held up a hand and the wagon drivers brought their horses to a stop. The riders ambled forwards a couple of strides before doing likewise, one of them dismounting.

Naida glanced at the two men on the wagon, sweat on their brows picked out in the light of the lanterns hanging from poles either end of the driving seat, before focusing on the dismounted rider. He was short and a little portly, grey-haired and red in the face, wearing a loose shirt and trousers. His face was friendly, split by a smile as it was, and he put his hands together in front of his chest in greeting.

Naida reciprocated but then held up a hand to indicate he come no closer.

'Do you know any of them?' she asked.

'No,' said Tan. 'Safe to assume whatever he says is a lie, unless he admits he's here to kill us all.'

'Really?'

Tan shrugged. 'He proves he's of good heart or he turns around and leaves. Look how he dismounted, barely able to ride. Seen people like him my whole life, and they're always on the make.'

Naida touched Tan's shoulder, message received.

'This is a quarantined plague zone,' she said. 'Stand fast unless you're here to tend to the sick.'

The man's smile broadened yet further and Naida feared for his cheeks. 'I can do better than tend to them. My name is Emilius Markan and I am delivering an end to the torment suffered by all the poor victims of this dread disease.'

Naida exchanged glances with Tan but it was Elias who spoke.

'You're doing what now?'

Markan gestured at the wagon. 'I am delivering the cure for Red Spot.'

Tan barked a short derisive laugh and spat on the ground. Naida was aware of her friends adjusting their feet.

'While I am, naturally, delighted,' she said, 'unless your wagon is full of the Gifted, you can't help us. There is no other cure for Red Spot.'

On the wagon, both drivers made the chest-to-hip Arbala sign. One of them swore quietly and Naida picked up on the accent immediately. Markan's smile faltered slightly.

'You are mistaken,' he said.

'No, I am Naida, head of the royal medical service and ten years a military surgeon. If there was a cure, I would know about it, and I would already be administering it.'

She did not miss the darkening of Markan's expression, though he lightened it with another smile.

'A pleasure to make your acquaintance, I'm sure,' he said. 'But not even the great Naida can know all that happens everywhere

235

across our great alliance of nations. This cure was not made here but by our friends in Cantabria. And it is here for you now.'

'Convenient,' said Kat.

'Fortuitous,' said Markan pleasantly, though his glance was scalpel-sharp. 'That our work of a decade can aid you now. As soon as we heard of the outbreak, we came. I can't understand your scepticism.'

'What's in it?' asked Naida.

'It is our secret, you must understand. What is important is that it works,' said Markan, evidently beginning to feel uncomfortable in a place where he had assumed he would be welcomed as a hero. 'Allow us to demonstrate.'

Tan spat on the ground. '*Cure*. Born yesterday, were we?'

'The mortality rate of Red Spot is over eighty per cent,' said Markan. 'You need what I have.'

'Oh, to make it up to a hundred per cent, is it?' said Tan, taking a pace forwards.

Naida put out a hand to slow Tan's ire.

'Markan ... Emilius ... feelings are running very high here. Suspicion runs deep. I'm in the business of saving lives, or at the very least, making people who are going to die as comfortable as I can. And I will not administer a medicine whose provenance is hidden from me. I cannot risk killing people I might otherwise have saved.'

Naida stared at Markan, forcing him to look away and wave to one of the wagon drivers.

'I have papers,' he said. 'We have authority to deal directly with the community here and have been instructed to provide the cure and oversee its administration to the sick. I will speak to you no more, only to a community leader.'

The wagon driver trotted across to Markan and handed over a flat leather folder. Markan recovered his poise and looked at Naida again.

'So ...?' he said.

Naida shrugged and took a pace back. Tan Delliher stepped up. Markan's face fell.

'I am Tan Delliher, co-speaker of the representative council for Old Landers, Fishooks and Ropers.'

'Oh,' said Markan. 'May I—'

'What's in your cure?' asked Tan. 'Once I have that information, I can discuss with my doctor whether we should allow it to be given to my people.'

'Perhaps you could ask our saviour which outbreaks of Red Spot the cure has been tested on, over the past decade,' said Naida. 'I'd love to see any results. Just for my own personal interest, you understand.'

'You heard the doctor,' said Tan.

'You'll find everything you need to know in these documents,' said Markan. He proffered the file which Tan took and handed to Naida. 'Now if you'll allow, we need access to the site to organise distribution of the cure. Every moment wasted is a life lost.'

'This is medically illiterate,' said Naida, riffling through the papers. 'There's no ingredient list here.'

'Oh dear,' said Tan. 'You see our problem.'

'I don't,' said Markan and he raised his voice to appeal to any who might hear. 'You're treating me with suspicion when all I am doing is bringing aid. I am no threat to you or your sufferers. I am not even armed. Let us help you.'

'Get me a sample of your cure,' said Naida.

'Of course.' Markan snapped his fingers and made a drinking gesture. One of the carriage drivers disappeared inside the wagon.

Everything Markan had said had been reasonable. The details of some medicines were kept secret. It was impossible for one doctor to know about every treatment being researched. If they did bring a cure, she was just being rude. But she could not

237

shake Tan's words. He was certain someone intended them all to die, and she believed him. And she could not dispel the feeling that this miraculous, unheard-of cure was way too convenient, and they had not expected her to be here. But she so wanted Markan to be an honest broker.

The carriage driver hurried over with a small wooden crate. She glanced at Naida with a cold expression. Naida smiled back sweetly, and Markan opened the crate, which contained six bulbous glass phials packed with straw. He plucked one out, removed the stopper and handed it to Naida.

'The answer to your prayers,' he said.

'No god has ever answered my prayers,' said Naida, and examined the contents of the phial.

It was a pale green, quite viscous, liquid when she swirled it and it smelled of basil, cardamom and ginger. But there was something else there too. Something sharper that she couldn't identify, something the blender had tried to disguise.

'I am told the taste is as pleasant as the cure.'

'By whom?' asked Naida.

'The apothecarist who developed it,' said Markan, as if talking to an imbecile.

'I'll give you another chance, a last chance as it happens because I have patients to attend to. What are the ingredients, beyond those we could smell from the other side of the river?'

Markan paused, rocking his head slightly from side to side, trying to frame his words. Naida almost felt sorry for him. He looked so uncomfortable.

'The ... the creators of this cure are very keen that its exact, um, elements remain unknown as, as I think you can understand ... there is a certain monetary element involved. They have, after all, invested considerable resources in its development and production.'

'Aye and there it is,' said Tan. 'We suffer, they make money, whoever *they* are.'

'Every time you go to the apothecary for a poultice, money is made, sir,' said Markan. 'And you never know what will work for you best until you try it. And this is being offered to you free of charge.'

'Hmmm,' said Naida. 'Interesting thought. Tell me, Emilius, to your knowledge, has the cure ... what is it called ...?'

'Kindar's Tincture.'

'Ki— really? Well, all right, I suppose. Not an apothecarist I am familiar with. So, can you tell me, has Kindar's Tincture been used to treat any victims of Red Spot during its decade of development?'

Behind Naida, the bell rang. Another had died and she was no further forward.

'I cannot.' Markan raised both his hands to ward off the anticipated backlash. 'But please, be assured that the creator guarantees each ingredient is safe and that individual elements have been shown effective against conditions displaying some of the same symptoms of Red Spot. I urge you to try it before more of your people die.'

This last was directed straight at Tan. Naida turned to him.

'So, maybe they don't want you dead, just for market research. Does that make you feel better?'

Tan's gaze never left Markan's face and the unfortunate man withered beneath it.

'This how it is?' he asked eventually. 'My people an experiment for you?'

'I don't understand,' tried Markan.

'Huh.' So much contempt loaded into such a tiny utterance. Naida had always thought that someone dripping with anger was a terrible overstatement, but here it was. 'We were infected deliberately. The barricades were up almost before the first case

239

reared its head. The Gifted were moved out, to make sure the plague spread unchecked.'

Tan was moving forward and Markan backwards. Markan's people responded, moving to support him, the other rider dismounting. Elias made Naida aware of people coming from the barricade, five of them, armed and in a hurry. Tan wasn't distracted.

'And so we were herded from our homes, the sick and the well alike, and forced here. And now, but half a day later, here you are with a cure, almost as if you were ready and waiting for the word to ride to our rescue. Tell me it isn't so. Tell me this isn't a deliberate infection, engineered to provide your masters with a test bed for their medicines.'

'And if it fails, no one will know because no one can get out...' said Elias. 'Or so you thought.'

'What if it works?' asked Markan, his face pale now and his hands trembling. 'You have nothing to lose by trying.'

'Only because you put us here. Turned my people into an experiment.' Tan grabbed Markan by an ear and dragged him back towards the camp. 'Well, congratulations. You're going to be the first to try it. How does that sound?'

The wagon driver carrying the crate made to move but Naida stepped in her way.

'Don't think so.'

Quickly, Elias, Willan, Kat and Adeile closed ranks in front of Naida to meet the oncoming Keelers and Markan's people. None had produced weapons, though the Keelers had swords and clubs.

'Elias,' warned Naida.

'I've got this,' he said.

Where Markan's people were circumspect, not people of violence, the Keelers were the opposite.

'Delliher!'

Tan just walked on, Markan not resisting him. Elias and the others barred the way of the Keelers. They were all angry faces and jabbing fingers, fronted by someone Naida hadn't seen before. A woman, hard-cheeked, dead eyes. Dangerous.

'You'll stop there,' said Elias. Still not drawing a weapon, his arms folded in front of him. 'Markan has agreed to sample the cure personally.'

'This is not how it works.'

Elias snapped out his right fist, connecting with the woman's chin. She went down in an eye-watering heap. Naida winced.

'It is now. Anyone else want to discuss how it works?'

They thought about it. Weapon arms tensed. But next to Elias, both Kat and Adeile showed two inches of blade and it was enough. The Keelers might have plenty of muscle but they were facing soldiers now.

'Bring your wagon through,' said Naida to the driver. 'No one's going to hurt you or make you enter the plague zone. Park it just outside the first fires.'

She was given a sullen nod in return. 'We'll be needing those documents.'

'I'll keep them safe for you,' said Naida. 'You'd better start praying your cure doesn't kill your boss.'

Elias had faced down the Keelers who were helping their semi-conscious comrade to her feet and moving back to the barricade. Markan's rider took the reins of both horses and hitched them to the wagon. The drivers mounted up and moved towards the camp.

Naida fell into step beside Elias and Kat.

'Keep a close eye on this lot, all right? Don't need anyone sneaking off.'

'Anything interesting in that folder?' asked Kat.

'Yeah. I think Markan handed it over in a bit of a panic, and he wasn't supposed to. I still need to get out in a hurry, how will we do it?'

Elias smiled. 'Well,' he said. 'We've got this covered wagon...'

Chapter 23

The documents Markan had thought would grant him access-with-awe, or something, had revealed far more than he might have wished. They were medically useless, but also contained a letter of authority allowing representatives of Genneran Apothecary (Cantab) access to any area of Suranhom to conduct their business. It seemed innocent enough and, Tan had told her, was not unusual except in its signatory.

Suranhom's trade regulatory bodies were attached to the administration arm of the Crucible, and it was they who would grant or deny access to the city for any trader, large or small. This one was signed by the office of the Queen's personal private secretary, not by Jaren Kerslan – though his seal was across the base of the letter – but by another in his absence. Naida couldn't make out who it was.

Even more interesting was an oblique reference in a separate document to a production and storage facility being planned for a dockside location, something that played into Tan's fears about the ultimate fate of his home and community. There was no map, but if she was reading it correctly, the land in question had been bought up recently. There would be a record of it in the archives, no doubt.

Naida had left Drevien and Kella in charge, under Rosa's

cynical gaze, of administering whatever it was Markan had brought them. Every patient was offered the choice; the vast majority deciding they had little to lose. The man himself looked nervous and Naida almost felt sorry for him. He had, as publicly as possible, taken the medicine himself and had been left in no doubt that to be where he stood meant inevitable infection. His investment in the cure had been made personal and his veneer of confidence had been stripped away.

Naida had wanted to head back into the city on her own but, instead, found herself in the company of Elias, Kat, Adeile and Willan; and grateful for it. Even so, she ensured brief physical contact with each of them to keep them free of infection. One of Markan's people, forced to drive Elias's wagon, was left under no illusion of the consequences of exposing them to the Keelers on their barricades and played her part well enough and they eventually pulled up at one of Ludeney's checkpoints.

'Willan, best you go back to the camp with our driver, maybe help load up a few more crates of Tincture on the way, so our story is not a total lie?' said Naida. 'And look after Drev for me?'

Willan nodded. 'Be careful. You start asking questions of the wrong people…'

'You too,' said Elias. He dropped his voice to a whisper. 'Be vigilant. Keelers will have spread what's happened, and they might get violent to get Markan back out.'

Willan nodded and swung up onto the driving seat.

'Shall we?'

The driver shrugged, clacked her tongue and snapped the reins.

'Right, where to?' asked Elias as the wagon disappeared.

'How long 'til dawn?'

Kat stared up at the night. 'Four hours?'

'It'll have to be enough. Got your tool kit, Elias?'

'Never leave home without it,' he said.

'Good. I'm not going to get another pass at the archives, so we're going to have to break in.'

They began walking the healthy distance to the Crucible.

'I distinctly remember telling you that is a capital offence,' said Elias.

'So is orchestrating a plague so that you can seize land and experiment on a helpless community, I reckon,' said Naida. 'We've got to find out who's behind it and then go and coerce a few answers out of them. You can help with that, too.'

★

'I'd rather assumed this was going to be some exciting adventure like in a fireside story but as it turns out, I'm terrified.' Naida's attempt at a smile was, she knew, pathetic.

'It isn't too late to change your mind,' said Elias, although it plainly was.

The two of them, Katarine, and Adeile, were inside the building that housed the furnaces, pumps and miles of pipe work that fed the archive heating system and was arranged over two levels, the second one below them.

Getting in had been simple. There was no particular security around the furnaces, which ran day and night with a constant stream of workers, deliveries, hawkers and, in the winter, homeless people looking for warmth. And while the doors and gates to the system of pumps, intakes, manifolds, feeders and returns were locked, those locks were no match for Katarine who, it turned out, had enjoyed a rather unique upbringing.

Inside, the dry heat was constricting, though the system of pipework was impressive. Naida didn't pretend to understand how it all worked or what would happen if that valve was shut or this lever pushed vertical. It demonstrated the absolute commitment of the Suurkene authorities to maintaining every scrap of paper relating to any form of authority and process.

It would have begun as checks and balances, then morphed into evidence. Now it was history.

'What happens now?' asked Naida.

The floor on which they stood was pierced by pipe and metalwork in dozens of places. Up here were the controls, down there, the way in. Elias had been eyeing up the stairs to the lower level ever since they entered and had clearly waited long enough for someone else to take the lead. He trotted down the wooden treads and they heard him creak across a timbered floor, tapping metal on metal with his bolt-handle.

'Down here,' he said, unnecessarily, and Naida's apprehension peaked.

She led the way, seeing Elias working on a panel atop a wide-bore pipe almost at the point where it disappeared through a stone wall and, presumably, into the archives. Naida stared at the pipe awhile, trying to decide whether she could crouch inside it or if it was going to be a belly crawl all the way. Neither option was attractive.

They stood in silence watching Elias, the protestations of the bolts as they came loose vying with the low thrum and roar of warm air barrelling through the system.

'We're going to need to get in fast and pull the plate closed above us,' said Elias, grunting with effort at a stiff bolt. 'The air pressure will fall off sharply as we enter, and we don't want sudden attention from some night-shift maintenance crew.'

Katarine, Adeile and Naida all stared at him. He stopped working.

'That was a hint to get up here because I'm all but done.'

The climb up the wooden structure elevating the pipe was straightforward, though the violent trembling in Naida's hands and the reluctance of her legs to do anything asked of them made it torturous. Eventually, Adeile hauled her up the last couple of beams.

'Last chance,' said Elias, looking at her. 'This is your party, Naida. Do we go in?'

Naida closed her eyes and focused her Talent on calming herself.

'Yes. I'll go first. Who's got the lanterns?'

'Me,' said Adeile. 'I'll follow you in. Elias, I suggest you bring up the rear, you're best able to slide the plate back in.'

'Get a lantern lit,' said Elias. 'I'm ready.'

The inspection hatch was recessed into the ventilation pipe to aid the pressure seal. Elias had fetched a flat-headed tool from his pack. With the lantern lit, they arranged themselves in order.

Elias took them all in with his gaze, his expression fierce. 'Get in fast; move further down the duct fast. If we delay, we get caught, and we're all ashed.'

'No pressure,' said Katarine.

'Hilarious,' growled Elias. 'Go.'

Elias prised the hinged hatch up and hauled it open with one powerful motion of his right arm. Hot air surged out like a slap, the roar of it masking Elias yelling at her to jump in. Down Naida went, landing in a crouch and skittering forward, the pipe brushing her hair and her shoulders. Down came Adeile, lantern in hand, Katarine almost landing on top of her.

'Move up!' she said.

Last came Elias, bringing the hatch lid down with a clang above him. He searched for a way to secure it from the inside, but found nothing.

'Have to hope the pressure loss round the seal isn't too great. But it will fall. We need to be quick.'

He pitched his voice loud and it still barely carried above the racing thrum of the heated air all around them.

'Although we're a plug in the hole right now,' said Katarine. 'Pressure might well rise behind us, which is just as bad.'

'Good point,' said Elias. 'Let's go. Lead on, boss.'

Adeile passed Naida the lantern. It was small, storm-sealed, and shone well against the steel. Naida moved forwards on her free hand and knees, the going made tricky by the curvature of the pipe. Moving through the wall into the archive building itself was signified by a change in the timbre of her knees on the steel; duller for a moment, before a return to the hollower sound.

Almost immediately, the pipe split into three. Naida stopped and took her sketched memory map from her jerkin pocket.

'Problem?' asked Katarine.

'No. Just want to get it right first time.'

'Kind of hot with the air on your back,' grumbled Elias.

Naida ignored him, shone the lantern on the map, turned it round in her hand and tried to remember if they'd reached the end of the archives on her tour and if they'd walked down the middle while Stabile was waxing on about his ventilation system. She thought they probably had. If that was the case...

'Straight on,' said Naida, looking over her shoulder and tucking the map away. 'It should lead down to floor level soon.'

Immediately, as it turned out. And steeply. Naida had begun moving forward before bringing the lantern back in front of her and by the time she saw the hazard, her hand was already pushing on thin air and she slid hard and fast down and forwards, her weight taking her straight through a grille and into the quiet and wonder of the archives with a rattling clang followed by a thump. Somehow, she'd managed to keep the lantern in one piece and, breathing a little hard, she got to her feet.

'I'm not hurt,' she said back up the pipe. 'Thanks for asking.'

The unmistakeable sound of poorly suppressed giggling filtered down the pipe.

'Sorry,' said someone, Adeile she thought. 'We're sorry.'

'You should have seen yourself, though,' said Katarine. 'Amazing disappearing act with an added foot flourish.'

'So pleased to have provided such fulsome entertainment,' said Naida. 'I mean, I've just broken into the archives, thereby committing a capital offence but it's good we can all laugh about my imminent ashing. I've broken the grille too so, Elias, when you've stopped giggling, you can fix it.'

The silence was a bit more contrite this time.

'We'll find another way in to join you,' said Kat. 'We won't be able to climb back up that slope you fell down.'

'Didn't anyone bring a rope?'

'Yes, but there's nothing to tie it to,' said Elias.

Naida huffed and gave her head an irritated shake. 'Just get down here.'

She saw light flicker down as they lit more lanterns and followed the sounds as her friends took the branch pipes, hoping to find a less dramatic entrance. With a swish, Katarine joined her in the archives, a broad grin on her face. Naida couldn't help but smile back.

'Probably more fun feet-first,' she said.

'Couldn't resist,' said Katarine. 'Right, we need to start breaking into locked rooms. Where shall I start?'

Naida held up her lantern. 'Good question. Not much is marked. I need to get back into the royal medical records section again. Beyond that, we're looking for Crucible paperwork – anything to do with trade approvals, names of businesses and investors, donation levels, that sort of thing. The question is, where will it be?'

'Okaaaay.' Katarine looked dubiously at the hall stuffed with papers. Naida didn't have the heart to tell her there were a dozen more just like it, and many, many, side rooms.

'Let's get the royal medical room open first. It's … down here on the right.'

'What do you need in there?'

'The whole move against the Gifted has something to do

with those records. It has its roots in the Esselrode trial, and that's connected to whatever happened to King Pietr.'

'Whatever you say.'

Naida traced the corridors on her map, trying to remember the way and the rooms they had passed. She recognised the door to the royal medical records right away and smiled to herself. Katarine took a look at the lock and nodded, whispering something technical about mechanisms to herself and knelt to her task.

'How can we hope to find what you need in all this?' she said, while she worked. 'It's an ocean of information, to search for a single drop.'

'Let's start by assuming they don't want us to find anything we're looking for, so it's most likely behind locked doors. You might be quite busy with your picks, Kat.'

'No problem.' Katarine stood up and pushed the door open. 'I hope you find what you're looking for quickly, so you can help us with the rest.'

'Speaking of *us*, where have the others got to?'

'Probably got their arses stuck in a grille somewhere. I'll find them.'

Naida walked into the small room, hearing Katarine walk away and feeling the weight of the archives, dark but for her small lantern, press in on her.

'Focus, focus,' she whispered to herself, setting her lantern on the desk and deciding where to dive in.

She tried to recall what had bothered her when she'd first been here, and it came back to her soon enough. It wasn't to do with Eva's health, it was to do with her father's.

There was very little information about King Pietr, which struck Naida as odd. There was plenty on Eva in the same room ... and it was telling that the trauma she had endured was undocumented. What else had been hidden? Naida sifted through, looking for specific dates and entries by senior royal doctors and attendants, and this time finding the gaps she expected. She laid a few individual papers, leather-bound files, and a personal notebook on the desk thinking to take away what she could not read now.

Her search almost complete, she moved a couple of boxes to see if anything lurked behind them and heard soft footsteps behind her.

'Did you find them, Ka—'

But it wasn't Kat, nor was it Elias or Adeile. A tall man in brown with a neatly trimmed beard, shaven top lip, and short, dark hair, stood in the doorway. Danger oozed from him like oil from a handfish tail. Naida stepped away reflexively, feeling the shelves dig into her back. She had seen him somewhere before ... he was one of Denharl's administrators, the one who had been seated next to Dmitry.

The man smiled and the room seemed to shrink. Naida thought to call for help, and then thought again. He had a knife in his hand and if he meant to kill her, a shout would surely trigger the attempt.

'Those who pretend to serve the Queen yet scheme behind her back are the worst, I find,' he said, his voice low in tone and volume. 'She is too trusting. Fortunately, those who protect her are not.'

'I am no traitor to the Queen. I'm here to make sure she lives,' said Naida.

'By skulking around her medical records in the dead of night?'

He moved forward and Naida held up a hand in warning.

'I have friends here. They are but a scream away.'

He pulled the door closed, produced a key and locked it, all so smooth. He left the key in the lock.

'Let them come,' he said. 'These doors are strong, designed that way. I can wait until morning. Can they? Can you?'

At least his intent was clear. And she knew she was on her own. She needed to play for time ... and for information, if she could.

'Why are you here?' She wondered if she would be able to communicate with her friends, if they came to the door, and whether it mattered. With the key in the lock, it couldn't be opened from the other side. 'You can't have followed me.'

He cocked his head. 'All the way from Fishooks. The view from atop the warehouses is really something.'

'I am committed to keeping the Queen alive,' Naida said forcefully.

'You make the mistake of thinking I work for the Queen.'

'Don't you? Or has Denharl sent you?'

His left cheek twitched. 'Well, we both know it isn't Lord Marshal Ludeney, don't we?'

'Do we?' Naida managed to smile through her shivers and the effort it was taking to appear strong. 'I wouldn't be at all surprised if he had me followed.'

'Oh, but your little tea meeting in the Upper Terrace Garden was so convivial. A meeting of allies and friends, I'm told.'

He was so confident he had her caught that he was bragging about it. Careless. But if there was one thing she had learned in all her years in camps on the edge of battle, it was that no outcome was certain until the action was complete.

A face appeared at the grille in the door. Elias. He must have heard the voices, to know not to try to open it. Naida saw him out of the corner of her eye but kept her gaze firmly on the man in front of her, who held his knife like he knew how to use it and was studying her for any signs she might make a move. Naida had seen it before; shattered throne, the army was full of people like him.

'What's your name? You might as well tell me, I know where you work, after all.'

The man shrugged. 'Darius.'

Naida's mouth tugged up in a wry smile. 'Does everyone in your office have a name beginning with "D"? Funny, I thought it was Dmitry I had to worry about.'

Darius laughed. '*Dmitry?* He is almost as naive as you. No wonder you get on so well.'

'He was watching me,' said Naida. Keeping him talking and distracted while, she hoped and prayed, Elias and the others found a way to get her out of this mess. 'You aren't the first member of Lord Denharl's staff to surprise me in this very room.'

'I'm sure dead-soon-Denharl asked him to keep an eye on you, but that would have been out of kindness and concern. Bit different to why I'm here.'

Elias's face had gone from the window and Adeile's had replaced it.

'What do you mean "dead-soon"?'

'That limp of his. Not just a dodgy hip. Those of us that use the latrine after him ... well, enough said. Still, his medical issues aren't your concern, are they?'

Naida's expression soured and she made no attempt to disguise her contempt. 'I can help him. Ease his pain even if he proves incurable. Why would you not want that?'

'Lord Denharl lacks the vision others have. He presents obstacles. And now it seems the earth has chosen to remove him from our path.' Darius drew his right hand from left breast to right hip, just as Vinald had done. 'What the apothecary cannot do for him should not be done. And I doubt your skills as a surgeon can help him either.'

'*Apothecary.* You'll all be relying on the pestle and mortar to ease your suffering before long if you have your way, won't you?

Rolling back hundreds of years of progress, denying your own people the surest means to save themselves.'

Darius shuddered. 'The Touched are a blight on our earth. The sooner the path is cleared of them, the better for us all.'

The path is cleared ... It had been staring her in the face and she'd chosen not to pay attention. Everything linked together. Hatred of the Gifted built up over fifteen years after her parents' execution for genocide in Cantabria; a plague on the loose in the slums with no Gifted there to halt the spread; and an apothecary 'cure' appearing into the treatment void. A *Cantabrian* apothecary.

'Shattered throne,' she muttered. Even if she were to die in here, she had to get the message to her friends. 'Money. It's only ever about money.'

'Sorry, I didn't catch that?'

Naida looked away from Darius and sat down. 'Your heart is already ash. I will not speak to you further.'

'Because I believe nature should take its course?'

'No!' shouted Naida. 'Because every fibre of my being desires nothing more than to help the sick and injured and you relate to me a story of pain and the likelihood of slow, agonising death, from the pathetic throne of ancient belief. Who would you turn to if this fate knocked on your door, Darius?'

Naida allowed her angry gaze to cross the door, slowly enough to see Adeile look at her then glance upwards, repeating the gesture twice before she settled her eyes back on the table and the papers it contained. She understood, and hoped the slight nod of her head and the flicker of the fingers on her left hand conveyed that message. How she was going to achieve what she thought Adeile wanted was another matter. To give herself time to think, she gave Darius a poisonous glance before selecting a folder marked with the moniker of King Pietr and signed, rather scruffily, by someone she presumed had been a doctor or senior close attendant.

'What do you think you're doing?' demanded Darius, an edge to his voice.

Naida focused on the top sheet, which gave a summary of the file.

'Filling in the long hours until dawn,' she said. 'Since you've not tried to kill me, I presume I'm under arrest of some kind. But even if I go to the cage, as you so clearly hope, I will never lose my desire to learn and understand. You should consider it yourself. It might save you from future displays of lamentable ignorance.'

Darius was moving closer. 'Close that file and step away from the table.'

Naida looked at him now, saw the ... *fear*. It was *fear* ... in his eyes and held up her hands, pushing her chair back and standing up.

'All right, Darius ... something someone wants hidden in there?'

'That is not your concern,' spat Darius.

Confirmation if any was needed. Naida's desire to take the folder was so intense she thought about trying to push him aside and grab it, but he was tall, young and strong, and anyway, he was right where she thought Adeile wanted him. Darius moved to close and tie up the folder.

The ventilation grille in the ceiling crashed in and a figure emerged fast, and feet-first. Grille and figure thumped into Darius's back. The breath was punched from his body and he was flattened against the desk, which broke under the combined weight, sending papers, wood and the lantern flying.

The lantern hit the shelves to Naida's left and shattered, oil spraying across floor and papers alike, and it was all alight in a moment.

'Ash and water!' muttered Naida.

She looked about her, grabbed a leather file and slapped the flames, dragging papers to the floor where she could stamp them out.

'Naida! The door!' shouted Adeile.

Smoke was starting to gather. Naida stamped out more flames, continued slapping at them with her leather file-turned-beater.

'It's a bit on fire at the moment,' she said. 'Just down the bottom. Hang on.'

She spared a glance at Darius, who was still moving but impeded by Katarine's knees hard in his back and the broken ventilator grille that she was pressing against the back of his skull. Naida stepped over low flame and reached out to turn the key in the lock and Adeile and Elias raced in, the latter with his jacket off, ready to smother the fire.

'Naida, do you want to see if your assailant needs help?' said Adeile, handing over her lantern. 'We can put this out.'

In truth, it was mostly out already. Naida nodded, turned and saw Katarine grinning from ear to ear.

'I was getting sooo bored of listening to him drone on,' she said. 'I cannot tell you how satisfying this was.'

'Let's see if anything other than his pride is injured,' said Naida, and gestured for Katarine to get off him. She took the grille and stood back, ready to use it to further subdue him if necessary. Naida shone the lantern over Darius's sprawled form. The pool of blood shone darkly. 'Oh no. Help me turn him over.'

Katarine dropped the grille and helped Naida put Darius on his back. Naida's heart sank. He'd still been holding the knife when Katarine struck him. The entire length of it was buried in his gut.

'What can you do?' asked Katarine with a shrug. If Naida

had expected any guilt in her expression, she would have been disappointed.

'Here, not much. We can try to stop the bleeding, and then get him to the royal infirmary.' Naida knelt down. Darius was unconscious and losing blood fast. 'I need a pad.'

'Save it,' said Elias.

'What? No, we have to save *him*.' Naida pushed her hands down on the wound, letting herself flow into him to assess the extent of his injury.

Elias put a hand on her shoulder. 'You know you can't.'

'Not here, but if—'

'That's not what I mean,' said Elias. 'You know we can't let him live. He's seen you; he could identify you. Do you think he'd be in your debt if you saved his life?'

Naida was on the edge of tears with anger. She kept her eyes on Darius, who would die without her help. Only Elias was right, and deep down she had known the moment Darius had challenged her that one of them would not survive their encounter.

'Isn't there any way—?'

'No,' said Elias gently. 'And right now, all we're doing is making more trouble for ourselves. Stop the pump, Kat.'

Katarine nodded, and Darius's eyes flickered open in the moments before her knife pierced his left orb and skewered his brain. Naida would never forget the accusation in his gaze. She scrabbled backwards, the sudden violence at such close quarters shocking and brutal.

'Ash and smoke, Kat! What are you doing?'

'Being real,' she replied. 'The sand is running down fast and our dreams of leaving without a trace are in tatters.'

'Bring more light,' said Naida, her voice quiet and frightened.

She was so very good at focusing on the immediate, it was part of what made her such a brilliant battlefield surgeon. But now she found she couldn't think beyond the inevitable consequences of the mess they had created. And when the lights lit up the room again, she saw it wasn't just a mess, it was a catastrophe.

Darius had bled everywhere, staining the floor. The table was shattered and documents, shelves, papers, boxes and crates and the door were all fire-scorched. The whole room stank of smoke, and the damned ventilation system would soon push the stink of it everywhere, alerting Stabile to a problem the moment he walked in.

The ventilation grille, though, that was the giveaway. The metal itself was bent in the centre and twisted on the frame. Where it had fitted to the ceiling, the wooden surrounds were torn and splintered and one part of it was hanging off.

All four of them stood and stared while the three remaining lanterns illuminated the evidence of their crime. There was no fixing it. Not so that Stabile wouldn't notice. There was no scrubbing the blood from the stone, because there was no brush, no water, and no soap. There were no tools for mending wood or re-affixing the grille, even if they could straighten it enough.

Naida stared down at Darius, then back up at the battered ventilation pipe. There was no hiding his body. But a plan had formed and she was half horrified, half proud that it had hatched in her mind.

'What do we do?' asked Adeile. 'How do we clean all this up?'

'We don't,' said Naida.

'You're going to need to explain,' said Adeile.

'Everything that's happened, has happened in here. All we need to do is make it look like a solo action.'

Elias made a long 'Ahhhhh' sound. Naida continued.

'So, we get all the papers from around and under the body. I want them anyway, bloodied or not. We tidy up the shelves again. We turn Darius back over, but we put the lantern handle

257

in his grip and a big piece of the glass in the eye Kat emptied for him. We put the vent cover under him too. Make it look like he fell through attempting, you know, a break-in.'

'Take his keys, too, lock him in,' added Kat. 'Make it seem even more like he was acting alone.'

They'd all got it now and the suggestions flew. Taking their boots off at the door so they didn't leave a trail; making sure the main doors to the archives were locked, assuming that was how Darius had got in; refit the cover Naida had rolled through and that, Elias assured them, had suffered nothing worse than a bent clip or two; and collect all the papers Naida wanted, or as many as they could find in the time they had.

All that and get out before dawn brought unwelcome attention.

'But someone sent him here. Whoever his master is knows he was here, looking for you, Naida,' said Adeile.

'Not going to admit it though, are they?' said Elias. 'Who has access to archive keys anyway?'

Naida felt a ping of excitement. 'Now that, my friend, is an excellent question. Who should have access, and who has access who shouldn't? Darius had his own set of keys. We should lock up and go, now. We don't want to be discovered here.'

But they only got as far as the main doors.

'Naida, how disappointing.' Stabile was at his desk in the dark, looking a little dishevelled at this early hour. His expression, that of a disapproving parent, destroyed her. 'Although at least it shows you were paying attention to my little talk on the ventilation system. It is impressive, inside and out, isn't it?'

'The part I saw, yes,' said Naida. Her whole body felt as if it had slumped, every muscle enervated, and exhaustion threatened to overwhelm her. 'What are you doing here?'

'Do you mean: why didn't I run away after Darius made me unlock the archives?'

'I suppose I do.'

'This is my home, it is my life. If I am to be killed, I should die here.'

'Back up a little, Stabile. Who's going to kill you?'

'You, presumably. After all, I've seen you, haven't I?'

Naida looked back down the passageway to see Elias standing there, palms spread. She held up a hand, and he shrugged and stayed where he was.

'None of us will hurt you,' said Naida.

'And Darius?'

'Darius is dead.' Lying was pointless. 'What you choose to do is up to you, I mean that. But I'd like you to choose to help me.'

'I don't help murderers.'

'But you helped Darius. He was down here to kill me. Had he succeeded, you would have been as complicit as I am now in the death of another. You don't have to wield the knife to share the guilt.'

'I cannot walk away and pretend I didn't see you,' said Stabile.

'I wouldn't expect you to. The question is what you do with that knowledge, isn't it?' Naida took a deep breath. 'Can I tell you what I am here to find, and what it means for the future of Suranhom – the whole country? I believe a great crime is being committed. Far greater than that committed here tonight. Stabile, will you hear me out? And if you believe me, will you help us find the information we need to prove it?'

Chapter 24

It was Cerrie who woke her. The young maid and dresser dragged her from a sleep: deep and dreamless, but short. She opened her eyes to Cerrie's ashen face and almost smiled because it wasn't soldiers here to drag her away to a cell and thence the cage.

Naida had crawled into bed maybe two hours before, wishing for Drevien's warmth and comfort to ease her mind and body. The haul of documents Stabile had found her were safely hidden. She had intended to read them today, and to put anything actionable into the right hands before returning to the plague zone from which she was desperate for news. And that was all before going to her offices in the Crucible where, Stabile said, the secondary medical records were stored while new space was made in the archives.

Her plan, however, was about to be upended.

'Cerrie?'

'Something terrible has happened. I was asked to wake you. I'm sorry about the hour.'

'What happened?'

Naida's exhaustion was compounded by the knowledge she was going to have to put on an air of ignorance, surprise and sadness over something she had done.

'I don't know,' said Cerrie. 'I will lay out some clothes for you.'

'Thank you. Working clothes. No skirts.'

Cerrie nodded and went to the wardrobes while Naida swung herself from her bed and walked into the hall and then to her drawing room, where she shook Kat's shoulder.

'What?' The soldier rolled onto her back and stared at Naida from the sofa.

'I think Darius's body has been found,' said Naida. 'I'm being summoned by someone. Start reading without me, and if I don't come back, get everything into the hands of Johan Temets. He's a pit speaker. If I come back, I'll need a brief on anything important and I'll go see him myself. Try to get news from the plague camp too. Is Aryn still there?'

Kat was very much awake now and Elias and Adeile were stirring on their makeshift beds.

'Yes. Well, as far as I know. He's good at fishing for information. I'll get Adeile to send Jess. Anything else?'

'Yes. Anything that might link the anti-Gifted movement with increased apothecary industry might prove very useful.'

'Would it?' asked Kat.

'Well, just ask yourself: if you're an apothecary, what's the biggest ongoing threat to your business?'

'Oh, right.'

'Right, I'm off. Be careful. Remember you aren't supposed to know anything about this.'

Kat smiled. 'You too.'

Naida hurried to the bathroom to wash and make herself halfway presentable before letting Cerrie help her into her clothes. She grabbed her medical bag. There was an aide waiting for her outside her rooms. It was Panoa, one of Vinald's original welcoming committee.

'How can I help?' she asked.

'Thank you for your haste,' said Panoa. 'Your presence is required in the royal apartments.'

Naida frowned. She'd only been here a few days but could already recognise some of the coded palace language.

'Not the Queen, then,' she said. 'Who?'

'My Lord Denharl,' said Panoa, his expression grim.

'What's happened?' she asked.

Panoa shook his head and Naida thought she could see his eyes moisten. 'I can't...'

'My apologies, Panoa. Let's go.'

★

The guards to the Queen's private apartments snapped to attention and opened the doors. Gone were the smiles in Naida's direction, replaced by straight-ahead stares and expressionless faces. At least they weren't staring at her, judging her and finding her guilty. Inside, lining the long corridor that was the spine of the apartments and the Queen's administration, more of the Queen's guard stood sentry.

Panoa led Naida straight into Denharl's offices, where Darius's desk was covered in a deep green sheet and strewn with flowers. The lamps were low, shrouding the front office in gloom and partially obscuring the three remaining administrators. The industry that had gripped the office the first time she had entered was absent. In his chair, Dmitry was crying.

'What's happened?' asked Naida, her self-loathing scaling new peaks.

Dmitry carried on staring, lost, like a soldier unable to take in the death of a comrade.

'Naida.' Denharl was at the door to his private corridor and office. He turned and limped away without waiting to see if she was following. 'It is the grimmest of mornings.'

Naida let her gaze linger a moment on Darius's desk,

reminding herself that she shouldn't even know his name, and walked after Denharl, noting the wince in his upper body with every step he took on his surely cancerous hip.

Denharl walked around his desk and sat down. Through the listening system she could hear sniffles and sobs. He gestured to a chair and Naida sat.

'How can I help, what's going on?' She was leaning forward.

Denharl regarded her with eyes dulled by tragedy. Naida was desperate to tell the story, to give them the answers they craved, and the knowledge that her silence would perpetuate their grief stained her soul.

'My trusted man, Darius, was found in the archives this morning. Dead. Died in the most awful and confusing of circumstances. A sweet, caring, talented young man snatched from the palace, from Suurken, from all the people he served with such diligence and grace, and I cannot comprehend it.'

'That's awful,' said Naida, reaching out a hand, which Denharl grabbed and held in both of his. She allowed herself to probe gently, trying to define what was killing him. The conflict inside her, feeling the dry, withered skin of his fingers and palms against hers, intensified, though she found it hard to reconcile Denharl's depiction of Darius with her experience. 'When was he found? How?'

'Stabile, poor Stabile, came across his body when he opened the archives this morning. The circumstances ... in a locked room, blood everywhere, signs of a fire – fortunately extinguished – horrible injuries and a broken vent ... as if he came in like a thief. I can't believe that. We are bereft and we don't know where to turn.'

'Tell me what you need,' said Naida, with a horrible sense that she knew what was about to be asked of her. She should have been delighted, but she wondered if she was walking into a trap.

'I know this is not a usual request, but can you examine him? It has to be done by someone trusted by both myself and Her Majesty. Can you determine how he died, if he died alone or if, as I strongly suspect, he was murdered...though the motive eludes me.'

'My Lord Denharl, of course I will examine him. I will need an assistant to help – to take notes, provide a second opinion, move the body if necessary. I can bring someone I trust, or you can appoint someone. It's up to you.'

Denharl looked relieved.

'If you can nominate a trusted person, I will back your choice.'

'Thank you,' said Naida. 'You must know Brin Gorvien, through his service to the Queen. He has a keen eye and is accurate and knowledgeable in areas where I am not.'

Denharl raised his eyebrows but nodded and pulled himself from his chair, wincing when his hip bore any weight. Naida rose too.

'Then it is settled. He is still in the archives, untouched and under guard. Please, go to work so his body can be returned to his family for the proper ceremony and remembrance rites. I have lost a colleague and a friend. They have lost a son and brother. I would see those guilty of this crime ashed and scattered while I watch.'

Naida dropped her gaze, covering the reflexive move by rubbing her face. 'I can quite understand. I will report back as soon as I am finished. Might I ask one thing?'

'Speak freely.'

'Did Darius have any cause to be in the archives yesterday? Could he have inadvertently been locked in?'

Denharl made a frustrated wave of his hands. 'He was in the office all day. I didn't ask him to go there and cannot explain why he was. Of course, there's…' Denharl wrinkled his nose and then shook his head in irritation. 'No, not him.'

'Not who?'

'People, particularly those working in the palace, quite often serve more than one department, if you understand my meaning. But not him. Pure of soul, pure of purpose.'

Either Denharl was trying to cover having sent Darius to ensnare her, or he was blinded by a paternal loyalty to him. Naida had to assume the latter. Unless he was baiting the trap. Whichever, she was committed now.

'I'll send Dmitry with you.'

'Thank you, Lord Denharl.'

'No, Naida, thank you. You are doing me a great service today.'

'And I will do a greater one when I come back and examine your hip, because it is clear your mobility is deteriorating as your pain increases.'

'I am fine,' he said.

'No, you are not.'

★

Naida's swift journey from self-appointed protector of the people of Suranhom to fraud and accomplice to murder was complete when she arrived to deduce the circumstances of the death of a man she had watched die.

Try as she might, she couldn't shake the slight tremor from her hands, and she was so grateful Brin was with her. Without the burden of complicity, he managed to drive the whole gory charade while making it appear that she was in command. Dmitry, who wandered off occasionally, still spent too long staring at Naida, which risked throwing her off her already-fragile stride.

She tried to ignore him, focusing on Stabile instead. The

archivist would not leave the room; he looked as if his whole world had collapsed on him. She supposed, in many ways, it had. He knew everything and the knowledge would torture him, especially knowing what Naida had told him in the early hours meant that he could not yet say anything. She had put him in a horrible position and would spend the rest of her life apologising for it.

When the body had been examined, she took the notes from Brin and released him back to the infirmary while she briefed Dmitry. Walking back towards the palace, keeping to the shade as far as possible against the blistering heat of the day, Naida used her Talent to calm herself as far as she was able, while she tried to tell him the facts without admitting her guilt.

'Darius was murdered,' she said.

Dmitry paused in his stride, his face a sad conflict of emotions. Relief won. 'It's so strange. He lay there like a common thief fallen foul of his own crime and even though I knew he wasn't, the evidence of my eyes was telling me different.'

'I'm happy to give you some peace, though it's scant comfort, I know.'

'I'm sorry if I was no help. There was part of me believing you could bring him back from the dead and another part that couldn't bear to see him like that.'

Naida put a hand on his arm as they walked. 'You react to shock and grief as you must. I'm so sorry.'

Her stomach was knotting, her face flushed and she was certain she must be radiating guilt. Poor Dmitry was broken up and she was to blame. She squeezed his arm a little harder and bit down on that last thought. She handed him the notes.

'Darius was murdered. Someone came through the vent and drove him to the floor, inflicting mortal injuries. It is fortunate the entire archive didn't burn down. You know who I'd be looking for as well as the murderer? The person who sent him

266

there to his death. The person who left him locked in a room, alone, to bleed out while the murderer escaped. Who was that?'

Dmitry nodded. 'I don't know what's going on. Why would *he* have been sent here in the dead of night?'

'Perhaps he had more than one master in the palace,' said Naida, hoping to prompt a reaction.

'Well, he kept it quiet if he did.' Dmitry couldn't hold her gaze but the pain within him was plain enough. 'Perhaps I didn't know him as well as I thought.'

One thing she was sure of was that she'd misjudged Dmitry. 'I'm sorry for my reaction down here yesterday. I know you were just trying to protect me.'

'Maybe we can have that drink then.'

'Maybe we can.'

Chapter 25

They walked back to the palace in companionable silence for much of the time, Dmitry lost in his own confusion, anger, and grief. Naida felt unable to offer more words of comfort because she could not bear to hear the hollow echo of her hypocrisy.

Walking into the Queen's private apartments, Naida's goodbyes and offers of support were interrupted at the door to Denharl's offices by the thud of leather shoes that were the precursor to the arrival of an obviously irritable Ianna Velez.

'I wonder what she wants?' Naida indicated the oncoming Minister of State for Royal Affairs.

'Can I help, Minister?' asked Dmitry.

Velez was not looking at him, though. Naida laid a hand on his shoulder.

'I think it's me who's done something wrong,' said Naida. 'You'd better give the report to Lord Denharl, and tell him I need to treat him.'

Dmitry loitered in the doorway and Naida smiled. You could never have too much information about what was happening in the palace after all. Velez waved him away with an impatient flick of her hand and beckoned Naida forward with the other like she was directing wagons in a tight courtyard.

'Good morning, Minister Velez,' said Naida. 'I'm flattered you came in person to meet me. How can I help?'

'Perhaps this will convey the gravity of the situation.'

'Poor Darius,' said Naida.

'I refer to your interference in our efforts to rid our city of the plague.' Naida stopped walking, having to flood herself with calm to avoid saying something she would regret. Velez moved on a few paces before realising she was walking alone. She turned. 'Oh. Surprised I know so much?'

Naida scratched her head. 'No. Surprised that you could make a statement of such staggering ignorance with a straight face.'

Velez checked around her to make sure Naida's words had not been overheard.

'How dare you?' she hissed.

'I was saving lives in Fishooks all yesterday, what's your excuse?'

'And now risking all our lives coming back here when you might be infected.'

'Don't presume me to be as ignorant as you. I know I am neither infected nor a carrier, and you know who I used to be certain of those facts.'

Velez's nostrils pinched and she straightened her whisper-thin frame. 'My office. Now.'

'The Queen—'

'Will understand.'

Ianna Velez's offices were just as Naida would have sketched them. Immaculate, filled with tall furniture and without a single concession to personality. A working space. She pitied those who normally populated the three desks in the outer office, so austere were their surroundings. Velez's personal office was no different. Small, efficient, and so tidy it was painful.

'You could do with Eva's duck in here,' muttered Naida.

'What's that?'

'Brighten the place up a little.'

'Colour is a distraction,' said Velez, walking behind her desk but not sitting. There was no seat for a guest.

'You must be such fun at parties,' said Naida. 'Anyway. Explain how saving lives interferes in saving lives, would you?'

'Our allies have been—'

'Kindar's Tincture. Yes, I know. We are using it on volunteers and a very nice gentleman called Markan tried it first to show it wasn't lethal. None of it would be necessary if the Gifted weren't too terrified to come out of their homes. How else can I help?'

Velez's stare was exquisite poison. Naida met it and held it.

'And because they are fearful, we must provide alternatives and so we have, through very delicate negotiations over the course of many years. Negotiations that are ongoing to ensure future prosperity, and which may be upset by meddling third parties.'

'Many years? How prescient of you,' said Naida.

'You will not obstruct the delivery of signed contracts with our allies.'

'I will obstruct anything that might risk the lives of the citizens … your citizens, Minister … that I am trying to save. And should Kindar's Tincture prove ineffective, I will not stand by and let it be sold to people believing it to be the cure.'

Velez nodded. 'Hmm. Then let us hope, for all our sakes, that it works.'

'I'm going now,' said Naida and she was halfway through the door before turning. 'You need to work on your veiled threats.'

★

'Naida! What a pleasant surprise on such a grim day,' said Eva, tying a silk gown around her as she swept from her bedchamber into the dressing room where Naida had been told to wait.

Her hair was wild, her face wrinkled from sleep, and her eyes bright with the sunlight flooding the dressing room. It was already hot despite the hour, the open windows and gentle breeze rippling the nets and drapes.

'It is a confusing and desperate tragedy,' said Naida. 'And I am afraid I've concluded it was no accident. A deliberate attack, leading to mortal injuries.'

The Queen sank into her sofa. 'Senseless. And in the archives too. A haven of peace and history. But your work is done and it's no longer a matter for you and me. So: cheer me up. Give me some happy news.'

'I wish I could lift your mood, but I fear we are walking into a crisis that could engulf the city and kill many thousands of your people.'

Eva's expression cleared and she waved the words away. 'I have been briefed about the plague. But how many have died of any disease this summer? I presume that's what you are talking about.'

She filled a glass with water as if the subject was closed, leaving Naida confused for a few moments.

'Perhaps you are not aware: there is a serious outbreak, right now, in the dockland areas. I have been in attendance myself. Your Majesty, should the disease breach the quarantine borders, it will spread unchecked throughout the city, but given a few of the Gifted we could—'

'There are Touched ... Gifted ... in my cells even now, accused of fomenting the disease. Is this the same outbreak we are talking about?' Eva frowned and rearranged herself into a more formal seated position.

'Ma'am, I believe those prisoners were deliberately escorted from the area so they couldn't stop the outbreak. They are blameless.'

Eva shrugged and Naida felt a growing frustration. 'Then

they will be exonerated at their trial. But they weren't always here, were they? We should ask the question: how did we cope with contagions before the Gifted began to suffocate medical developments?'

'We didn't cope,' said Naida, despairing that she had to repeat such obvious truths. 'Thousands died every year, even with quarantines and a determination to isolate the source of the outbreak. The very first outbreak of Shine Fever killed over half of the population. Old, young, rich, poor. Disease does not discriminate.'

'So *dramatic*, Naida,' said Eva, another expansive wave of her hand exemplifying her complete lack of self-awareness. 'We will cope. We are—'

'No, we won't!' snapped Naida, raising a hand in apology when she saw the ice in Eva's eyes.

'Subjects do not interrupt monarchs,' said Eva. She drained her water and rose. 'I'm hungry.'

'I am sorry, ma'am, but we will not cope. This city, this country, has built its good health upon the miracle that is the Talent for over two hundred years. We have no natural defences against any of the diseases that might ravage the city, and never have. It takes but one accident, one misstep, and there are no cures. Without the Gifted, we cannot hope to halt a spread. Nowhere and no one will be safe.'

'But I understand a cure for Red Spot has been found, and is being administered now.' Eva smiled indulgently. 'And I so worry that we have become too reliant on a capricious ability that can kill as easily as it cures.'

Naida weighed her next words carefully. Eva had clearly received a comprehensive, if biased, brief. And not for the first time, she wondered about the Queen's involvement.

'Kindar's Tincture is untested,' she said. 'There is no certainty it will work, though we all hope that it does. The only certain way to help these poor victims, and to stop the outbreak, is to get the Gifted back in there and protect them with the royal guard. Will you authorise that? I have five brave souls there, but they are in no way enough.'

For a moment, Eva looked discomfited. 'Everything is possible, but not everything is desirable. You are my chief medic, and I have every confidence in you to protect the health of the city. I wish you all the luck in containing this outbreak and I look forward to our next, more cheerful, meeting.'

★

'You're joking, right?' said Kat. 'She can't ... I mean, can she?'

'I have to believe she's being deliberately misguided, or I might have to revise my earlier view of her.'

'Misguided by who?' asked Kat.

She, Elias and Adeile were sitting amid all the paperwork, which had been arranged into piles. Atop each pile was a page of notes.

'Well, my dressing-down by Ianna Velez puts her right at the top of the list. I'm hoping we can find the connections in this little lot. What have you discovered?'

Adeile laughed a little ruefully. 'I think your first question ought to have been about how much of it we understood. Not a lot, to be honest.'

'More than I'd grasp, I'm sure,' said Naida, feeling a pang of guilt that she'd asked them to do her work for her in the first place. 'So, what's in these piles, then?'

'Stabile pulled out all sorts of information about Cantabrian apothecary importers as well as ship-building and construction, like you asked him to. We've sorted it into subject piles as best we can. Up to you or Temets to see if it's legal or not.'

'There's got to be a timeline here,' said Naida, sitting down and starting to pick at the nearest pile. 'The working hypothesis is that anti-Gifted sentiment has been driven by those seeking to replace the Talent with apothecary treatments and make cartloads of money in the process. More than that, it's the establishment of a whole new industry, involving transport, infrastructure and products at the expense of wider public health.'

Clouds parted on Adeile's face. 'And if there are no Gifted to help you ...'

'You have nowhere else to go but the local potion-maker.'

Elias straightened. 'Hang on ... sorry, I didn't mention this earlier because I didn't think it was relevant but, where I was walking at least, there was talk of local apothecaries, people who'd been there across the generations, being bought out, or forced out.'

'By who? Forget that, I know already.' Naida felt a little more hope bleed away. 'This plan has been a long time in the making.'

'What makes any of the big stuff illegal, though?' asked Adeile.

'If I understand anything at all, we have to find a link between foreign investment and the anti-Gifted legislation,' said Naida. 'Temets will know; he'll have access to the sponsors of the legislation. I wonder what he'll make of the apparent palace involvement, too.'

'Be careful, Naida,' said Elias. 'You're painting a target on your back.'

'Paint's already dry,' said Naida. 'Keep an eye on the plague camp for me. Bring me good news ... like that the tincture works, or something.'

Chapter 26

Johan Temets was not happy to see Naida. He clearly wondered how she had even tracked him to his office, buried in the administration wings on the first level below the pit. They were labyrinthine, seasonally damp, pleasantly cool, and laced with the sounds – and often the sight – of a large number of rats.

Naida had asked Misha, rather than Dmitry, for help gaining access to him, desiring as much secrecy as she could muster. Misha was back in her rooms to continue her convalescence and the mischievous look in her eyes delighted Naida, evidence her health was returning. Misha was a repository of everything useful. One of the benefits of a long life of gleaning information and retaining a sharp mind in which to store it.

Not only could she provide Temets' location, but also how to get into the administration level using her name and position. All she need do, apparently, was tell the guards she was going to her office. Perhaps she'd fall in love with bureaucracy after all.

'Well? I am busy.' Temets was very tall, this close up. Stick-thin yet imposing in his expensive suit, pince-nez on the bridge of his nose, standing behind his paper-strewn desk. His thin grey hair was slick to his head and his wild eyebrows gave him a fierce countenance. 'I am due in the pit shortly and have cases to review first. I'd be delighted to make your acquaintance on

275

another occasion when you have not surprised me in my own office – where I never host guests and do keep confidential documents.'

'I was in my office,' lied Naida, 'and needed to see you regarding the legislation you debated with Francesca Oliari, concerning the registration and restriction of the Gifted. I was moved by your passion and skill.'

Temets' expression turned bleak. 'I lost.'

'As you knew you would. Didn't you?'

He raised those wild eyebrows. 'The outcome of a pit debate is never certain.'

'Johan, it's just you and me in here and I am not an idiot.'

'What do you want?' Temets waved her to a chair and sat down himself. 'Going over old debates is never productive. And I am *Honoured Temets*, to you, Lady Naida.'

Naida had sifted through Stabile's documents before coming here and had a pile of papers she considered important with her. She opened her sack and pulled out the summary sheets covered in names and connections between the palace, Cantabrian apothecaries, construction and ship- and dock-building, some Suurkene, some from further-flung shores. She pushed them all across the desk to Temets, who adjusted his pince-nez and read, eyes widening almost comically, his face reddening in concert. Temets was no fool, and she saw him make the obvious connections.

'I'm surprised this isn't drenched in blood. How did you come by this information?'

'Wow, dramatic stuff, Johan. You should be a pit speaker or something.'

'Your attitude is not endearing. What I can see here appears to be clear evidence of a conspiracy to create an outbreak in order to force a cure on a population denied Gifted intervention, presumably for financial gain. But none of it is admissible because of how it was obtained. You have brought me information I am not at liberty to view and I, and the rest of the Crucible, am very much aware what happened in the archives overnight.'

'Look … Honoured Temets, and honestly, that's a right mouthful when Johan suits you far better, does it matter how I came by it? Look at what this represents, given the legislation you are fighting at the moment. There's a link in here to the sponsors Oliari was representing on the floor of the pit, I'm sure of it … but I don't have that evidence and you have access to all the sponsor information. You could find out who is orchestrating this murder in the name of profit. Please.'

Temets stared at Naida and then back at the notes. He swallowed once, a long affair.

'You have the proof to go with this list of names and alleged associations?' Temets waved Naida's paper at her.

'I know where to get it,' said Naida.

Temets almost smiled. 'Naida, it's just you and me in here.'

'Yes. I have it here.' She put the heavy files on the desk. 'I know having this is against all sorts of laws. Darius died trying to kill me and keep this information hidden.' Naida paused while Temets absorbed her partial admission. 'Can I take you through what's happening in Old Landers right now, and why it threatens everyone in the city?'

Temets pressed his lips together, and she could see him thinking through the implications of working with her, or of turning her in. His eyes never left hers.

'We've come this far,' he said finally. 'It can't get worse, can it?'

But it could.

Naida laid out what she knew: the ganger barricades, the removal of the Gifted from a plague zone … and the convenient arrival of a Cantabrian merchant with a supposed cure that it seemed was to be sold throughout the city. She watched him join her statements into a very disturbing picture, his brows arching together, his jaw setting tight. Every now and again, his eyes would drift back to her notes, and Naida could see him trying to walk paths of contacts and influence, just as she'd hoped he would.

Temets was silent when she finished. Out in the corridor, bells were ringing.

'I am called,' said Temets, looking towards his office door and removing his pince-nez. 'And this information is dangerous to any who hold it without due authorisation. If I can find a link between the sponsors of legislation against the Gifted, the docklands, and medical supplies, that involves foreign influence, it will represent a serious enough breach to halt further legislation relating to any of it. A rematch of all recent connected legislation will also be forced. It would mean the publication of all current sponsors' names and their interests, so you will understand that there will be powerful forces unwilling to let it happen.'

'Do not risk yourself,' said Naida.

'That is advice you should heed,' said Temets. 'I support the Gifted, but I know enough that this won't sway the tide of hate. I'll follow the threads as far as I can, put some information into the right ears among my proposers. I'll update you here in a day.'

'Thank you,' said Naida, standing to go.

'But if I find out you are lying about Darius, I will see you ashed and scattered.'

★

Hope. That was the feeling. It surprised her and there was a bounce in her step as she hurried back towards the daylight, pausing just a moment at the door to her own office. She had the key, it was part of the kit she'd received on her first day in the city. It was back in her rooms, though, discarded because she'd assumed it ceremonial, so ridiculously ostentatious was its design.

Heavy too. She'd need Elias to carry it. Still smiling at that image, she reached the top of the stairs and almost walked straight into him. Seeing his expression, she realised that hope, like time, was fleeting.

'What is it?' she asked, as he grabbed her arm and ran with her through the Crucible crowds, heading for the southern doors.

'Can you ride?'

'No, why? Elias! What's happened?'

Elias didn't break stride, just pulled her a little closer as he pushed through the crowds.

'Aryn got here. He's beaten up pretty badly but he made it. There are Keelers massing at the barricades. Got mercs with them too. Lots of weapons. He could see Tan trying to organise a defence, but it's going to be a slaughter.'

'Ludeney's soldiers—'

'They won't act to stop it unless someone, like you, lights a fire under them. We've got to get there. Willan's inside. Drevien and Kella too.'

Drevien... that she should be under threat and Naida was not standing by her chilled her to the marrow. Outside, there were four horses in a small courtyard that let on to the main street running from the Crucible towards the old docklands. Kat and Adeile were mounted up already.

'Hurry!' shouted Kat.

'Why would they attack?' Naida felt the kind of fear she normally reserved for a desperate retreat from a marauding enemy. 'Why now?'

'Aryn says they've heard Gifted are in the camp.'

The heat of the day could not melt the frost that rimed her veins, nor could the hubbub of a city, unaware of what threatened to engulf it, fill the void that had been torn in her gut. Their blood would be on her hands... because she had let slip that the Gifted were there to Velez and the Queen. And unless someone had been listening at the door, or down some concealed pipe, that meant one of them was part of this conspiracy. She knew who her money was on.

'Naida can't ride,' said Elias, climbing into his saddle with the easy fluidity of experience.

'Climb up behind me,' said Kat. 'Ridden like this before?'

'Once or twice.'

Naida adjusted her medical bag, and the document wallet containing her evidence, to lie across her back, and pulled herself up behind Kat.

'Hang on,' said Kat. 'And lean with me, not against me.'

'Just get me there, fast as you can.'

Naida put her arms around Kat's waist and pressed herself into the soldier's back, the smells of sweat, leather and horse strong in her nostrils. She put her head just to the left of Kat's so she could see the way ahead.

'Is Kindar's Tincture working, Kat?' she asked, trying to distract herself from the disaster approaching the camp.

'Early signs are encouraging, apparently.'

Behind Naida's flush of relief came a sickening realisation.

'Tan was right, wasn't he?' she said.

'That's my reading. They'll use the Gifted as a pretext to kill everyone in the camp. Then they have their successful trial *and* an empty dockside for redevelopment.'

'I thought I was saving them. Seems the Gifted will be the death of them all.'

Kat snorted as she dug her heels into her horse's flanks. 'Bloody melodramatic nonsense. We both know they'd have found a way to instigate a bloodbath one way or another.'

'I'll take the lead, make a path,' said Adeile. 'Kat, behind me. Elias, you all right to bring the other horse?'

'No problem. Fast, Adeile. Really fast.'

It was a personal torture of noise and smeared colour for Naida, worsened by the memories of the other time she'd ridden like this. Then, escaping the clutches of Ludeney; now, with her life and those of her loved ones at no lesser risk.

Her friends shouted people aside, galloped their horses through the streets and squares of Suranhom, swerving, sprinting, hauling back. Collisions were inevitable and frequent, the tirades of insults and threats thankfully lost in the hammering of hooves on cobblestones.

Naida stopped looking ahead, preferring to cling to Kat's back while her panic blossomed, and imagined enemies chased her into exile once again. Worse was the thought that those she had believed safe ... if a plague zone could ever be termed safe ... were in a potential conflict zone, and the speed the horses were being urged to said everything about how worried the others were.

Rattling through the cloth market, the closest marketplace to Old Landers, the horses were forced to slow by the sheer volume of people. Naida raised her head, looking for the patrols by Ludeney's people, and whatever hope she'd had of changing the mood deserted her.

On the stage that should have been hosting entertainment for those touring the colourful stalls selling fabrics, the Arbalers were holding a rally. Four priests stood there, dressed in deep brown and green, chains like woven roots around their necks, heads shaven and painted in the colours of the earth. Arms raised in the symbol of the living forest.

The chants she heard, and the obvious popularity of the messages being called to the crowd, would shrivel the soul of anyone possessed of the Talent. This was a mob, being riled up in order to be set on the innocent with a single baseless accusation. An army, assembled to destroy the very people who could save them. It was heartbreaking and the speed with which it had been mustered was terrifying.

Adeile rode hard around the back of the crowd, navigating between the few open stalls with consummate skill and extraordinary fortune. They pulled up at the checkpoint, where a soldier eyed them.

'Who are you? This is a quarantine zone.'

'I am Naida,' said Naida, unpeeling herself from Kat's back. 'I have letters of authority.'

The soldier stepped aside. 'Not necessary, Lady Naida. Go. Be safe.'

'The camp is under attack. We need your help,' said Elias. 'Now.'

'We can't abandon this post.' The guard shrugged. 'I'm sorry. But I will send word for reinforcements.'

'Do it fast,' said Naida. 'People are going to die.'

They spurred on and, rounding a corner, they approached the community barricade.

'Move aside!' Adeile yelled. 'Move aside!'

Locals, with scarves over their mouths and noses and hats pulled low against the heat, dragged the barricade chains aside. Ahead, the Keelers' barricade stood closed against them. The five gangers in front of it turned as they approached, spreading out, cautious.

'Elias, go right!' called Adeile. 'No chatter. These are enemies now.'

Adeile guided her horse left, digging her heels in again, the animal leaping forwards. Elias galloped up on the right, letting the spare horse go, leaving Kat to take the centre. The gangers readied weapons, looking to one another, shifting stances. Scared. Without hesitation, Adeile dropped a hand from her reins, drew a short blade from her left hip and swept it straight into the face of the first ganger.

Elias pulled his horse to the left and dismounted on the run, landing in a crouch and racing forwards, blade in hand. Two squared up to him, unconvincing, one held a blade, one a club, and Elias roared as he ran in.

'Run, rats! Get back to your holes.'

One broke, dropped his blade and ran. The other stood taller, gripping his club in both hands. Elias ducked the wild swing and buried his blade to the hilt in the Keeler's gut. He dragged it clear and hurried to the barricade while Adeile wheeled her horse, chopping her blade into the back of a Keeler looking to attack Elias. The ganger pitched facedown to the cobbles and lay still. The other two were already clear and running back towards the community barricade.

Elias put his shoulder to one of the armoured wagons and pushed it aside.

'Go, go!'

Adeile and Kat, with Naida tucked in tight again, rode through the gap. Naida saw Elias throw himself back into the saddle, sword still drawn, and gallop after them. She turned towards the camp and, for a few moments, she thought they weren't too late.

Perhaps twenty or so Keelers were advancing, still forty yards or so from the border fires. Lined up facing them, a mix of Elias's soldiers and the unmistakeable shapes of Tan and Rosa Delliher amid their own people. In the camp itself, there were others standing ready, defending the spaces before the canvas shelters and, she thought, protecting the entrance to the ware-house. It looked solid enough.

Twenty yards from the fires, with Adeile still perhaps sixty yards away, the Keelers stopped, the front rank spread out, and the second rank moved in front of them and knelt.

'Shattered throne, they're professionals,' shouted Kat over the sound of their galloping horse. 'Crossbows!'

Tan had seen the danger. The defending line scattered into a loose arc but at that range each one of them was rolling the dice. The Keeler crossbowmen loosed. Naida held her breath … and every bolt found its mark. Six people fell, incapacitated, dying or dead. More jerked under the impacts, staggering with leg wounds, one clutched at a shoulder but still came on.

With no time to reload, the crossbows were discarded and the Keelers, though they evidently weren't all true gangers, drew weapons and charged. Naida looked on helplessly. Elias was to her right, Adeile ahead and about to engage. Kat urged their horse on, but it was tiring beneath their weight and in the heat of the day.

The Keelers stormed hard into the defenders. Three of the fighters Elias had brought with him were at the heart of the line, providing a bulwark, but elsewhere Tan's tired, sick and inexperienced crew fought and fell. Naida saw a woman fall with a blade sunk halfway to her spine, and another had a leg chopped from under her. Tan was old and wise, working as a team with the equally wily Rosa, jabbing and dodging, bringing enemies onto other blades. It couldn't last, though, not without help.

Panic was sweeping the camp. The Keelers broke through just as Adeile and Elias rode into the back of their second line, swords sweeping through unprotected backs. They wheeled to deal more mayhem, spill more blood, while Kat rode straight through. Naida glanced back and saw Elias lean out and chop his blade into the collar of a mercenary. Adeile was chasing another pair, sword high, ready to strike.

'Drop me at the fires,' said Naida. 'I'm more use there.'

'They'll go first for anyone defending the sick,' shouted Kat. 'The rest they can take later.'

Naida's heart skipped. 'Hurry.'

Ahead, the fight had turned into deadly running skirmishes. Naida saw Tan on the ground, Rosa standing over him while others raced to help, and the enemy swept past them. More local people were moving to face them but from behind, there was fresh panic. More Keelers were coming in from the western barricade. Flame surged into the sky from canvas. Trapped between the fires and their attackers, the sick were trying to rise, to run. Naida searched the crowds, seeing Willan bringing defenders to him, standing in front of a shelter where the Gifted were still treating plague victims.

'To the left. Willan needs help.'

'Got it,' said Kat.

Once more, Elias and Adeile moved past them, this time sliding down from horses that would be a hindrance in the midst of the mass of friendly forces and patients. Kat pulled up and moved with her as Naida dropped to the ground and ran towards Willan. Kat shouted to Elias for support.

Willan was trying to defend too wide a front and didn't have experienced soldiers with him. Naida could see him shouting orders and waving poorly armed locals into position as best he could. He ducked a sword sweep and buried his own blade in the gut of his attacker, pulling it clear just to be knocked down by a defender with a hideous gash in his side.

'Willan!' shouted Naida, trying to run harder, hurdling a body. 'Your left, your left!'

She didn't know if Willan heard her but he looked up, saw the danger and got his blade up to deflect an axe blow. Moments later, Elias brought his raw power into the attack, forcing attackers back, creating space for Willan to scramble to his feet.

Adeile was right behind him, pulling him clear before hurling herself into the fray beside Elias.

'Breach to your right!' yelled Kat, leaving Naida in her dust.

Elias looked up and saw the Keelers knock the last of the defences aside and run under the shelter where Gifted and medics still worked.

'Run!' he shouted but none of them so much as turned his way. 'Run!'

A Keeler pulled a Gifted from her ministrations by one shoulder, opened her throat with a short-bladed knife, and suddenly the shelter was full of screams and blood and suffering. Willan blocked another from his innocent target but a third got through and hauled his victim away from her patient. But it wasn't a Gifted, it was Drevien.

'NO!' screamed Naida. 'She's not—'

The blade ran through Drevien's gut, and when he pulled it clear she collapsed across three patients, hands pushed hard into the wound, blood flooding between her fingers. Kat's blade carved through the Keeler's back as Naida screamed.

'Turn to face!' shouted Elias. 'Reform!'

Out in the camp, the Keelers were marauding almost unchallenged. Heedless of risk, Naida pushed through the skirmishing, around the bodies of terrified, immobile plague victims and their screams of terror, their expressions of confusion and pain.

She dropped to the ground next to Drevien, memories of battlefields crowding her mind.

'Drev,' she said. 'My love, it's me, it's Naida.'

Drevien was lost to her pain and the life flowing from her body. She was clutching so tight, Naida couldn't move her hands from the wound.

'Help, I need help here!' She turned and saw a Keeler die, her face opened by Adeile's blade, and heard what she thought might be horses, but it hardly mattered. 'Someone, please!'

'I'm here,' said Kella and her voice was balm on a fresh burn. 'Let's make her comfortable at least.'

Naida stared up into Kella's eyes, brim with tears, then turned back to Drevien.

'No,' she said. 'We can—'

'We can't,' said Kella, helping to move Drevien off the plague victims and onto an area of bare earth. There was so much blood. 'The Gifted are all dead. You saw the blade go through her. We can't. But we can stop the pain. What do you have in your bag?'

Kella reached out and Naida thrust the bag at her, pulling the strap over her head. She began to straighten Drevien's body to see the wound and Drevien groaned, barely conscious, hands still pressed into her gut.

'Get the resentha oil, get dressings. Needle and thread, too.'

'Naida, not this. All we can do is stop the pain now.'

'Oh, I think we can do much better than that,' said Naida, knowing exactly what it would mean, as she pushed her hands against Drevien's terrible wound. 'Get what I asked. Do as I say.'

Kella frowned, then smiled as a tear fell on to her dusty cheek and she opened Naida's bag.

'I cannot let you go. Not like this,' said Naida, hearing the thundering of hooves loud now, a metaphor for the torrent of betrayal and hurt she was about to unleash. But there was no choice. She could not let Drevien die. 'I'm so sorry. For everything.'

'What do you mean?' asked Kella.

'You'll see.' Naida focused on Drevien. 'Drevien, my name is Naida, and I'm going to save you.'

Despite her pain, the critical blood loss and the knowledge of her imminent death, Drevien opened her eyes and managed a chuckle.

'You're funny, Naida,' she gurgled. 'I love you.'

'I love you, too,' said Naida, about to betray her all the same. 'Try not to judge me too harshly.'

Drevien's eyes closed again, the last of her energy spent.

'Have the resentha and dressings ready, Kella. Pour the oil into the wound – just a half-dozen drops.'

Naida pushed her index fingers into Drevien's wound, and pushed her energy deeper, and deeper still, able to feel the ragged cuts to her flesh, muscle walls, intestines... it was a horrific wound. Impossible to treat without the Talent. Even with it, there was so much to do, so many bleeds to stem, so much contamination from the blade and Drevien's clothes to neutralise.

Kella dripped the resentha, mixed with mandragora and opium, into the wound. Drevien relaxed immediately, allowing Naida to work fast, sealing nicks and gashes in her large and small intestines. She allowed her Talent to flow through Drevien's entire body, pouring herself into the woman who thought she was to die, feeling it soothe bruises, and marry up flailing veins and nerve endings. Making Drevien whole without considering whether she would ever want such an intervention. She hoped Drevien would forgive her eventually. And still love her.

By the time she was done, the fighting was all but over. There were dozens of soldiers in the livery of the Suranhom city guard walking through the camp. Ludeney's people had heeded the call of the soldier on the barricade.

'Do you want to sew her up?' asked Naida, looking up.

She became aware of a wider audience than just Kella. Willan was there too, with Elias and Kat. All four were staring at her. Pushing herself to her feet, she wiped her hands on her trousers in a futile effort to clean off the blood. She pointed to the wound.

'Front and back, Kella. The bleeding won't stop, otherwise.'

Naida picked up her bag and put it over her shoulder, feeling tired, feeling altogether different to the woman who had ridden into the plague camp. At least they all knew the truth now. Some of it. It didn't make her feel any better.

'She ... she'll need clean dressings every four hours and the wound cleaned with saline.' She gestured towards the rest of the camp. 'I should go and see who else I can fix, eh?'

'You do that,' said Kella, crouching to arrange dressings, needle and thread instead of looking at her. 'Kat, can you help me?'

'Sure,' said Kat, looking away from Naida. 'What do you need me to do?'

Chapter 27

Naida fought back sudden tears while she hurried across the camp towards Tan and Rosa. Ludeney's soldiers and riders were in control now. Surviving Keelers and mercenaries had been rounded up, the panic was subsiding and there was movement of the healthy among the sick. But the atmosphere was one of shock and loss. Naida could hear crying, the particular sound of people staring at terrible wounds in their own bodies, unable to comprehend them.

She wanted to help them all but, as on the battlefield, it had to be one at a time. Approaching Tan and Rosa, sitting alone amid the bodies of friends and foes, Naida hissed in a breath at Tan's stillness. He was lying on his back, Rosa at his head, smoothing his hair. His arms were by his sides.

'Rosa,' said Naida, coming to Tan's other side and examining him, seeing the blood all round his mouth and down his chin, the pool soaking into the ground beneath his body. 'What is his injury?'

Rosa raised a tear-stained face. 'He's going. Nothing anyone can do. Gifted are gone and his chest was crushed by a club.'

Naida looked back at Tan's face, seeing a faint exhalation and the red bubbles forming and bursting. 'Let me see what I can do.'

'Just take away his pain while he dies.'

'Open his shirt,' said Naida, unshouldering her bag and looking for a soothing balm. 'Let's see what we've got.'

Rosa smoothed Tan's hair again. 'Naida is here, you'll be all right now, my life.'

She untied his leather coat and unbuttoned his shirt, carefully pulling it away to expose the appalling wound below. Blood surged out of the hole smashed into his ribs. Naida laid her hands, thick with a balm of ginger and Gorsen leaf, onto Tan's chest, letting her energy spread across his ribcage and reveal the full extent of his injury. It had been a colossal blow, splintering his ribs above his right lung and driving shards of bone into the delicate tissue.

It didn't matter how good a surgeon she was, or how great her Talent, with such an injury. It was incredible he still clung to life. Naida massaged the balm into the wound, though he was beyond pain now, slipping away as if he'd just been waiting to say goodbye.

'I'm sorry, Tan. I'm so sorry.'

'Don't apologise,' said Rosa. 'Just find out who's doing this.'

Naida felt a clear anger wash away the guilt at what she had hidden from her friends. She looked back, where Kella still tended to Drevien. Elias, who she wanted, was helping move the bodies of the slain Gifted from under the canvas shelter.

'I've got a pretty good idea already.' She stood up, bag back over her shoulder. 'And I'm going to blow this whole thing open. We will have justice for Tan. Because, make no mistake, this is murder, and it was committed for profit.'

Rosa wasn't listening. She was staring down at Tan, smoothing his hair again, her strong shoulders shaking with grief.

'I'll send someone to be with you,' said Naida.

Rosa nodded and reached out a hand, which Naida squeezed before trotting over to Elias.

'Elias, I need you.'

Elias straightened and turned, his face not unkind as she had feared it might be, just not as warm as it would otherwise have been.

'How's Tan?' he asked.

'That's why I need you,' said Naida. 'He's dead, and I need answers, and I can't be bothered to ask politely anymore.'

'Sounds like my line of work,' said Elias. 'Who are we asking?'

Naida walked towards the warehouse, taking in the bodies, the wounded, the feverish activity of those dealing out aid. She waved at Sennoch, whose clothes and hands were covered in blood. He nodded back and she was so thankful he was here, casting his calmness across all in his orbit.

'Markan,' she said.

Elias smiled. 'I was hoping you'd say his name. Pity you didn't let me persuade him earlier.'

'If his tincture really is working, I have to have proof of its part in the conspiracy. He can provide it.'

'He's over by the warehouse door,' said Elias.

Naida saw him, standing unmoved by the carnage around him. He was unharmed and still handing out phials of his tincture, making a finger-wagging point to every recipient, who then hurried away to one canvas shelter or other.

'Markan!' called Naida as they approached. 'Work goes on regardless, I see.'

Markan's smile was thin enough to be transparent. 'There are a lot of people to save.'

'So there are. And your friends have managed to kill many of those best able to help, while you are blissfully untroubled.'

'I am not Touched,' said Markan. 'I am doing the work of the pure.'

Naida tensed and Elias, armed with his new knowledge of her, growled, making Markan flinch.

'The Gifted cure wherever they lay their hands, and you will accord them the respect they deserve.'

Markan raised an eyebrow. 'The Cantabrians have evidence to the contrary.'

'Take a walk with us to the riverside. We need to talk,' said Naida.

Markan glanced at Elias. 'Talk...' he said. 'Right.'

'Given this attack, you'll excuse me if I feel the need for a little... security.'

Markan smiled, no fool, and put down his box of phials. 'Going fishing, are we?'

'In a manner of speaking,' said Naida. 'It does seem your tincture, while unproven as a cure, is having some effect in alleviating symptoms. Which makes it all the stranger that mercs and gangers, clearly acting under orders, have attacked the camp, intent on killing everyone in it but you, apparently.'

Markan swallowed but said nothing.

They walked in silence along the side of the warehouse and across cobbles strewn with weeds towards the old dockside.

'What do you want to know?' asked Markan eventually, staring down into the river just below his feet where foam, sticks and other debris had collected.

'Those documents you didn't want me to have were very useful,' said Naida. 'I know about purchases of land here in the docklands. I know about deals signed with Cantabrian apothecaries. But I don't know who the lynchpin of it all is. I don't know who is enabling the Keelers, or arming them and their mercenary friends to murder mine. And I want you to tell me.'

'I think you have overestimated my importance to the enterprise,' said Markan. 'I am, sadly, little more than a delivery boy.'

'Your role was described somewhat differently when I

mentioned your name to an ally in the Crucible earlier,' said Naida, the lie slipping easily from her mouth. 'Try again.'

'It never hurts to underplay it,' said Markan.

'Sometimes it does,' replied Elias.

Markan shot him a nervous glance. 'My employer, Genneran Apothecary, sent me here to oversee our end of a deal with Suurken. I am a senior advocate for Genneran and am often in the field, overseeing trials, construction developments, and negotiating low-level contracts for our goods. That's it. I'm sorry I can't help you more.'

'I see,' said Naida, nodding. 'What do you think, Elias?'

Elias unleashed a massive punch to Markan's gut. 'I think he's lying.'

Markan, shocked and winded, dropped to the ground and curled into a ball, coughing and retching. Naida dropped to one knee next to him.

'My friend is an astute judge of a situation, and he likes hurting people. Especially when he's cross because those he cares about have been hurt or killed. I need a name.'

Markan turned his head. 'Can't give you one ... It was all handled by the family.'

'Who organised the plague outbreak? Was that the family's idea or some traitor from inside the palace?'

'No one organised the plague!' said Markan.

Elias's boot struck him hard in a kidney. He jerked with the pain, and cried out, but no one was listening.

'You'll give me names, Markan. Anyone can hand out your tincture and wait for results. You're expendable.'

Elias grabbed the back of Markan's collar and hauled him to his feet, marching him to the water's edge. 'Can you swim?'

'Yes, actually,' said Markan. 'Can I go now?'

Elias laughed and almost dropped him. 'You've got balls, I'll give you that. Still best you answer Naida, though. Hard to swim with two broken legs.'

Naida dragged Markan's face towards her with a hand around his chin, letting her expression go cold and feeding her Talent through her body to steady her as she issued a rare threat.

'Don't lie to me again or I'll have Elias kill you. Your people murdered my people and I am all out of mercy. Names. Was it Kerslan? The Queen? Velez?'

Naida stared into his eyes and could see his fear warring with his loyalty. There may have been the slightest reaction to Velez's name. He shook himself and both she and Elias let him go. Markan straightened and tugged his clothes straight, dusting himself down.

'I'm dead either way,' he said. 'But I really do want that tincture to work.'

And he threw himself into the river.

'Dammit!' shouted Naida, watching him struggle in the current that was already sweeping him out of reach. 'Elias, can you get to him?'

Elias ran a few paces down the bank and threw himself flat, reaching out, trying to snag Markan's coat.

'I need a branch, anything to hook him!'

The bank was clear and Naida ran alongside Markan, who was struggling under the weight of his clothes, his head bobbing no matter how hard he tried to swim.

'Make for the shore!' called Naida. 'We can save you. Don't be a fool.'

Elias overtook her. Markan was beyond the reach of any branch, but he had a length of rope in his hands.

'Grab a hold!' Elias tossed the rope towards Markan. Naida saw it splash into the water close to his head. 'Grab it. I'll pull you in.'

The flow was strong and Markan was tiring quickly. He

turned to face them, ignoring the rope, treading water though his mouth was all but submerged.

'You cannot stop what's coming,' he gasped. 'And I won't help you.'

He drifted further away, his face serene. Naida stopped walking and watched him go, hating what he represented, yet taken aback by his courage.

'Shattered throne,' she said.

'It's not bravery,' said Elias, pulling the rope back in and coiling it up. 'He was just more afraid of his masters than he was of us.'

'What now?'

'Before or after you explain yourself to Drevien, Kella and Willan?'

Naida sagged. 'I know. I owe you an apology too. And Kat, Adeile … everyone.'

Elias shook his head. 'We hardly know you, not really. We knew the stories, the legend, and it's disappointing it's not true … but it doesn't change who you are, not to me.'

'Thank you, Elias. I'm sorry anyway.'

'Why did you hide it?'

'It's … complicated. I hope I can tell you all soon.' She looked across to the shelter where Drevien lay. 'But not until others know. Can you fetch the document wallet? I need to go over everything again, see if there's anything we've missed.'

★

Naida sat with her back to the warehouse wall as the afternoon light and heat began to wane. She looked out over the river in which Markan had drowned, to the fishing villages that studded the opposite bank, and took the papers, folders and files out of her satchel. Her heart was full of regret and her mind was whirring, wondering how she could navigate herself, and her friends, to a place where they would forgive her; understand what she had been forced to do. It was so hard to see a path.

It didn't help her unease to remember that Temets would strive as hard to uncover Darius's murderers as he would to follow the trail of money and influence driving the purge of the Gifted. And she had handed him evidence of her link to that murder. It would not be difficult to deduce.

Among the few files she had gathered from the archive was a set with an unbroken seal. The cover was signed by a former head of the royal medical service, a man called Rius Denharl.

'Well, well, well,' said Naida. 'Must write me a song about nepotism sometime.'

She broke the seal, unwound the green ribbon and opened the file, seeing the beautifully scripted list of contents on top. She scanned down the list, its dates and titles, and felt a grim twinge of excitement. She sorted out some papers and hunched over them, trying to remain calm while she read about the King's health during the time her parents were being tried, tortured and executed.

The notes reported a rapid and sustained deterioration in King Pietr's condition during the time leading up to, and during, this critical period in Suurken's history. That he was already in serious mental decline before her parents were put on trial was not in doubt. All his cognitive functions were compromised with scant, brief periods of remission. What was also clear, she read, was that as the trial and torture played out, the strain on the King was, quite literally, killing him. His decline was sharp and distressing for all those around him.

It was no surprise. Her parents and the King had been close friends and confidants and the magnitude of their crime, of which he had been unaware, must have been a mortal blow to his already-weak mind and body. In her youth, Naida had complained about never being allowed to visit the palace. Perhaps Pietr's deteriorating condition had something to do with it.

Naida sighed, put down one set of notes with a weary hand and picked up another. By the end of it, she was in tears.

> '...it was notable today as it would have been yesterday and will be tomorrow, that the only relief His Majesty enjoys as his confusion clouds him further and his distress intensifies, are the visits from his beloved daughter, the Grand Princess Eva. She spends time with the accused every day, easing their agonies as best she can, trying to persuade them to admit their guilt, counselling them with the skill of one much more experienced in the ways of world affairs. She reports their condition to the King daily, which is of great comfort and the only time His Majesty appears fully aware. It is upsetting to note that when she leaves, his subsequent descent is swift indeed. As and when she ascends to the throne, her capacity for mercy, for even the nation's most hated individuals, marks her out for greatness.'

Now, more than ever, Naida was frustrated by her life-saving change of identity. Despite her frustration at Eva's attitude to the inevitable disaster heading in Suranhom's direction, she wanted to embrace her, weep her gratitude into Eva's shoulder. How fitting that this most human of monarchs had been the one soul whose capacity for care of other human beings had outweighed her revulsion at their crime.

And Ludeney wanted her killed for not wanting a continuation of the monarchy. It showed the glaring gap between the ever-monarchists like the Lord Marshal and the march of a more liberal, people-led, way. Naida knew which side she was on... but to get there she had to persuade the Queen to back away from her more extreme positions. Not an easy task, particularly when Naida sympathised with her refusal to bear an heir.

Naida shook her head and wiped her eyes. A yawn blossomed long and deep. She needed sleep, and she wasn't about to get any. Getting closer to the truth of the events surrounding her parents' death gave her hope, and she couldn't rest. Naida stood, stretched extravagantly and almost lost her grip on the papers, some of which fluttered to the ground, threatening to follow Markan into the river.

She snatched them back up, having to stand on one to prevent the faint breeze taking it from her forever. Stooping to pick it up, she saw a scrawled note on an otherwise blank page. It was written by Rius Denharl and seemed to have been done in a rush. It was unsigned and that piqued her curiosity.

'We showed Pietr the evidence today. He would not read it. He cannot face the injustice and so retreats within his already devastated mind, there, no doubt, to suffer yet further. Without his attention and his decree, we cannot save them.'

★

Naida had no idea how long she stared at those words while the lies that had defined her life since she was fourteen rotted and fell about her feet.

Every assumption she had made; every step she had taken on her lifelong journey inside her new identity; everything that had driven her into a life dedicated to saving others to salve her assumed familial guilt; every day she had shed tears of hate and regret and shame and disbelief; every time she had feared she would be unmasked; every time she had sworn not to be her mother's or father's daughter but something better, kinder, more merciful; every time she had denied her own ability in order to avoid the fatal connection being made; every emotional

299

and psychological blow she had taken when she had heard her name used as insult and slight.

Every moment she had hated her parents anyway, despite believing in their innocence.

All of it lies.

The burdens she had carried her whole life had been unnecessary. The desperation she had felt; the times when killing herself seemed the only course of action. All those people who had hidden her, many at the cost of their own lives. It had been a waste; a cruel, pointless waste.

For a few moments she wished it wasn't true. Going on in ignorance would be so much easier than living with the truth. And yet ignorance was a feather on the breeze – the more she clutched at it, the further away it flew.

She sat unmoving. She was aware time was passing, a lot of time, but it didn't matter. The page had slipped from her hand and lay on the dirt, trapped between her feet.

Naida wiped tears from her eyes but more came and she couldn't stop her hands from shaking. It was as if she had a high fever. Snatches of coherence were swept away by a tumbling, dizzying array of memories, the sight and sound cascading through her mind as within her, somewhere, some part of her fought to make sense of her discovery.

There was no sense, though. Two innocent people had been tortured and killed over a period of seventeen days, then ashed and scattered like the worst of criminals. All the while, the proof of their innocence was ignored, suppressed, so her parents died while the guilty...

The guilty.

Naida opened her eyes, a dreadful calm settling on her and a strange relief beginning to run through her body. Amid all the wrongness and the lies and betrayals, there was something she could cling on to, and it lifted a deep-seated terror from her mind, allowing her to breathe deep, free from a fate she had, until this moment, assumed inescapable.

Her parents, her wonderful mother and father who had wanted nothing but good and happiness for everyone they came across, the mother and father she had been taught were evil, were exactly the people she had believed them to be. But more than that: there was no darkness, not in them and not within her. There was no unbearable malice waiting to be unleashed should she take a life.

Strange. There was no way she *would* ever take a life, but to know that even that action would not render her an unrecognisable monster was liberating. Even though she had never believed in that darkness, had proved to herself so recently that it could not be so, the final, irrefutable proof was a priceless gift.

Naida had read enough over the long years to believe that the plague spread in Cantabria had been started deliberately. It was not a disease that had ever afflicted the country before and there had been no defences against it whatsoever.

It was the perfect weapon, you might say.

It meant that, while the Esselrode name was still the most hated in Suurken, those who had perpetrated the outrage had walked free to ... to see their plans come to fruition. Someone for whom the wholesale slaughter of large swathes of an indigenous population, and the resultant demonisation of the Gifted, could be used for profit. Or power, or influence, or a return to religious fundamentalism.

Someone was using misery and murder to make money. And if they had been willing to set a plague fifteen years ago, they would not hesitate to do so again. Perhaps all they had been waiting for, along with enough anti-Gifted sentiment, was a treatment, or a cure, for any of the diseases which rose up in the hot summer months.

Naida tidied up the papers and returned them to their wallet. She needed to think through the deepening fog of her anger, grief and screaming sense of injustice, hard though that was. Her parents had been blameless innocents. So was she.

She needed the evidence Rius Denharl alluded to ... and that meant getting back to the Crucible and the palace – and doing so with enough protection to get the information she needed. The notes were likely within her own medical records. She would have to get them to Lord Denharl and maybe, just maybe, to the Queen – who might know more than Rius Denharl had reckoned. It was doubtful. But nothing could be set aside. Eva was, after all, a likely suspect in telling the Keelers that the Gifted were in the camp. Though more and more the storm's eye seemed to settle about Ianna Velez.

Hard though it was to believe, there were more immediate concerns. Naida needed her friends. She could count on Elias, but she wasn't so sure about Willan and Kella. And she needed Drevien's blessing above all. She had already rocked them once by revealing part of the lie she had been living. Should she risk revealing the rest? Her family was innocent, and she could all but prove it ... but speaking her name would have a dramatic effect on people long-schooled in its evil.

It was her name though, her true self. And they already knew she'd deliberately hidden her Talent. They would want to know why, and her explanation had to be convincing.

Naida laughed to herself. A hollow, broken sound. She'd revealed that she had been lying to those she professed to love ever since she met them, and here she was contemplating which lie might convince them she was telling the truth this time.

★

Drevien was dozing when Naida returned to the shelter. Kella took one look at her and walked away to treat another patient and Naida couldn't tell if it was out of respect or disgust. Probably both.

Naida sat, stroked Drevien's face, held her hand and checked her stitches and dressing, impressed as always by Kella's deft needlework. She had imagined a hundred different ways to explain when Drevien opened her eyes, and it was all entirely inadequate. In the end, she didn't even get to speak first. She'd looked away for a moment, her eye caught by Willan walking with a bandaged arm but otherwise unharmed. He'd nodded to her which was something.

'Why did you hide your Talent?'

Naida's breath caught and her gaze snapped back to meet Drevien's. She'd feared hatred and anger but what she saw was disappointment, and it hurt more. Tears welled up. She wanted to say that the army wouldn't have accepted her as a surgeon if she was a Gifted but that would have been less than half the truth.

'I had to hide everything back then.'

Drevien frowned. 'What does that mean?'

'I couldn't bring any of my past with me when I joined the army medical corps.'

'That's the same answer but with different words.'

Naida laughed but it came out a sob. 'You never let me get away with anything. It's why I fell in love with you. One of the reasons, anyway.'

'Who did I fall in love with, then? Who are you really and why couldn't you be a surgeon with the Talent? Not in the army but you wouldn't have been the first.'

Drevien had been so close to death and the Talent had brought her back, but if Naida had hoped she would be exhausted and not ask difficult questions, she was disappointed. She found herself reaching for another lie, backed into a corner, needing to fight her way out.

'No, I won't,' said Naida.

'Won't what?'

'Lie to you.'

'Not anymore, anyway.'

That stung but Naida nodded her head. 'I deserve that.'

Drevien's hand sought and found hers and lay on top of it. 'Just tell me, you idiot, it can't be that bad. Who were you hiding from?'

There was no judgement in Drevien, just a yearning to understand. Exactly what Naida would have felt. And here it was, the decision to be made. She'd thought she'd have more time. She almost blurted it out right then ... but she caught herself. If she was to admit the truth, she couldn't just drop it like a boulder from a mountain top.

She had hidden this for fifteen years, terrified of the loathing her name would inspire. And wishing to spare those she loved the danger they would be in if they did not disavow her.

In a way, it was the ultimate test of a relationship, but she didn't want Drevien to take it. Ash and smoke, she didn't even know which reaction was a pass and which a fail.

'Have you forgotten?' Drevien's face was kind, her expression edged with humour and affection.

'Don't be daft,' said Naida. 'Did you want me to save you? Did you want to live, Drev?'

Drevien raise an eyebrow. 'As a deflection from the matter in hand, that's a pretty stupid question. When we are dying, we all want to live, don't we? Of course, I wanted you to save me, I just knew you couldn't, not without, well, you know ...'

Tears spilled from Naida's eyes unbidden, a reaction Drevien misunderstood.

'Hey ... I'm here and if you weren't Gifted, I wouldn't be. I don't hate you; I love you. I just wish you could have trusted me with the truth.'

'You don't understand,' said Naida through a sob. 'You couldn't.'

'So help me, Naida ... if that's really your name.' Drevien smiled and squeezed Naida's hand.

Naida's heart raced so hard she thought she might faint. She felt breathless, sweaty beyond the heat of the day.

'I need you to remember that I have dedicated my life to saving others, risking my life to rescue wounded soldiers. I have fought to prolong the lives of other women and men, and I will die with my conscience clear.'

'Why do you need to tell me that?' asked Drevien, and there was trepidation in the way her gaze danced across Naida's face and in her deepening frown.

'I lied so that I could prove my own truth, as a healer. I lied because I had to believe in myself, in who I was. I lied because I didn't want more people killed while trying to protect me.'

Naida saw Drevien begin to withdraw. 'You're scaring me a little. Why must you say all this? Who are you? Why would people die if they knew who you were?'

Naida wondered if she had already guessed. That last question had faded in her throat. To Naida, it was obvious. She breathed deep and savoured her last moments of anonymity. In her daydreams, she had swept into a room and announced herself, tall and proud, and the blank faces around her had welcomed her and loved her.

She had to smile. Here, under a makeshift shelter, outside a warehouse in a dockside slum surrounded by plague victims, was about as far from her daydreams as it was possible to get. But not as far, perhaps, from her nightmares where she screamed her name as they broke her bones.

'I love you, Drevien. I would die for you.'

Drevien had pressed her lips together to keep her from breaking down. 'Naida...'

Naida closed her eyes, made peace with herself, and leaned in close to Drevien's face so no other could hear her.

'I am Helena Esselrode.'

Chapter 28

It was the fear in Drevien's eyes that broke Naida's heart. She had hoped that perhaps there would be understanding, even forgiveness. Or just acceptance that she was the person she had proved herself to be. A name shouldn't change that. But it did.

Esselrode. The one name in Suurken's history that inspired revulsion like no other, and Naida had just made it her own. How stupid to think that anyone would be able to accept it and look on her with anything other than apprehension bordering on terror.

Naida wanted Drevien to say something, anything. But she just stared, still processing what she'd just heard. Naida would have taken a slap in the face, a barrage of abuse, rather than this shock. There was nothing more she should say, but the silence went on so long, or so it felt, that she could not remain silent.

'I have been running from it all my life.'

Drevien removed her hand and made tiny shakes of her head to stop Naida saying more. The fear had gone and in its place was a chasm of disappointment and loss, and Naida realised that she had forced Drevien to live a lie too.

'You made me fall in love with the daughter of monsters,' said Drevien slowly. 'All that time and loyalty and love I invested in you, with no idea what you were. Of course you saved lives, your guilt would demand it. Of course you've tried to believe you are different, but how can you be?'

'Because they were innocent,' said Naida and it felt liberating to be able to say it out loud. 'But if you believe otherwise of me after all that you have seen and all we have shared, denounce me.'

Naida could see Drevien's memories warring with all she had been taught. Now she had revealed her name, Naida was desperate for allies. It was quiet around them. People had moved out of earshot, and they were as alone as they could be.

'They were innocent, Drev. I don't expect you to believe their daughter, and I didn't know it for sure until just now. But I found some evidence – it's right here – and there's more I have to find. For the Gifted who are being framed now, just as my parents were.'

'How can you be you, and also be her?' asked Drevien, as if to herself, as the shock began to settle. 'How can you have your heart, and their blood?'

'Because I am not *her* and they were not what were painted.' Naida held Drevien's gaze. 'They were murdered. My parents were murdered, and their deaths were a part of what's happening now, in this city. You can hate me, you can be disgusted by me, you can shun me … but please don't stop me proving it, so the right people are brought to justice for the murders they have orchestrated.'

Drevien looked so sad it broke Naida all over again. Her face was pinched, her eyes brim and lost.

'I don't think I can hate you,' said Drevien. 'I should, but you saved my life when it would have been easier to let me die and remain Naida.'

'If I had, I wouldn't have remained Naida. What do you call someone who lets another die when they could have saved them?'

Images of Litvin, and her utter hypocrisy, swamped her mind.

'I can't do this,' said Drevien. 'You need to go, let me work this out.'

'I understand. Tell the others the truth. Tell them what I'm doing. And if you decide you must denounce me, I understand. But give me a head start, so I can prove what I say is true. I can show you what I already have.'

She reached into her satchel but Drevien stopped her.

'Don't show me. Go. When I tell them, I don't know what will happen. They don't all know you like I do. Like I think I do.'

'I love you, Drevien.'

Drevien nodded but was silent. Naida stood. 'No walking for two days or you'll break your stitches. Keep those wounds clean.'

She turned and walked towards the fire-marked boundary of the camp, trying not to look back, trying to walk as if she had a noble purpose and wasn't the most wanted person in the country. She so needed her friends' help but the sands had shifted and she had to do it alone now. She couldn't risk dragging them down with her if it all went wrong.

Approaching what had been the Keelers' barricade but staffed now by Ludeney's guards, she paused, giving into the temptation to look back. She couldn't see if Kella was already speaking with Drevien, hearing the words that would change her world, but she could see Elias; he was, after all, hard to miss. He had come to the boundary fires, his big frame picked out in the fading sunlight, staring after her. She raised a hand, receiving a nod and raised hand in return.

Ludeney's guards waved her through, pointing out the quickest route to the palace for her and even offering her security, but she turned it down, not wishing to draw any attention to herself.

She hurried to the borders of the cloth market, which

transformed into an entertainment arena once the traders had packed away for the day. Ludeney's soldiers were discouraging people from journeying down to Cotton Row, which she'd just trotted along, though in truth few wanted to get closer to the plague zone.

Naida only had to mention her name to gain access to the market square and she moved through the fire-eaters, story-tellers, acrobats, players and musicians; past the throngs of happy faces that were unaware or uncaring of the crimes that had been committed just a short stroll away; and between stalls selling everything from dubious stews to exquisite kebabs.

She knew how they could play while the plague raged: it was the confidence the Gifted had given them and they were yet to realise their safety net was gone.

'Dancing while the dead burn,' she muttered.

She checked her position, seeing the tallest of the palace's spires in silhouette away to the north, and walked through the crowds. There were far too many people gathered around the stage where Arbalers still peddled their lies and stoked fears.

Naida blew out her cheeks and her head was in mid-shake when her eye was caught by a frenzy of movement at the guard post she'd crossed to get into the market. Looking back over the heads of the hundreds, thousands, in the square, she saw the guards ridden down, swords flashing in the late afternoon light. The southern end of the square filled with riders as the sounds of laughter and chatter fell away.

The mood of the marketplace darkened to fear in a ripple as riders kicked flanks and horses began to move. The crowd panicked, then scattered like a flock of birds taking flight, the main wave heading straight for her. She turned on her heel and ran.

Naida was fast but the spreading panic, charged by the in-creasing volume of shouts and screams behind them, propelled people to greater effort. The riders had split to drive straight through the crowd and ride around its borders to cut off all routes of escape. They were after her, she was certain of it. She had to stay ahead of the crowd to hide, and to escape before the encirclement was complete.

Ahead, the crowd was as dense as it was behind her. With every pace, she had to move around those slower than her. People sprinted in every direction, were pushed aside, pushed over or in some cases helped by those with more kindness than terror.

To a galloping horse, the perimeter of the square was no great distance. Naida could see riders moving up to her left and right. The exit to Silks Approach was nearing, but even though it was a wide avenue, the crowds would be packed closely, and the danger of injury or death would increase.

Naida tried to move faster. Someone came by her as if she were standing still, pushing her to the left. She stumbled and carried on, sensing she would just make it out before the riders trapped her. Behind her, the mass of the crowd felt as if it was closing in, full of urgent shouting and the thrum and drum of thousands of feet.

Naida burst into Silks Approach with them, the mass tightening to try to avoid the clutter of stalls, chairs and tables set outside the shops, inns and dwellings. All of it was engulfed by the crowd, and more and more people fell in the unstoppable charge.

'I have to get off the road,' Naida muttered.

She was closest to the right-hand side and glanced that way, seeking a way out. In the same moment, the man in front of her stumbled and fell. She tried to hurdle him but her satchel caught against another runner and threw her off balance. She knew she was going down a moment before she sprawled, an ugly fall, her legs already scrabbling to drive her back upright.

She almost made it too, half falling, half running and gathering momentum when she was pushed hard to the right, crashing into what was left of a display of colourful jewellery and hitting the ground hard once again. Naida tried to get up but the crowd was on her, buffeting her like waves.

The first foot to land square on her back was shocking, the force driving her body into the uneven cobbles. Then another foot trod on the back of her calf and she squealed, barely having time to draw breath before a third clipped the fingers of her left hand. Still she tried to rise, and again she was knocked down.

'No,' she said. 'Not like this.'

Another boot caught her in the side and she could see nothing but legs all around her, feel nothing but the reverberation of those thousands of feet through the ground. She was kicked in the side of the head and rolled onto her back with the force of it, winded. She needed shelter, a friendly face, anything.

But no one as looking down. A woman tripped over her and tumbled to the ground, screaming as the crowd battered her as they had Naida – who tried to roll again to get her feet beneath her. There was blood on her face and up her nose, her hand was on fire and her head throbbed. She shook it but her eyes had blurred. She brought her legs up, was knocked down once more and cried out in frustration, taking blow after blow.

One more time, she gathered herself, and then hands gripped her under her armpits and drove her up and right, feet barely touching the ground.

'First door!' shouted a voice she recognised. 'Take it down.'

Tucked under the arm of a powerful figure, Naida looked up through the haze of her vision and the blood running from a cut in her forehead. A figure ran hard into a door, shoulder-first. The wood and iron didn't stand a chance and both door and figure disappeared into shadow. She was bundled through, and down a narrow wooden corridor and out into an inner courtyard where she was sat down against a wall.

'Well, you've caused quite a stir,' said Elias.

The quiet in the courtyard, where the sounds of the stampede outside were muted and echoing, was so blissful Naida slumped. She put her hands over her face and stopped her bleeding, focusing her energies into sealing the cuts and alleviating her thumping headache. She looked up to see Elias and Kat staring down at her.

'You followed me?'

'Dangerous being one of the Gifted in this city right now,' said Kat. 'Anyway, Ludeney ordered us to keep you safe when we left the battlefield. That order is yet to be rescinded.'

Naida cursed her stupidity, her belief in her invincibility and, yes, her naivety.

'Thank you.' She had other questions, but they had to wait a moment. 'Who were they? The riders?'

'Keelers. Well, whoever the professionals are, fighting with the Keelers today. You're a prized head all of a sudden. Have you been rubbing people up the wrong way again?'

Naida's mind was still in Silks Approach and Kat's question caught her on the hop, though it was clear from her tone that she hadn't spoken to Drevien yet. The speed with which the news of the Gifted being at the plague camp had reached the Keelers' ears had bothered her. Now it seemed someone, probably the same someone, had wanted to capture her – or at least keep her in the camp.

'Ianna Velez, certainly, and with Temets asking questions on my behalf, there's reason enough to want to silence me. I need to get back to the palace. And I need to warn Temets to be even more careful.'

'Sure, but you're being hunted now,' said Kat. 'Some of the riders'll be caught up in the market but there'll be plenty of others looking for you, on horse and on foot, and they know where you're going.'

'We'll get you there,' said Elias. 'Somehow.'

'Where are we now?'

'Good question. Kat?'

Kat shrugged. Naida had her first real look around. They were in a courtyard the architects had seemingly envisioned as an escape from the hurly-burly of Silks Approach, complete with calming fountain, benches, and flower beds. And no doubt it had been blissful before the riches had moved elsewhere and the slum landlords had moved in.

The fountain was a burbling ruin, its original marble having been stripped down to its foundations. What would once have been a network of flow pipes was gone too, leaving a fractured, algae-encased feed stump amid weeds, moss, and the remaining shards of the fountain's base.

The shells of the benches remained, as did the outline of beds and lawns, but all were gone to weeds and mud, while the walls were grey, run with mould; and the windows and balconies that looked down into the mess, those that remained intact, were festooned with rags, drying in the heat of the decaying afternoon.

Elias indicated a passage at the other end of the courtyard. 'Reckon we get to Fincher's Alley that way? We weren't seen coming in here so the Keelers will be concentrating on Silks Approach and up towards the Barrows and the Spice Market, I would have thought.'

Kat glanced up at the sky to get her bearings. 'Maybe. So long as we can head left at the end, we should be all right. Worth a try.'

'No other choice, I'd say,' said Naida, pushing herself to her feet.

'You all right?' asked Kat.

'A bit sore, but I can't complain. I could be dead.'

They hurried through the passage. At the end, Kat pointed to their left. The bells still rang. People must still be running.

'This is one of the alleys that bleeds off the Martyrs' Market, I think ... Back behind us, it runs off towards the Carriage Road and the Old Stockhouse complex. We can pick up Heron Lane if we cut right when we hit the square and then get on to Fincher's.'

'Good.' Naida nodded. 'Look, before we go on, did either of you talk to Drevien before you came after me?'

Both of them shook their heads.

'Then I need to tell you something, because you have to know what you're getting into.'

Chapter 29

'If you openly support me, you'll make yourself a target,' Naida said into the unsettling silence that followed her announcement. Kat had backed away a pace and her hand had strayed to her sword. Elias too. She respected their reactions. Here they were in a darkening street, with a woman who was the most wanted person in Suurken. She hoped they would help her anyway.

At least neither of them had made the heart to hip gesture of the Arbalers. That would have been the beginning of the end. Instead they had stared at her, clearly wondering whether to believe her and, once deciding they had to, not having a clue what to say.

'Target how?' asked Elias eventually.

'They'll ash and scatter you too. So if you want to go, to deny everything you've just heard, or to turn me in, I understand completely. I won't try to run, because I am innocent and, given the chance, I can prove it. I know it's hard but I need you to remember how many lives I have saved.'

'Yeah, but your parents were the same until they committed genocide,' said Kat, managing not to be unkind, just matter-of-fact.

'Except they didn't... can I show you something? From my wallet.'

Elias and Kat shared a look and shrugged at each other. Naida unshouldered her satchel and pulled out the papers she needed, positioned right at the top. She so wished Drevien had seen them and wondered what was happening in the camp now. What Willan was thinking, Sennoch, Adeile ... all the friends she had lied to from the moment she had met them.

What would Hazza think? The archetypal grizzled old soldier who thought she was a miracle-worker would hate the thought the Talent had been used to save him. But without it he wouldn't be seeing his family, hugging his children or kissing his wife right now. What confusion she would sow in so many minds.

Naida shared Rius's notes about King Pietr's mental state and Eva's work with both him and her parents, saying nothing, leaving her friends to draw their own conclusions. Then she showed them Rius's note about the evidence Pietr wouldn't, or couldn't, read.

'I have to find that evidence,' said Naida. 'It is the keystone to everything that's happening now. My parents committed no crime. They were not evil, and neither am I.'

Kat handed the documents back and Naida replaced them in the wallet.

'I'm not sure I understand,' said Elias.

'Look at the hatred being stoked against the Gifted, the same people who are in jail awaiting trial for laying the plague in Old Landers, though we know they were escorted away before the outbreak. Look at the Arbalers, out there again as if they were never discredited. Then look at what happened to my parents, and at who, miraculously, has a cure for the Red Spot and tell me there is no link.'

'The Queen could help, no?' asked Kat. 'I mean, she was in Cantabria heading a trade and aid delegation when the plague kicked off and she was evacuated.'

317

'What?' said Naida.

'I remember it because I was just signing up. We'd battered the Cantabrians—'

'Slaughtered more like. Battle of Errind Bay...'

Kat flapped a hand at Elias. 'Right, exactly. Then we sent over a big delegation to bully them into trade and security deals that benefited us. A fair price for stopping the killing. I wanted to join up, to win us more victories like that.'

Every time Naida thought she had worked out the conspiracy – because that's what it was – it got bigger. Even at sixteen Eva would have been a figurehead to give weight to Suurken's sincerity in dealing with their defeated foe. So, who else from the palace had travelled to speak with the Cantabrians? Had someone who was there laid the plague, knowing her parents would carry the blame? And how convenient that a significant force of Suurkene dignitaries and military would have been in the right place to help deal with the disease.

'I can't ask her,' said Naida. 'I won't know who's listening. And would she tell me? Why would she, unless I reveal my identity to her? And without the evidence, that would lead to a quick trip to the cage in Traitor's Square.'

'Then carry on as you planned,' said Elias.

Relief was an unlooked-for pleasure and knowing these two were still with her was something she'd savour if she survived the night.

'Are you sure? I mean, I'm the daughter of monsters and everyone hates me,' she said, managing a smile.

'I hope Elias agrees when I say that whatever you are, there is plague that needs eradicating and we have to help. And that'll give you the chance to find your proof, if it exists. Just don't make fools of us.'

Naida's smile faded. Kat's tone was hard, not suspicious but not accepting either, not yet.

'I get it, and I'll leave word for you in the palace infirmary. My plan is to head into the Crucible, catch up with Temets, and then search my offices. Then, the palace, I guess. Thank you, both of you.'

'Let's get moving,' said Kat. 'I can get us there unseen.'

★

Naida called into the medical centre on her way to the Crucible as she'd promised, ensuring no one saw her with Kat and Elias. Making her rounds was a breath of fresh air, taking her from the immediacy of her problems. There was nothing more serious than apothecary-treatable infections, some healing bones to assess, and a couple of bad teeth to extract. Normality in microcosm, while outside everything felt like chaos.

Hurrying down to the Crucible before the doors were shut for the night, Naida picked up her expensive coffee from Sammel's stall on the way to Temet's office, making sure to pop her head round the door of her own offices to check in on the administrators patiently creating records to be placed immediately in the archives, never to see the light of day again. Well, mostly.

Her initial knocks on the speaker's door were greeted with silence so she tried again, doing that half knock, half walk-in action, complete with apology. The moment she did, she caught the scents of blood and urine. She closed and secured the door behind her and ran to Temet's desk.

'Oh no,' she crouched by him. He lay on his front, curled into a ball by his chair. There were bloodied smears on its arms and his desk. 'Johan, can you hear me?'

Naida felt for a pulse and found it, strong enough that she didn't have to panic. He groaned at her touch and she was relieved he was conscious, if only just and in bad shape. What she could see of his face was swollen and laced with contusions and

319

cuts. It was clear the beating had concentrated on his stomach as well. She needed to assess his internal organs for damage.

Naida pushed his chair aside then laid a hand on his shoulder.

'Johan, it's Naida. You're not in danger but you need help. I have to lay you on your back, can you help me?'

'Leave.'

'I'm sorry, what did you say?' Naida could not have heard clearly.

'Go.'

His voice was clogged, either by blood or swelling. He rolled on to his back and Naida tried hard not to react. His eyes were both so swollen he'd have trouble seeing her. The bruising to his face was as severe as she had ever seen, and she could see more running down his throat and onto his chest through his torn and bloodied shirt.

'You need medical attention,' she said, feeding into him enough to ease his pain and allow him to relax a little.

Temets rasped in a breath. 'They did this because of you.'

'What?'

'I asked ... questions ...'

Naida sat back on her haunches, ashamed but hoping her suspicions had been correct. 'Ashes and water, I'm so sorry.'

'Just go. My family next.'

Naida's heart was palpitating and she felt clammy. She glanced back towards the office door, but when it didn't burst inwards, she turned back to Temets.

'I'm here now, and that makes you my patient. I'm going to clean you up enough that you can get yourself to Brin at the medical centre. Agreed?'

One eye fixed her with a stare so laden with fear and pain that her breath caught.

'Yes.'

'Good decision. Can you get back in your chair? Any broken bones?'

'Ribs, I think.' He coughed and spat blood. His mouth was a mess of broken and missing teeth. 'Some fingers. I can stand . . . help?'

Naida turned the chair then crouched down to offer him her strength, letting her Talent further dull his pain and seek out the extent of internal injuries. 'Easy now. Easy, easy . . .'

Temets pushed himself up on one forearm, Naida seeing at least two fingers on that hand dislocated. It was a slow process, every moment of progress punctuated by shivers and gasps despite her help. Naida blew out her cheeks. Whoever had done this knew what they were about. He had been disabled without endangering his life. It left him a walking . . . limping . . . warning.

Naida put a hand under his shoulder to help him into an upright sitting position. He shuddered and moaned as his stomach muscles, beaten to jelly, tried to engage to steady him.

'Sure you can do this?'

He bared his teeth, nodded and brought his legs under him, Naida taking as much of his weight as she could from behind him. He was trying not to put his hands out to steady himself and ended up levering himself up with the inside of his right upper arm braced against the desk side.

'Just have to . . .' he said and with a single, agonised push he came up high enough to collapse into his chair, the pain dragging a whimper from his lips and tears from his eyes.

'We can start to fix you from here,' said Naida.

'I'm all right,' said Temets, his words barely audible.

Naida cocked an eyebrow and poured some water into a metal cup from the jug on his desk. She handed it to him, helping him curl enough bruised fingers around the cup so he wouldn't drop it, before opening her bag, inadequate though its contents would be after all her work at the plague site. She

321

fetched out what remained of her clean cloth and an alcohol solution, her few dressings, a bottle of lavender and peppermint, and a pot of capsicum and ginger balm.

'You're going to smell amazing,' she said, but it didn't raise the mood.

Naida got to work, feeling his upper body for broken bones, deep bruising and the telltale signs of internal bleeding. She fed a little of herself into him again to help diagnose his injuries accurately, and to give him information to take to the medical centre.

'Tell me what happened.'

'They will kill me if I talk, after they've killed my family.'

Temets had two cracked ribs, bruised kidneys, gut and testicles, but no bleeding. Medically, she relaxed a little.

'I'm so sorry,' said Naida. 'Then say nothing, I understand. Let me clean up your face, make you look presentable at least.'

'Thank you.'

Naida had felt his fear when she had examined him. The shock would settle on him when he left the office and every passing person scared him, staring at his face and after him as he shuffled past them. It would be worse still when he got home to his family and his inability to protect them pressed down upon what was left of his emotional resilience.

'I'll have someone watch your house. No one will touch your family while I'm breathing,' said Naida while gently cleaning Temet's face, lifting the dried and smeared blood from around his nose and mouth, leaving her with a clearer canvas to treat. He had deep cuts in his lips and cheeks, some needed stitches, all needed proper, stinging cleansing. He lifted a broken hand and pushed hers away.

'You cannot save us from them. No one can.'

She nodded. 'This is going to hurt.'

Naida tipped some alcohol onto a cloth. Temets raised an eyebrow and shrugged.

'I define pain differently this morning,' he said and almost smiled. 'Get on with it.'

Naida worked fast, feeling Temets tense and wince with almost every stroke of the cloth. He would still be barely recognisable through his bruises and grotesque swelling but at least the risk of infection would be minimised. Next, she would need to relocate those two fingers, or he wouldn't be able to open his office door.

'I will have your house watched all the same. I have power at my back too,' said Naida. 'Of whom did you ask your questions?'

'The Registrar,' said Temets, after a long silence, forcing the words out with the utmost reluctance.

'Who?' Naida frowned. 'I'm new to this.'

'The Registrar of Interests. They record every proposer and opponent of legislation. They had to know there was illegality.'

'Thank you,' said Naida. 'I'll ask no more. I will find out who did this, because they're after me, too. And I'll keep you safe, trust me. Gifted can help you, if you can find one.'

Naida left Temets in as good a condition as she could, and before his nerve gave out entirely. He had passed on his address, which was something, and she managed to get back to her office without seeing another soul, which was something else. Temets was going to knock on the door as he went past, assuming he wasn't being followed. The poor man had shuddered when Naida had reminded him to be careful.

None of the administration team were there now, which suited Naida perfectly. She liked to think that she wasn't paranoid but she preferred not having someone looking over her shoulder while she snooped around.

The office was cramped by the sheer volume of paper shoe-horned into it. The first room had two desks back-to-back at its centre. Both were stacked high with papers and leather-bound files. The walls were hidden by floor to ceiling shelves bowing under the weight of labelled box upon labelled box of medical files.

The second room was down a short shelf-lined corridor, behind a heavy door. It was locked but a quick search through desk drawers revealed the key. Inside, the smells of leather and paper mingled with those of damp and rodent. The sight that greeted her when she shone an oil lamp from one of the desks into the darkness was of a wall of paper.

She waited, wanting to rush in, until she heard Temets' knock on the outer door.

'Good,' she said to herself. 'Good.'

Naida closed and locked the file-room door behind her, memories of Darius's unwelcome appearance fresh enough to cause a prickle on the back of her neck. It all had to be here. Everything about King Pietr, still awaiting transfer to the archives. She took a close first pass at the labels on boxes, files and ribbon-bound stacks.

'Oh my,' she whispered. She shone the lantern on the ground, confirming that she was walking through a coating of dust, and wondered how long it had been since anyone had walked in here. 'Oh my.'

Every box that she could read, every file with a title insert she picked up and every bound stack of papers with a cover sheet carried the mark, signature and/or seal of the office of the head of the royal medical service, Rius Denharl. All filed in chronological order and detailing everything to do with King Pietr, his Queen, and the young Eva.

Odd then, that a couple of file boxes had found their way to the archives when where she stood now was likely to be an otherwise complete record. Naida pulled out a file at random, dated during the period when Eva would have been just a baby, her mother already dead and her father struggling with grief. Leafing through the pages, she saw information about meditation, maximising time with his daughter, sleeping draughts and sunlight and scent as treatments for dark moods.

Naida wanted to feel sorry for Pietr but with every pang of it, his monstrous treatment of his daughter corrected her. She skimmed over the dates, looking for the most recent and then spreading it on the dusty desk. She recognised the date; every child had it drummed into them. It was the day King Pietr had died.

The file was slim, containing the official recording of his death and various notes from the five days leading up to his passing. The notes were fascinating, noting a shocking decline in mental capacity and physical function, and linking this swift journey to death with, according to Rius Denharl's notes, the ashing and scattering of her parents.

Aware her time was short, she read the rest of the file, noted Eva's almost constant attendance on the King and how even this could not stop, nor even arrest, his decline, and ... oh, here it was again.

'...His Majesty, in perhaps his last moment of true lucidity, lamented his refusal to believe in their innocence and railed against himself and any who would hear him that they were all to blame, all complicit. All guilty. Happily only the King, Princess Eva and I were in his chamber at the time. I can rest easy knowing I did my best, as, I am sure, will the princess, who appeared unmoved by his outburst and far more concerned at the blood dripping from his nose...'

'Too late...' whispered Naida.

She gathered up and retied the file, placing it in her wallet though it proved nothing. To most eyes it would be the last rantings of a dying man.

'Where will it be?' she asked of the shelves. 'Where are you?'

Anxiety threatened her. She had so little time and the room, though small, held thousands of files, papers and boxes. Rius Denharl had presented Pietr with written evidence that her parents were innocent. It must be among these papers because these were *his* papers.

'Think, Naida, think,' she whispered.

So much could be ignored. Anything before the date her parents were arrested and brought back to Cantabria. Probably anything before their trial, too. She checked the date on the document on which Rius Denharl had scrawled his note and followed it to the shelves. Then sighed. Even working from this point would take a day at least, And she couldn't guarantee it was even here.

'What was I thinking?' she asked of the locked door.

Someone would know what the evidence was and where it was hidden. Maybe she needed Elias and Kat to help persuade a few people to talk. Naida stopped, a thought popping into her head that should have presented itself the moment she'd read Rius's note the first time. She picked up the lantern and left the room, closing and locking it again behind her. Misha. If anyone knew, she would. She walked along the shelved corridor and came to an abrupt halt.

Standing in the middle of the room was an imposing figure. He was dressed in the blue and grey uniform of the Crucible militia though it was short at wrist and ankle and with a poorly executed top knot at his neck. His hair was cropped and blond, his face scarred, eyes bright and cruel.

'It was all supposed to be burned, never to reach the archive.' He smiled warmly.

Naida, initially threatened, frowned and smiled back reflexively, a little confused. She moved forward and he backed off to give her space, almost back to the door. Naida placed the lantern on the nearest desk.

'I thought nothing was ever destroyed?'

326

The man shrugged. 'That's for others to decide.'

'You are aware this is a restricted-access office?' she said pleasantly. 'I am Naida, might I have your name?'

The man, he was no soldier despite his uniform, tugged at his clothing, tight enough to be uncomfortable, and wrinkled his nose. He carried an easy threat.

'My name is unimportant, but my message is critical,' he said. His accent was unfamiliar, perhaps not even Suurkene at all. 'And since you dodged my riders, I have to tell you in person. You will confine yourself to your duties. You are a valued member of the palace and, as such, immune to the type of enforcement that, regrettably, has been necessary to deter those who ask questions they should not. That status is not permanent, however, and so you must comply immediately.'

'Oh dear.'

Whatever he had expected her to say, it wasn't that. Naida supposed it was because he didn't know her that he half laughed, shifted his position, frowned a little and said:

'What?'

Naida leaned back against the desk and folded her arms, reckoning she had this man's measure. He wore no long blade, was heavyset enough to be slow, and lacked the confidence to back up his words. Words someone else had written for him, she reckoned.

'On who's authority are you issuing these... orders?'

'That is none of your concern.'

Naida's smile was thin.

'I see. So—' She pushed herself away from the desk. 'You, whoever you are, march in here and tell me, head of the royal medical service, how I must conduct myself henceforth, and I am supposed to agree without question. Is that it?'

He straightened. This was clearly not how he had expected the conversation to go.

327

'That's it,' he said, already realising that was the wrong answer.

'Let me tell you how this works, as someone who is actually, unlike you, from the military.' He was about to protest but she put up a hand. 'I work in a chain of command, always have. I take orders from my immediate superior, those orders having been handed down by their superior and so on, I'm sure you understand. You are not my superior, nor will you tell me who your superior is, nor can you offer any proof that these orders you spout carry any weight. Indeed I am sure they do not. So: I do not take orders from you. Is that clear?'

'I ... no,' he said. 'You will do what I say or what has happened to others who asked what they shouldn't, will happen to you.' He tipped his head in the direction of Temets' office.

'Thank you for clearing that little mystery up,' said Naida. She walked up close to him – he was almost a head taller than her – and smiled up at him. 'Poor lackey. You're not allowed to hurt me, are you? Your orders are to scare me, right? Bet you thought it was going to be easy. Career thug terrifies poor defenceless doctor. You should leave now.'

He glowered at her, anger warring with doubt.

'No,' he said, and he moved to bar her way to the door. 'I won't. And neither will you until the message gets through.'

'Your masters don't know me at all, do they?'

Naida was scared. Who wouldn't be? Threat hung in the air, and he was far bigger and stronger than she was. She was gambling that his orders not to hurt her, not today anyway, would outweigh his desire to scare her.

'What?'

'People who know me, know that no one threatens me successfully, and no one gets in my way. So, I'll ask you once again to leave.' Naida moved closer to him, trying to look threatening. 'I don't want to cause you any pain.'

'What?'

His confidence that she was no threat to him got the better of him. As an expression of ridicule bloomed on his face, Naida stepped up and clapped her cupped palms over his ears, hard and fast. He howled in pain, staggering backwards against a shelf stack, his hands to the sides of his face, eyes screwed shut.

Naida took another pace forward and struck the heel of her left palm into his nose, breaking it comprehensively. Even as the blood started to flow and his head rocked backwards, she smashed her foot into his testicles. He collapsed to the floor, flailing, not knowing which pain to bring his hands to first.

Naida crouched by him, aware the ringing in his ears might obscure his hearing, even if his eardrums hadn't ruptured. 'For your future reference: people like me are fast. People like me trained to face actual enemy soldiers. Tell your masters I will do my job the way I see fit and the only person I take orders from is the Queen, in person. Try to hurt me, my friends or Honourable Temets again and we will find you. I will not kill you, but my friends will have no such scruples.'

Naida stood and took a pace towards the door, stepping over her victim. His eyes, already beginning to puff up, followed her.

'I won't come after you,' she said. 'You don't have to live your life looking over your shoulder. Not unless you come after me and mine again. Your choice.'

Naida adjusted her bags on her shoulder and walked out, closing the door behind her. She took a few deep breaths, slowed her heart rate to a more comfortable level, and walked towards the stairs back up to the main floor of the Crucible. The guards at the head of the stairs nodded as she passed them and smiled back.

'You know where the medical offices are?' she asked.

'Yes, my lady,' replied one.

'There is a man in there, quite a large one. He's wearing a uniform too small for him because he is not a soldier. He threatened me, and I acted in self-defence to get away. He should be arrested for impersonating Crucible Militia. You might need to take him to the medical centre before the cells.'

Nadia smiled and walked away. At the coffee stall she treated herself to a large mug and savoured it.

'Are you all right, Lady Naida?' asked Sammel. 'You look a little flushed.'

Naida laughed.

'I've just done something I shouldn't have,' she said. 'But it felt so good.'

'Then maybe it was the right thing to do.'

'Maybe it was. Oh, and I left a mug downstairs. I'll bring it back tomorrow.'

'No rush.'

But there was, and her next meeting would not wait.

Chapter 30

Walking through the palace corridors, having left a message about her whereabouts at the medical centre again, Naida felt that every eye was on her, judging her and finding her guilty of murdering Darius, or being Helena Esselrode, or being one of the Gifted ... take your pick.

It didn't help that she couldn't quite remember the way to Misha's rooms, and she refused to ask for directions because she didn't want anyone to know her destination. She repeatedly arrived on the correct floor, the third, of the principal and oldest palace building, and had to pretend head-down urgency when she kept passing the same sets of guards.

At last, though, she recognised a bust of Queen Ceanne, the monarch credited with founding the Crucible, and knew Misha lived three doors down on the left.

It was a quiet corridor, nothing fancy in palace terms though the ceilings were high, the paintwork crisp and clean, and the drape-framed alcoves boasted bust after bust of monarchs and military personnel. Misha's door, like the rest, was polished oak, carved with roots and leaves. Naida knocked as gently as she could, trying to tamp down her desire to shake answers out of the old woman if she had to.

Her fury at her parents' murder had subsided, replaced by a

brooding anger bubbling away beneath what she hoped was a tranquil exterior. Misha had lived through it all and had spent her life listening and assimilating information to make herself indispensable. It was inconceivable that she knew nothing about it. If she could prove their innocence beyond doubt and uncover who had laid the genocidal plague, the whole conspiracy would fall apart; one pulled thread that unravelled the tapestry.

The door was opened by a young attendant, no more than fifteen and dressed in the pale greens and greys of the junior palace service. The attendant smiled through a gasp that made her face a picture of joy and awe, things Naida currently felt unqualified to inspire.

'My Lady Naida,' said the attendant, blushing deep. 'Please, come in.'

'Only if dear Misha is awake and well enough to take visitors. May I have your name?'

'Lisele,' she said, opening the door wide. 'Please, go straight on into the bedroom. Misha will be delighted to see you, as am I. I wanted to thank you for saving her life.'

Her words came out in a rush.

'Thank you, you're very kind.'

Lisele closed the door and tried not to let her excitement get the better of her. She failed delightfully, though Naida was able to raise just the smallest of smiles.

'Misha, it's Naida! You said she'd come and here she is. Ashes and water, it's *actually Naida*!' the words echoed from the carved plastered ceilings, bubbling over like boiling milk.

Lisele rushed past Naida and into the bedroom, dropping the hint of a curtsey and hurrying left and out of sight. Naida heard Misha muttering some admonishment before walking into the palatial room complete with flower arrangements, a hot breeze blowing at the net curtains and drapes, and a staggering four-poster bed decked in green and red and gold with an intricate dark wood frame.

Misha was propped up atop a landslide of pillows while an ocean of white cotton and pale wool hid her frail form so effectively, she looked like a disembodied head.

'It is lovely to see you, Actually Naida,' said Misha, producing a trembling hand from all those covers and holding it out. Naida crossed the room to take it in hers, feeling a welcome warmth and, extending herself very gently, finding no hint of infection remaining. 'Thank you, Lisele, you can leave me in Lady Naida's hands.'

Still blushing, Lisele backed away. 'Shall I bring water or juice or tea? A herb infusion?'

Naida shook her head. 'No, thank you. But I'll see Misha drinks enough.'

'Thank you, Naida,' said Lisele, eyes widening each time she said her name.

'Let us speak privately,' said Misha, voice still tainted by fatigue but much improved.

Lisele bobbed her head and withdrew, the doors closing with a heavy clunk. Naida switched her gaze to Misha who dropped her hand back to the bed.

'Can we be overheard?'

'No,' said Misha. 'You know how careful I am.'

'I'm sure that care has allowed you to play all sides,' said Naida, a little more tartly than she'd intended.

Her tone did not escape Misha.

'I knew you were here for something other than to enquire after my health. What's troubling you? Are you discovering the Queen is not quite the paragon she likes to seem?'

'She has her faults, but none so egregious as an individual who would let others die knowing they were innocent.'

Misha noted the tears glistening in her eyes, threatening to spill over.

'What do you think you know?' she asked carefully.

Naida leaned in. Her jaws were tight, her voice threatened to strangle in her throat, and it came out in a rasping, viper-like hiss.

'My parents *were* innocent!'

Naida couldn't sit still. She got up and walked to the end of the bed, the window, a mirror, distracting herself by unbuckling her satchel to fetch out Rius Denharl's words and brandish them in Misha's face.

'*My parents were innocent.*'

She made no attempt to stop the tears, feeling them track down her cheeks as she turned from the mirror. Outside, the sun beat down on a busy city. Horses, markets, laughter, colour. In here, misery and fury in a monochrome miasma.

Misha's sheets rustled and Naida glanced round. The ancient lady-in-waiting was sitting up a little more, her face was supposed to be neutral, but her eyes betrayed her. She was worried. Naida walked back, slowly, gauging Misha's expression. She bit back on the question she wanted to ask and let the old woman speak instead.

'How are you able to make such a claim?'

'I read it,' said Naida. 'Written down as plain as new blood on a fresh dressing.'

'You have evidence?' Misha's eyes widened. 'In your possession?'

'Right here,' said Naida, handing her the paper. 'A reference to their innocence, made by Denharl's brother or father – I don't know which. It's good enough for me.'

'Brother,' said Misha. She was tense. She couldn't hide it. 'This is incredibly dangerous information for you to have. Where did you find it?'

334

'Don't change the subject.' Naida chewed on her top lip, growing more and more sure of her initial assumption. 'Did you know?'

'We spoke about this, Naida. I only knew what your parents managed to tell me.'

'*Did you know?*'

Misha started. 'I ... heard rumours. Things are always swirling around the palace.'

Fresh tears pricked Naida's eyes and she smiled, so brittle, so angry. 'And you dismissed it, did you? That their words, and your rumours, might have substance? Ignored the possibility that Lord and Lady Esselrode should not be having the skin stripped from their feet, or bolts driven through their shoulders, or each knuckle broken by a hammer or crushed in a vice. None of that troubled your sleep?'

'You don't know what it was like,' said Misha, trying to retreat into her pillows. 'I told you already. To raise any doubt was to be complicit. The fear of saying the wrong thing ... it was horrible.'

'Should I feel sorry for you? *You* were scared to say the wrong thing while my mother and father were slowly murdered? Rius Denharl found courage. Why didn't you?'

'And it got him dismissed from his post. He was lucky to escape the city with his life. What do you want from me?'

Misha stared at her, strong within her frail body. Not looking for sympathy but for clarity. Naida checked her ire and sought an answer to Misha's question.

'I want to know who knew the truth and did nothing. I want to know who gained from scapegoating my parents. I want to know who was behind it because they are behind all that is happening now. And I want to know why I was supposed to spend my life believing my parents were evil and that that same evil lay dormant within me.'

Misha relaxed a little. 'No one confided in me, I overheard no one speaking of proof. That evidence existed was one of the briefest palace rumours. Now I know why.'

'It was stamped on. Crushed, like my parents, by those who sought to profit from death, and by guilty minds needing plausible deniability.'

Misha nodded. 'Yes.'

'Who are they? I have to know.'

'No. You need the evidence, not a few references to it. Until you have that, you have nothing.'

Misha reached out for her glass of water and Naida gave it to her, waiting while she took several tiny sips.

'Where will it be? Who else travelled to Cantabria with Eva and my parents? Someone who was there planned the plague, and who to pin it on. I need a name.'

'And what would you do with it, this name, if I knew it and gave it to you?'

'Use your imagination,' growled Naida. 'I'd light the fire in the cage myself after dragging their confession from their bloodied, toothless mouth.'

'No, you wouldn't,' said Misha, her gentle admonishment deflating Naida's passion. 'But I worry you would confront them and condemn yourself. You have to be careful. You have to get the evidence, and get it into Lord Ludeney's hands, for he is the only one who would not destroy it in front of you.'

Naida sat on the bed, shoulders slumping. 'So do you know who it was?'

'It was a sizeable delegation, if memory serves. Those who took the risk to travel to a conquered territory were promised senior positions later.' Misha smiled. 'I was there, you know, but I think I can discount myself.'

Naida relaxed a little more. 'Who can you not discount?'

'It's quite a list, though I can't believe evil purpose in the heart of the, then, aspiring Lord Denharl. Velez, Kerslan, Galiari, Ordshin ... half the council went. High-powered stuff was supposed to be going on.'

'Velez does keep on popping up.'

Misha shrugged. 'Well, she's all over everything but then, Ministers for Foreign Affairs should be, right.'

'I suppose ... And what did you see? What happened?'

'It's easy to see why they were accused,' Misha said slowly. 'It was so hard to believe they were guilty ... but just as hard to see how they weren't. I barely left the castle during our stay, and neither did the princess. She was there to demonstrate our sincerity ... the army was there in case the Cantabrians didn't accept it. The delegation did all the boring talk, and we saw them sparingly. Meanwhile, your parents were out in the city, overseeing aid and setting up medical facilities.'

Naida could picture them again, the way she had before being taught that they were evil, going to the places no one else would visit, teaching about hygiene, educating others about apothecary treatments, administering to those who couldn't afford treatment, bringing light to dark places.

'I only know what I was told. So: how did they come to be accused? Why did it stick?'

Misha paused and her already-pale face paled yet further. 'Oh, Naida.'

'What is it?' A tear spilled onto Misha's face and Naida realised it was the first time she'd shown emotional weakness or vulnerability. 'You believe me, don't you?'

Misha nodded. Naida fetched a green-edged lace handkerchief from her bedside table and handed it to her.

'Thank you.' Misha dabbed at her eyes. 'The sin of pride is among the most grievous and I have been committing it for so long. I saw, yet chose not to see.'

'What are you talking about?'

337

'Of course they were innocent, and if this was all planned, Cantabria was the obvious victim. They had no Gifted, but they also had none of the diseases we saw every year because they had closed their borders to us for so long. So, when the plague was sparked, and spread so fast and killed so many, starting at the very point where your parents were working, it was the easiest thing in the world to blame them. And I never questioned it. Even as we were hurried out of the city and the country, even when I was comforting Eva – she was bereft, as if your parents were dead, so much did she love them – I never thought to wonder. It seemed the sad but simple truth.'

'You cannot blame yourself.'

'Yes, I can! I have made myself a place here by listening to and investigating rumours. I have made it my life! But had I been even the remotest bit suspicious instead of just accepting what appeared so obvious... what was cleverly made to seem obvious... I would have been able to drip the truth into the right people's ears. But I didn't. I believed what I was told, and then there was the fear of questioning the given truth. I accepted that even the best of us can turn out to be monsters. Perhaps trust is a bigger sin than pride because I trusted the real monsters.'

Misha's hands were shaking, and her face was lined by both her age and cares.

'So who were the real monsters? Where are they now?'

'It could be anyone. It doesn't have to be someone who was there, after all. And so well-hidden now, they may be beyond us.'

'Find the evidence, you said. What did Ludeney know?'

Misha frowned. 'He has always been a true loyalist, but he is a man driven by the need for truth. I presume he believed in their guilt because he could find no evidence for their innocence.'

'But he didn't ever speak to you about it?'

Misha shook her head.

'Hmm.' Naida raised her eyebrows. 'Where is he?'

'Confronting him would be an error.'

'Torturing and murdering my parents was a bigger one,' said Naida.

'Naida,' said Misha. 'Look at me.'

Naida inhaled deeply, not wanting to hear what Misha was about to say while knowing she would impart wisdom. So, she looked.

'You have no idea how dangerous this knowledge is. And, as yet, you have no proof, just this allusion to some. You do not know if it still exists. All we can say for certain is that if someone has orchestrated all of this, then some very powerful people will be desperate to keep such evidence suppressed and will have destroyed whatever they can. Whoever this is, they will not hesitate to silence anyone who threatens them.'

'I get that—' began Naida.

'No, there's more. The whole tide of hate against the Gifted has been built on the assumed evil perpetrated by your mother and father. Even the Queen has involved herself in it, and she loved them. Add up the risk. I already know that your entreaties to Her Majesty were dismissed … It seems clear the Queen's rooms are not as secure from listeners as these.'

That gave Naida pause, remembering all of Eva's precautions when they had eaten together. If someone had overheard her and Eva in her rooms, then perhaps someone other than Velez had informed the Keelers that the Gifted were in the plague camp.

'What do I do?' asked Naida, feeling trapped when she'd come here to free herself. 'Where do I turn?'

'Do nothing until you have your proof.'

'But what if I can't find it?' Naida spoke more loudly than she intended, her desperation beginning to get the better of her. 'I'm already being chased by Keelers and being warned off by thugs.'

'You are?' Misha pressed herself back into her pillows. 'Then you've already upset someone with influence. Do you know why?'

Misha knew nothing about Old Landers, Markan, or the foreign interests behind the anti-Gifted legislation. So Naida told her.

'So even here, you will be watched. And your task was already so hard.'

'Then help me,' said Naida.

'Help us remove the Queen,' Misha urged. 'When she is gone, the new monarch will sweep the palace clean and finding what you seek will be so much easier.'

'Has the Lord Marshal found our saviour yet?'

'Some things I am not privy to, for my own safety as much as anything,' said Misha.

'Ludeney wouldn't tell me either.' Naida puffed out her cheeks. 'I told him what you said my parents had told you... about the monarchy.'

'I know,' said Misha. 'He spoke to me at some length about it.'

Naida frowned even as her heart fluttered. 'Could there be something in it? Might they have been killed for knowing something damaging to the Rekalvians?'

'No idea but he's a thorough man.' Misha smiled mischievously. 'Fancy being Queen?'

'Shattered throne, no. Worst job in the kingdom and that's up against some pretty stiff competition. Anyway, I don't recall 'Esselrode' ever being a name mentioned in royal terms.'

'Shame,' said Misha. 'It'd be a pretty compelling motive.'

'I'm not going to kill Eva just in case my parents weren't mad when they made their end-of-life claims.'

'Your refusal to understand the danger she represents to the country remains the key problem in our strategy.'

'I understand that her actions against the Gifted are misguided and rooted in a flawed desire to be in tune with the public mood. How else is she risking the country?'

'You're forgetting she wants to end the monarchy. Isn't that enough?'

Naida gaped. 'No! Of course it isn't. It's progressive and sensible and founded on love for as-yet unborn princesses.'

Misha raised her eyebrows. 'Whatever you choose to believe, your standing will be enhanced by completing your appointed task.'

'Oh, thank the Spires for that.'

'Sarcasm doesn't become you.'

'Honestly, right now I could not care less.' Naida got up and headed for the door. 'This has ended up being a waste of time.'

'I'm sorry you feel that way,' said Misha, sounding like a gently scolding mother, something Naida remembered distantly. 'Being heard is always of value. As is knowing who you can trust.'

Naida turned sharply. 'And who is that, exactly?' Now she advanced back towards the bed and Misha looked alarmed. 'Ludeney? Denharl? *You?* I've no idea who hid the knowledge that would have saved my parents' lives, which seems to be the keystone to all of this. Until I know, anyone who was in this ridiculous palace of lies and whispers at the time is under suspicion. Anyone.'

She spat that last, then felt guilty for it as Misha recoiled and looked frail again. But the fire still burned in those eyes.

'I told you—'

'Nothing! You told me nothing that I could not guess for myself. You've warned me off, said I must find evidence but not where to look. So, if you want me to trust you, help me and I'll reassess my judgement of anyone I need to.'

'I'm sure. But when you start looking under rocks, anything can crawl out.'

Chapter 31

The palace was as busy as ever, though between the plague in Old Landers and the surging purge against the Gifted, there was a tension in the air. That it had reached these corridors of privilege was a message in itself.

On the tortuous journey to her rooms to rest and eat, perhaps bathe, she became aware of something more than the bustle of cleaners, servants, artisans of every stripe, courtiers and aides. Every step on stairway or passage felt as if it had an echo. Whether she sped up or slowed to examine a bust or chat to a guard, it was the same.

Naida had walked past the guards many times and that was a comfort. This echo was unsettling and intolerable. Taking a sharp right towards a stairway down to her floor, Naida stopped and spun on her heel, waiting. A few paces later, Vinald appeared, smug insincerity bleeding from his smile.

'Lady Naida, what a pleasant surprise. Can I be of assistance?'

'Someone's following me. Perhaps you could wait here and let them know that following me can lead to nasty injuries to delicate areas.'

'Why would someone be following you? Are you hiding something?'

'Oh, Vinny, you know me. I hide nothing but my disdain for

gormless lackeys. I'm extra nice to them.' Naida smiled sweetly. 'How are you, anyway? In the full flush of perfect health, I hope?'

Vinald stared. 'If you're being made to feel uncomfortable, perhaps you should be under suspicion.'

'Suspicion of what, do you think? You're doing the following, presumably you know.'

'People, particularly those so new to the palace, cannot expect the levels of trust enjoyed by those' – he gestured at himself, a vague wafting movement of the hand – 'who have been loyal servants throughout their lives.'

'Oh, I see.' Naida turned and walked away, confident Vinald would continue to follow her. In fact, she was discomfited that he had neither denied, nor tried to hide what he was doing. 'Well, while you ensure I don't commit any crimes on the way to my rooms, they are perfect by the way, I'd love to hear what has so upset your masters, or mistresses, that you have to trail around after me like some love-sick puppy.'

Naida smiled to herself, aware of the tension radiating from him.

'Everyone employed by the palace should confine themselves exclusively to their duties.'

The ice that ran through Naida's body would have been picked up by any Gifted within a hundred yards but Vinald, two or three paces behind her, would be oblivious to the effect of his words. Words that she could only presume he had given to the Keeler thug who had confronted her in her offices.

'My remit is to keep the Queen alive and manage the city's medical service. I have not stepped outside those duties.'

Naida was near her rooms now. The comforting thought of being able to close the door in his face calmed her, though not as much as what she saw behind him when she glanced back.

'Actually, don't bother, I know,' she said. 'And it disgusts me that some people are so desperate to see their city kin die that they'll speak against the Gifted in favour of a foreign apothecary company. Am I close?'

Vinald's face took on an unhealthy hue and he moved forward to fire his words straight into her face, his finger jabbing out his every point.

'Stop sticking your nose into areas it doesn't belong. Do not mistake the Queen's temporary patronage for a lifelong loyalty I—'

Vinald was half-hoisted from the ground by the back of his collar and his last words were a strangled yelp.

'Need this irritant removed?' asked Elias.

Naida smiled but shook her head. 'No. I'm sure Honoured Vinald has tasks he must attend elsewhere, urgently.'

Elias shrugged and let him go. Vinald spun round to confront Elias.

'How dare you! Common soldiers do not address, let alone touch, Aides of the Palace. I will have your name and that of your commanding officer.'

'Common. Huh.' Elias grabbed Vinald again, this time by the lapels of his coat and spun him around, putting his body between the aide and Naida. 'I'm only not breaking your jaw 'cos Naida doesn't have the time to set it for you. Run along. If I see you harassing her again, you'll be scooping mash into your broken mouth for a season.'

Elias shoved Vinald hard and he stumbled backwards, falling in an untidy heap. Though he was on his feet again in an instant, his fall had been seen by other staff who would no doubt dine out on the story for days to come. Vinald knew it as he straightened his clothes and glared at Elias in a fury.

'You have not heard the last of this. I will see you behind bars!'

'My name is Elias and my commanding officer is the Lord

Marshal Ludeney. I am protector to Lady Naida and you violated her space; I acted, as I feared you would strike her. Start with that and see how far you get.'

★

'I'm not sure that was wise,' said Naida when they were in her rooms. 'He's a grudge-bearer.'

'Status bully,' said Elias. 'Seen his type a hundred times. Nothing in him but empty threat and foolish pride.'

'He'll probably send another one of his thugs,' said Naida, thinking to draw a bath.

'What do you mean *another*?'

'Oh, nothing. I was threatened by one in my office in the Crucible.'

'What?' Elias stopped her heading for the bathroom. 'What happened?'

'Well, he parroted the same words at me that Vinald just did, and when I told him I only took orders from the Queen, he got a bit cross.'

Naida shrugged at Elias's concern.

'And when you say *cross*...?'

'He wasn't going to let me go 'til I swore I'd do what he said, so I bloodied his ears, broke his nose and hoofed him in the plums.'

Elias laughed out loud and sank into one of the chairs in the hall.

'You've been with the army too long. I almost feel sorry for him. Short man, was he?'

Elias put a hand up to chest level.

'How dare you,' said Naida, smiling. 'He was enormous, actually. A mountain. Tall, big frame, blond hair, and lots of squiggly tattoos on his arms. I think they were supposed to be roots. What?'

346

Elias had stopped laughing. He'd stopped smiling too.

'Naida, this is important. Did he have a scar on his face? It'd be from the corner of his right eye and ragged down to his right ear lobe.'

Naida thought briefly. 'Yes. Badly stitched when it happened, I would think.'

'This isn't good,' said Elias. 'That thug was Geth Herron, enforcer for hire. He is bad, bad news, and he'll come after you again. Paid to or not.'

'He has orders not to touch me.'

'That won't make any difference. Not now. No one downs Geth Herron.'

'I did.' Naida flashed a smile.

'This isn't a joke,' said Elias sharply. He blew out his cheeks and Naida was taken aback by how nervous he appeared. Her bravado wilted like a leaf in hot water. 'Herron is a flint-eyed killer and, if you're right, he's in Vinald's employ. If you see him again, run. I'll get in his way.'

Naida looked long at Elias. 'If he's so bad, won't he kill you, too?'

'Yes, but I can at least buy you some time.'

★

Naida tried to relax in her bath but it was tricky, what with Elias prowling the hall as if he expected Herron to burst in at any moment. And whenever his pacing stopped, and a moment's peace fell, her mind would not rest and her anger would not settle. While she soaked and scrubbed the dirt from her body, Naida absorbed and nurtured a hitherto alien emotion: the desire for revenge.

For the torment of her parents; for the love and time with them that she had been denied. For the life she had been forced to lead and the fear she had lived with every day. For every time she had denied her own name and cursed those of her mother and father. And for Drevien who lay badly wounded in a plague camp, knowing the person who claimed to love her the most had been lying to her the whole time.

Naida dried and dressed quickly, the soak no longer holding any pleasure. Elias was sitting in the drawing room and rose immediately.

'We can't stay here,' he said.

'Why ever not?' asked Naida. 'This is the Palace of Spires.'

'And if I can get in waving a letter of access, so can Geth Herron.'

Naida nodded. 'Where's Kat?'

'She's at the camp. She'll report back to the infirmary if the tincture is really working or not. Does that matter right now?' Elias, thrown by her sudden change of direction, scratched his forehead. 'Actually, you know, we'd be safer there than we are here. Plenty of Ludeney's soldiers about.'

'I can't get stuck at the camp, though, tempting as it is to hide there and look after Drev,' said Naida. 'So much is going to happen here. Gifted trials, legislation ... and the truth. It's here somewhere.'

'Where? And where can we go that Vinald can't find you?'

Naida looked out of the window. The sun had set on an uneasy city and the normal throng and hubbub of night was muted by the haunting threat of plague in the docklands. Misha had likened her to a pebble dropped in a mill pond. She felt more like a round of flay-shot landing among the defenceless. People were dead and injured because of the Naida-effect already. And she feared there was far worse to come.

Never mind that it was night, she could not afford to rest. She pulled the cord she knew would bring Cerrie scurrying. The knock on her door came impressively quickly.

Naida turned to Elias before opening the door.

'Just follow my lead, all right?'

Elias rolled his eyes.

Cerrie, still in her uniform and neat to the point of obsession, stepped into the hall, glanced at Elias's powerful frame and smiled. Naida ushered her into the bathroom, a place she had to hope had no listening tubes.

'Expecting trouble?' she asked, reddening at her own comment. 'I'm sorry...'

'Don't be,' said Naida, her voice low. 'And no, not at all. Elias has brought me news that the Lord Denharl is unwell. Sadly, he can't tell me where his rooms are. I hoped you would know.'

'Of course, Lady Naida. I can take you there directly.'

Elias drew in a sharp breath and Naida shot him an equally sharp look.

'We need to be... discreet. We don't want the Queen's doctor being seen visiting a member of the Queen's Council late in the evening or tongues will start wagging.'

'I would never tell a soul,' said Cerrie.

Naida reached out and took her hand. 'I wouldn't have called you if I thought otherwise. But perhaps you know a way to the Lord Denharl's rooms that avoids prying eyes.'

Cerrie's eyes lit up. 'There are at least two paths to everywhere and my lord's rooms are no exception. But I will have to show you the way, it's a little complex.'

'I'm sure we could find our way,' said Naida.

'Begging your pardon, but I heard you got lost on your way to Misha's apartments,' said Cerrie, mischief in her expression.

'Thank you, Cerrie. Word travels fast, doesn't it? Very well. Please, could you put out my night things for me while we gather the equipment? We'll wait for you in the hall.'

Cerrie bobbed her head. Naida ushered Elias out of the bathroom.

'What are you doing?' hissed Elias, following Nadia as she

collected and checked her medical bag, tucking key papers into an unused pocket that sealed with a clasp.

'Making us disappear from Vinald and putting me in front of someone I'm pretty sure can help us.'

'Willingly?'

Naida shrugged. 'Well, you're here to help if he's not willing.'

'I'm not roughing up an old man,' said Elias.

'Correct,' said Naida. 'Just stand around looking cross. A bit like now.'

Whether or not she sensed there was more to Naida's request than it appeared was a concern for later, but Cerrie proved herself a most capable guide of the maze of passages and accesses that were designed to keep the lowest ranks of palace workers from the paths of the landed and feted.

They travelled baking-hot corridors run with pipework feeding hot water to every part of the palace. They walked quietly through staff quarters, lines of doors below-stairs, dark and damp. They hurried along corridors servicing laundries, linen stores, kitchens and maintenance rooms. And they climbed dark back staircases that led into disguised storage closets that, Cerrie told them, sat at the end of most corridors. She opened the one that sat closest to Denharl's rooms.

'Where are we?' asked Elias, voice still a whisper.

'Second floor, west building, where many of the QC live when they are resident in the palace,' said Cerrie. 'You can tell by the high ceilings and the gold-flecked green wallpaper.'

Elias chuckled. 'You're good. We might need you again.'

'Lord Denharl's attendant will be inside. She'll be either drunk or asleep, but a knock should wake her to let you in.'

Naida smiled. 'We'll be polite, I promise.'

Cerrie shrugged. 'I wouldn't bother, she never is.'

'What's her name?'

'Lauren. She's my aunt.'

Naida and Elias shared a look then Naida kissed Cerrie's cheek.

'Thank you, you've already done more than you know.'

Cerrie looked at her cryptically. 'I hope Lord Denharl recovers.'

'I'm sure it's a temporary affliction.'

Elias and Naida moved into the corridor, the soldier trotting to the end so he could look left and right for guards or night staff. He gave her a nod and she rapped on Denharl's door, wondering how drunk or asleep Lauren might be at this hour. She glanced at Elias, still keeping watch, still unflustered. Nothing moved within.

Naida knocked again, a little harder, and put her ear to the door. There was movement inside, unhurried. As footsteps approached, Naida could hear grumbling and saw Elias walking towards her, cycling his hands in a hurrying gesture.

A key turned in the lock and the door opened to reveal a pale-faced, middle-aged woman hastily tidying her grey hair under a maid's bonnet. She had a round face, lined with care, and the weight of the years of service and all the sacrifice it entailed were reflected in her cold brown eyes. She weighed Naida up in an instant.

'Yes?'

'Lauren, I am Naida, here to treat Lord Denharl. I—'

'He needs no treatment,' snapped Lauren.

'I promised to assess his hip and have just finished my other duties. Please, he is expecting me.'

'He mentioned nothing of the sort and has retired for the night. Good evening to you.'

'Please, Lauren...'

The ageing maid looked at her, brown eyes narrowing. 'Perhaps your other duties should not have come before the Master of the Spires.'

Lauren made to close the door only to have it slapped back by Elias.

'Yeah, well, plague's a bitch like that, ain't it?' he said, a hand on Naida's back, pushing her inside and closing and locking the door smartly behind them. 'Prying eyes, Naida, sorry for the rush.'

'This is an *outrage!*' hissed Lauren.

'Just like your breath,' snapped Naida. 'Now I suggest you sit very quietly while I tend to the Lord Denharl who, it should come as no surprise, does not share his every medical need with a servant. My friend here will sit with you.'

Elias smiled and gestured through an open door to a drawing room. Lauren glared at him and then Naida.

'You have not heard the last of this. I will see you dismissed.'

'That's something we hear a lot,' said Naida. 'Your niece was far too complimentary about you, apparently.'

'Huh. Trusting the word of that common tart.'

Naida raised her eyebrows. 'Ash and water, you really are horrible, aren't you? Elias, I apologise for having to leave you in such poisonous company.'

'I'm sure we'll have a fine time,' said Elias and growled at Lauren, sending her scuttling into the drawing room and, doubtless, another tot of cheap spirit.

In outline, the hallway in which they stood was very much like her own, but on a far grander scale. The ceilings rose to dizzying heights, the decoration was lush and richly coloured, and seven heavy oak doors stood along its walls.

Naida opened the door to a second bedroom, a bathroom, and a linen cupboard before she found one that revealed a large study with comfortable seating in front of a grand fireplace, a huge desk and an ancient leather chair. The walls were bedecked with paintings of landscapes and portraits punctuating towering shelves of books. The room smelled of old leather and paper, tainted by pipe smoke and the merest hint of damp.

Opposite her was another closed door, which she was certain was Denharl's bedchamber. Walking in, she found him propped up in his bed, a pot of tea on his nightstand, papers in his hands and a startled look on his face.

'Forgive the lateness of the hour, my lord Denharl, but we need to talk.'

Chapter 32

'It seems a little late for room calls,' said Denharl, his voice a quiet rumble. 'Tea?'

Naida shook her head. 'I fear we are beyond the rattle of china while we share irrelevances.'

Denharl frowned. 'I offered you my support and patronage. No doubt the trouble in which you find yourself now could have been averted had you come under my wing.'

'Wow, that's ... confident ... of you,' said Naida. 'And, as it happens, wrong. Listen to me, and when I'm done we can discuss how to prolong your life from the cancer eating through your hip. How's that for an agenda?'

Naida hadn't come in meaning to confront him about his health but his defences had to be torn down before he would listen. Denharl's lips narrowed and he took his teacup with slightly shaking hands.

'It is small wonder you have turned against you, people who could help you,' he said.

'In my experience, some who offer help do so with a poisoned hand.' Naida smiled bitterly. 'One of the benefits of my upbringing, you might say.'

'You've come to recount your life story?' asked Denharl, recovering somewhat.

'In a manner of speaking. Because what is happening now is the last act in a conspiracy born fifteen years ago. Plague is running in the city while the Gifted are hounded and rounded up, facing legislation that will outlaw their practice and leave all our lives at risk from the ravages of the Red Spot. Why? Because the way had to be cleared for an unproven apothecary treatment to be used on an unsuspecting test population. Profit, Master of Spires Denharl, has been placed before the health of the city, and the wider country.'

'I'm afraid I do not follow what you are suggesting. Or how it impacted your upbringing?'

Naida watched him, searching for signs that he knew about the conspiracy of which she spoke. And she saw them – but how deeply he was complicit, or whether he was on the outside watching, was another question.

'I have uncovered the original crime, the one that underpins today's conspiracies, and I need the truth to hold the right people accountable for it. I need your help to do that, to avenge those I loved and to save others now.'

Denharl's eyes flickered over her face and his confusion deepened. 'Of course, if I can help, I will.'

Naida took the critical document from her satchel and gave it to him, watching him read it and knowing the inevitability of the conclusion he would, eventually, draw. Denharl read his brother's hastily written words regarding her parents' innocence before looking at the other side of the parchment, where there was the conclusion of a report and a signature. He handed the paper back and settled himself against his pillows.

'My brother struggled to understand that good people could harbour evil,' said Denharl. 'He tried to change King Pietr's mind even when there was no mind left to change. He failed.'

'What evidence did he have? He must have confided in you.'

'Why do you need to know? What difference could it possibly make?'

'Humour me.'

Denharl shrugged. 'He was a great doctor but a renowned trouble-maker. He said a great deal to me, normally berating my weakness in supporting the monarchy, and usually angry that I didn't believe him.'

'About what?'

Denharl, plainly uncomfortable recalling details of events decades old, paused for a considerable time before speaking.

'He made two claims, one leading to the other, without showing me the merest thread of proof. First, he said the Esselrodes had learned something that changed them. Not from good to bad in his eyes, you understand, but in their dealings with the palace household. They became more distant, though they continued their work, which he said would bring great change to the palace.'

'He must have given you some hints,' said Naida.

'He did not. Our relationship was always rather strained, I'm afraid.'

So tantalisingly close she could almost touch it, yet the truth remained a mystery.

'And the other thing?'

Denharl smiled. 'He said he had proof they were innocent but, again, he could not or would not show me. He said it went to the top of the palace, and that the King would see it and have to act. He was wrong. Beyond his medicine, he was wrong about a great deal.'

Naida looked away, fresh tears threatening. She focused instead on a portrait of a young man on horseback in full dress uniform, sword held high above his head.

'He kept it to himself,' she said quietly, voicing her fear. 'Why?'

'Why not share proof that the most hated traitors were innocent, at the most tense and contentious time? Why not casually implicate someone else? Imagine the risk of saying anything to anyone.'

'Like to you, you mean?'

Denharl chuckled. 'He was my brother. I would never have betrayed him, but I was happy to see him fail. He never understood the way things work here.'

Denharl sipped his tea again and put the cup down before indicating her with a lazy movement of his left index finger.

'But what about you, Lady Naida? Who were they to you?'

'Their betrayal, their murder, was the seed from which the distrust of the Talent has grown. A seed grown to ripeness and fit for harvest now – while I am responsible for the welfare of this city.'

'No, no, no, that isn't the whole of it. This is personal. People you loved, you said. You knew the Esselrodes? Sad to say, I did too and thought them good people until they turned. You seem to see their goodness too, not their evil.'

Naida could see him withdrawing, his disdain for her position obvious, but she needed more from him.

'I understand,' said Naida, moving forwards and touching his arm, a fleeting contact which was broken when he withdrew, but enough for her to discern the exhaustion in his sick body, driven forward by the strength of his heart. A stubborn old goat and a man who, like Misha, she didn't want to end up hating. 'It all seems so obvious from the inside, but the truth is rarely so straightforward as it seems.'

Denharl studied her and she wondered if her connection to the Esselrodes was so unthinkable that his mind was preventing him making it. Just like accepting that her parents were innocent was unthinkable.

'What were you to them?' he asked. 'Or them to you?'

Naida, reaching her decision and knowing he would survive it, rummaged in her bag and pulled out an analgesic balm, and an infusion she could add to his tea.

'You're in pain,' she said, uncorking the balm. 'Rub this on your hip, or allow me to do so. It'll let you sleep properly, by the looks of you for the first time in a season.'

Denharl stared at her, confused by her every response. She hadn't thought it would be so easy to disarm him, but she still had to be careful. His mind remained sharp even when he wasn't fully alert.

'I'm asking you to help me. And I want to help you,' she said. 'I don't know if I can save you, ultimately, but I know I can ease your pain and prolong your life if you want.'

'Every day I breathe the air and see the beauty of the world, I want another,' he said. He pushed his covers down and rolled to present his right hip, beneath his long white nightshirt. 'Please.'

Naida hitched up his nightshirt, careful to maintain his modesty, and rubbed a generous amount of the goral balm into his hip, feeding her senses into him to comprehend the scale of his cancer. She concentrated hard on massaging the balm into his skin to avoid reacting.

There were growths spreading from his prostate – which must trouble him when emptying his bladder – into his large intestine, and all across his pelvis, threatening his left hip and seriously impairing his right one. Naida let her energy soothe the inflammation and encase the worst of the tumours, draining them of their fervour, and slowing the cancer's progress. But nothing, not even she, could save him for long.

'How does that feel?'

Denharl smiled. 'Like I should have listened to you the first time you spoke to me.'

'Well, better late than never. Let me examine you properly

tomorrow and we can work out a treatment plan to give you as many days as we can.' She showed him the infusion, a porous bag of dried leaves. 'If you will allow, I'll refresh your tea with this. It aids rest.'

Denharl inclined his head and she dropped the bag into the pot, swirled it, and poured the tea into his cup, the heady aromas of bluebush and serron root adding to the camomile he was already enjoying. It was quite the dose and would act quickly. She watched Denharl breathe it in before draining the cup, and Naida rearranged his covers for him.

'And now your pain is fading and sleep is coming – a long sleep to take you refreshed into tomorrow – tell me who has their fingers deep in the deals to bring Cantabrian apothecaries to our shores, and to redevelop the docks.'

Bluebush and serron were powerful sleep agents. They also loosened the tongue.

'How do you know about that?'

'By watching and listening. Who is pulling the strings?'

'Trade brings peace following war, and peace brings harmony, and harmony brings profit,' said Denharl as if quoting another.

'A mantra to line the pockets of the few at the expense of the masses. Who said that?'

'I can't remember ...' said Denharl. 'Vinald or Dmitry. Something they'd heard someone else say, maybe.'

That was a name that reared its head uncomfortably. 'Does the Queen know of all such arrangements?'

Denharl chuckled. 'Oh no. A Queen must trust her council and they must do right by her.'

Ludeney hadn't grasped the enormity of the problem. He knew that Eva wanted to end the monarchy, and that was an affront to his loyalty, but right now, killing her would only feed the flames of corruption. Eva was a pawn, repeating what she was told was the will of her people. She did not need replacing, she needed educating.

'But they are not doing right, are they? I will, though. I will see this tide reversed and the Gifted returned to their rightful place among the people they serve. And in so doing, I will cleanse my parents' reputation, and see justice done for them.'

Whether she had vowed that to Denharl or just to herself, Naida couldn't say, but he had been fading towards blissful sleep when his eyes widened and shock infused his face, turning it grey enough for her to worry she had misjudged the strength of his heart. She patted his hand and he hadn't the strength to withdraw it. Tears threatened.

'You need not be afraid. I will prolong your days, I promise. It is the way of all the Esselrodes, to seek to cure and heal, to ease pain and lengthen lives, to the ends of our abilities. It was so with my mother and father and so it is with me, their daughter, Helena. You are safe in my hands, Lord Denharl.'

He was terrified, poor man, so long had he, like everyone else, been convinced of the evil that ran in Esselrode veins. And here he was, facing an Esselrode who had given him what she said was a sleeping draft.

'They will kill you. I will see to it,' he mumbled.

Naida smoothed his palm with her fingers. 'By the time you awake, and awake you will, whether you believe me or not, all will be over, for good or ill. Either I will be dead or the guilty will be facing the cage for treason.'

Denharl was asleep and Naida wondered whether the fact that he would awaken feeling refreshed, and in less pain, would convince him of her good intentions. It was doubtful. She rose, packed her bag, and picked up the teapot, hurrying into the drawing room where Elias stood over Lauren. She was a long way into a bottle of spirits and muttering expletives.

'I've learned all sorts of new words,' said Elias. 'I think my ears are bleeding on the inside.'

Naida grabbed Lauren's glass and threw the contents out onto the floor, refilling it with tea.

'Your lives are over,' spat Lauren. 'Whorescum.'

'Drink this, shut up and sleep tight. Bright new dawn tomorrow,' said Naida. She pushed the glass to Lauren who spat in it. 'That'll add to the flavour. Elias. Hold her.'

'Pleasure's all mine.' Elias wrapped one huge arm around Lauren's chest, trapping her arms, the other hand slapped harder than necessary against her forehead and pushed back. 'Open wide, sweet one.'

Lauren hissed and spat like a cat, jerking her body against the chair and Elias's prodigious strength, and she kicked out until Naida stood on both her feet. If she'd forced fluid down the throat of one reluctant soldier, she'd done it a hundred times, and Lauren was no soldier. Naida grabbed the hinge of her jaws and squeezed hard. Lauren opened her mouth to squeal her pain and spit more vitriol only to find her mouth full of tepid tea. Naida shut her mouth for her and Elias rocked her further back, ensuring she swallowed plenty before coughing the rest up.

Naida stepped back and Elias released her.

'There, that wasn't so bad now, was it?'

'What was that filth?'

'Something to help you sleep. Feel it already, don't you? Good, and as you drift away, you awful, embittered excuse for a woman, console yourself that you have just been ministered to by an Esselrode and lived.'

Lauren lunged forwards but Naida stepped smartly aside and the maid crashed gracelessly to the floor, the bluebush combining with the alcohol to speed her towards unconsciousness.

'Sleep well. Come on, Elias, we've got another meeting.'

361

'We have? Where?'

'A couple of doors along.' Naida pointed, leading the way out and right. There were only two other doors in this section of corridor, so she knew where she was going. 'There's something I have to know before I can sleep again.'

Chapter 33

'This is the stupidest idea I have ever heard,' hissed Elias.

'He's supposed to be an ally and he is your commanding officer.'

'And famously grumpy,' said Elias. 'And you're going to ask him about your parents, aren't you?'

'I have to know,' said Naida.

'You'll be the death of me.'

'Very probably but not tonight.'

Naida didn't knock, and surprised Ludeney's servant who was folding cloth in the small hallway. She could hear the sounds of pen on paper and see bright lights from a room to the right.

'I do beg your pardon but I must see the Lord Marshal on a matter of extreme urgency. I am Naida.'

'This is most irregular,' said the servant, looking beyond her at Elias's hulking frame.

'My friend is happy to wait elsewhere if he makes you nervous. But I must see the Lord Marshal.'

'He sees no one at this hour.'

'He'll see me. So, if you could . . .' Naida made a motion towards the room she assumed him to be in.

'I think it unwise,' said the servant.

'Shattered throne!' thundered a voice that caused the servant's face to drain of all colour. 'Show the Lady Naida in. The noise you're making is giving me a headache.'

'My apologies, sir,' fluttered the servant, turning and then flinching as Ludeney appeared in the door frame to wave a finger at Elias.

'And make this man some tea. If we had longer, I'd have you draw him a bath. Looks like he could do with it.' He waved Naida in and as she walked past him, continued. 'What can I do for you?'

Ludeney closed the door and indicated the plush furniture but Naida shook her head. She fetched the note from Rius Denharl out of her bag and passed it across to Ludeney. He gave her a quizzical look, read the scribbled note, turned the page over to confirm the author and then read it again.

And again. And each time Naida watched him *age*. His proud bearing sagged, shoulders hunching, head dropping as if his neck could no longer support its weight. He drew the back of a trembling hand across his mouth, the frown on his forehead so deep it looked ploughed. The muscles around his eyes tightened as he fought off tears.

Nonetheless, Naida needed to hear his confirmation.

'Did you know?'

Ludeney sat down at his desk and gestured once more at the plush chairs but still Naida wouldn't sit.

'I wasn't here,' he said, his voice a cracked shadow of its normal self. He gave a short, bitter laugh. 'I was hunting you.'

Ludeney looked at her and in his eyes was so much sorrow for both of them. For the life he had forced her into and the years he had wasted. So many lies, so much damage.

'I'm so sorry,' he said.

'You had your orders,' she said, seeking to salve him of his guilt, which was an extraordinary feeling given the figure of terror he had been to her for so much of her life. 'You could not have known.'

'I could have been braver,' he replied. 'Stood up for them, for what I knew them to be in my heart.'

'And where would it have got you? The cage next door, that's where.'

Ludeney nodded and tried to hand her back the note. 'What now?'

'Keep it. What happens now is that I find out who is behind this whole grand conspiracy, the one that began with the murder of my parents, and expose the whole thing. With your help.'

'Of course.'

'Denharl confirmed that my parents had discovered something that affected how they thought about the King, and I cannot help but feel that whatever it was, put them in the malevolent sights of the powerful. Have you found anything?'

'We're following a couple of paper trails but, as is often the case, they may lead nowhere.'

'My guess is it had to do with the apothecary trade and Cantabria.'

'That wouldn't be enough but I'll bear it in mind,' he said, then frowned. 'What are you doing wondering about the palace at this time of night?'

'I need to break into a few more important offices of state so I can prove to you it isn't the Queen who is the danger to the country, so we can bring her to her senses together. I need you not to get in my way.'

'Except if Eva is a usurper, as I believe, she is a fundamental danger,' said Ludeney. 'And I am prepared to stake my reputation that your parents had found that out too.'

'I will not kill the Queen whatever you find out,' said Naida. 'All I care about is ending the plague and clearing my parents.'

'Do what you must but promise me that you pass to me anything you uncover, however small. I'll try to keep malign eyes away from you as far as I can. You've already given me a new direction. One pulled thread can unravel the entire tapestry.'

'Thank you.'

'Likewise.'

Naida walked from the room, sweeping past Elias on her way to the door, feeling all the threads beginning to coalesce around an uncomfortable conclusion. What if it *was* knowledge about the monarchy that led to her parents' murder? And if it was, how much did Eva know?

'Where are we going?' asked Elias.

'Nowhere special.'

★

'I don't think the offices of the Queen's Personal Private Secretary are *nowhere special*,' said Elias. 'And we could really do with Kat for this.'

'We're a bit short of time,' said Naida.

'And I think you telling everyone who you are might not be helping.'

They were back in the linen cupboard and heading down the back stairs, hoping to remember the labyrinthine route Cerrie had shown them.

'Let's just get there, get in, get out, and go and hide somewhere.'

At the bottom of the stairs, Elias, who was unusually tense, stopped in the gloom.

'We need to pause and think for a moment,' he said.

'We don't have the time.'

'Tell me when Denharl and the witch will wake up.'

'Not before noon,' said Naida. 'So—'

'It's not yet midnight, so we do have time.'

'To do what?'

'To get this right, Lady Esselrode, and keep you from the cage.'

Naida focused on herself for a moment and found her heart was racing and her energy low. Her mind was snatching at possibilities, driven by assumed urgency. Now they had paused for a moment, she realised Elias was right.

'I didn't learn much in the army beyond how best to kill the soldier in front of me,' he said. 'But one thing that went into my thick skull was that if you fight when you are tired you do not think properly, and when you do not think you make mistakes, and when you make mistakes in war, you end up dead. And those who do not stop to look across the line never see the strike coming until it is too late.'

Naida squeezed one huge bicep. 'You don't have to speak in allegory.'

'Bloody good job because I don't know what one of those is.'

Naida chuckled, feeling the full weight of her exhaustion begin to bite now the adrenaline was receding. 'Any other nuggets of wisdom?'

'Yeah, actually,' said Elias. 'Did a bit of burglary, like most of my friends when I was younger. Best hours to get in and out are just before the dawn. Even in a palace, I reckon. Quiet, dark, slow hours. Guards are waiting for the shift to change, and sleeping folk are deep in their blankets.'

'So what now?' Strange how tiredness affected you. From complete certainty to needing help with the simplest of decisions in the blink of an eye.

'Back to the infirmary. We'll be safe there. And have time to get a few hours' sleep, and get word to Kat and the rest, cos we'll need some help. We can make a plan. It might be a long day.'

'Might not, if I get unmasked and burned in the cage.'

'Good, you're keeping positive.' He held out a hand, which she took, and they walked down a pipe-run damp passage. 'It's not over 'til we're all afire. Come on, sleep is waiting.'

★

The seeds Naida had sown before she crawled into one of the medical centre's solitary beds to embrace a deep and dreamless sleep for a few hours had developed green shoots of both hope and despair by the time she awoke, her shoulder shaken by Elias.

'Burglary hour,' he said. 'But there's some stuff you need to hear first.'

'Where?'

'Garden.'

'I'll see you there in a moment. I should check the patients first. How bad is it?'

'Terrible.' Elias flashed a grim smile. 'Hard to believe what's going on unless you assume it was all organised this way.'

Naida stood up and pushed her hands through her hair, feeling barely refreshed but, when she sought within herself, she found her body was less strained, less stretched. And she took some comfort in that. Today, after all, could be her last. If only she had Drevien here to tell her it would all be all right.

She rearranged her clothes, laced on her boots and patted Elias on the arm before slinging her bag over her shoulder and walking down the short corridor and on to the ward. Brin was there, a constant comforting presence, moving through the ordered beds arranged in their neat rows backed by freshly painted walls. Two other staff were helping him, even in this dark hour before dawn. There was progress here at least.

Seeing Naida, Brin came across, questions on his lips.

'I understand you're in charge, but it would have been decent of you to tell me you'd be using this place as a hub for whatever

368

you're doing … ideally before inviting soldiers here,' he said. 'What is going on? No one will tell me anything.'

'Short answer is: I'm trying to stop a disaster engulfing the city. Walk through the wards with me on the way to the garden and you'll understand … though you won't like it.'

Brin took her on the briefest of tours, introducing her to patients with various minor ailments, some post-op recoveries and one very elderly man in palliative care as he moved towards death. Brin's impatience made him quite brusque and Naida smiled, seeing in him plenty of herself, desperate to learn, keen to understand.

The garden was lit with a quartet of lanterns on the walls. Elias, Kat, Willan and Adeile sat there in the warm still air that heralded a blazing hot day to come. All of them knew who she really was, and none of them shied away, though Willan wore the lies hardest. Her old friend had deserved so much better and she hoped she could find a moment to say so, help him come to terms with it. He was a soldier, brought up on the battlefield, her betrayal would run deep. He must still believe in her, on some level, or he wouldn't be here.

'Thank you, all of you. You're all taking a great risk in standing with me and I will not think less of you if, once you hear my plan, you need to step away. I may not live out the day, and if I fail, you will be dragged down with me.'

'It's not easy,' said Willan. 'I trusted you, protected you, and you lied to me.'

'To everyone, though I hope you at least understand why. To confide in you would have been to incriminate you.'

Willan shrugged. 'So many soldiers believed you saved them with the skill of your knife.'

Naida nodded, feeling her guilt deepen. 'I know. But they lived to fight again, to see their families, to be angry with me. Believe me, Will, for every moment you have spent battling with the pain I have caused you, I have spent a season battling with my conscience. I do not ask for your forgiveness, just your understanding.'

Elias cleared his throat. 'This has to wait because the dawn will not.'

'Sorry,' said Naida. 'I need news. From the camp first. Will?'

Willan drew in a long breath and his expression was bleak, sending anxiety through Naida's heart. He pulled a piece of paper from his jacket and handed it to her.

'Sennoch wrote this for you about Kindar's Tincture: Kella and Drevien both have the Red Spot. The tincture does slow the infection, which means more might survive it, but it is not a cure. Kella and Drevien are really sick, Naida, and there is no more tincture.'

Naida had begun to shake and she put a hand to her mouth to help steady herself before she spoke. 'Are they dying?'

Willan had tears in his eyes too. 'Most of them die, don't they?'

'But right now, we still have time. If we can get Gifted down to the camp, we could save them. Tell me we can do that. Kat? We *have* to do that.'

'Honestly, I don't know where to start,' she said, looking taut and tired. Naida might have slept, but Kat had not.

'Why?' Naida's pulse was painful in her throat. 'She cannot die.'

'It's horrible out there. The plague has escaped the dockland slums and is spreading fast in the city. Meanwhile, the first Gifted trial is starting tomorrow, and that has unshackled the hate mobs. The Gifted are already being blamed for the outbreak and I've heard stories of them being hauled out of their beds, hunted down if they fled. The lucky ones have been marched to the holding pens by Traitor's Square. If you can call that lucky. Plenty of others have been murdered where they were found. No Gifted is going to risk going to the plague camp or out into the city but, contrary to Will's information, there is plenty of tincture. It's being sold all over the city, demand for it spreading faster than the plague.'

'What?' Naida's worst fears were all being realised at once. 'What's it being sold as?'

'Preventative or cure, whatever will sell it for the highest price. The Arbalers are everywhere, touting it as the answer; saying the Gifted have stained the city for too long and must be cast aside. Purged. The atmosphere is horrible.'

'I don't understand,' said Naida. 'How can they think this will work? If the tincture doesn't cure the Red Spot then tens of thousands are going to die and the survivors will know they've been lied to.'

'Too late then, isn't it?' said Brin. 'Think about it. If what your friend says is right and the tincture slows the disease, then the deaths will be delayed, perhaps, conveniently, until after the legislation banning and criminalising the Gifted has passed. The lie about the outbreak being their fault is already believed, isn't it?'

'It's open season on the Gifted, and the markets are flooded with apothecary remedies...' said Adeile.

'...that don't work,' whispered Naida. 'But a few get rich while thousands die because a bad apothecary is all they've got. We need Aryn to get to Temets, give him Sennoch's report and make sure he draws out the debate for as long as he can, so the evidence of the failure of the tincture starts to appear. If he can sway opinion in the Crucible, it will affect the Gifted trials.'

'This is an appalling crime,' said Brin.

'And we're going to try to stop it,' said Naida.

'How?'

'Prove to the Queen that the Gifted were never to blame,' Naida said firmly. 'Prove to her the plague was set by those pushing Cantabrian medicine. Convince her, by about lunch time today when Denharl wakes up and starts shouting.'

'How?' repeated Brin.

'I've got a couple of leads on the proof we need. We have to break into Jaren Kerslan's office while Aryn does his best with Temets, and I have to explain the crime to the Queen and how it all began with the murder of my parents for a genocide they did not commit.'

Brin stared at her, overwhelmed, and seized on the one detail he thought he could understand. 'You've lost me. Your parents?'

Naida glanced round her friends. Elias and Adeile shrugged, Willan was staring at the ground, and Kat managed a smile.

'They're doing to other Gifted what they did to my parents fifteen years ago: blaming them for a plague they did not cause, only sought to cure. I've never truly believed in my parents' guilt and now I know, despite all the energy spent in demonising them, that I was right. Brin, I am Helena Esselrode.'

Brin took a sharp step away from her and gaped around those assembled in the garden, searching for a sign she was making some kind of sick joke.

'You ...?'

'...have, like my parents, dedicated my life to saving those of others? Yes. Any other questions? I normally invite people to denounce me if they want to at this stage, but I'm afraid we don't have time for that today.'

Every time she said her true name, Naida felt the thrill of release, of freedom. Brin stared at her.

'It's not about me or my family, Brin. It's about a deliberate conspiracy to start a plague, frame the Gifted, and sell Cantabrian medicine that doesn't work for a vast profit. Someone is trying to make money out of thousands of lives, and we can't risk you standing against us now.'

'You don't need to threaten me,' said Brin. 'I knew your

parents ... well, I came into contact with them around the palace. I believe you.'

And yet he looked unsure. Naida smiled and put a hand on his shoulder.

'Thank you, Brin.'

Over his shoulder, though, she glanced at Elias and her message was clear. *Watch him.*

'How can I help?' asked Brin.

Naida was about to speak but Kat got there first.

'May I? We've been thinking, Naida. We need to gain access to state offices in the palace apartments, and us wandering up looking like a bunch of mercs and asking to come in isn't going to cut it. We need a reason and now you've drugged Lord Denharl, we have one ready-made.'

'I don't understand,' said Naida.

'We're going to disguise ourselves as medics and take Denharl to the Queen's personal medical rooms as an emergency. How's that?'

Naida felt proper hope blossom. 'That's brilliant! Brin, a stretcher and a few orderly and medic gowns and uniforms, please? The soldiers are going to do some dressing up.'

★

'Remember, all bustle and professionalism now, absolute quiet when we get inside,' said Elias. 'Naida, once we've got you in, I'll get help to Drevien and Kella. Somehow. I promise.'

Naida nodded and managed a smile though, with every pace, she felt Drevien's grip on life was being further weakened. Yet she had no choice. To run to the plague camp as her every loving impulse desired, would be to consign the city to ruin and thousands of its people to a horrible death. If she was sacrificing Drevien, it had better be worth all the grief to come.

They were hurrying through the dark back corridors of the

palace, trying to avoid unnecessary contact, using Elias's remarkable memory of Cerrie's route to Denharl's rooms. Brin was with them to add gravitas, and because Elias was keen he stay in sight, until he'd incriminated himself enough that denouncing Naida wouldn't save him.

They reached the Master of the Spires' rooms unseen by anyone other than night porters and the first of the early morning cleaning details, all mops and cloths and steaming water. Naida produced the keys and in they went, the acrid odour of vomit in the air.

'Brin, check on the maid in the drawing room ahead. She was drunk before she was drugged. The rest of you, with me.'

They hurried into Denharl's bedchamber where the sick old man was in a sound sleep, his face serene, with a hint of colour in his cheeks. Naida wondered if in drugging him, she might have done him a favour.

Will, Kat, Adeile and Elias loaded Denharl onto the stretcher. Naida covered him with a sheet up to his shoulders.

'Anyone know the way?' asked Willan once the soldiers had picked up the stretcher.

'I do,' said Naida. 'This one's easy. Left at the door, head to the end, go right and follow it. I'll show you. And walk in step, bit like when you're marching, or you'll jostle him on the stretcher as well as give us away.'

They met Brin back in the hallway.

'How is she?'

'Alive,' he said. 'She reeks of cheap spirit and puke but I've cleaned her up and resettled her. I'll get someone to sit with her until she wakes up. Blackbush and serron, was it?'

'What else?' Naida shrugged. 'Come on, let's go. You stay in the middle of the stretcher and keep a hand on his chest. Look concerned.'

'I'm no actor.'

'Well, imagine you're putting your faith in the daughter of monsters, that ought to do the trick.'

'How can you joke about it?' asked Brin, discomfited.

'Like everyone else, I would rather laugh than scream. Let's move.'

With Naida at their head, Brin and the stretcher team hurried through the predawn palace corridors towards the Queen's private apartments, past maids, guards and aides, all of whom saw what they were supposed to see and no doubt scurried off to share the big news.

Reaching the guarded main doors, Naida felt the nerves settle on her and she had to reach within to calm herself and not gabble when the soldiers moved to block their path.

'The apartments are locked until first bell,' said one, her voice rough from a long shift on her feet without food or water.

'We have an emergency,' said Naida. 'Lord Denharl was found unconscious in his rooms. Let us pass, so we can treat him in the Queen's private treatment rooms; we don't have much time.'

The soldiers did not move. 'The royal medical centre is nearby,' said the other.

'It does not have the stores I need,' said Naida.

'Our orders are very specific,' said the first.

'So are mine!' said Naida. 'And they don't include letting senior members of the Queen's Council die.'

'Naida,' said Brin, his voice urgent. 'His pulse is weakening.'

'Unlock the door,' she said. 'Now. I am the Queen's personal physician and this man is dying.'

The soldiers shifted, unsure of their ground.

'On whose orders is this door sealed?' snapped Brin. 'Not on Her Majesty's. Whose?'

'Aide Vinald,' said one and Naida cursed. Aide Vinald knew too much, and suspected even more. 'Get his permission, we can stand aside.'

Elias, who was front left of the stretcher, grumbled deep in his throat, drawing their attention.

'You don't look much like an orderly,' said the first, she of the rough voice.

'What's that supposed to mean?' asked Elias, glancing at Kat. Naida knew that look, and she readied herself.

'It means I don't recognise you.'

Brin picked up the rising tension and threw oil over it, leaning in close and listening to Denharl's heart while searching for a pulse.

'Set him down,' he said to the stretcher-bearers. 'Naida, help. He's fading. What have you got in your bag? He needs a kick or he'll die.'

Naida was at his side.

'I've got jastoria root.'

Brin didn't flinch. Naida was aware of the guards staring down at what was becoming feverish work.

'It'll have to do.'

Naida managed to tap Elias's ankle. 'Gently now.'

Elias straightened. 'I'm sorry,' he said to the guards.

'What for?' asked the first, understanding what was coming as she uttered the words.

Elias's fist smashed into her gut and she doubled over. Kat grabbed her hips and swung her hard into the wall, her head making a solid connection, and she slumped to the ground. The second soldier, stunned for a moment, made to grab for his blade only to look up straight into Willan's boot, the wily fighter leaping clean over the stretcher. The boot caught him in the chest and he staggered backwards against the door frame. Elias cracked a fist into his chin, putting him down.

Naida grinned at Brin. 'Good work.'

'What, by ash and water, is jastoria root?' Brin's eyes were wide with excitement and fear, his face flushed.

376

'No idea, but it sounds good for restarting hearts or some-thing.'

Naida stood up. Kat was already working at the lock, having determined that the guards didn't hold the keys. They'd be the other side of the door.

'So what do we do with these two?' asked Naida.

Both were already stirring. Elias knelt by them, looking hard at them, inspecting their uniforms.

'Something's not right,' he said. 'Kat, how are you doing?'

'It's a multiple lever with a double mechanism. Not easy but I can do it. Why?'

'Check this out.' He was holding the collar of one of the guard's deep green shirts. 'Anything strike you?'

It was Willan who spoke. 'That isn't military cut. Those shirts have been dyed.'

'They aren't guards,' said Elias. 'Vinald's stooges, probably Keelers.'

Naida looked at the doors. No wonder they didn't want to let her in. 'We have to get inside. The Queen could be in danger.'

'Working on it,' said Kat. 'There will be top and bottom bolts. Start praying they are attached to the second mechanism.'

They were so vulnerable here. Anyone could come up the wide stairs, or head round the corner and see them.

'Adeile, keep an eye out. Will, down one flight,' said Naida. They moved, fast. 'What do we do with the imposters?'

Elias turned a bleak expression on her. 'Best you look away for a moment, Naida. You too, Brin.'

'You can't—' began Brin.

'They are the enemy,' said Elias, his voice, normally so jovial, was flat. 'Here in the palace, outside my Queen's door. I am sworn to protect her.'

'No,' said Naida. 'We didn't come here to kill people. We'll drug them, same as Denharl. It'll put them out of the game until it's resolved one way or another. They should face proper justice.'

Elias thought to argue but withdrew. 'Be quick, though.'

While she and Brin mixed the root with water and forced it down the throats of the guards, Naida's head filled with fears of what they might find within, whether whoever it was, Velez, Kerslan or any of the Queen's Council, had taken Eva captive or whether she was blissfully unaware of the turmoil in her own corridors. She flirted with the notion that Eva might even be dead, but that was far-fetched. No one could wield authority without either the ear, or control, of the monarch.

Chapter 34

'All right, we're in,' said Kat. She stood up and backed away. 'Back on the stretcher?'

'Yes,' said Naida, relief flooding her. 'Get in, act normal, assess. If it's quiet, bring in the two sleepers and hide them. There's storerooms right by the door.'

Adeile came round the corner at a run. 'We've got company. Kitchen staff, I think – maybe breakfast is on the way – and they're unarmed but we can't be seen.'

Elias hissed Will's name and he came bounding up the stairs.

'Naida, Brin, in you go,' said Kat. 'Two on the stretcher, one to a body.'

Naida took a breath and opened one of the doors, finding a dimly lit and empty corridor. 'Clear. Hurry.'

In came the stretcher with Kat and Will. Adeile and Elias dragged the bodies in and tried the nearest doors. 'Kat, lock the door. Can you disable it, somehow?'

'That bit's easy,' she said.

Brin closed the doors, slid up some hand bolts and knelt by Denharl who had been laid on the ground again. 'He doesn't look great, as it happens. He's going blotchy.'

Naida glanced down. 'Shattered throne, that's all we need. He's having a reaction to the drug. The apothecary cupboard in here has everything so we should find some Alianza or Hythewort.'

'I know,' said Brin. 'I built and stocked it.'

'Right, let's get him moving. Adeile, Will, take the stretcher and follow Brin. Kat, Elias, with me to Kerslan's office. We'll need to be quick. If anyone finds us, we need to be treating Denharl, not ransacking an office.'

The palace apartments in early morning carried an atmosphere of anticipation for the bustle and flow of the day to come. Portraits of monarchs, consorts, princesses, and princes, complete with favourite animals or a trophy from a hunt, maybe sitting taking the air in a formal garden, looked down on them as they hurried along the rug-strewn corridors.

Naida's earlier fears dissipated at the sight of guard patrols, and occupied guard posts everywhere they turned or looked. Offers of help were welcomed though turned away, with soldiers recognising her, Brin and, more particularly, Denharl.

'So why were the Keelers outside?' she asked.

'To keep others out, I suppose. Well, you, anyway,' said Kat.

They slowed as they approached the Queen's rooms which, as always, were guarded. The medical rooms were at the end of a short corridor near Eva's dressing room, Kerslan's office was the closest to her. Both were in view of the guards on the door.

'Go with me,' said Naida. 'Kat, if you get a chance, Velez's office door is the next one you can see on your right.'

They moved on, the two guards showing an interest but no alarm as Naida waved them forwards.

'We have an emergency for the medical rooms.'

'Yes, Lady Naida,' said a tall soldier with short-cropped hair and a very young face. 'Lord Denharl...'

'Yes. We can save him, if we act fast.'

'Can we help?' asked the tall soldier.

'Yes, and thank you so much,' said Naida. 'If you … what are your names?'

'I am Keer and this is Pellor,' said Keer, indicating his shorter, equally youthful comrade.

'Thank you. Could you take the stretcher from my colleagues, accompany them into the surgery and help them make the Master of the Spires comfortable? That would be such a help while I get what we need from the apothecary supplies.'

Even if she said so herself, that was smooth. She, Elias and Kat watched while Keer and Pellor took themselves from their duties, Kat examining the lock on Kerslan's door and chuckling to herself.

'My, my.'

They were inside in moments, the door locked behind them, open drapes admitting the dim predawn light.

'Let's hope they're as careless with their incriminating documents as they are with their security,' said Kat. 'What are we looking for?'

'Anything to do with Cantabria and trade,' said Naida. 'It's a live issue, so papers could even be on a desk. But pull open every drawer, and never mind the mess.'

Kerslan's office was a smaller copy of Denharl's. Two administrator's desks sat in the front office, while Kerslan's private office was complete with huge desk, drinks stand, tapestries, fireplace, luxurious seating and an enormous painting of the personal private secretary himself in a terrible attempt at a heroic pose.

'I thought Velez was prime suspect, or am I missing something?' said Elias.

'But here's where we find what's happening right now with Cantabrian representation in the city, and whether it's government, business or both. I don't know … I need to see names I recognise on incriminating documents.'

'Loosing in the dark,' said Kat.

381

'I don't have anything else.'

While Kat and Elias searched the outer office, Naida went to work in the private office, sorting through Kerslan's papers, delighted that she would never be the resident of such an office, so mundane was it all. Receipts, invoices, reports on meetings with senior figures from home and abroad, invitations, requests, maintenance schedules, decoration plans, furniture orders, artist sittings, jewellery design days, menus. Everything to be read, assessed, filtered and diarised.

Diarised.

Naida scattered papers and opened drawers in a flurry, finding several leather-bound volumes and placing them on the desk. She opened the first of the diaries, skipping to today's date then going back ten days. It was Kerslan's personal diary and he was impressively busy with mundanity. But there was nothing. Barring his daily briefings with Eva, every other meeting was deep in the weeds of palace life, including a meticulous note about Her Majesty's medical examination by the new head of the royal medical service.

Naida smiled. Seven days ago seemed another life entirely. She slid the volume from the pile and opened the next. It was a purchasing log and diary, exhaustive in the details, and it looked as though everything bought on behalf of the palace was co-signed by Denharl. She slid it aside. The third was the Queen's diary, and Naida flicked through to today. There was nothing of interest, though her own name appeared a few times, which felt good.

Naida began going forward and, there, the day after tomorrow, was a lead. The whole day was blanked out for a reception, tour and various meetings with the Cantabrian royal family and their heads of trade and foreign affairs. Perfect timing. Naida read the entry, particularly the boxed note at the bottom of the page, '*reference briefing docs at seven-four-three (four-one), Canta-org-seven-nine*'.

'Ash and smoke, that has to be it!' Naida ran into the front office. 'How are the files organised?'

Kat looked at the top of the one she was holding. 'Three numbers, two more in a bracket, a few letters, two more numbers.'

'Perfect. Find me seven-four-three, forty-one, Canta-hyphen-org. Quick!'

Kat knew exactly where to look, pulling open a cabinet and then drawer after drawer, searching for the number, her fingers running over file covers while Naida and Elias watched as if it was the finale of a mummer's show in Festival Square. By the time Kat pulled out a big, fat laced leather file, bursting at the seams, Naida felt almost faint with tension.

They laid the file on a desk, pulled it open and spread out the documents. Kat scanned them greedily. Naida could already see, from the headers on some tied bundles, that it contained everything they needed. Names, payments, premises purchasing, signatories...

Pulling the bow on a file dated just thirty days ago, Naida found the ratification papers on a trade agreement to bring in enormous quantities of Cantabrian medical supplies in the form of raw material and pre-prepared treatments. Profiles and intelligence on the Cantabrians involved in the deal was there too, food for the influencers and blackmailers.

'Look at these names...' said Naida. She tapped the page. Kerslan, Velez, and Markan. Not Emilius who had taken his own life rather than divulge secrets, but a relative, his brother or father, listed as a co-owner. It was signed by Velez, next to the Queen's seal. 'This is solid. Anything else?'

'Yes,' said Kat, handing her another document. 'This was in the same drawer.'

Naida sorted through the pages and her pulse quickened. The paper detailed how to clear the market for the incoming products. Its focus, beyond buying or wrecking local apothecary concerns, was focused upon fomenting distrust of the Gifted and recommending legislation to maximise potential profit, and it was dispassionate and blunt. There was even a proposal for a sliding percentage profit to be paid to those driving out the Gifted, depending on the level of their success. An addendum detailed a plan to set Red Spot in an 'easily contained' area in order to test a market-breaking product.

It was not signed but there were indents on its surface of what looked like a signature.

'This is it. If we can identify that signature ... got to be Velez or Kerslan, hasn't it? They're working together, aren't they?' said Naida, her anger burst through again. 'We've got to make them suffer.'

'Who do we take it to?' asked Elias, still sifting through papers.

'The only person who can stop the trials and the debates is the Queen, surely,' said Naida.

'Except she signed something here,' said Kat. 'Look. It's the licensing agreement, which allows bulk importation. Has to be signed by the monarch.'

Naida looked. Eva's signature was there.

'She can't say she knows nothing about it,' said Kat. 'So, the question is: how deeply is she involved?'

'Look at the date,' said Naida. 'Well before any legislation was passed. Well before that report was written. And all it does is confirm licences to import and trade, granted against profits for the Exchequer. But she'll know the key players. I wonder if—'

The key had turned, and the door was already half open before any of them realised. Naida looked up and met Dmitry's eyes, and his expression of comical surprise turned to one of disgust.

'What are you doing here?' he demanded. Kat stepped smartly behind him, shut and relocked the door. Dmitry took in both Kat and Elias. 'Need protection in the palace now, do you?'

'Given who was standing outside the apartments, yes,' said Naida, facing him down but understanding the seriousness of the situation. 'I came here to find the evidence to expose a vast corruption and halt a public health disaster. How about you? I believe your office is further down the corridor.'

'I bring the public petition papers, collected here, to Her Majesty every Fair's Day. Today.'

Naida couldn't quite believe it. 'Lucky you. And you seem entirely unsurprised about corruption in high offices.'

'Aide Vinald said you poked your nose where you shouldn't. I'm sad you've proved him right.'

'Safeguarding public health is on page one of my job description. The question is, how much do you know? What names are you protecting?'

Naida knew her voice had gone cold. Dmitry's mask of confidence slipped. Elias moved around the table separating them, his frame huge in the tight space.

'I will not be intimidated by you or your thugs.'

'No, though your buddy Vinald thinks I can be intimidated by Geth Herron. Mind you, he was wearing his balls as earrings by the time I'd finished with him. And I'm really short on time today, so don't think I won't do the same to you. This city is on the brink of self-induced destruction and one sore groin is a good exchange for a life, do you get me?'

'There are guards on the Queen's doors, and there are medics in her healing rooms. All I have to do is shout.'

Kat thumped a fist into his right kidney. He gasped and staggered, having to reach out to the back of a chair to maintain his footing.

'Yeah, but you're not going to do that, are you?' Kat said into his ear. 'And they're our medics, so ...'

Dmitry stood tall again, despite his obvious discomfort. 'You know this leads to a life behind bars, or maybe a short and painful one in the cage, don't you?'

'Only if we're wrong,' said Naida. 'But we're not, are we?'

Dmitry stared at her, defiant.

'I so wanted to believe the best of you,' said Naida. 'How much do you stand to gain, Dmitry? Do you get Darius's share as well, now?'

'I don't know what you're talking about.'

'When the plague takes you, it is like you're aflame. Your organs melt inside your living body, your eyes cloud over and darken and your head hurts so much that to lose it would be a blessing. But death won't come. Not for a day, maybe two. At worst, three. And all the while you are helpless, lying in your own faeces, your tongue swollen, your body a seething mass of pustules. It is a death to be feared, and yet you would visit it on the very people you are sworn to protect and serve. On yourself, if you don't help me.'

Dmitry didn't flinch. He showed no fear, just disinterest. The charming man she had first met was gone, replaced by someone else entirely.

'Nature has provided a cure that is even now safeguarding the people.'

'But it *doesn't* work properly, does it? And you have forced the Gifted out, leaving the city facing death.'

Slowly and very deliberately, Dmitry drew his fist from his heart to his hip. Naida felt sick, right in the base of her gut.

'The plague will take the weak, and the strong will survive. When we are summoned back to the earth, we may not ignore the call. Nature must prevail.'

Naida felt the chains on her temper break and she slapped him hard across the cheek.

'A deliberately started outbreak is not *nature's way*,' she hissed. 'And the Talent is a gift from nature, pure as the ocean, natural as the dew. Who ordered it? I want a name.'

Dmitry did not raise a hand to his smarting cheek. 'I will gladly give my life to my cause. I am sworn to the true way and you cannot break me. What began in the slums of Cantabria ends today and the light will shine again.'

Elias's haymaker scattered teeth and blood from his mouth. Dmitry crashed into the cabinets lining the wall before hitting the floor heavily. Groggily, he hauled himself up on hands and knees and spat more blood.

'Lady Naida asked you a question,' said Elias.

'You cannot stop what's coming,' said Dmitry, his words muffled by his broken mouth. 'We are returning to purity.'

'Wading through the blood of innocent people. Is that what your God advocates?' Naida was snarling, experiencing a fury she had no wish to dissolve. 'Thousands will die as you march this country back two hundred years and unleash all the old fears of disease and pain that we had overcome. This will not stand, not while I breathe.'

Dmitry managed the most crooked of smiles. 'We have already won.'

'One more time, Dmitry: who is *we*? Who is your master?'

'We are the real Suurkene, the true patriots, who follow the ancient paths and reject the infection of the tainted. We are the pure, and Arbala is our mistress.'

'You're wasting your time with him,' said Kat. 'I'll deal with this creature; you need to find the Queen. City's waking up, Crucible is about to go into session.'

Dmitry chuckled. 'What do you think Eva can do? She cannot stop the avalanche any more than you can.'

'What will you do?' Naida looked down at Dmitry, now sitting with his back to the cabinets. 'He needs help. He'll learn nothing from being killed.'

'I'll deal with him,' repeated Kat. 'Go. Elias, go with her.'

'I will see you ashed and scattered, Naida Erivayne.'

'Dream on, Dmitry. You will come to see and understand the horror you've unleashed.'

Elias unlocked and opened the door. 'Naida.'

'Goodbye, Dmitry.'

Naida followed Elias back into the corridor. To the right, the guards on Eva's rooms barely registered their reappearance as they hurried towards the surgery with papers tucked under their arms. Inside, the atmosphere was calm. Brin was mixing ingredients in a flask, Denharl was on one of the two beds, and Adeile and Willan were very much on guard, the scabbarded blades they had hidden beneath Denharl on the stretcher evident beneath their orderly's gowns.

'Find what you need?' asked Adeile.

'Enough, I hope,' said Naida. Elias was strapping his blade around his waist. 'Brin, how's Denharl?'

'Responding well. Breathing and pulse are steady. He'll be fine.'

'Stay with him,' said Naida.

'No. He doesn't need me and your friends in the camp do.'

'But—'

'I will get a Gifted there. One of my friends. Trust me.'

Naida kissed his cheek, tears threatening. 'Thank you. Please hurry. Kat will have to help you out of the doors. She's in Kerslan's office.'

Brin nodded and ran away out of sight, all of Naida's hopes going with him.

'Let's go find the Queen,' she said. 'Follow my lead and remember you aren't guards until there's a problem.'

Naida strode out, her trio of soldiers keeping her in sight and trying to appear casual as she walked up to Eva's door guards.

'Is my lord Denharl improving?' asked Keer, the very tall one.

'He is indeed. Sleeping comfortably, his natural colour returned to his cheeks. Thank you for your aid. I shall mention your names to Her Majesty.'

Keer and Pellor both smiled, the latter blushing. 'It is our pleasure and our duty.'

'I must report his condition to Her Majesty. May I be granted access?'

Keer looked apologetic. 'I can check with her lady-in-waiting?' He indicated through the doors.

'Thank you.'

Keer knocked on the door, a coded tap of five, then three. There was the sound of a key in the lock and the door opened to the extent of an internal chain. Keer asked to be admitted and he disappeared inside. Naida smiled at Pellor, then wandered back towards her friends, her nerves taking control of her stomach, muscles and head. She blew out her cheeks and wiped her face. There was something else too, a creeping anxiety. This was all taking too long.

'You all right?' asked Willan.

'It's just a little ... surreal.'

Willan made a face. Back along the main corridor, there was the sound of a heavy impact. Naida started. Elias spun round.

'The main doors,' he said.

Kat appeared at a dead run. 'Trouble.'

'Did Brin get out?'

'Barely but yes. We have to get out of here.'

There was another heavy impact, then a third, accompanied by the splintering of wood, shouting, and running of booted feet. Bells were ringing without, alarms to bring soldiers from their beds to protect the Queen.

Elias, who had disappeared briefly after a look from Kat, came charging back.

'Naida, run. Now.'

'Run where?' The apartment and offices were sprawling and multi-floored, but as far as she knew, there was only one way in or out.

'Away. Anywhere, I don't know. It's Vinald, he has Herron and more with him. Quickly!'

Naida turned to Pellor. 'Where's Eva? We must protect the Queen!'

The young soldier was wide-eyed, trying to comprehend what was unfolding before his eyes.

'I...' he

'Naida...' warned Elias.

The enemy was closing. Alarms had begun to sound within the apartments.

Keer pulled open the door and looked towards the noise.

'The Queen may be in danger. Is she in there?' Naida was terse, Keer was scared, staring past her to the oncoming threat. The notion that, as a Queen's guard, he might be called upon to guard the Queen, had clearly not occurred to him. 'Keer!'

He turned his gaze to her.

'Fair's Day,' he managed. 'They said she went very early.'

'Yes?' Behind Naida, medical gowns were being discarded, clips loosened from the top of scabbards. 'What does that mean?'

'Naida!' barked Elias. 'Kat, Will, flank me.'

'Throne Room,' stuttered Pellor, as frightened as Keer. 'Public petitions.'

'Which way? Which way!' Pellor gestured helplessly towards the main doors behind them. Naida cursed. 'Keer! Is there another way?'

He pointed along the corridor past the medical room. Naida kissed his forehead in gratitude.

'Hide,' she whispered. 'Take Pellor, go inside and hide. Elias, all of you! With me!'

Naida ran down the corridor, past the medical centre, the glowering busts of the royal dead, and door after door letting into offices and guest suites. She could hear the other three behind her and the sounds of pursuit, the shouts to stop.

'Where are you going?' called Kat.

'Throne Room,' said Naida.

'How?'

'I don't know,' she muttered. 'Downstairs, it's downstairs.'

But where were the back stairs? At the back of a closet, no doubt. How she needed Cerrie right now. But there was no Cerrie, instead there was the clatter and echo of boots and shouting, and the thundering of her heart, the oppressive atmosphere, and the strong possibility they were running into a dead end.

Reaching the end of one luxuriously appointed corridor, Naida turned sharp right.

'Oh no.'

There it was. The dead end, a door in a frame that would either give them a way out or trap them in a confined space with Suranhom's most vicious killer. She picked up speed, feeling Elias right on her shoulder.

'This better be what I think it is,' he said.

'Got to be,' said Naida. 'It's *got* to be.'

Behind her she could hear Vinald's shouts for them to stop growing louder. They were about twenty yards back and had just rounded the corner. Naida pushed herself harder than she ever had. Elias cruised past her, his boots thumping dully on the carpet that ran down the centre of the corridor, itself flanked by cabinets containing decades' worth of gifts from foreign dignitaries.

He reached the door and Naida held a breath until she saw him push it open and spin round.

'In! In!' he shouted, looking past them, eyes wide. 'Go! Go!'

Kat and Adeile all but lifted Naida from her feet and rushed her into a dark storeroom that was lined with shelves stacked with all manner of apartment and office supplies. Willan raced in behind them.

'Keep it open long as you can,' said Elias. 'We need the light. The way out is locked from the other side.'

Naida's heart fell. She could see Vinald and Herron leading the charge towards them, Willan was poised to push the door shut. Kat and Adeile had their hands on some shelves, ready to pull them over to block it.

'Will ...' warned Kat.

'Closing,' said Will, and he did so with admirable calm, ducking and retreating, and Kat dragged the heavy wooden shelves across the door where they lodged at an angle against those opposite.

The storeroom was plunged into darkness. Elias swore; and hands, feet and then weapons began to beat on the door from the outside. Naida reached out and found both Willan and Kat, resting a hand on their backs as they faced the door, calming them with her touch as she stayed her own fears. She spoke softly to herself, senses picking up on Kat's energy and readiness; and Will's pure determination. She wished she had a third hand for Adeile.

'What did you do to Dmitry?' she asked Kat.

'He's still alive,' said Kat. 'He's a bit groggy, though.'

Naida kept her eyes closed, listening to Elias work on the door behind them and Herron attack the door ahead of them. She allowed herself a smile based in her faith that her friend would win the grim race. There was control and process behind, fury without.

Wood splintered. Blades bit deep, through the door and into the shelves, smashing and ripping. The door moved inwards, the shelves back towards them. Herron roared his promises of their painful deaths as light speared into the storeroom. Kat and Willan readied themselves for the fight.

'Got it,' said Elias. 'Let's go.'

'Come on,' said Naida. 'I'll follow you out.'

'Don't be stupid,' said Kat, and pushed her towards Elias who held the door for her to run through and on to a flight of stairs.

Naida began to run down them, pausing when she didn't hear enough footsteps behind her. She turned. Only Kat was with her.

'Come on,' she urged.

'I can't block this door,' said Elias. 'I had to break the lock.'

'So run.'

'No, not this time.'

'What are you doing?' she stared at Elias, Will and Adeile.

Elias smiled. 'Buying you some time.'

'No,' she said. 'We can all make it.'

'Don't waste it.'

Elias closed the door on them and she stared at it.

'I can't let them die for me.'

'Neither can you stop them,' said Kat. 'And they may yet survive.'

But she didn't believe it, either. She pointed down the stairs and they ran together, to save what lives they could.

'Hold on to your anger,' said Kat. 'Save it for those who need to see it.'

Chapter 35

Kat discarded her blade the moment they first heard voices, stowing it out of sight underneath some pipes in a service passage that was so much like all the others they'd run down, or up, that Naida had no real notion where they would emerge. They needed to get back into the palace proper and find the Throne Room.

Any thought that they might reach the Queen before the palace became too busy with petitioners was dispelled the moment they reached, with help from three aides, a packed reception hall. The light through the east-facing, glorious and enormous, tree and root stained-glass windows told her it was just dawn and yet hundreds stood here, awaiting their chance to beg help from the Queen.

They were overwhelmingly poor, wearing their best clothes – which were mostly drab, ill-fitting, patched and worn. But pride shone from every scrubbed face and was evident in the gifts so many carried... flowers, bread, cloth, jam, vegetables... anything and everything the citizens of Suranhom grew or made. The scents of perfume and soap filled the room.

The people were standing cheek by jowl in a rough snake line that crossed the reception room and wound out into a palace courtyard beyond. The head of the snake faced the

Throne Room and Naida moved through the crowd, apologising, asking for access. Most moved aside, some grumbled, others refused until they heard her name.

'Wouldn't believe there's a plague threatening to consume the city, would you?' said Kat.

'No ...' And it was strange. She wished she knew how the Queen could be protected from the risk this many people posed. Closer to the Throne Room door, though, the answer presented itself. 'Oh, very clever.'

Each and every individual who passed into the Queen's audience was greeted by an aide, in perfect dress uniform, offering the warm clasp of a hand, and a friendly touch alongside words of encouragement.

'What do you mean?' asked Kat.

Naida leaned towards Kat and spoke very softly. 'Gifted on the door, testing everyone.'

'That's ... surprising, isn't it? Y'know, given what Her Majesty said about them?'

'I think the word you're looking for is hypocritical.'

'Probably,' said Kat.

They manoeuvred the last few paces to the door and caught the eye of one of the quartet of guards stationed there, aware of the voices of some petitioners being raised as they feared someone attempting to jump the line.

'Lady Naida,' she said. 'Can I help you?'

Naida wondered how long she had before Vinald or Herron would enter to cause chaos and demand her arrest.

'I need urgent access to the Queen. It cannot wait.'

The guard wrinkled her nose beneath her helmet. 'That's difficult. This is a citizens' affair. With respect, this is their one chance, while those in the circle of the Queen have far wider access while I have orders—'

'Not to let time-wasting courtiers occupy the citizens' time because they won't wait for their official appointments,' said Naida, glancing back over her shoulder, fearful of pursuit. 'But this is a matter, quite literally, of life and death.'

'So is mine,' said a nearby voice and Naida turned to see a balding man, old beyond his years, his eyes exhausted by care. 'For dozens and dozens of people.'

'Then I will take up your case personally, but I beg you: allow me a brief audience that could halt a citywide disaster.'

She probably shouldn't have been so dramatic, but as she swung back to appeal to the guard and the Gifted aide again, both of whom were looking a little anxious, the voice piped up again.

'We all got problems. Get in line.'

'Please, honoured gentleman, I don't think you understand the gr—'

'Oh, I understand all right. You think you're more important—'

'No!' snapped Naida, turning once more, aware of Kat moving past her towards the door as the tension rose and other voices began to be heard. 'I think *you* are more important, and I am trying to speak to Her Majesty for you and everyone you love.'

Naida knew she'd made a mistake and could hear Kat speaking, though not what she said. The crowd erupted with noise, from the man in stitched rags and scrubbed skin in front of her, to ten jabbing fingers, shouting that everyone was equal today. And Naida agreed with them all... but for once her mission *was* more important than theirs and there was no way she could explain it.

The crowd was pressing, the guards moved to protect the door and Naida felt a strong hand on her shoulder.

'Come in, before you cause any more problems.'

She turned and Kat propelled her to the door. It opened to admit them and a brief blast of outraged voices before closing on them, leaving them in the abrupt silence of a packed Throne Room.

Both Naida and Kat stopped dead. Seeing the Throne Room of the Palace of Endless Spires in paintings was nothing compared to standing within it.

A glorious carved and vaulted roof, hung with flags of country and family crest, ran the centre of a column-run room as big as the pit in the Crucible. The polished marble floor glinted in the dawn sunlight that was flooding through high-set etched windows, which threw patterns of trees, rivers and animals across the yellow-stone walls.

Alcoves along the length of the room, on both sides, sheltered the busts of monarchs across the centuries, glass-topped cabinets displayed the texts that had formalised the structure and constitution of Suurken and, at the far end, the royal flag hung from wall to wall, a fitting backdrop to the glory that bled from every stone, every timber.

A blue-edged, emerald-green carpet runner ran from the doors of the Throne Room across the floor and up a shallow set of wide marble steps to a stage, upon which sat the Shattered Throne. Naida knew that every eye was on her, that she had interrupted the Queen, who would not be impressed, but here she was, in the presence of history and she could not drag her eyes from it.

It was the most painted and idealised chair ever created. Its back reached up towards the rafters, deep brown timbers carved to resemble ivy climbing and clinging some thirty feet and more; and where back met seat, carved as roots springing from the earth. The arms were the boughs of mighty trees, the legs were trunks standing proud from the earth and the coverings were leather, cracked and ancient.

And the whole throne was stitched, glued or braced together. A militia, supporting the embittered and banished Konstan family's baseless claims to the throne, had breached the palace and shattered the throne with hammer and axe, reducing it almost to firewood.

It was a moment that might have broken ... shattered ... the nation, but instead the incumbent monarch, the wise and brave Queen Jasmeen, had used it, turned it to a time of national repair, rebirth and unity. And central to it had been the rebuilding of the Shattered Throne in the geographical centre of Suranhom, with every skilled tradesperson invited to take their part in the restoration and make their mark.

Naida smiled, imagining what had been perhaps the clearest single defining moment in history for Suurken, forgetting where she was for just a moment, before reality intruded.

'Naida?' said the Queen, dressed in simple pale green and brown robes, moving away from the petitioner with whom she had been speaking. 'That was unnecessarily dramatic. Surely the usual channels would suit you far better?'

That comment was not meant for her but for the hundreds gathered inside, who chuckled, dutifully. Naida took a breath and moved up the emerald carpet.

'My apologies, Your Majesty, and to all of you honoured citizens, official recorders and palace guard. But I must speak with you on a matter of the gravest importance. It will not wait.'

Eva spread her hands to include the room. 'There can be no favouritism on Fair's Day, my lady. Like everyone here, you must wait your turn to be called.'

'No, ma'am, I will not,' said Naida.

Eva's head movement was tiny, a very slight raising of the chin combined with a slow lowering of her arms to her sides. The extraordinary pressure of her focus was entirely upon Naida, carrying all the authority of a decade as monarch; and within the Throne Room, the silence was deep enough to steal the breath and crush the chest.

'Clear the room,' Eva said slowly, holding Naida in a constricting gaze. 'Except her.'

It took an age, though it was surely done in a matter of moments. Aides and guards barked instructions, doors were opened, people herded outside, Kat among them. All the while, Eva stared at Naida while she shrivelled inside. She tried to cling to her reasons for being here, the righteousness of what she had to say and how she had to say it.

Everything came down to this.

The doors closed with a dread finality and Naida knew enough not to speak first. She was standing close to the bottom of the steps and Eva remained at the head of them, moving closer to the throne and resting a hand upon one of its arms.

'A queen does not hear *no*, not even in her private chambers. To hear it in a public forum while surrounded by her citizens as witnesses is a crime punishable by a lifetime beyond the sunlight.'

'I will accept any punishment you deem fit, ma'am, but I beg you hear me out.'

Eva's index finger traced a pattern on the arm of the throne and she looked away for a moment, letting the sun fall on her face before looking back to Naida, her expression now one of a disappointed parent, which was an improvement on murderous.

'I do not have to hear anything you have to ask of me or tell me,' she said. 'It is a perk of being the Queen. I should have had you marched away to await me at my pleasure. And I am so ... saddened ... that you have chosen to abuse your perceived influence in this way.'

Naida hung her head. Eva was right, that was what she had done, though she had done so in the absence of a viable alternative, given who was pursuing her.

'If I may have the opportunity to explain, ma'am?'

Eva made a wafting motion with her hand and sat on the

throne, accentuating her power, and deliberately separating herself further from Naida.

'Thank you, ma'am,' said Naida, feeling their relationship shift from personal to formal and fearing it was permanent. 'I believe tens of thousands of your people's lives hang in the balance, while those best placed to save them are persecuted, as part of a grand, corrupt conspiracy to profit from an ineffective Cantabrian treatment while the stricken die on every street in the city.'

'That is quite the catastrophe that you describe. I wish I could be surprised that is what you wished to speak about. You seek to advance your own agenda—'

'I seek to stop you making a mistake that will have generational consequences! I am here because I love you, and because others seek to make a profit and leave you to carry the blame.'

Eva managed an indulgent smile. 'I am delighted to hear that you love me, though it is hoped the majority of my subjects share this emotion. But what, pray, is the mistake you think I am about to make?'

'I must stress that it is through no fault of your own but, allowing legislation to pass that outlaws the Gifted in the midst of a plague, when the supposed alternative treatment does not work, leaves the city and your subjects completely without protection from our most virulent disease. Your subjects' lives are in danger, ma'am.'

Eva slapped her palms on the arms of her chair, her irritation flushing her face. 'Did I not tell you that I must reflect the will of my subjects in this matter?'

'Yes, and you also told me that you intend to dissolve the monarchy, whatever your people's will on the matter, to be revered forever as our last queen.'

'Really? Wonderful. Forever is such a long time and I do intend to enjoy it.'

It was a confusing statement, leaving Naida none the wiser whether she had changed Eva's mind or whether she was joking, or something else entirely.

'I don't...'

'No, you don't,' said Eva and her ire was gone, replaced by an earnest sadness. 'And it is why I need you, and fear for you, and why you mustn't expose yourself like this. You have been here but a handful of days, Naida. There is so much you don't understand.'

Naida felt totally disarmed. There was more she needed to say, about the plague, her parents and what Eva needed to do but for the moment, she was lost.

'What do you mean?'

'You are so honest and passionate. Everything you believe in is writ large on your face and in each word you speak. It is an essential goodness that does you such credit but that is wholly unsuited to a snake-pit like this palace and the Crucible.'

'We must always seek to do right, surely?'

Eva smiled and gestured to one of the luxurious seats near her throne. 'Come and sit with me.'

Naida walked up the stairs, allowing herself a glance backwards to enjoy the sight that greeted Eva each time she stood here, and sat, hoping Kat was safe, and praying Elias, Will and Adeile had survived Geth Herron. With every passing moment, as armed men did not arrive, that outcome seemed more likely.

'We fight battles where people conscripted into armies are killed for reasons they often don't understand but trust are in the cause of right. And being right in war is always the result of some unpalatable decisions. Decisions that, as monarch, I have no option but to make. You would laugh if you knew how powerless I really am.'

'But you aren't, ma'am...'

There was an urgent knocking on a side door to the Throne Room. Naida froze, certain an attack must follow.

'Wait!' snapped Eva. 'This is a private session. When I am ready, I will summon you.'

Naida sucked in a deep breath. She had faced down the most belligerent generals, stood up to ranting colonels and commanders alike, but for all their bluster, none had the Queen's instant authority. It was quite something to behold. She turned a smile on her and her tone was warm as a summer morning, kissed by first sunlight.

'I think you can call me Eva again, don't you? Now we're friends again.'

But Naida wasn't at all sure that they were and she wondered if she should have taken Misha's warnings about falling under Eva's glamour far more seriously.

'Eva ... you aren't powerless. You can change how the public views any issue with a word. You do not have to reflect them, that is a choice, isn't it?'

'The Suurken monarch is not all-powerful, Naida. The Crucible has seen to that, and I am in full support of it, as you know. I do have influence, but I must take care how and where I exert it. I know to my cost that to lean in too hard and too often can be counterproductive.'

'How can saving the lives of tens of thousands of your citizens be counterproductive?'

Eva tilted her head as if considering the point. As though it needed to be considered. And, apparently, it did.

'Every decision is a step taken along a tightrope. The health of my citizens today is critical to me, but so is their long-term health and prosperity. There is never an easy answer. Sometimes, pain today is calmed by the joy of tomorrow. It is never binary.'

'How is the baseless accusation that the Gifted set the plague not binary? It's a lie – I know, because I have been to Old

Landers and know it was set by those seeking test subjects for their substandard tincture. How is it not binary to legislate against the Gifted who could cure the disease, solely for the benefit of those who are scamming and killing your people? Especially when the ban on the Gifted now is predicated on *their* decades-old lie?'

There was a shake of the royal head and an arching of the brows, a lifting of the shoulders. 'You are making serious allegations, Naida.'

'I have proof. Proof that the removal of the Gifted was carefully planned and is critical to an effort to flood Suranhom with Cantabrian apothecary products. It will enrich their country and the coffers of a very few ... with a small benefit to the Exchequer, as per the licensing agreement you signed. It is corruption, Your Majesty. Not by you, but in your name. I know who is behind it.'

Eva stiffened and she was off balance. The first time Naida had seen it.

'You are treading perilous ground.'

'I know. But the truth must come out if I am to save lives, and your reputation.'

'Or if you seek to incriminate me.'

'No!' Naida reached out and touched Eva's arm, feeling her tension. 'The absolute opposite, Eva. I am afraid that the conspirators' goal is to profit from the death of your people and walk away leaving you with the blame. But if you think that of me, I will withdraw from your service immediately.'

Eva was unused to being challenged, and unused to reviewing decisions she thought – literally – signed and sealed.

'That's perhaps a step too far. But you must be cautious.'

'It is too late for caution,' said Naida. 'The petition to ban the Gifted is in debate now and it will pass ... unless you make a stand against it. If you don't, I fear a terrible purge will be unleashed.'

'I wish you were right that I have such influence. The truth is, there is no real weight I can bring to a debate in the Crucible. Some will heed the word of their monarch, but you have to understand that this legislation has been coming for over a decade, ever since … well … we all know the history. For many people, those scars will never heal and nothing I say will move them.'

'Even if my … the Esselrodes were innocent?' Naida froze but the slip went by unnoticed.

'Does that really matter now?' asked Eva earnestly.

Naida wanted to shout that it did, that it mattered more than anything. She wanted to reclaim her name, and her position as the daughter of innocents, not the daughter of monsters but not yet … not yet. She hoped the colour she felt rush to her cheeks at the Queen's careless injustice was less visible than it felt. She tried to gather herself.

'You were there when it happened. I have read the reports of your kindness, your mercy to people thought pure evil. It is extraordinary, but I suspect very typical of you. You must have spoken to them, heard the truth.'

Eva looked lost for a moment, and a fragile smile crossed her face, a reaction to memories buried by time, locked away to hide the trauma.

'Mercy … yes … I suppose it could have been seen like that.'

Naida gave a surprised laugh. 'What do you mean? How else could it have been interpreted?'

'I mean, it wasn't how I ever saw it,' said Eva, eyes searching Naida's face. 'I was just doing what I had to. Like you say … the right thing.'

'What did the Esselrodes say to you?'

Eva shifted on the throne, smoothing the arms with the palms of her hands.

'They never begged for an end to the torment. They maintained their dignity, their unshakeable confidence in their innocence, and their belief that they would be exonerated. It was admirable, courageous. And they suffered for so long, never giving up hope.'

Naida was desperate to appear neutral when every word Eva spoke was a claw dragged across her heart.

'And did you believe them?'

'It was very hard not to when admitting their guilt would have saved them so much suffering. They said that, for their daughter's sake, they had to remain true to their beliefs. Confessing to a crime they had not committed would have undermined everything they stood for and believed. They were so determined to protect their little girl.'

Naida wouldn't be able to hold the tears back for much longer.

'That isn't quite what I asked, Eva. Did you believe them to be innocent?'

'I knew they were,' said the Queen without hesitation. 'And I could do nothing to save them.'

The tears came then, Naida couldn't stop them. They were the words she had wanted to hear all her life, she realised, but she had buried the dream deep so she could move on with her life. So she could survive. The sobs shuddered through her body and she hid her face in her hands, dropping her head towards her chest, helpless to resist the tide of emotions.

It was exoneration, it was the ability to hold her head high and speak her name without friend and foe alike recoiling, stepping back in fear or wishing her dead. It was walking from darkness into light, from dream into reality.

She could speak her own name, and it would not be a death sentence.

Naida lifted her head to look at Eva, finding her standing close, wringing her hands, unsure what to do. Naida stood too.

'I'm sorry, I'm so sorry,' she said. 'I don't know what came over me.'

'It *matters* to you that I thought them innocent,' said Eva. 'Why? Did you know them?'

Naida nodded, there was no other way out. 'Why couldn't you help them?'

'Oh, Naida, there is so much you don't understand.'

'Let me show you something,' said Naida, and opened her medical bag to search for Rius Denharl's scribbled note.

'I was only sixteen,' said Eva. 'A princess trying to salve my friends' horrible injuries, to help people my father loved. Of course I told the judges, and the torturers, and my father about their innocence. But it ended there. A naive young princess swayed by the honeyed words of genocidal maniacs. So easy to dismiss.'

Naida could understand now. Eva had so wanted them to stay alive, her parents had wanted Eva to help them … all of them were waiting, hoping that the truth would come out, that someone would stand up and prove the crime. But no one did. She unfolded Rius Denharl's note and handed it to Eva, who read it with a gasp.

'It wasn't just you,' whispered Naida. 'Rius knew as well. So did others. The truth was suppressed for a reason … because all that is happening here now was part of the plan, which began with embedding mistrust, pinning the blame on the Gifted, leading, slowly and inevitably, to outlawing the Talent. You cannot nod this lie along. So many lives depend on the truth. Everything the Esselrodes stood for depends on it.'

Even uttering her surname brought fresh tears and she tried

to wipe them away only to find Eva got there first, cupping her chin, smoothing the tears away with her thumbs before enveloping her in an embrace, letting Naida sob into her shoulder despite the breach of protocol it represented.

'You must have loved them very much,' said Eva, stroking her hair. 'Their deaths hurt you so deeply.'

'I still love them. I miss them every day, with every breath.' Naida was almost talking to herself, as though no one else was there. 'I thought I hated them for what they had done but I knew ... *I knew* ... that they were innocent. I should never have lost faith in them.'

Eva clutched her harder. 'What can I do?'

'Tell the Crucible they were innocent! Tell them the Gifted aren't evil! It is all they would want. It is all I want, too.'

Eva pushed back, still holding Naida's hands, a smile animating her face. 'But if you were so close to them, how did we never meet? They practically lived here at one time.'

'I was never allowed to travel to the palace. My parents thought I would get delusions of grandeur.'

'Oh, what a shame! And to think we might have been friends forever.' Eva's look of disappointment could have graced the mummers' stage. 'Naida Erivayne ... It's not a name I can recall.'

'It isn't my real name.' Naida braced herself. 'I am Helena Esselrode.'

Eva's smile never faltered. She embraced Naida again, so warm and loving, but her words were frost riming a bough.

'I so wish that you were not.'

Chapter 36

'What do you mean? They were innocent! I am innocent!'

'I know, I know.' Eva broke the embrace and smiled before turning her head to the side door. 'Enter!'

She gestured for Naida to stay where she was and walked over to the door, which was tucked away in the right-hand corner, down the stairs from the throne. Someone stood in the doorway, shadowed by the ornate stone lintel. Naida, shivering, wondered if she had made the greatest mistake of her life as she strained to hear. But the voices were whispers.

'Wait there,' said Eva after a while. 'Outside.'

She moved back up the stairs with effortless grace, a frown on her brow and her eyes back on Naida who, berating herself for her paranoia, felt like a new species of fly that had collided with the spider's web.

'There has been violence in the palace today,' said Eva.

Naida relaxed and felt a flush of guilt at her reaction. 'I am aware. Indeed, I am partly responsible.'

'Yet you are an innocent?'

'I make no apology for attempting to uncover injustice and corruption,' said Naida, aware of the narrow ledge she walked, that her true identity hung in the space between them. 'And the violence I witnessed, that my people instigated, was against gang members masquerading as palace guard. We feared for your safety.'

'I've just heard a version of events involving break-ins, beatings and the theft of official documents. Who am I to believe?' Eva's tone was light, even playful, and it made Naida nervous.

She glanced at the sunlight, which had moved far across the walls since she entered the Throne Room, or so it seemed.

'Me,' said Naida, attempting a smile. 'Because I have evidence that must lead to the arrest of Velez, Kerslan and Vinald, among others. It means the anti-Gifted legislation must not go ahead but the Crucible is well into session, and the plague will spread unchecked. Time, Eva, is so short.'

'So it is, on so many fronts.' Eva's eyes sparkled with sudden joy, barely suppressed. 'We are on the verge of something quite remarkable.'

Naida couldn't help but be swept up in her enthusiasm and energy. 'So, what will you do?'

'Visit the Crucible, of course,' Eva said decisively, leaving Naida feeling light-headed, giddy with excitement and bathed in the warm light of hope. 'Let's waste no more time. Enter!'

Naida started and Eva laughed.

'Visiting the Crucible will require both assistance and armed guard,' she explained. 'Come on.'

Eva extended a hand and Naida walked towards her, only to see who had come through the door, and backed away, reflexively.

'No, no!'

Vinald walked up the steps to the throne, and behind him was Geth Herron, a sack over his shoulder, blade at his hip. Just when she had dared to hope they had been stopped, there they stood by the Queen, leaving her plan hanging by the merest thread.

'Why, Naida, whatever is the matter?' asked Eva, her concern giving Naida a glimmer of hope.

'These are not your allies.' Naida stared at Eva, pleading with her to understand. 'You have a killer and a traitor next to you. Call your guards, ma'am.'

'The palace's work is occasionally unsavoury, it's true,' said Eva. 'And I entrust such work to the most effective forces. Aide-to-court Vinald, who is no traitor … what terribly emotive language … assures me that Honoured Herron is the best.'

'Please, ma'am. You are in danger.'

But if she was, then no one could save her … either of them.

'We should update you on the whereabouts of your friends,' said Vinald, grabbing her attention like a steel gauntlet about her chin. 'You must be concerned.'

Herron's face was as cold as it was cruel. There was bruising on one cheek and a smear of blood across his forehead. Naida began to crumble inside, the inevitability like incoming flay-shot. Herron took the bag from his shoulder, then opened and shook it all in one motion. Blood scattered across the floor, trails from two severed heads that bounced down the steps, past the impassive Eva and onto the carpet where they rolled a little way apart, finishing scant feet from Naida.

The strength went from her legs, there was screaming inside her skull, and she dropped to the ground, desolate. Unable to drag her eyes from them, Naida felt her body collapse inwards, her back slump and the nausea threaten to overwhelm her.

'Sorry, I'm so sorry,' she said, her voice a broken whisper, reaching out a hand but not able to touch either Willan or Adeile's heads. Eventually, she stared up at Herron. 'What have you done?'

'What I am so very, very good at,' he said through a sneer, not caring to disguise the hatred he felt for her. 'More to come, I am assured.'

'Where's Elias?' She had to ask, though she had no desire to know.

'He's safe,' said Vinald.

'What do you mean?' Naida's confusion deepened. The world had spun on to its head so fast and she was lost, the lives she was fighting to save slipping through her fingers. 'I don't understand.'

Eva stood over her and held out her hand once more.

'Come on,' she said as if encouraging Naida out for a stroll in the rose gardens.

'I don't think I can stand.'

'Ah, but I am your Queen and I command it. Take my hand.'

Naida reached up and in that moment saw Eva with Vinald and Herron behind her, framing her, and she knew her failure was complete. Misha had warned her, and yet she had fallen under the Queen's spell, fallen for her charm and vulnerability while ignoring the signs that must have been so obvious. Naida might as well have locked the door of the cage herself.

Moving from the floor, her eyes crossed those of her friends one last time; Adeile who she had known so short a time but who had trusted her nonetheless; and Willan, whom she had betrayed after a decade of friendship but who had died for her anyway.

She should burn for them, if nothing else.

'Is everything I believe about you wrong?' she asked Eva, her body a pit into which her folly had been poured to suffer for eternity.

Eva brushed her fingers down Naida's cheek and she had to steel herself not to flinch. 'Probably, my sister. Let's find out, shall we?'

'Where are we going?'

'To the Crucible, Naida, just like you wanted. It'll be fun. I've so much to tell you, now I have found you, and so much to show you.'

'I came here to save you,' said Naida, wilting beneath that unstinting gaze, her words falling like empty husks.

'Oh, believe me, you have. Walk with me, laugh with me. Everyone will be watching.'

How can I do that? I can barely walk, barely breathe.

Naida nodded, mute and Eva clapped her hands, delighted, and led Naida through the small service door. Vinald bowed while staring at Naida, his face as despicable as Herron's. They've won, she thought. How stupid to think she could beat them. Where was Ludeney now? Or Kat or Misha? Elias was either captured, or escaped and they would not admit it, but that seemed unlikely, knowing what she did about his honour and loyalty. The only person she knew who was more loyal than him was Willan...

To her infinitesimal credit, Eva made conversation easy, discussing issues – plague excepted – concerning the city's health service. She agreed with Naida that health should sit in the order of institutions along with education and vocational skills, as it could also increase the capacity of citizens to make money for the Exchequer. She was, in some respects, remarkably enlightened. It was a tragedy, both personally and societally, that in the most important respect of all, she was looking to a bleak past with summer eyes.

Despite her misery, on this slow walk to her doom, Naida found she hadn't quite given up on Eva. There was room for manoeuvre, she thought, maybe. Slowly, approaching the Crucible and attracting the expected attention, which Eva adored, and even with Geth Herron providing snarling security, Naida began to clear her mind.

She had no hope for herself. What she had to do was drag proceedings out for as long as she could, perhaps allowing those with influence and power to take up the torch that had cost at least two of her friends their lives.

And she had to know, to understand, if only before she died in the cage, what motivated the Queen. Whether it could all be traced back to her father's monstrous treatment of her. It was a sadness that Naida was with her on so many issues.

They walked to the Crucible, the Queen waving at various people, wishing any in earshot a safe day and assuring those same people that the plague was under control allowing the Crucible to be as open and welcoming as ever. They were ushered through an elaborate private entrance to the pit, and the moment they were inside, servants fussed about the Queen, offering her food, drink, and touching up her make-up.

'How did they know we were coming?' asked Naida.

'They didn't. They are always here, just in case. Have a drink, Naida, you look as if you could use one.'

'It's a little early. Perhaps coffee from Sammel's stall?' she ventured of one of the servants. If it was to be her last day, she might as well have an expensive coffee.

No one moved and the Queen stared and spread her hands. 'Go! And I will have one too. Make sure this... Sammel... is well rewarded, whoever he or she is.'

'Shall we?' said Vinald, gesturing to a set of carpeted stairs that wound up a tower, presumably to the best viewing area of the pit. 'The session sounds lively.'

Naida should have noticed it already, but she had other things on her mind. Muted though it was, the mood of the crowd soaked through the walls. Cheers and boos reverberated. Foot-stamping shook dust from rafters and set ripples across wine and water.

'Yes, we shall,' said Eva to Vinald. 'But I would sit with my unfortunate sister alone and unheard. You will stay here.'

'But if you should—' began Vinald.

'Naida, are you planning on harming me?' asked Eva.

Naida laughed in spite of it all. 'No, ma'am. Not you, never you.'

413

Eva raised her eyebrows at Vinald. 'There you are, see? I have a bell pull if I need anything.'

Eva swept up the stairs. Naida was blocked by Geth Herron, his breath stinking of last night's malt.

'Your friends died begging for their lives.'

'I think we both know that's a big lie. Now, unless you want me to smash your balls into your throat for a second time, you'll want to get out of my way.'

Herron glowered down at her. 'She can't protect you forever. I'll be waiting.'

Herron moved aside, making sure to bump her shoulder on the way.

'Have a grown-up explain to you how to behave,' said Naida.

She climbed the stairs after Eva, who had gone on ahead without a backward glance. The spiral was beautiful. Deep green rope handrails to the outside, a matching carpet runner up its centre and every stone polished and spotless, shining in the light of wall lanterns.

Naida turned three full spirals before the stair gave onto a wide reception area with a fireplace, seating, food and drink service and a single pair of carved wooden doors in its centre. Eva was standing in front of them.

'Did you get lost?' she asked.

Naida's bravado with Herron was forgotten in an instant. He was merely cruel muscle where Eva was true power and Naida's life was in her hands.

'No, I was delayed by Herron.'

Here, the noise from the pit was thrilling. She could hear Temets speaking but couldn't pick out his words, so many of which were drowned by boos and hisses. She could feel the waves of energy and emotion and, when Eva ordered a servant to open the doors, the sheer force of sound was breathtaking.

Eva beckoned Naida close and the two of them walked out

on to a wide, drape-hung balcony that sat around halfway up the auditorium, opposite the High Gavel. Six richly upholstered chairs sat in a line across the space, and as soon as Eva moved in between them and into view, the High Gavel slammed his gavel down on the wooden plate three times, bringing a halt to Temets' speech and total silence to the Crucible.

The Queen clasped her hands over her heart. The crowd responded in kind.

'Please, don't let me interrupt any further.'

Naida caught Temets' eye and nodded. He looked terrible, his face purple and swollen, his hands claws of damaged fingers. He made the tiniest acknowledgement back, a raising of his chin. The gavel came down again, the crowd's chatter picked up and Temets returned to his speech.

'Your Majesty is most welcome, and I am honoured by your presence, as are we all,' said Temets, his voice muffled by his damaged jaw. 'Whichever side of the divide we sit today, we are united in our loyalty to you.'

The crowd roared its approval. Eva inclined her head, sat down and indicated Naida to sit next to her.

'It is instructive to note,' said Temets, 'that accompanying Her Majesty today is Naida Erivayne, the new and most welcome head of the royal medical service. I don't say this because it infers any bias on either of their parts. Indeed, both of these most honoured women are neutral in this debate. But what is the royal medical service if not a holistic approach to the health of the city? Doctor, surgeon and Gifted, working in concert.'

Naida and Eva shared a glance.

'Neutral,' said Eva. 'You? Right.'

The crowd, perhaps a little inhibited by the presence of the Queen, gave Temets a little leeway, their boos and jeers reduced to grumbles and dismissive or obscene hand gestures. Many appeared to be mimicking sleep. Naida felt like an exhibit, unwillingly thrust in front of a curious public.

Thousands of eyes were on her and Eva, seduced by the lure of royalty and celebrity. And there she sat, the severed heads of two of her friends lying in the Throne Room, their killer guarding her escape route and beside a woman whose reactions to Naida's name and those severed heads were frightening.

Eva looked radiant, excited... expectant. Naida, who was already fearing the worst yet trying to cling on to any glimmer of hope, still feared what might come to the floor of the pit.

'...and we are in the midst of a serious outbreak of Red Spot in the city,' continued Temets. 'An outbreak that appears to be spreading without pause. And although our city forces are doing an extraordinary job of enforcing quarantine and infection zones; without treatment, the death toll among our people will be unconscionable.'

Temets let that hang in the air. Across the pit, people in the public benches, Uppers and Lowers alike, shifted in their seats.

'So let me ask you a question, all of you. Who would you turn to first if you contracted the plague and faced almost certain death? Who have all of us turned to for decade upon decade?'

Naida had never experienced a massed awkward silence before. A few coughs echoed around before the odd brave voice called out *Gifted*. As if a switch had been thrown, a storm of noise swelled and Temets spread his hands in agreement with the crowd.

'Point of order!' called Oliari, again speaking for the petition. She was dressed in an array of bright colours, robes flaring and sweeping about her as she strode forwards. The gavel came down twice and the crowd quietened. 'Honoured Temets is trying to slow down what has already been an interminable opening address.'

'I posed a question, which is within the parameters of the debate,' replied Temets. 'I can only imagine Honoured Oliari was delighted at the weight of voices which were previously calling in her favour. And it shows how far the lies have spread. Kindar's Tincture... chanted over and again. And all of you who are placing your faith... your health... your lives in this medicine might be interested in this report from Old Landers where, we all know, the outbreak began.'

He reached inside his dark blue topcoat, his broken and bruised fingers struggling for a firm grip and making his unfolding of the paper a torturous affair. Naida felt a moment of satisfaction within the enduring anxiety. Aryn had clearly done an exemplary job, and Kella's words were about to be heard by everyone inside the Crucible. She wondered if it would be enough to even pause, let alone suspend, the legislation. Perhaps, with the revelations she knew Temets would unveil concerning the illegality of the first anti-Gifted legislation.

There was a knock on the door behind them and Naida almost jumped from her skin.

'Enter,' said Eva, and a servant scurried in, handed her a note and scurried out. Eva read it carefully, first sighing and then making a squeaking sound as if the recipient of good news. 'Well, I think that would be the perfect backdrop.'

'I'm sorry, Eva?' asked Naida, half-listening to Temets reading Kella's report to uncertain jibes from the crowd.

'Talking to myself,' said Eva. She turned to the door. 'Aide!'

Vinald was through the door with obscene speed.

'Your Majesty,' he said.

Eva waved the note. 'This is excellent. See to it immediately.'

'I know you want it to be the panacea... that Cantabrian medicine will cure all ills and render the Gifted obsolete, but I'm afraid it isn't so,' said Temets. 'That testimony from an army medic, herself now a victim of the Red Spot, must... must give you pause. You want to entrust your life to untested, unverified apothecaries' efforts over the guaranteed cure the Gifted can bring you? Do you? Stand and tell me why.'

Temets, limping heavily, walked a circle around the pit, exhorting anyone who could, to stand and defend the indefensible. Not a soul had the courage to do so. Temets shrugged.

'I could give way to the Honoured Oliari now because, in all honesty, my work is done. Outlawing the Gifted will, let me be clear, sign the death warrant for tens of thousands in this city ... and for who knows how many of you, sitting in this place now?' He locked eyes with someone in the Uppers, and then another, and another. 'It could be you. Or you. Or you. Are you really prepared to take that risk, now that you know the much-advertised *cure* ... Does. Not. Work?'

Naida felt true hope bloom. The mood of the Crucible had been high when they entered but had changed completely. Temets had managed to turn the debate away from the Gifted and make it both personal and mortal.

'Before I give way, and really, I will enjoy my colleague's arguments to ban the only group of people who can save us from this plague, I will mention just one more thing ...'

'Naida,' said Eva, demanding attention. 'Although I could call you Helena in here, couldn't I?'

'I doubt I'll ever be comfortable using that name,' said Naida.

'You have been a spring breeze through the palace,' said Eva. 'From the first moment, you were someone I could trust, confide in and rely on. A combination I had never enjoyed before. And you're funny and honest.'

With every compliment, Naida felt herself shrink a little more. Her world closed in and Temets' words were muted.

'That doesn't have to end,' said Naida, like a lover begging for another chance. 'You know I wish you no harm. You know my parents were healers, not killers.'

Eva looked at her with an expression of such complete sympathy she almost burst into tears again. Shattered throne, she needed to sob over the deaths of Willan and Adeile; cry out her fears for the ordinary people who were destined to die because of a desire among a few for even greater profits.

'I wish life were as simple as you see it,' said Eva. 'But it isn't. Events must unfold as I have planned, which means my feelings for you are irrelevant. I cannot chase my dreams of what might be, instead. Do you see?'

'No,' said Naida. 'It doesn't make sense at all. But I am on your side, Eva. I can still help you stop the deaths which are coming.'

'Hmm.' Eva raised her eyebrows. 'You're making some interesting assumptions and I'm going to have to put you straight.'

Eva held out her hands for Naida's. After a moment, sweaty and trembling as they were, she reached out, feeling the comforting warmth and softness of hands that had never felt the abrasion of a scrubbing brush. Down in the pit, Temets had wound up his address and although a few dissenting voices were raised against him, his words had struck deep. The High Gavel invited Oliari to respond and she walked into the middle of the floor.

'I don't fear you might to do me harm, Naida. Let me demonstrate why,' said Eva. 'Try not to overreact.'

Naida's body went rigid. Healing warmth was spreading through her, easing aches she had felt it too trivial to soothe, and cupping her head so gently she felt her tension and confusion diminish. She moved her gaze from her hands, which were being massaged gently by Eva's thumbs, to the Queen's eyes which were fixed on her with a zealous, almost maniacal, energy.

'You're *Gifted*,' she whispered. 'I don't—'

'Oh, one moment,' said Eva, withdrawing her hands and leaving Naida bereft at the loss of their touch and her extraordinary ability, a Talent which went far beyond her own. 'History is about to be made down in the pit.'

Chapter 37

Francesca Oliari did not look at the audience, the Uppers or Lowers, or at Temets who was standing to the side, his bruises and abrasions unable to disguise his satisfaction. She was waiting for the High Gavel, who was surveying his papers, to return his attention to the floor.

'My honoured High Gavel, it is clear that Honoured Temets seeks to talk this legislation as far into the future as he can, and we all know that his prevarication, obfuscation and procrastination skills are unmatched. We believe this to be injurious to the health of the population. Surely, whatever fears they harboured, the Gifted would have travelled to Old Landers to snuff out this outbreak. If only to prove their worth to a grateful population. But where were they? Absent. They abandoned those in their hours of direst need in order to save their own skins. Meanwhile, despite my colleague's unverified and most likely false claims concerning the efficacy of Kindar's Tincture, it is available now and working to ease the suffering of the people.'

A round of chuckles from the audience and a smattering of applause.

'Therefore, it is the unanimous decision of the petitioners to this vital piece of health security legislation, to invoke section seventeen, clause twelve. Seventeen twelve, aye.'

'WHAT?' Temets all but exploded. The fury and injustice surged from him in waves into an ignorant Crucible pit. 'Are we savages now? Honoured Oliari knows she cannot win this debate with reason, or with evidence, and so now stoops lower than a sewer rat to pluck out seventeen twelve to back up the blatant lies? This is the morally corrupt act of an ethically and intellectually bankrupt petition. I'm sure she is ashamed to have even spoken the words and I give her the opportunity to retract her invocation.'

Naida, like the vast majority within the auditorium, had no idea what had provoked this reaction, though an explanation was clearly spreading, provoking consternation, opposition and excitement in equal measure. Naida glanced at Eva who was leaning forwards, face alight.

'Can you feel that energy? It's incredible,' she said.

'What's going on?'

'Hush now,' said Eva sharply. 'Watch.'

Oliari was making a face at Temets. 'Retract it? No. Seventeen twelve, aye!'

'Then I move that the High Gavel strike this demand from the record,' said Temets. 'It is against every precedent, every advance and every ethic on which the Crucible operates, and to permit it would destroy trust in the Crucible, perhaps fatally. This debate must be heard. Arguments must be heard, and a vote must be taken. It is the right way; it is the only way.'

But Naida could see there was no expectation behind Temet's words, and when the gavel fell, so did his head to his chest.

'Honoured Temets, Honoured Oliari. I have heard the proposer's request and I have heard the response to that request. I share Honoured Temets' horror at the invocation of seventeen twelve, but the act is still written in law and we must abide by all our laws, not merely those with which we agree. I approve the request to settle this petition under section seventeen, clause twelve: trial by combat.'

The eruption of noise in the Crucible would have eclipsed the southern army's battle cry on a clear dawn. Naida could feel the force of emotion like a blow in the face even as she digested the moral and ethical atrocity being committed right in front of her. All around, people were on their feet. Order papers were hurled into the air to flutter and spiral down all over the pit floor.

Temets was yelling his objections at the High Gavel who had his head in his hands. Oliari stood to one side, an inscrutable expression on her face. Uppers and Lowers either howled their protest or, in the case of petition supporters, applauded this unexpected chance for the will of their paymasters to pass without their involvement.

Naida, in a state of disarray herself, seeing what was left of her desperate plan fall to pieces, had barely the wit to remember her history, which told her that each speaker, advocate and opposition, either fought in person or had to nominate a champion. Way back through the centuries, the champions would sit on chairs opposite the Upper and Lower benches but these days, she doubted anyone gave the appointment of a champion a second thought. And, when the noise abated slightly, aided by the frenetic rapping of the gavel, she was proved right.

'I will have your attention!' roared the High Gavel for a final time. 'Advocate and opposition, I will have the names of your champions.'

'This is ridiculous!' called Temets, his outrage undiminished. 'Who in the last hundred years has nominated a champion? This is a farce, it is pure theatre, and a departure from all reality while a plague rages without. Where is the sense that will stop this descent into madness?'

'Nominating a champion has always been a requirement of

423

your attendance, it is a stipulation that has never been removed,' said Oliari, handing a note to the High Gavel, which he read with a brief flicker of an eyebrow.

Nadia watched as the last of Temets' respect for Oliari evaporated. Even from here she could see the depths of his disappointment and the height of contempt on his face.

'I do not have a champion. I represent the present and the future, not the past,' he said. 'I will take no part in this monstrous perversion of our legal system. Shame on you, Gavel. Shame on you, Oliari.'

The gavel rapped once, sharply. 'These are comments unbecoming of the floor of the pit. You will withdraw them.'

Temets laughed, a harsh bitter sound. '*My* comments are unbecoming? I withdraw nothing. Look at me! I have been assaulted already for attempting to ensure this place is not subverted. I have bled for it. I fear no sanction you choose to hand down. Do what you must, sully this place as you will, stain it for generations. I will not support it, or retract my words.'

Cheers and applause rang around large sections of the crowd. People who had come to support Oliari were as dismayed by the turn of events as those few still brave enough to stand up for the Gifted. Only Oliari could bring the Crucible back from the brink now, and she had chosen to put victory above the cost in trust for years to come. The damage could well be permanent.

The High Gavel, his face a mask, waited for the crowd to quieten.

'Honoured Temets, since you have no champion, one will be provided for you.' Another rap of the gavel. 'Return to your benches and await your champions.'

Oliari bowed and strode away. Temets shook his head at the High Gavel in disgust before clearing the pit floor. Oliari sat, Temets did not, his protest silent and pointedly against protocol, or so Naida assumed. The High Gavel stood and smoothed his deep blue gowns. He gestured left and then right, beckoning gestures. Naida heard doors open out of sight along short, downward sloping corridors between rows of benches.

Strutting like a peacock from the right, bare-chested, barefooted and wearing three-quarter length trousers, came Geth Herron. His face was swollen where Naida had broken his nose but he still exuded menace. He wore shining knuckle steels and, with a withering sense of dread in the depths of her stomach, Naida knew who would appear from the left.

It was Elias. Bewildered, shambling, his face also bruised and swollen, his chest part bandaged, the blood soaking it at the front, and with one foot which could not take his weight. He stared around the auditorium, wincing in the light and the noise, with one half-closed eye, the other mercifully undamaged. He too wore knuckle steels and he stroked them with his fingers, an unconscious, nervous gesture.

'No!' shouted Naida. 'You can't—'

'Sit down!' snapped Eva. 'You embarrass yourself and me.'

Naida turned on her. 'You *knew*. You brought me here to watch a friend die at the hands of your hired murderer?'

'No,' said Eva. 'You were brought here to see how power really works, to understand that I have won. Your friend being the exemplar of that power is a delightful bonus.'

Gone was the sparkle and lightness of touch. In its place, an edge sharp enough to split flesh, a tone to silence any grievance and an expression that bled belief in her absolute authority. Naida sat.

'What are you talking about?' asked Naida. 'Stop this, please. You can see Elias is injured. This is not a fair contest.'

'Fair? *Please* ...'

Elias was shown to his place, one of two tarnished brass plates in the centre of the pit floor. Herron moved smoothly to his, taking the time to turn and bow to the Queen, his eyes flickering to Naida, mouth turning up in a callous smile. Naida shivered, her heart going out to Elias, hoping his suffering would be brief but knowing it wouldn't.

'Fight, Elias!' she shouted down. 'You can take him. I did!'

Elias looked and found her and he smiled through his blood-ied features. Other voices added to her call and she could see Temets complaining to the High Gavel about the state of his champion and, no doubt, this further blow to the reputation of the legislature. But it would make no difference; the Queen was enjoying it.

'Your Majesty, I beg leave to treat Elias. To at least give him a fighting chance.'

'Gladly denied,' said Eva. 'And no more shouting. On this balcony, we are neutral.' She smiled at her hypocrisy.

'This isn't you,' said Naida. 'This is not the monarch I admire.'

'Haven't you understood yet? I appear as the monarch the individual desires.'

'We are not as opposed as you think,' said Naida, desperate now, her heart beating hard.

'Oh, but we are, and you know it. It's why you're here, after all, isn't it?'

'Lord Marshal Ludeney sent me to be your doctor.' Naida was fighting the recollection of why Ludeney had sent her here. 'And that is all I desire to be.'

'Yes, I'll have to speak to him about his recruitment skills, won't I?' said Eva, laughing at her own joke. 'I think he might have forgotten a few important questions in the interview.'

Naida's confusion deepened. 'Like what?'

The gavel came down three times, slowly, bringing silence to the pit. Naida and Eva both looked down to see Elias and Herron facing each other from their brass plates. Herron was as a statue, his confidence armour-plated, his eyes on his victim.

Poor Elias, unable to balance properly, shifted and swayed, favouring his injured foot and a swollen knee.

Her eye was caught by a movement just behind Temets on the public benches. It was Kat. Wearing a long dress and bonnet to disguise herself, but definitely Kat. Naida would never forget that face. While she watched, Kat slipped Temets a note. The opposition speaker read it, nodded to Kat who promptly disappeared.

'High Gavel, I would address my ... champion,' said Temets.

'Last words for the condemned?' asked Herron.

'Don't bet on it, Geth,' said Elias through swollen lips. 'Apparently just talking to women makes your balls hurt.'

'Your pain will be mine to savour,' said Herron.

'Did someone have to teach you that one?'

The gavel rapped. 'The champions will be silent. Honoured Temets, please speak with your champion.'

Temets, his face and body as battered as Elias's, spoke quietly to the big soldier. At one stage, Elias glanced behind him and another time he made the merest of glances to the balcony. Temets put a hand on each of his hulking shoulders. Elias nodded, said a few words himself and refocused on Herron.

'Champions, you fight to see this petition pass or fall. In the statutes, this combat is deemed complete when one of you is dead. But there are addenda to the original regulations, and I shall invoke one of those now. While the combat *can* be fought unto death, it is in the gift of either speaker to concede the debate. Honoured Temets, Honoured Oliari, to concede you must step on to the plate of your champion, thereby symbolically summoning him home.'

'Oh, bravo,' whispered Eva. 'Such a trial for our speakers... well, for one of them.'

'I'll laugh in your face when Elias has your man bleeding out over the feet of the Lowers,' muttered Naida.

'Oh, Naida, no need to be nasty.'

There is every need.

'Do you all understand?' asked the High Gavel.

Oliari and Temets both nodded and Naida could see the conflict on Temets' face. He could save Elias's life right there and then, but he knew the cost to everyone of letting the Gifted ban pass. The question was how long he would let the fight go. And as if sensing his indecision, Elias turned a stern look on him.

'Remember what you just told me. Don't even think about it.'

Whatever Kat had told Temets had energised Elias too. He was standing taller. Even so, he was a head shorter than Herron, if broader across the shoulders and, when fit, was possessed of as much raw power. But Herron was as close to a predator in human form as she had ever seen. Built of muscle, reliant on instinct and lightning-fast on the strike. She dared not hope for anything more than Temets stopping it before Elias was killed.

Something was clearly happening away from here, though. Something that might turn the tide once more. But it seemed obvious that whatever it was, would take time. So, Elias had to try to stay in the fight as long as he could.

'Seventeen twelve has been invoked to settle petition sixteen twenty-seven mark one four seven A: the removal of the right to practise the Talent, the introduction of penalties for practising the Talent, the prohibition of use of the Talent in Suurken, the wider territories of Suurken, Evontide and the greater archipelagos of Northern, Western and Central Gerestova, its oceans and rivers,' intoned the High Gavel. 'Combat will begin at the fall of the gavel.'

Silence. Naida, her body rigid, pushed aside her fury at how easily she had been taken in by Eva and sent all her strength to Elias. He stood proud, his body calm. She so wished she could touch him, lend him her Talent to ease muscle and defray bruise. He was ready. Herron, with his back to her, was ready too.

Animal instinct and speed would play against determination and intelligence. If the world was fair, Elias would win, his cause was righteous. But the world wasn't. Only while he stood, while he fought, was there hope.

Whatever you're doing, Kat, do it fast.

Around the pit, no one dared breathe. Temets was seated now, shoulders slumped. Every eye was on the High Gavel. He brought his gavel down and a roar sounded around the pit. Eva clapped her hands, excited as a child, and it was all Naida could do not to punch her in the face.

Herron ran straight for Elias, who waited a beat before diving to the left and rolling back up, wincing when his left leg took his weight. The ganger turned and ran at him again. Elias waited a beat more, dived left, rolled, came up. Herron slid to a stop and growled. The was a cheer from the crowd.

Herron paced around Elias, who was standing right in the centre of the floor, and following him, turning, watching and waiting, ready. Herron spread his arms, inviting Elias on. Elias shrugged and stayed where he was. The crowd hushed again.

'Frightened little man,' sneered Herron.

Elias shrugged again. 'Just enjoying the attention.'

Herron paced forwards, arms by his sides. 'You can't keep it up forever, Elias.'

Another shrug, and Herron's face darkened. Good.

★

'Do you know what I learned as a young princess, shut away in my room for hour upon hour?'

Startled by Eva's sudden closeness, leaning across her chair to put her mouth by her ear, and her decision to talk during the fight, Naida recoiled.

429

'What?' She glanced at Eva, then back to the floor where the combatants still sized each other up to the increasing frustration of Herron. 'I don't...'

'Let me tell you,' said Eva, her tone demanding attention. Naida dragged her gaze from the pit floor. 'I learned about the true nature of the Talent. I learned what it can do, and what it cannot; for instance, it cannot engender an invasive disease in a human body, because its essence lies in eliminating disease, in healing.'

'I'm an Esselrode, I know all this. What's your point?'

★

Movement caught her eye. Herron rushed Elias a third time. Elias dived a third time, but Herron had anticipated his move and correctly guessed which way he would go. Mid-dive, Herron collided with Elias and the two of them sprawled on the floor, Herron trying to get a hold, Elias trying to scrabble away.

He almost succeeded but Herron grabbed his shoulder and pulled him on to his back. Elias made to roll aside. Herron, quick as a snake, lashed a foot into his kidney, lifting him from the ground to gasps from the crowd. Herron was ready to pounce, Elias got to his hands and knees and dived straight forwards into a roll, winning space to regain his feet.

He was hurt, but he was also skilled and determined to survive. Herron swore, but he knew he'd scored. Elias was upright but sagging to one side, perhaps nursing a broken rib, and suffering the blooming pain from the blow to his internals.

★

'The Talent can be made to see pregnancy as a disease,' said Eva.

'I beg your pardon?' Naida, feeling Elias's pain, reeled at Eva's statement and fostered fresh anger she had no desire to quash.

'I didn't lose the Haronic prince's child. And when he was

gone and I realised my father still wanted me to give birth to the heir, I made my decision and my Talent did the rest. And shall I tell you something else?'

Naida, whose sympathy for Eva's suffering was undimmed, was shocked by the Queen's brutal choice but understood the mental and emotional torment the sixteen-year-old princess must have been suffering.

'I am sorry you felt forced to use your Talent in such a way,' said Naida.

'Oh, don't apologise, I'm rather enjoying telling you things about your gift that you haven't grasped. The next one is even more amazing.'

★

Herron sized Elias up, seeing how he could be forced to move, which foot he had to favour and where he was already weak. Elias knew it too, knew that diving aside was a spent tactic. The ganger moved in, bouncing on his feet, taunting Elias with his easy balance. Elias waited, arms loose, stance wider but still favouring his right side.

Herron struck hard and fast, a fist snapping out, catching Elias a glancing blow on his cheek as he tried to duck under it. Herron followed with an uppercut. Elias knew the combination, swayed aside and in his enemy's follow-through, stepped in and slapped a palm across his right ear.

Herron cried out and stumbled away, his hand to the pain that would have reached deep into his already damaged ear canal and drum. Naida felt grim satisfaction. Herron was temporarily disoriented, his cocky balance gone. He turned, only to meet Elias's steel-shod fist slamming into his already-broken nose.

Blood smeared across Herron's face and flew in an arc behind him as he spun away. Elias moved in again, Herron dropped low and swept out a leg, snatching Elias's from under him and dumping him hard on the ground. Herron bounced up, ignoring the blood pouring from his smashed nose and cracked his right heel into Elias's face, knocking him flat, the back of his head thudding against the timbers of the pit floor.

The crowd quietened again, some turning away. Herron dropped onto Elias's chest and powered blow after blow into his face. Elias reached up with both arms, trying to defend himself, trying to pull Herron off him, the skin of his cheeks split, his nose flattened.

★

Naida felt every blow, they were all being taken for her.

'Make it stop,' she whispered.

'It can be made to see age that way, too,' said Eva, her eyes on the fight, her voice pitched loud enough for Naida to hear. 'As a disease. One that can be cured.'

'I ... what?' Naida couldn't process it. Elias's beating, Eva trying to distract her with lies. 'Don't be ridiculous.'

Eva's face appeared in hers. 'You know so little, Helena Esselrode. I'm betting my life on it. Ha. My immortality, I mean. And I'm right: the Talent renews, the Talent heals. The Talent, when directed properly, will stop the ageing process. Isn't that amazing?'

'It's nonsense,' said Naida. 'Besides, aren't you ending the monarchy?'

'Yes. Because there can never be a threat to the throne from another line,' said Eva and she withdrew, taking Naida's gaze with her. 'I intend to be enshrined in law as the last monarch of Suurken, not to step down as Queen. I will live on as that Queen forever. And as the last of the Gifted too, so that no one, no other pretender, will be able to challenge me. And you still think I don't know why you are really here?'

But Eva couldn't, because she had no idea why Ludeney had

sent her here. And surely, if Eva thought Naida was here to kill her, they would not be sitting together now.

'Why do you think I kept your parents alive, *Helena*? How did you think I kept them alive for so long?'

Naida gaped.

★

Elias took another blow to the head but had managed to grab one of Herron's arms. He struck up with his free fist with enough force to catch Herron on the chin, heaved him off with a roar of exertion, and scrabbled free. The crowd was foursquare behind the underdog, and howled its support.

Elias was groggy, leaning heavily on his right-hand side. His face was puffing up anew, his mouth and nose dripping blood, his eyes closing, his cheeks red. Herron fared a little better but there was a wariness in his eyes now. They faced each other across a few yards of space, Herron nodding a grudging respect. He glanced across at Temets.

'You'll have to finish this yourself, Geth. Unless you're quailing at the thought of another killing on your hands.'

'Blood never bothered me, Elias, you know that, and this fight is as good as over. I will win and just be doing my job. He'll be the one with your death on his hands.' Herron jabbed a finger at Temets, who looked tortured.

Elias shook his head. 'I'm still standing. It's my decision. Come and finish it, if you think you're able.'

'If you say so,' said Herron and he strode across the space between them.

★

'Oh, you're sad now, so maybe it's all starting to fall into place, no?'

Naida was stunned. Nothing made sense. She felt the tears flow down her face.

433

'No,' she whispered. 'What are you doing?'

'Making it all make sense,' said Eva, delighting in Naida's pain, making every moment of their relationship, their *friendship*, a lie.

Naida laughed, a tragic, bitter little sound. 'You're killing me.'

'You have no idea how much I hated my father and his obsession with his bloodline.' Eva grabbed her dress above her chest and made a fist. 'In here, he killed me, and it was the joy of my life to watch him suffer while your parents died. Day after day he had to witness it, and even his failing mind knew their endurance could not possibly be natural.'

'You kept them alive to torture *him*? I don't believe you.'

Eva's smile was frightening. 'And still you cling on, poor Helena, poor Naida. He knew he couldn't save them or stop me. My father knew your parents were innocent – that bastard, Rius Denharl, told him, showed him the evidence – but Father understood the risk they posed too because of what they had discovered. He knew they had to die, but he had wanted it to be quick. The best part of my day was reminding his dribbling heart what your parents had suffered, how I had prepared them for the next day's torments, and when he asked me the same question, every day, I would tell him: no. And then I would remind him I would never bear children, and watch another little part of him die.'

Naida put her hands to her face, her stomach churning, her breathing shallow and painful. She couldn't even feel rage anymore, beneath the pain of Eva's revelations.

'What question?' she managed, mouth quivering, barely able to get the words out.

★

The sound of the crowd changed, receded like a long-fingered wave from a beach. Herron had got behind Elias and had him in a chokehold. Elias kicked backwards but couldn't shake him.

434

Herron had his arms trapped at his sides, his other arm cutting off his air supply. He tightened and tightened, a constrictor administering the death squeeze.

People were shouting for Temets to move but Naida, through the chaos entrapping her, could see the tragic sight of Elias refusing to let him yield, minute shakes of his head enough to keep Temets in his seat.

'He will die here,' shouted Herron, moving Elias nearer to Temets. 'And nothing will give me greater pleasure. Here, you can watch him fade, since it is your silence that ensures his death.'

Elias gave a great cry and broke Herron's grip on his chest and arms. Herron tightened the arm around his neck and Elias flailed his arms, landing blows on Herron's head and managing to grab him around the back of his skull. He pulled, and Herron used both arms to choke him harder.

★

'It was pathetic. He would start crying at the trap he was in. "Did they confess? Did they renounce it all?" And I would shake my head and stroke his cheek and whisper to him how much they would suffer tomorrow, and he would cry some more and his mind would slip away another notch. My only regret is how quickly he died after your parents had gone to the cage and burned.'

Naida's rage rekindled at the image of her parents dying over the flames, the cage lowered to give them a long, slow end. And all for Eva to ... what? Torture her father. She fought for clarity.

'What was all this for?' she asked, careless of her tone, of the hatred she felt for this woman.

'Everything has unfolded as I planned,' said Eva. 'All except you. I'd given up on finding you, and it is such a bonus to have you here, today of all days.'

'I don't…' Eva. It had been Eva all along, and none of those who did her bidding had understood her plan. Perhaps Vinald… but none of the others, who only saw a piece of what was ordered. The Queen was smiling at her, delighting at the shock she was delivering.

'Your parents were so *loyal* to me, but they had found out who they really were, their birth right, and that made them so dangerous. I took your mother and father to Cantabria to betray them but even I couldn't have imagined how perfectly it would play out. Not just how the mistrust of the Talent was sown that day, and how I could use it as and when I wanted. When I was ready. But the investment we made in Cantabria in the years that followed they can never hope to repay. Not with all the apothecary or ships in the world. We own Cantabria, or rather I, as Queen, own Cantabria.'

'Great, so you'll make a lot of money from importing useless Cantabrian apothecary while your loyal subjects die of plague. How proud you must be.'

Eva wafted a hand. 'Efficacy will improve with refinement. My subjects must live with the choice they made to embrace Arbala once more. In the meantime, I will be fulsome in my sympathy for the bereaved.'

'You are unfit to rule,' said Naida. 'I am so sorry I ever thought you a friend. My parents were no threat to you. All they ever wanted was to heal, to help. You sacrificed them.'

'No. I stopped them because of who they were. And what you, therefore, are. You must know that in my place you would have done the same. You have to use every weapon in your armoury to hold on to power. I could brook no opposition, not with my father on the path to his demise, not before I was confirmed on the Shattered Throne.'

'How were they your opposition?' asked Naida but deep down she knew, she just wanted Eva to admit it. 'How am I?'

Eva frowned. 'Are you really trying to tell me you don't know? Ash and smoke ...'

'Enough.' Naida rose from her chair and moved to the front of the balcony. Elias needed her more than she needed answers from Eva. They could come later.

'You will sit,' ordered the Queen.

'Make me.' She looked instead down on to the floor of the pit.

★

Elias was all but done. Herron let him go and backed off a pace and Naida hoped he would stay down, be at peace, but she knew he would not. Coughing and gagging, his throat crushed, Elias dragged himself to his hands and knees, head hanging. Herron lashed a kick into his side, knocking him back down.

Elias rolled onto his back. His feet pushed to gain purchase, roll him, but they were so weak. Herron walked around and straddled him. He leaned down and grabbed one of Elias's shoulders, hauling him up to a seating position before driving a fist into his nose and mouth, rocking his head back.

The crowd were shouting for Temets to end it. Proposer and opponent alike, Upper and Lower, even Oliari was screaming for him to act, and Temets finally moved, standing from his bench. Herron clubbed Elias again, knocking his head to the other side. Naida saw movement in the benches behind him. Ludeney and Kat, forcing their way forward. Kat was shouting but in the tumult of the crowd, Temets couldn't hear her. He approached the brass plate: Elias's salvation, and the Gifted's extermination.

★

'End it now,' said Naida, swinging back to the Queen. 'Right now.'

'Make me,' mocked Eva.

'Last chance ... ma'am.'

'One does not issue last chances to queens,' said Eva. 'Besides. This is all so perfect. Because you know, deep down, don't you?'

'Know what?'

'Why you have to die. Why your parents had to die. You know who you are. How wonderful. Because you have failed, entirely, and I have won.'

And suddenly, for Naida, it all came down to this moment. She leaned down, grabbed the front of Eva's dress and hauled her from her seat, the Queen too shocked to do anything more than open her mouth in outrage.

'I made a promise, a very long time ago. Never thought I'd break it, but now I think perhaps I will.'

'Unhand me.'

'You don't understand, do you? How fragile life really is? Stop the fight. Now.'

'No.'

Eva stared at her, put her hands over Naida's and tried to push her away. But Naida, a lifetime on the battlefield behind her, was far too strong.

'Someone once told me that a distraction is the best way to stop two dogs fighting.'

Eva frowned, half-smiled. 'So?'

Naida spun her around and shoved her towards the front of the balcony. She cocked a fist and smashed it into Eva's face. The Queen staggered back, bleeding from her burst lips, incomprehension across her face, thighs against the plush rail. Naida lashed a kick into her gut, doubling her over, then dragged her upright with her hair.

Eva screamed. Naida put a hand around her throat and pushed her back over the balcony rail, off balance, her feet scrabbling, her hands gripped around Naida's, trying to pry them off. Naida merely increased the pressure, pushed a little more and gazed down onto the pit floor.

'Stop this farce right now or she dies!'

Chapter 38

Eva was screaming to be set free in the moment's silence before the crowd understood what they saw and began to howl, to cram towards the bottom of the balcony.

Down on the pit floor, Herron dropped Elias and stared up at Naida and his Queen. Temets had stopped a pace from the plate; Kat had raced over to see if Elias was still alive; and Lord Marshal Ludeney strode to the centre of the floor. The High Gavel was hammering for order.

Soldiers ran in, hundreds of them, forming a protective ring around the edge of the pit floor. More surrounded Herron. Behind Naida, the balcony door burst open and Vinald ran in.

'One more step, you weasel, and I will drop her,' rasped Naida, her eyes on his, leaving him in no doubt she would do it.

He stopped and backed up a pace, holding out his hands. Servants and soldiers crowded the doorway behind him and the sound of booted feet echoed up the stairs.

'Naida,' said the Queen, voice small now. 'Naida. Let me go.'

Naida pushed a fraction further, her gaze still on Vinald whose face was drawn and white.

'Shut up, Eva.'

Order was being restored. Ludeney's soldiers were every-where, moving people away from the balcony, back to their benches. More pushed past Vinald, and Naida was for once relieved to see their livery. She turned her attention back to the pit floor, ignoring Eva's struggles and pathetic wheedling. Ludeney was waiting for her to speak and she let him wait. Instead, she called down to Kat.

'Is he alive?' she asked, clearing her throat and repeating the question. 'Kat?'

Kat nodded. 'Barely. He needs help. He needs you.'

'Get Brin, get anyone. Get Misha.'

'Naida!' Ludeney's voice carried clear.

'I told you I would not kill her and I will not.' Naida pulled Eva back from the brink and shoved her into the soldiers who took her arms gently but firmly.

'Unhand me!' demanded the Queen. 'How dare you touch me! Lord Marshal, you will explain yourself or be beside this traitor in the cage.'

'With all the respect due to you, ma'am, be silent,' said Ludeney. 'Bring her down.'

Eva stared at Naida. She was scared and caught. A frightened princess in a prison of her own making.

'What have you done?' she asked. 'We are friends.'

'*Friends?*' said Naida. 'No, Your Majesty. This is what your defeat looks like.'

Naida watched the soldiers march Eva from the balcony, Vinald went with her, under guard, leaving six soldiers with Naida.

'The truth has been uncovered now, Lord Marshal, and I can go to the cage with my soul at peace,' she said.

Ludeney chuckled, a sound so at odds with the situation it clawed at her ears.

'The cage? Oh no, Naida. And you do not have the whole truth by any means. There is so much work for you still to do.

There is no need for you to hide anymore. Come down. No one is going to harm you.'

Naida moved in a haze. She had just attacked the Queen and now what looked for all the world like an honour guard was whisking her to the floor of the pit. Outside, in the concourse, crowds were forming as rumour and fact mingled together, leaving a web of half-truths in its wake. Crucible militia, bolstered by platoons of city guard, had closed every entrance to the pit, moving aside to admit her. The guards shadowed her to the floor before withdrawing and once there, she took in the crowd.

There was muttering, there was accusation, but overriding it all was confusion. Ludeney's presence was a potent restraint on their assumptions while, beside him, the Queen stood silent, present enough to realise that further protest was going to be futile.

Naida took a step towards Ludeney, but then looked to Elias, prone and still, Kat sitting by him, speaking to him, smoothing his hair. The Lord Marshal noticed, how could he not, and tipped his head in Elias's direction, a warm smile on his face.

Naida ran over, and dropped down beside Elias, hands on his chest, feeding herself into him. She inhaled sharply. Nothing was undamaged. He had broken ribs, internal bleeding, a fractured skull, every bone in his face cracked or splintered, his trachea crushed all but flat, his testicles burst, a broken ankle, fingers and a dislocated shoulder. But he lived.

'Hey, big man, you still there?' she asked, flooding him with everything she had, beginning to soothe inflammation, repair the most critical of damage and ease his agonies.

Unbelievably, his eyes fluttered open.

'Did we win?' he slurred through a mouth of broken teeth and swollen lips.

'Yes, we won.' And then for the last time, and with a feeling of incredible warmth and satisfaction, she said, 'My name is Naida, and I'm going to save you.'

Kat kissed her on the cheek and she got to work while Ludeney spoke behind her, quelling the anxious fidgeting that had come over the crowd.

'My Honoured High Gavel, speakers Oliari and Temets, esteemed Uppers and Lowers, official recorders and all of you herein. I am the Lord Marshal Ludeney, and I speak for Suurken. There are times when history is made before our eyes and today is one of those days. Today you will witness justice being served.'

At those last words, Naida paused for a moment and the whole crowd shifted. Ludeney held up his hands.

'One hundred and eighteen years ago, almost to the day, a great crime was committed. One which changed the course of Suurken. Those historians among you will know I refer to the death of the childless Queen Arianna and the accession to the throne of the first Rekalvian king. But he should never have ascended the throne. The Rekalvian dynasty should never have taken root in our country.'

Now the crowd's mood darkened, fear growing. But Ludeney still had their attention. He waved a hand and Stabile walked onto the floor, carrying a sheaf of papers to the High Gavel, indicating he read the top sheet. Ludeney continued.

'More than a century ago, in the shadows of the Palace of Spires, a conspiracy was born, one which saw the rightful monarch and her family murdered, records falsified or destroyed, testimony forced from unwilling mouths. But some survived, hidden, their name changed, their rightful role hidden even from them, lest they too be killed.'

Medics had entered the pit floor and Naida moved to let them tend Elias. She had sealed the ruptures within him, eased bruising and inflammation, and sedated him to a state of semi-consciousness. He would live, but he might never be back to his old self.

'Kat,' whispered Naida. She looked round. 'Did he make it? Brin?'

'Last I saw him, he was riding with another surrounded by a dozen of Ludeney's guards. He'll make it.'

Relief and hope flushed through Naida and she allowed herself to dream of Drevien's embrace again. She gathered herself and turned her attention back to Ludeney.

'Future generations did not even need to be hidden,' said the Lord Marshal. 'The story was over, after all. Except that it wasn't. Suurken is beloved of its records, and not even those who created the false trail handing the Rekalvians the throne could hope to find and destroy all the evidence. A hundred years later, I have uncovered it. High Gavel?'

'These records are genuine,' he said. 'Lord Marshal Ludeney will be heard. All other business is suspended.'

'Lies. It's all going to be lies,' said Eva.

The gavel came down. 'Silence!'

The crowd quietened, desperate to hear more, to watch the drama unfold.

'A single thread unravelling the tapestry, Naida,' said Ludeney, before turning back to the crowd. 'Fifteen years ago, by chance, the only surviving members of that wronged family discovered their true identity, their true destiny. But that luck was to turn to torture and murder.'

Ludeney was drowned out by the shouts demanding who, demanding to know the name, until the High Gavel ordered silence once more.

'Only the keen historians among you will recognise the name. In the days of Queen Arianna, they were the family Morantal.'

'Lord Marshal,' intoned the High Gavel. 'While we all love

our history, if you have a name to present and a rightful monarch to put before us, do come to your point.'

'I do,' said Ludeney. 'But I beg your indulgence because this will not be easy to accept. Not only was this family almost eliminated entirely, when Queen Eva discovered descendants still lived, she moved to complete the job, ruining their reputation, demonising and murdering them. Yet even then, not all of the family was destroyed.'

'Lies!' shouted Eva. 'Treason!'

Ludeney ignored her. 'With recent new information I could focus my search and what I discovered delighted me because I had seen our true monarch prove herself, showing the values of mercy and care for our city and our people. Her ascension to the throne will bring a new age.'

Naida felt she might faint yet she resisted admitting who he was talking about. Ludeney beckoned with his left hand and the four pit recorders came into the arena, their faces sombre with knowledge, grey with shock.

'Are you all in accord?' asked Ludeney.

'We are,' said their speaker.

'Does what you have recorded today constitute an official record of the Crucible?'

The speaker breathed hard and handed Ludeney a document. 'It does.'

The silence in the crowd carried a power Naida felt deep in her body.

'I am now going to read the relevant section of a conversation that took place on the balcony between Queen Eva and Naida Erivayne during the combat you have all just witnessed.'

'No,' screeched Eva. 'NO!'

'You really should remember where you install your listening tubes, Eva.' Ludeney turned to her guards. 'If she interrupts me, you may gag or remove her.'

444

Naida must have stumbled because she felt Kat's strong arms supporting her. Not all of Ludeney's words registered, but enough filtered through.

I took your mother and father to Cantabria to betray them ... He knew he couldn't save them or stop me ... He knew your parents were innocent ...

'Do you deny it?' demanded Ludeney, bringing Naida back to herself. Eva said nothing, attempting to stare him down instead. 'I thought not. Those innocent people she betrayed, and tortured, whom we have all been taught to hate for a crime they did not commit, were Lord and Lady Esselrode.'

The name still brought consternation, but the crowd was rapt with this revelation. It was the first time Naida had heard their names in public, spoken without disgust.

'Esselrode was not their true name, but the name which hid them – which saved the Morantals. The rightful heirs to the Shattered Throne. There was no evil inside them, as there is no evil within *any* of the Gifted. Nor does evil lie within their daughter.'

'So it's true,' breathed Naida and she would have fallen but for the squeeze of Kat's arms and the soldier's laugh of delight.

'I like this story,' said Kat.

'Today I right a great wrong,' said Ludeney. 'Today, we put a queen on the throne who will bring to Suurken the peace, justice, love and honour that we deserve.'

'Oh no.'

Ludeney held out his hand and put the other over his heart, bowing his head.

'I give to you your Queen, Suurken's greatest healer, their daughter: Naida Erivayne.'

The announcement was greeted in almost complete silence. It was only when she moved towards Ludeney and the centre of the arena, Kat still holding her arm, that the crowd began to make themselves heard.

The stamping of feet and the clapping of hands echoed around the pit. Support for Eva came from all sides and she supposed she shouldn't be surprised. But the depth of hatred for her that she had always feared was not evident, or it was drowned out.

'This is quite some promotion, Your Majesty,' said Kat.

'Don't ever call me that. Not you. Not Elias. Not any of you,' said Naida, beginning to weep that Willan was not here to witness it.

'By your actions shall you be accepted,' said Ludeney, his looming presence still intimidating, his complete calm so re-assuring. 'Trust is hereby repaid.'

'I can't process this, Lord Marshal. I need space.'

'I can.' Eva's voice brought instant quiet and an unease to the Crucible. 'The Lord Marshal is a traitor seeking to replace the rightful monarch with a puppet dressed as a doctor. Speculation and falsified documents are all the armour he has. Pay him no heed. Stand with me, my people!'

Fists punched the air and threats echoed around the Crucible. Ludeney's soldiers stood impassive. The Lord Marshal moved to respond but Naida stopped him with a gesture, choosing to stand in front of Eva herself.

'Speculation? The High Gavel holds historical records, brought from the archives. A demonstration of the Suurkene administrative system in perfect working order, wouldn't you agree?'

'I—'

Naida shook her head. 'You'll have your time to speak but it is not now.'

'You were not born to be Queen.'

'Neither, apparently, were you,' said Naida, causing Eva to

446

recoil at her tone. 'And yet, so desperate were you to be so, you organised a genocide and the torture and murder of my parents to deflect the blame. Worse, and yes, it is worse, you set in motion events that led to your own people turning on those whose only desire was to keep them alive and well.'

Naida would not look away from Eva, trying to see in her eyes some guilt, some acceptance of responsibility. She found none.

'All to keep you in power and wealth. What sickens me most is that you are one of us. You are a Gifted.'

In the still of the Crucible, the revelation drew gasps and a flurry of conversation.

'You are one of us, and yet you would have seen us all burn so that you could be Queen forever, over a sick and dying country.' Naida turned to the nearest Crucible guards. 'Get her out of here. Treat her well.'

Eva made a strangled sound. Almost apologetically, guards came to either side of her and took her arms.

'Unhand me,' she spat.

Ludeney shook his head at the uncertain look thrown him by one of the soldiers and Eva was led away, her head held high, eyes forward, dignified in departure at least. The mood in the crowd was unsettled and turning sour. Hundreds were calling out their support for Eva and while Naida turned a slow circle to take them all in, the calls grew in volume and intensity.

'You will hear your Queen!' Ludeney's voice, carrying all the heft and power of decades of authority, brought hush. Naida nodded her thanks while standing in awe of his power over an angry crowd.

'My friends. Not my subjects, my *friends*. Today, whether you accept me as your Queen or not... whether I can honestly ever call myself your monarch, doesn't matter.'

447

That stilled the muttering that had already begun. Ludeney, stood beside her, was smiling.

'Red Spot threatens our city. It is relentless, and remorseless, and lethal, but we have the means to defeat it and save countless lives. And if we do not embrace that means, every one of us in this city will be touched by the death of a loved one, a friend.'

As if facing the reality of their situation for the first time, an anxious murmur ran through the audience.

'All the Gifted will be released immediately and, with armed protection and support, will go out on the streets now, beginning in Old Landers where the sickness is most acute, to begin healing our people. This purge of the Gifted ends now, this moment, by my decree and backed by the irrefutable proof that my parents were innocent.' She thought a moment, seeking the right words. 'Our first business, our most important business, is to heal.'

Ludeney looked to his left. 'Lieutenant! You heard Her Majesty.'

'Yes, Lord Marshal.'

Ludeney smiled at Naida and the memories of that day in her house when he had come to arrest her lost their power.

'You will make a fine queen,' he said, and his mind had clearly travelled back to the same place. 'I am forever grateful for the day you escaped me.'

'You and me both.'

'I am eternally sorry for my part in what befell your family, Your Majesty, and I will of course resign my commission immediately.'

'Don't be ridiculous. I will need your help, and your wisdom. I still don't believe this is happening.'

Ludeney bowed. 'I am at your service until my last breath.'

'Thank you,' she said and turned to Kat, throwing herself

into the soldier's arms. The crowd applauded. 'Thank the throne for you.'

'Not sure this is protocol,' said Kat.

Naida laughed and pushed back. 'Yeah, but I'm in charge of protocol now and hugging friends is definitely allowed.'

'I'll get the word out,' said Kat.

'So, what next?' asked Naida. 'I honestly have no idea.'

Kat spread her hands. 'Well, before you go to see Drevien, you still have an audience. Did you have anything else to say...?'

'She's going to be cross she missed this. Even crosser that she's about to be a Queen's consort.'

Naida grasped at her thoughts, hoping they'd fall into order while she spoke. There was so much to say, and so much to do. She cleared her throat, faced her people, and felt tears begin to stream down her face.

'I came in here today the head of the royal medical service, and walk out of here the head of the royal family,' she said. 'I came in as Naida Erivayne, and I leave as Queen Helena Morantal. But my heart has not changed.'

Applause and booing in equal measure.

'I understand that this is all a great shock, seismic ... just think how I feel ... and I know that to persuade all of the people to accept me, to accept the truth of the Esselrodes, will be difficult and take time. But you were here, you have heard first-hand, and you can tell your story.'

Naida paused to watch them begin to contemplate what they had just witnessed.

'Your testimonies will be more powerful than any decree nailed to a board. Your words will reflect the history you have seen here this morning and I need your help. And help must be rewarded. So, when we are done here, I will meet each and every one of you and, if you allow, lay my hands on you to confirm you are clear of the Red Spot. And to thank you and

449

to learn your names for the next time we meet. Because we are nothing if we do not work together, nothing if we do not support each other. So whether you are ready to accept me as your Queen or not, let us begin today to make a better Suurken for every single one of us.'

The roar that greeted her words took her aback, her eyes widened, and she exhaled through a smile that broadened with every heartbeat. Ludeney nodded his approval and for some reason that simple gesture by her – so recently – sworn enemy, was exactly the affirmation she needed.

'Thank you, all of you,' said Queen Helena and she couldn't deny it, this felt *right*. 'Now let's get going; there's a lot of work to be done.'

The End

Acknowledgements

This book has been a long time coming and my editor, Gillian Redfearn, has been behind me all the way. Gillian, your support, guidance and insight have been incredible. Thank you.

Author's Note

The first draft of this novel, which included all of the central themes, characters and events that appear in these pages, was completed in May 2019. Make of that what you will.

JB.

Credits

James Barclay and Gollancz would like to thank everyone at Orion who worked on the publication of *The Queen's Assassin*.

Agent
Robert Kirby

Editor
Gillian Redfearn
Claire Ormsby-Potter

Copy-editor
Abigail Nathan

Proofreader
Gabriella Nemeth

Editorial Management
Jane Hughes
Charlie Panayiotou
Tamara Morriss
Claire Boyle

Audio
Paul Stark
Jake Alderson
Georgina Cutler

Contracts
Anne Goddard
Ellie Bowker
Humayra Ahmed

Design
Nick Shah
Tomás Almeida
Joanna Ridley
Helen Ewing

Inventory
Jo Jacobs
Dan Stevens

Sales

Jen Wilson
Victoria Laws
Esther Waters
Frances Doyle
Ben Goddard
Jack Hallam
Anna Egelstaff
Inês Figueira
Barbara Ronan
Andrew Hally
Dominic Smith
Deborah Deyong
Lauren Buck
Maggy Park
Linda McGregor
Sinead White
Jemimah James
Rachael Jones
Jack Dennison
Nigel Andrews
Ian Williamson
Julia Benson
Declan Kyle
Robert Mackenzie
Megan Smith
Charlotte Clay
Rebecca Cobbold

Finance

Nick Gibson
Jasdip Nandra
Elizabeth Beaumont
Ibukun Ademefun
Afeera Ahmed
Sue Baker
Tom Costello

Marketing

Lucy Cameron

Production

Paul Hussey
Fiona McIntosh

Publicity

Will O'Mullane

Operations

Sharon Willis

Rights

Susan Howe
Krystyna Kujawinska
Jessica Purdue
Ayesha Kinley
Louise Henderson